Chasing Amanda

When the secrets of the past hold the hope of the future

Melissa Foster

ISBN-13: 978-1481190800
ISBN-10: 1481190806

Publishers Note:
This is a work of fiction. All names, characters,
places, and events are the work of the author's
imagination.
Any resemblance to real persons, places, or events is
coincidental.

Melissa Foster ©2011
WORLD LITERARY PRESS

For Leon, Evelyn, and Sidney Alice Shulman, who
will never be forgotten

One

Molly kissed her husband goodbye and closed the front door of her colonial home, listening to the silence that echoed in her ears. It had been eight years since Amanda's death, eight years since she'd escaped the painful memories of Philadelphia, and moved to the quiet community of Boyds, Maryland. In the stillness of the mornings, Molly found herself missing the incessant background noises of the city, which seemed amplified in the six weeks since her son, Erik, had left for college. Her bare feet lightly slapped the ceramic tile as she padded into the kitchen, stopping in front of the picture window to watch Stealth, her rambunctious Rottweiler, and Trigger, her playful black lab. Molly briefly envied their carefree lives, then turned to look at the calendar that was clipped to the refrigerator with an enormous magnet that read, *Dance like nobody's watching!* The calendar was blank, as it had been every day this month, except for the third Thursday, where she had scribbled,

Civic Association Meeting. Molly sighed, remembering a time when every day had held a different list of assignments and chores, schedules for Erik, and important meetings for Cole. Eight years ago she had needed a calm, almost boring, lifestyle to save her sanity. Now, she wondered if she hadn't let it go on that way for too long. She coyly lifted her eyes to the magnet once again, remembering when Erik was young, and they'd danced unabashedly around the kitchen to silly songs from Sesame Street. The edges of her lips curled upward at the memory. That seemed like a lifetime ago. She raised her eyebrows, glancing around the empty kitchen, like a child about to reach into the cookie jar, and suddenly burst into spasmodic movements that did not resemble a dance by any stretch of the imagination. The phone rang, saving her from feeling any more ridiculous. "Yeah, right," she said to the magnet, and answered the phone.

"Hey, Ma, what's up?" Erik's use of "Ma" rather than "Mom" made Molly smile. When Erik was about twelve years old, he'd suddenly started calling Molly "Ma" when he needed her help or was simply in a jovial mood, and he'd used the term "Mom" when he was angry, scared, or upset, just as Molly had called him Erik Michael Tanner when he'd misbehaved as a child. Molly had seen it as a sign of his maturing, testing the waters.

Molly blushed, her lame excuse for a dance fresh on her mind. "Not much. Are you okay?" A shadow of doubt about her mothering skills momentarily gave Molly pause. There had been a time, just before finally moving away from Philadelphia, when she'd been unable to care for herself, much less for Erik. Cole had stepped into the roles of both mother and father while Molly struggled to come to grips with the trauma that had befallen Amanda. Even now, years later, that fleeting trepidation was enough of a reminder to keep Molly on her toes.

"Yeah, 'course. I wanted your opinion. There's this girl, Jenna? We've been hanging out a lot, and, um, well, she used to hang out with this guy down the hall, and—"

"And you're his friend, and you aren't sure if you should keep hanging out with her, right?"

Erik breathed a sigh of relief. "Yeah, exactly."

This was nothing new for Molly. She'd been helping Erik with everything from skinned knees to breakups forever. When Erik was younger, he'd draw Molly outside to discuss matters of the heart, as if the fresh air had somehow made things easier for him to discuss. Molly pictured the way he'd drop his eyes as he spoke, the way he bit his lower lip between thoughts, just as he had since he was four, and the nervous, crooked smile that always accompanied a relieved sigh when he'd heard her thoughts. She pictured that smile while she spoke with him, gently asking about his relationship with the other boy, how much he liked Jenna, and generally getting a feel for his long-term intent, of which, of course, he wasn't really sure, although he "really liked" her.

"Okay, so basically, I need to decide if I'm good enough friends with this other guy to be worth the pain I'll cause him if I keep seeing her?" The conflict in Erik's voice was tangible.

"Yeah, in my opinion, anyway. Is she worth hurting someone else, and are you good enough friends with the guy to care?" Molly thought about how cold the latter sounded, quickly revising, "It's all about karma, Erik. Would you care if you were him? That's what you need to think about. Put yourself in his situation. Was it a painful breakup? Were they madly in love, or was it a college fling?"

"Right. Okay."

Molly knew the meaning behind that particular response, *This isn't easy, so I don't want to think about it right now.* "You'll figure it out," she said. "Everything else okay?"

"I guess. Thanks, Ma, for making it a little harder," he laughed. "I gotta run. I've got class in five minutes, and it's across campus. Love you."

Before Molly could answer, the line went dead, and Molly longed for a hug from the boy who was no longer little, the boy who was now a young man and only needed to touch base with his mom rather than follow her around, hanging onto her every word. Molly missed those moments, feeling as though mothering a young man came with a whole different set of guidelines than mothering a boy, and accepting a phone dismissal without being hurt was one of the requirements. She missed building school projects and chaperoning field trips, taking pictures at soccer games, and standing at the sidelines, painfully silent, as her son had ordered her to remain because he was embarrassed by her cheering him on, "Go, Erik! That's my boy!" Molly shook her head, missing the child that he'd never be again, and smirking at the trials and tribulations that accompanied youth—and motherhood—then she headed upstairs to put on her running clothes.

Molly had wondered, recently, if they'd done the right thing when they'd uprooted from Philadelphia and moved to the country. Those thoughts were immediately chased by painful memories of Amanda. Nine years ago, Molly hadn't been sure she'd make it through each hour, much less each day. After Amanda's death, she'd spiraled into an abyss of depression, wrapped in the guilt of her silence, paralyzed by the truth—if she'd only spoken up, told somebody besides Cole, then maybe she could have saved her. Memories of that dreadful afternoon haunted her, the nightmares that followed suppressed her only hope of escape from the mental torture. She couldn't eat, and sleeping was out of the question. Losing her job had come as no surprise, since the commute to and from work, the sounds of the busy streets, had brought constant panic— an obsessive need to search the face of every child, looking for that hint of fear, looking for the deceit in the eyes of adults. Every screeching child had reminded her of Amanda, bringing forth a gut-wrenching visceral reaction, causing parents to guide their children away from the crazy woman who wouldn't stop asking them, *Are you sure this is your parent?* Molly remembered the unease she had felt as Amanda's abduction had unfolded before her.

It had been a cool October evening. Molly had left Walmart with an armful of groceries. She popped open the trunk and threw the bags in, trying to ignore the little girl's screams coming from the black minivan two cars over. She settled herself into the driver's seat, and rolled down the window. The deafening screams continued. Molly backed out of her parking space and inched slowly past the van's rear bumper. The child's father frantically tried to settle the little girl into the van, the little girl's arms and legs thrashed wildly. The frustrated father's eyes shot in Molly's direction.

"She didn't get the dolly she wanted," the man had said through gritted teeth.

Molly hadn't realized she was staring. Embarrassed, she had driven away. It was three days later, when Molly had seen Amanda's face on the front page of the newspaper, that Molly put her nightmares and the image of the man together, and realized that it had not been the little girl's father she'd seen, but Amanda's abductor, her murderer.

Molly shuddered. It had taken her years to understand the post-traumatic stress she'd been experiencing, to relearn normal reactions, and to retrieve her confidence. In small increments, she'd begun to move forward, to accept her failure. *You did the best you could,* her therapist had told her, and eventually Molly had found her footing again, slowly moving forward with her life. She pushed the distressing memories aside and reminded herself of how she'd come to grips with the nightmare she'd lived. For years, she had been confident that she would never slip back into that panicked, anxious state, but at times like these, when she remembered, she wasn't so sure. Determined to remain strong, she employed the coping mechanisms the therapist had taught her, reminding herself how far she'd come, and telling herself, out loud, that Amanda's death wasn't her fault. *Yes*, she thought, *moving to Boyds had been the right thing to do*. Erik had quickly fallen into favor with the kids at school and neighbors, and Cole had transitioned seamlessly to a nearby practice. Molly liked the close-knit flavor of Boyds, where most of the residents of the small farming community had grown up and still remained. She found safety in knowing who her neighbors were, and that strangers were few and far between in the three thousand acres that made up the small town.

The parking lot of the Boyds Presbyterian Church was empty, save for Pastor Lett's Corvette, which, it seemed to Molly, was ever present at the church. Molly's hamstrings burned as she stretched toward the sun, feeling each muscle pulsate as it was drawn to life. She stretched her arms above her head and let out a long sigh, thinking of the day that lay ahead, and wondering what she would do to keep herself busy. She yearned for her morning run, her escape from the mundane errands that barely filled her days.

Molly bent her lean body at the waist one last time to loosen her hips, pulling her head almost between her shins, her long, auburn ponytail flipped toward the ground. A faint clicking sound caught her attention, and she let her gaze move in its direction, but from her upside-down view, she couldn't see anything out of the ordinary. She turned and faced the aged white clapboard church which loomed behind her. Molly shielded her eyes from the bright sun and watched a blue bird whisk by. *Blue bird, blue bird, fly away home. Your wings are signs of peace for none.* Molly heard her mother's gentle voice ring in her head and cringed. *Great,* she sighed. Throughout her life, Molly's mother had often made random comments that Molly had later realized were psychically-charged warnings. Her mother had been clairvoyant for as long as Molly could remember, and when Molly had first realized that she had the same ability, she had thought of it as normal. She called the powerful episodes the Knowing, as her mother had. Now, she'd give anything to be able to close her eyes against her ability, wash it away like dirt from a fall.

Before Amanda, Molly's visions had been vague and sporadic, sand under a breaking wave, morphing from one second to the next in unclear shapes and patterns. Amanda's death had changed every aspect of her life, including the clarity and frequency of her visions. Molly didn't mark time like most mothers, cherishing each of their child's milestones. For Molly, there was only life before Amanda and life after Amanda.

Molly caught a glimpse of Pastor Lett standing alone in the shade of the church. Her long arms hung limply at her sides. When Molly had first moved to Boyds, she had thought it very progressive to have a female pastor in such a small town. Now, as Molly watched Pastor Lett crane her neck and look into the cornfields behind her, she couldn't imagine anyone else taking her place. She was a bit aloof and even slightly mannish, but Molly didn't find either of those traits unappealing. Molly had quickly confided in Pastor Lett about the tragedy that had befallen her in Philadelphia, and Pastor Lett had been patient and supportive of Molly's need to visit her at the church several times each month to cleanse the chaos from her mind. That's what Pastor Lett had called it, *Cleansing the chaos*. She'd said that everyone had confusion in their minds about things they'd done, or not done, and that one needed to resolve that turmoil in order to move forward with a productive, sane life. Molly smiled as she thought of their visits, which had become less frequent as the years had passed and Molly had come into her own once again.

Molly waved, "Pastor Lett!"

Pastor Lett's head turned toward Molly. She thrust her hands deep into her pockets, hunched her shoulders and lifted her chin in curt acknowledgment, quickly retreating into the church.

Molly disregarded the slight brush-off, thinking that perhaps she was just in a hurry, distracted. She jogged out of the parking lot toward White Ground Road, a three-mile stretch of secluded rustic road that wound through the historic section of Boyds, Molly's typical morning run.

She ran at a strong and fast pace for the first half mile, pushing the worried thoughts of Erik and his latest female conflict to the back of her mind and focusing on the sting of the crisp fall air as her lungs expanded with each breath, until the familiar rhythm of her feet pounding the earth lulled her into an easier pace, and she found her groove.

Every morning, her own body surprised her. At forty-two, she was still able to run several miles without issue, but the fact that she could run was not what surprised her the most, it was her desire to run—almost an insatiable need—and the confidence she felt as she ran. Her therapist had wondered, maybe rightfully so, if running was symbolic of Molly running away from her past. Molly had never quite been able to shake the similarity. Before Amanda, Molly had run to stay in shape. After Amanda, running had centered her mind. With the absence of the responsibilities of work, Molly had still been plagued by thoughts of Amanda. She craved the escape that running provided—the escape from her own thoughts.

No sight was more beautiful than the graceful branches of the tall oaks that lined the rural road. She knew every rut and pot hole, the areas that deer favored as their highways, and even where the sun shone through the brightest, up around the bend near Hannah

Slate's farm. She anticipated the shift in her footing as the paved road ended, fading gently into dirt and gravel, and felt her body relax as she inhaled the smell of the bright fall day.

At first, the change in temperature seemed imagined. Molly's eyebrows furrowed. She sped up her pace and her heartbeat followed. Within seconds, the air around her became cold. Goose bumps rose on her arms and sent a chill down her spine. She swallowed hard. Her calm slipped away, overshadowed by dread and certainty of what was yet to come.

A cold sweat replaced the perspiration she had earned. She swiped at her brow with a shaking hand. Her shorts and tank top clung to her small muscular body. An eerie silence took shelter in her eardrums as her vision dimmed, and an acidic taste settled in her mouth. Each breath became a fight for air. Her feet stopped moving. *No! Not now!* She closed her eyes and tried to will away the pressure in her head. There was no escape. She clenched her fists and brought them to her forehead, bracing herself for what she knew was happening. A fog enveloped her mind, and her legs became weak beneath her. A passerby, seeing her body shake and thrust, would have thought Molly was having a seizure. A passerby wouldn't have been able to distinguish between a seizure and the Knowing. Molly could.

She cursed herself for allowing the Knowing to continue to control her, year after year, yet she had no power to stop it. She felt like a puppet on a string. Visions flashed in her mind: *A cavern-like room surrounded by shadowy darkness; a young girl huddled in a corner, scared and shivering; the smell of rancid, wet earth.*

Molly fell to the ground and cried out in fear and frustration, "No!" She lay there, amidst the dirt and gravel, too spent to move, her mind in turmoil. A war raged within her—a battle of fear and denial—fear for what the Knowing had shown her and her own denial to believe it. She held onto reality by a thin thread, her trachea refused to open, to breathe. She stood on shaking legs and staggered, grasping at her neck and trying desperately to take air into her lungs. She spun around, looking for anyone, anything that might help her. She finally gasped a breath, a tortured inhalation. Molly pushed on, trying to make it out of the secluded area, to the clearing around the corner. Her mind saw flashes of the little girl and instantly replaced the images with one she knew—Amanda. Tears ran down her cheeks, and a familiar weight bore into her gut.

Breathe, breathe, breathe. She stumbled forward. *It's not my fault,* echoed in her head. The visions were now part of her. Molly scanned the edges of the forest; the mass of tangled branches and fallen trees were thick, the underbrush unforgiving. She couldn't maintain her focus. Her mind was too foggy, her body too weak. Nothing made any sense.

She limped up the road in a stumbling jog. As she neared the bend of the road where White Ground ran into Old Bucklodge Lane, she found her footing, pushing forward, faster, trying to make it to Hannah's before the Knowing disabled her once again.

Adrenaline coursed through her veins, and she ran faster than ever before. She ran up the hill and sprinted the last half mile to the old red farmhouse where Hannah lived. As if she had passed into another universe, the air lightened, birds chirped, horses gamboled in the pasture. Normalcy abounded. Hannah was outside with one of her many hunting dogs, a small beagle with floppy brown ears and a little tuft of brown fur in the center of its white and black body.

"Hey, Molly!" Hannah hollered, waving.

Molly grabbed her left side, kneading a stitch, her renewed energy left her as quickly as it had come. She lifted her arm in a limp wave and lowered herself to the grass of Hannah's yard, her mind in a bubble of disbelief.

Hannah came running over, "Molly, are you all right? You look like you've seen a ghost." She crouched next to Molly, reaching for her hand. "Molly?"

The feel of Hannah's large calloused hand, hardened from years of farm work, brought comfort to Molly.

"Molly, what happened?" Hannah's voice was hurried, concerned.

Molly longed to take refuge in Hannah's arms, to feel the protection of another human being. How could she tell her that she'd reached beyond the tangible? The secret of the Knowing was excruciating. Fear and stress locked inside her like a rabid animal in quarantine, yearning for escape. Yet she would not speak of it. Molly had learned years ago that the Knowing was not something most people possessed, much less understood. They feared her ability to see into the lives of others or simply dismissed her visions and defined Molly as crazy or attention-starved. She'd lived with the ill-defined visions, the ability to be shown just enough details to drive her crazy, since she was a little girl. Some saw her visions as a gift. Molly felt imprisoned by her mind. The psychic ability was as much a part of her as her hazel eyes and the birthmark on her left thigh.

"Hard run," she managed. In her mind she pleaded for the images to leave her. It was happening again, and she had no way to control it. She silently began her mantra, *I'm okay. It's not my fault.*

"My goodness, Molly," Hannah said, looking over Molly's dirty legs and shirt.

"I tripped in a pothole," Molly lied.

Hannah frowned, her brown hair, absent of the typical streaks of gray seen in other sixty-year-olds, swept her shoulders. Molly crawled to her knees, and Hannah helped lift her to her feet. "Molly, why don't I take you back home? You can't run in this condition. Is Cole home?"

"My car is at the church," Molly said, distracted. "Cole's at work." Her body felt awkward, too heavy for her legs to carry.

Hannah guided her to her car and settled her in the passenger's seat. "I'm headed to the church anyway."

As Hannah drove, Molly could feel the pressure lift from her chest. Slowly, her mind became her own again. Her first rational thought was that Cole could check her out when he arrived home from work. There were definite advantages to being married to a doctor. Her second was that if she were losing her mind again, she didn't want Cole to know.

When they turned onto White Ground Road, Molly was surprised to see a mass of cars. "What's going on?" Molly squinted at the traffic jam. "Is there a funeral today?" The question was in contrast to the attire of the gathered crowd, none of whom were dressed to honor the passing of a loved one.

"Oh, Molly, if only. It's much worse. I thought you knew," Hannah's face grew grim. "Celia and Mark

13

Porter's daughter, Tracey, went missing late yesterday from the Germantown Adventure Park. The community is gathering for a search party today. It's awful, poor little thing."

Comprehension hit Molly hard and brought with it a feeling of dread. Amanda. Panic grew in Molly's chest, the hope she'd had of the visions being flashbacks was now crushed. The Knowing had wrapped its claws around her mind and now prickled her limbs, commanding her attention. Molly was terrified of going down the rabbit hole again, and equally as frightened not to.

Two

Tracey's small body trembled. She grimaced as she pulled her knees, scraped and bruised, up to her chest. Her red hair, which was normally so carefully coifed, was thick with dirt and stuck to her forehead and cheeks. She tentatively lifted her hand and pushed the sticky strands away from her face—every careful movement a torturous reminder that she was not alone, magnifying her desperation and bringing more tears, which slipped silently over the newly-torn skin on her cheeks, stinging her face. She squeezed her eyes closed in an attempt to keep from making a sound but could not suppress the memory of the terror-filled night that had led her to the tiny chamber where she now huddled, shivering and scared, on a dirty, torn mattress.

She listened carefully to the slow and steady breathing of her captor, barely visible in the dark chamber. Tracey's gaze shifted to a lone candle, standing sentinel on a crude table and casting scary shadows of jagged shapes across the room. The smell of the dank dirt floor lingered in the air, making her feel sick to her stomach. She suppressed the urge to gag and concentrated on her surroundings. She saw makeshift wooden shelves stocked with canned food, batteries, and something else that she could not identify. Her eyes settled on a warped piece of plywood resting cockeyed against the dirt wall, blocking her only escape—an escape that Tracey knew would be impossible. Even if she could escape the chamber, she could never find her way through the twisted, narrow passageways that had brought her there. Tracey also knew that at seven years old, she could not outrun an adult.

A chill ran through her like ants crawling along her skin. She shivered and drew her legs in tighter, swallowing the sounds of fear that vied for release as she thought about the person who had lured her there with empty promises and lies. Her eyes spilled tears from the pain in her legs and the fear that consumed her. She shifted her body, making a slight scratching sound against the stale mattress. Her heart pounded in her chest, and her hand flew instinctively to cover her mouth—but it was too late. The terrified sound had already escaped her trembling lips.

Her captor stirred.

Three

Molly desperately wanted to talk to Pastor Lett before leaving to help with the search. She needed to flush out her feelings, to feel safe, and Pastor Lett had always managed to help her wash her mind clean of the demons. Pastor Lett was the only one in Boyds who knew about Amanda, and Molly was thankful to have her to lean on. Now she pushed through the crowd and saw Pastor Lett walking toward the cemetery, glancing backward every few minutes. "Pastor Lett!" Molly called out, noticing that her pace had quickened. She jogged up the hill, "Pastor Lett! Wait, I need to talk—"

Pastor Lett had vanished. A moment later, Molly reached the field and spread the dead stalks with her hands, wondering why in October they were still standing. The fields around Boyds were usually harvested by late September. "Pastor Lett?" she yelled. There was no response. The stalks were still, there was no rustling of husks, no crunching of leaves and stalks under hurried feet—just the noise of the crowd in the meadow below.

The grassy fields of the Adventure Park were spotted with volunteers searching for Tracey. The playground equipment stood unused, unnaturally empty, and eerily quiet. Molly knew she was on dangerous ground and hoped she was strong enough to handle the emotions that swirled within her. She turned her thoughts to Celia Porter, shuddering as she remembered the look on Cclia's face as she had told the crowd of volunteers that it was her fault that her daughter, Tracey, was missing.

"Tracey wanted one more chance to play hide and seek. It's her favorite game. I found Emma right away. I ran to her and she laughed, and we just sort of ran around for a minute. Then we started looking for Tracey. We found her. She was in the tall grass on the other side of the ship. It's just that…something was wrong. We found her, but she wasn't herself." Celia had wiped her nose on her sleeve. "I should have known. I saw that she was quiet and forlorn, but I just thought that she had seen me laughing with Emma and was jealous or something."

Perplexed, someone had asked, "But you found her? She didn't go missing at the park after all? Was she hurt when you found her?"

"No," Celia had said. "She wasn't hurt. She was just—"

Mark Porter had interrupted, "She was scared shitless. That's what she was. Something happened in that tall grass, and we have no idea what it was."

Molly had seen the guilt consume Celia, had seen her shoulders slump.

"Emma and I both asked her what was wrong. She just gave us this look. So I just thought—"

Mark reached out and held her, and she had continued, "After we found Tracey, I said we had to go. We walked to the car. I was talking to the girls about what we were going to do that evening and about what they wanted to be for Halloween, and Emma's hair got caught in the clasp of her dress, so I was focused on that for a few minutes." Her husband had pulled her closer, giving her a look that told of years of support. "When we got to the edge of the parking lot, I reached back for Tracey's hand, and she wasn't there. I thought she was still upset about me and Emma. I figured that I had made it worse by just ignoring her sulking." She looked away. "So I started shouting her name.

"I kept calling her and looking everywhere—in the slides, under the ship, inside each of the little playhouses on the opposite side of the castle. I was thinking that she was there, just hiding from me." Tears streamed down her cheeks, "I called and called for her. A woman had been sitting on the bench when we were playing hide and seek, and she told me that she'd seen Tracey walking toward the long grass. The woman said she asked Tracey if she was alright and Tracey just nodded," Celia said. "I should have known." Melting like wax in the sun, Celia's body collapsed against her husband's. Celia had looked at the volunteers, pleading, "It's my fault!" she sobbed, uncontrollably, "I thought she was hiding."

Her fault! Molly seethed to herself. *It's not her fault! It's the fault of whatever sick fuck took her!* Molly looked for a path, some hint that a little pair of feet had ventured back into the field or beyond. She tried to ignore the growing unease within her, the old feelings

19

rushing back in. She stopped and closed her eyes, taking a deep breath, and reminding herself of how far she'd come, *Coping mechanisms*. She turned and scanned the volunteers who wore mixed looks of fear and concern. She wondered if one of them was the abductor, acting as if he or she was there to help, but really listening for clues that the police and volunteers had found. Some volunteers carried sticks, batting at piles in the dirt. The thought that they might be looking for a body suddenly occurred to Molly, setting loose anxious thoughts of the past. She turned her thoughts inward, repeating the mantra that what had happened to Amanda was not her fault. Then she reassured herself about Tracey, *She's not dead! I saw her alive.*

Every few minutes someone called to Tracey, and each time, the crowd silenced for a moment—a hopeful pause in the midst of the search.

Yellow police tape roped off sections of the field, creating an illusion of a maze. The police hadn't made public any findings. By simply allowing volunteers to traipse through the field where Tracey had gone missing, Molly assumed they had found it devoid of any clues.

Molly reached the end of the field where it eased into the woods, thorns gnarled with trees and bushes. The density of the forest was forbidding and lonely at the same time.

The voices from the volunteers carried in the cool fall air, leaves crackled under their feet. Molly lifted her right leg cautiously and stepped out of the sunshine into the shadow of the tree line.

The forest summoned her. She took a careful step. A tingling sensation whispered across her skin. An oppressive feeling, like an invisible balloon, pushed hard against her sternum. The air felt warm against her pounding chest, making breathing difficult. She'd never encountered anything like this before, but she somehow knew it was all part of the Knowing, and she was determined to continue on, to find Tracey. She pushed into the aura and was surrounded by the smell of cold dirt and wet rocks, the smell of a creek bed after a storm when the dirt begs to be touched by the sun. Feeling faint, she crouched down and let her head hang low, resting her elbows on her knees.

C'mon, damn it! Be clear, she thought. *You're not doing this to me again!* She cursed the malediction that possessed her. *Damn it! Give me more or go away!* She loathed the obscurity of her visions. Tears of frustration welled in her eyes. She silently urged herself to pay attention, to read the signs that she'd so obviously missed years ago.

Molly lifted her eyes and caught sight of Hannah in the distance. Hannah stooped down slowly, her age showing in this simple motion, and she seemed to be clearing leaves from the ground. She shifted her body, swiftly looking from side to side. She walked forward and turned, dodging tree limbs and bushes with agility that could only come from familiarity. Poking at the ground with a long branch, she stooped again.

A volunteer approached Hannah from behind and tapped her on the shoulder, startling her. She stood too quickly, and her stick fell to the ground. Hannah took a few steps backward, as if to cover the spot where she had been investigating. They talked for a few minutes. The volunteer picked up Hannah's stick, and together they walked back toward the park, passing Molly on their way.

"Are you going back already?" Molly asked Hannah.

"Some things are better left untouched," Hannah said.

Confused by Hannah's comment, Molly turned back toward the forest, and readied herself for the pressure that was sure to come. She moved forward with determination. The pressure waned. She was left feeling little more than uncomfortable and bewildered. She eased deeper into the forest, over broken twigs and branches, pushing through thick, prickly bushes. She caught her foot and tripped, catching herself on a small tree. A pain shot through her palm. *Shit!* Sucking in air between her clenched teeth she inspected the wound. The gash was deep. Blood dripped down her wrist. The cut formed the letter T.

Pastor Lett plodded up the gated-off, overgrown driveway towards the old Perkinson House, mumbling under her breath, "You better be there. Please, Lord, no trouble this time." It was just after dusk, the sky gray with few clouds, the brisk air stung her cheeks. The center of the drive, a long mound of earth between two ruts from tires gone by, seemed to go on forever. The grass on either side was knee high. Pastor Lett walked with her head down but keenly aware of her surroundings, making certain she was alone. Her dark hair poked out under a knit cap, the ends making a C that turned out just below her shoulders. Her left hand, shoved deep in her coat pocket, held an open bag of sunflower seeds like a security blanket. She thought about the search that was likely still taking place and ignored the shame that flushed her cheeks. She couldn't quite calm the guilt that wrapped around her as she thought of Molly. She'd heard her calling her name, even seen her running in her direction, but worried that if she'd stopped to chat—with Molly it was always more than a brief chat—she'd run out of time. *I do what I can,* she rationalized.

The Perkinson House had been strategically built atop a wooded knoll and expertly camouflaged behind enormous oak and elm trees. Only one turret was visible from the main road, and to see it one would need to be in just the right location when the trees were bare. The private yard sloped gently toward what used to be Ten Mile Creek, until it was dammed and the man-made reservoir had swallowed the valley and the few houses within it. Many residents didn't even know the home existed, much less that the Perkinson House had been entrusted to Pastor Lett some twenty-seven years ago by Chet Perkinson, the sole living family member, who some say was lucky to have escaped the home's deadly curse.

Pastor Lett slipped into the thick woods as the driveway curved toward the train tracks and became visible, only momentarily, from the road. Fatigue and regret filled her body, as it always did on her nightly journey.

She approached the Victorian house cautiously, concerned about the possibility of vagrants and curious teens. She stood at the edge of the woods until she was sure she was still alone. She stepped quietly out of the woods and onto the leaf-covered grass, taking note of the hanging shutters, loose boards on the wood siding, and the broken window upstairs on the left which winked mysteriously in the sunlight.

She started toward the ivy-covered stone walkway, sighing deeply at the thought of what lay ahead. The two entrance stairs cried out for repair with cracks in the second riser and a non-existent handrail save for the posts. Dwarfed by the looming trees, she turned, heading down the path that led around the side of the house, and moved swiftly to the rear cellar entrance. The smell of wet leaves hung heavily in the air. She quickly brushed the leaves off of the old wooden doors. The sound of twigs snapping caught her attention. She cocked her head to the side and listened intently. *Squirrels.*

She knelt close to the familiar wooden doors, her knees sunk into the cold, moist ground. She perspired under the weight of her thick coat. Taking one last look around, she removed a key from around her neck and unlocked the thick chain that held the wooden doors closed.

Cold damp air brushed Pastor Lett's face as she pulled the doors open. The musty smell hung in the air as she walked down the narrow, stone stairway and into the pitch black cellar. She ignited a lighter, pleased to see that nothing was out of place. The dirt walls of the small chamber sent another rush of culpability through her body. *Lord, please forgive me*, she prayed.

A claustrophobic pressure engulfed her as she became accustomed to the darkness and silence. She lugged the cheap metal shelving unit from the far end of the chamber into the center of the room, the old tin cans and few tools that were spread on the shelves knocked and clanked against the cold metal. She slid the marred plywood away from the dirt wall and moved it to the side, leaning it against the shelving unit. Sweating despite the cool air and feeling every day as old as her fifty-seven years, Pastor Lett worried about the day that the plywood would become too heavy for her to move alone.

Her body sagged as she tucked her head to her chest and moved slowly through the hand-dug hole and into the next chamber, where she could stand her full height of five feet nine inches.

Small battery-powered lights sat on an abused end table. An unlit candle lay tilted on the floor. Tucked into a nook in the dirt wall was a mattress, a cream comforter thrown haphazardly off the edge. An old, stained sofa sat an angle, inches out from the wall. The chamber was silent—too silent. Pastor Lett's heart pounded against her ribs. She stared at the black hole behind the sofa, calling out in a sweet voice, "Honey, you in here?"

Worry grew in her heart as she moved through the empty chambers, then retraced her steps back to the main chamber. She replaced the plywood and shelves, roughly arranging the tins and tools, her face tight with frustration. She left the cellar, locking the heavy chain securely in place.

Pastor Lett paced the back yard, worrying. She looked up as a shadow moved past the window of one of the upstairs bedrooms. Mumbling under her breath, she fumbled with the keys, unlocking the thick wooden door that led from the back porch into the butlers' pantry. *I've got you.*

"Ow, shit!" Molly grimaced at the pain in her palm as she lifted the spaghetti pot from the hot burner.

"Baby, let me get that," Cole said as he walked into the kitchen and saw his wife struggling. "What happened to your hand?"

Molly backed onto a white kitchen chair and laid her arm across her thigh. "Did you lose your pager today?" she asked, annoyed. "I tried to page you all afternoon."

"No. It was crazy, seeing patients, doing procedures. I must have forgotten to put it back on." He set the pan back on the stove and knelt in front of Molly. "I'm sorry, baby. What happened?" He kissed her bandaged palm, "Let me see that hand." He unwrapped the bandage. "Where are the pups?"

Molly had almost forgotten about their dogs' earlier escape. She shrugged, "They jumped the fence again. I'll get them later." She sat back in her chair, exasperated, and looked down at the crown of his beautiful dark hair, her frustration beginning to subside. "I had a terrible day," she sighed, "well, not terrible, but scary and confusing to say the least! Did you see the paper? The story about the little girl who's missing?"

Cole quickly glanced up at her, "No time this morning. I was running late, remember?" He fiddled with her bandage, his face grew concerned, "What did you say about a girl?"

Molly told Cole about Tracey's disappearance. "I met her parents today and helped with the search. That's how I cut my palm."

"Yeah, your palm," he said with a sigh, as he inspected her hand. "You could use a stitch or two."

Molly snatched back her hand, "What? No! I don't need a stitch or two. It'll be just fine!" Molly was petrified of needles—any needles, whether they were aimed at her or anyone else. "Don't you remember when Erik hit his head on the counter and needed stitches? I nearly passed out at the sight of the needle!" she exclaimed. She'd had to leave the room, and still felt guilty for not being strong enough to be there for him when he'd needed her—neither then, nor for the two years after Amanda's death. "I don't think so." She stubbornly shook her head.

"Honey, look at the gash! How did you do this?" Cole stood, right hand on his hip, left hand running through his hair—the familiar nervous movement that had toyed with Molly's heart for the past twenty-one years.

"I tripped over a log," she said sheepishly, wrapping her hand back up. She stood and snuggled into the familiarity of him. The smell of his aftershave faded into the unique smell of strength, of man, after a long day's work. *I love your smell*, she thought. His once-lanky arms and skinny chest, now full and muscular, held her tight. She wished the last few hours had never happened, that she'd open her eyes and realize it was all a bad dream.

"Mol, are you sure you're okay?" he asked.

She pulled back from him and looked up. The concern in his eyes did her in, and tears that she hadn't realized she'd been holding poured down her cheeks.

"Oh, Mol," he pulled her close again, caressing the back of her hair. "It's not Amanda, baby. It's not her. You're okay."

"It's like reliving my worst nightmare," Molly said, although that wasn't really the truth. Her worst nightmare would have been if it were Erik that was missing. She thanked God that Tracey was not her own child and was sure that there was some sort of sin woven into that type of thought—taking comfort that someone else's pain was not her own.

Cole gently reminded Molly of her coping mechanisms and that this child was not Amanda. "Mol, it's probably not safe for you to be involved in the search. The police don't even know if the abductor is a serial killer, rapist, or something even worse."

Molly knew what Cole really meant but was too kind to say: It wasn't safe because Molly might not be able to control her own emotions. She turned away.

Cole tried to lighten the mood, joking with Molly about how she was still making up for lost time with Erik, and still slightly over-protective of him. "Didn't you call him a few nights ago because you had a bad dream about him?" He kissed her cheek and headed into the family room.

Molly watched Cole leave the room, annoyed with his ease in pushing aside the significance of Tracey's disappearance. She took a deep breath, told herself to let it go, and hurried into her den, where she sent an email from her Civic Association account to the residents of Boyds about the search for Tracey. She chided herself for not checking her email sooner—there were already three messages about Tracey's disappearance.

Five minutes later, she dished the spaghetti onto plates, then went into the family room and ran her hand lightly across Cole's shoulder, "Come on, dinner's ready." The feel of him sent a tingle through her body, reminding her of how lost she'd been in his arms the evening before. With Erik away at college, they'd rekindled their sensuality like love-sick teenagers.

"I'm coming." He sauntered into the kitchen and sat at the table, "So, what else?" He picked up his fork and looked at Molly, "I assume you're not going to get a stitch, right?"

Molly pursed her lips into a crooked smile and tilted her head in answer. "What do you mean, 'What else?'?"

"There's more to this. It seems so…" he hesitated, running his hand through his hair and looking away. Molly waited, nervously. She knew where he was headed. "It's Amanda, isn't it?"

Molly twirled her spaghetti and stared intently into the little chunks of tomato in the sauce. Anytime she appeared worried or showed the littlest bit of apprehension in her confidence, Cole drew a connection to Amanda. She hated hearing the accusation in his words but knew she could not divulge the truth. The guilt ate at her so deeply it burned. "I just had a feeling, that's all." She couldn't tell him about the pressure as she had entered the woods or the visions that had engulfed her while she was running. Cole had never fully believed that she experienced visions, and she worried about how he'd immediately categorize her, as he had with her visions of Amanda, like a patient. As a physician, he believed in facts, tangible data—not paranormal episodes.

"Is that all? Nothing else?" he asked.

"No," she said, swallowing the desire to tell him everything. The need to keep her thoughts to herself saddened her. "I need to call Erik." She abruptly got up from the table, set her full plate onto the counter, and left the kitchen before the truth could escape.

"Of course you do."

Molly heard the rustle of the newspaper and the clank of fork to plate behind her.

Upstairs, Molly paced, her desire to call Erik forgotten, replaced with frustration. She knew Cole was right, her emotions were at risk. Her mind retraced the steps of the search, circling back to Hannah's actions, whose quick retreat nagged at her. She pushed the curtains to the side and looked out the window into the evening at the sunset. Staring into the vast woods beyond her yard, she realized that Stealth and Trigger's disappearance provided the perfect excuse for her to get out and investigate.

Her heartbeat picked up momentum as she grabbed her flashlight and notepad and stuffed them into her printed fabric backpack. I'll do this for Amanda, she thought. She threw the duffle over her shoulder and crept downstairs. Hearing the television in the family room, she circled around and grabbed her car keys off of the entrance table. "Honey," she called out, "I'm going to look for Stealth and Trigger." As an afterthought, she grabbed their leashes from the hook and hurried out the door.

Cole heard the door shut and worried about what his wife wasn't telling him. He remembered the morning of October 12, nine years earlier.

Molly had been sleeping fitfully toward the morning hours. When she'd finally awakened, she'd been scared and shaking. She'd anxiously relayed a dream she'd had of the little girl she'd seen in a parking lot days before. In the dream, the child screamed and cried, frenzied with terror. He had told her that it was her subconscious working overtime, and he'd gone on with his day. The next morning, she had again been tossing and turning. When she'd awakened, she'd stared straight ahead, tears streamed from her eyes. As if in a trance, she'd described her nightmare, the searing pain that ripped through the little girl's body, the stale smell of alcohol and sweat pouring off of the man's body as he climbed off of the damaged child, the knife being drawn from its sheath, glistening as it plunged through the air and into the child's chest. Again, he'd rationalized. It was just her subconscious fears—she'd seen a stressful scene between father and daughter, and her mind had run with it.

He had gone about his morning routine, and Molly had been furious, accusing him of not caring, not believing in her. It wasn't until two hours later, when he'd picked up the newspaper and seen the headline, "Body of Amanda Curtis Found," that finally, after all of those years of his wife professing that she had some strange type of sixth sense, he pondered, truly considered, the possibility that she was empowered, or hindered, with some sort of ESP that he could not comprehend.

Cole stuffed the memory into his subconscious, not wanting to revisit the tumultuous years that almost tore their family apart—or to think about the "T" emblazoned on his wife's palm.

Four

Tracey sat on a large rock, shivering and scared. The air around her was musty and cold. Her breathing was shallow, her clothes torn. She tried to be quiet as she eyed the tall woman who stood at the other side of the dirt chamber. Tracey's body trembled in fear. *I hope Daddy finds me. What if he's mad at me and doesn't look for me?* Tears welled in her eyes.

The stranger smiled, sending a chill down Tracey's back. Her body stiffened, her eyes grew wide. Her abductor walked closer, the friendly smile remained on her face. She took long strides, her strong arms readied at her side.

Tracey curled herself into a ball, backing her quivering body further onto the rock and into the dark corner. She looked around the menacing cave for someplace to hide, an escape route. The candles illuminated the small room just enough for Tracey to see the small table and the dirty mattress she had slept on the night before, casting shadows across the earth floor. Tracey's heart beat frantically as the woman reached for her hand.

"It's time to pray, Tracey," she said in a calm, gentle voice. "Let's put on your church clothes for Mummy." Her voice was low, husky.

Just as her large calloused hand touched Tracey's, Tracey pushed off the rock, tugging her hand away from her captor and crying out.

"Now, now, Tracey, crying will do you no good. There's no one coming for you. No one can hear you." Her voice became hard, cold, "Put these clothes on— now." Her smile morphed into an angry sneer.

Tracey reached her spindly, shaking arm out slowly, snatching the dress and pulling it to her chest. She looked down at the ground to avoid the woman's piercing eyes as she backed into the corner of the tiny cell-like chamber. *You're not my mommy! I want to go home!*

Facing the dirt wall, Tracey could feel the woman's eyes trained on her back. She trembled in fear.

Her captor turned, took a photograph from a shelf, and stared at it. Tracey heard her say, in almost a whisper, "I did it, Mother. I saved her!"

Tracey pulled her soiled clothes off of her petite body quickly, crossing her thin arms to cover her nakedness as best she could. Her soiled panties stuck to her bottom. She tried to ignore the smell of dried urine that permeated the air around her. She pulled the stiff, dirty dress over her head. The mildew smell wafted up and mixed with the putrid smell of the cave. She crinkled her nose and breathed through her mouth. It repulsed her senses, and she had to stifle a gag. Her teeth chattered, and her body shook. *I hate it here! I want to go home!* she silently screamed.

"That's Mummy's girl," the lady purred.

Her smile appeared friendly, though Tracey wasn't falling for that again. Friendly people didn't take you away from your family.

"You don't need help, do you?" the woman asked.

Tracey's eyes grew wide, and she vehemently shook her head.

Mummy approached her. Instinctively, Tracey crossed her arms over her chest again, huddling deeper into the corner. *No! No! Don't touch me!*

The lady reached over and grabbed Tracey's shoulder lightly, turning her to face the wall. She zipped Tracey's dress.

The feel of her rough, cold knuckles made Tracey want to scream. She bit down hard on her lower lip to quell the urge, knowing that a scream would bring a punishment, and Tracey had already spent time in the bad spot. She wasn't sure she could endure it again. Tracey closed her eyes tight and tried to calm herself. Her heart felt as though it were lodged in her throat.

The woman spun Tracey around, and Tracey took in a deep breath. Her heartbeat chased the bile in her throat, surging it into her mouth. She swallowed hard. The sound of fear escaped her lips softly, a withered mew. She tried to keep a courageous face, but her lower lip failed her. It jutted out, and tears sprang from her eyes. *Don't cry! Don't cry!* She tried not to whimper, remembering the early hours of the night before. *There is no place in this world for crybabies,* her captor had said, just before putting her in the bad spot.

The woman looked into Tracey's tearing eyes. "Crying," Mummy said. "You'll stop that soon enough!" The woman placed her strong hands on Tracey's back and prodded her toward one of the endless dark tunnels. "Stop that now and make Mummy proud."

You're not my mummy! I hate you! Tracey kept her thoughts locked inside. *Please don't hurt me.* She tried to stop crying. Her fear was too big. Had it not been for the lady pushing her, she hadn't thought she'd be able to continue walking. The dark, rancid tunnel went on forever. She silently prayed her parents would find her, and rued the lies Mummy had told her about the fun place where she lived—*where girls could play for hours with no rules*—but mostly, she hated what Mummy had told her once they were in the tunnel—that her mother didn't love her as much as she loved Emma, and that she would be glad to be rid of Tracey. *Liar! My mom loves me!* Tracey's anger grew, tamping down her fear, but not overtaking it.

Tracey reached up and touched the indentation just between her collar bones, as she'd done unconsciously so many times before, the very spot where the cold metal of her necklace used to sit—the necklace with the heart-shaped charm that her first grade teacher, Mrs. Tate, had given her on the last day of school. Fresh tears pooled in her eyes.

Mummy pushed Tracey deeper into the dark passageways. Tracey's heart pounded faster, fresh goose bumps riddled her skin. She could still feel Mummy's large body as it had slid in against her side while she had lain in the grass playing hide and seek with her mother and little sister, Emma. She could still see Mummy's smiling face when she had held her

35

necklace like a prize in her enormous palm, luring her in. Tracey had believed Mummy's promises of giving back her necklace and even letting Tracey try on her special diamond ring. As Mummy pushed Tracey through the dark tunnel, Tracey silently scolded herself for not listening to her parents' warnings about strangers, but Mummy wasn't really a stranger to Tracey. She had played with her many times in the park when Tracey's own mother had been busy with Emma.

Five

The night was cool with few stars in the sky. Molly parked by the Adventure Park, hitched her pack over her shoulder and tried to talk herself out of turning back and going home—the evening cast an eerie glow around the playground equipment. She hoped her dark clothes would keep her from being seen and couldn't help but wonder if the abductor had pondered a similar thought. *The abductor.* Amanda's abductor had never been caught. His face, his scraggly brown beard, his unruly, thick dark hair, and his cold eyes, still haunted Molly. Most of the time she could replace the image with one of happier thoughts, as her therapist had taught her, but now, in the dark, his face came back to her. She trembled, desperately trying to push away his cold stare, his rough voice. *She didn't get the dolly she wanted*, he'd said from the vehicle. *I should have known!* Molly berated herself. *I should have fucking done something, anything!* She jogged along the grass, trying to outrun the memory, and headed toward the woods. Molly thought she must be crazy to be out alone at night, looking for god knows what, but she had to do it. She wasn't going to let Tracey down. She prayed the Knowing would give her a sign, guide her, yet it had not given her anything more than the terrifying image of Tracey she had seen earlier—and it hadn't been enough to save Amanda. Her foot caught in a rut. "Damn!" She looked around to make sure no one heard or saw her. She found her footing and continued past the playground equipment to the crest of the field where it fell away into the woods. The forest looked completely different in the dark—intimidating, villainous. Molly crouched down and removed her flashlight from her sack. She did not turn it on for fear of calling attention to herself, but it made her feel more secure just having it in her hand. She forged forward, momentarily flinching from the pinch in her ankle. "It's now or never," she whispered to herself. As she lifted her leg to step into the woods, she once again felt pressure against her chest. She gritted her teeth, pinched her eyes closed, and pushed her slight frame through the strange energy field, fighting her way into the depths of the forest. Her vision began to blur, her heart raced against her ribcage so hard she was afraid she might pass out. The Knowing was upon her. She concentrated on moving forward, holding onto branches as if they were lifelines. She squeezed the flashlight in her hand so hard that it hurt. Each inch she gained was a struggle. Her surroundings closed in on her, fading quickly to black. She fell to the ground—a vision of a baby girl seared into her mind. She could smell the infant's milky-gray skin, wet with birthing fluids. The baby's body lay rigid, dead.

Molly came to in a fog, the pungent odor of death, the smell that had accompanied her dreams of Amanda, smothered her senses. Her palm bled through the bandage, caked with mud and broken leaves. She sat up and looked around frantically, putting together the pieces of what she'd seen and trying to breathe without tasting the sickening stench. The silence around her was unnatural. Molly's heart continued to race as she sat on the chilly ground, gathering her thoughts. She scrambled forward, grabbed the flashlight, turned it on, and scanned the area, nervously pulling herself to her feet and grimacing as her ankle complained about the hundred ten pounds of her weight. She spotted her bag a few feet away and reached for it, pulling her hand back quickly, the ground beneath the bag was hot. With the exception of the leaves and dirt being unusually dry, she noticed nothing remarkable. She quickly removed her notebook from her backpack and sketched the area, scribbling details about every tree, branch, and bush. She pushed leaves over the spot where her bag had lain and suddenly felt as if she were not alone. She spun around, facing the dark night. Amanda's killer's face flashed before her and disappeared just as quickly. "Shit!" She shoved the notebook into her pack, hitched it over her shoulder, and with the flashlight to guide her, sprinted back out of the forest, oblivious to the pain in her ankle.

Molly was mauled by Stealth and Trigger as soon as she entered the house—all paws and tongues—reminding her of what her supposed mission had been when she'd left the house earlier in the evening. In a voice loud enough for Cole to hear, she said, "Where were you guys? I looked all over those woods for you."

39

Molly hurried into the mudroom and stashed her bag behind the freezer. She eased her feet out of her muddy shoes and wriggled her ankle to see if it was any better without them. It was not. She washed her hands and face, patted dry her bandage, and went to face Cole.

The television blared in the small family room. It was not uncommon for Molly to wake up to hear the television as far upstairs as the bedroom and to find Cole fast asleep in front of it. Tonight, he was awake, sitting in his t-shirt and jeans and talking on his cell phone.

"She has no clue," Cole said with a smirk.

Molly walked quietly into the room.

"Gotta go," Cole ended the call and stared intently at the movie playing before him.

"Hi, honey," Molly said. "When did the dogs come back?" Her efforts at sounding casual were strained. She sat next to Cole and stretched her arm casually across the back of the sofa.

He leaned forward, his eyes remained trained on the television. "Maybe an hour ago."

Molly cringed. She glanced at the wall clock and went for a fast recovery, "I looked all over the woods behind our house. I'm surprised you didn't hear me yelling."

Cole turned to look at her with the "uh-huh" face she'd come to know all too well.

"I went across White Ground and searched the Hoyles Mill Conservation Trail for a bit, thinking that they crossed into those woods." Molly remembered that the Hoyles Mill Trail, part of the county's Legacy Open Space project, ran through the woods adjacent to White Ground Road and continued south, abutting the Adventure Park. She made a mental note to check out that area and rationalized that it wasn't a complete lie if she *planned* on doing it.

Cole gently took Molly's wrist in his warm hand. He ran his finger along the dirty bandage. "You know, Mol, I would have gone with you," he said. "I don't like you in those woods alone."

Molly was unsure if he was talking about those woods looking for dogs, or if he knew where she had really gone but was not yet ready to call her on it directly. She looked away. "I know," she said tentatively. "I was going stir crazy with the stress of the day, and I was worried about the dogs."

"Uh-huh," he laid her hand on her thigh and turned back to the television.

Molly desperately wanted to tell him the truth. She hated to lie to him, but she didn't want to face his disregard for her senses. She could just imagine what he would say: *What you think of as the Knowing is really just your repressed anxiety about Amanda and your desire to do something about it,* or something just as scientifically explainable.

Cole turned to her with a mixture of concern and anger on his face. "Baby, you can't keep putting yourself at risk." He said seriously, "You shouldn't be in the woods at all. You should be here, with me." He reached his arm around her and pulled her close. "You're going to hurt yourself so badly that you won't be able to run, and then you'll be miserable." His words were spoken with sheer love and concern, and just a sprinkling of frustration. Thankfully, what Molly had picked up on as anger had dissipated.

She snuggled into him, "I know," she said. "I had to go." It was the truth, plain and simple.

Six

Pastor Lett looked down at the scratches on her arms and was glad it was fall and that long sleeves were in order. She was exhausted from the prior evening's scene and the chase that had ensued. It had taken her hours to catch and settle down the kid, and when she had, her old body wouldn't move as fast as she'd needed it to. She needed to find a way to ensure that the kid could not escape again.

Figuring out a way to seal off the entrance to the house from the cellar wouldn't be difficult, she knew, she simply rued the energy it would take to do the job. In all of the years she'd been caring for the Perkinson House and utilizing the cellar, no one had ever found the entrance behind the sofa. She wondered how her observations could have been so sloppy. She'd been doing this for so many years that it had become a routine that she no longer enjoyed, a duty she loathed.

The idea that the kid could have wandered out of the house and down the driveway scared the dickens out of her. Her heart beat faster just thinking of the scene that could have transpired. She'd board up the windows and doors, just in case—lock the doors from the outside, too. Her heartbeat settled as she formed her plan. *I've put enough fear in that kid that it won't happen again*, she thought, and if the kid did get into the house again, there would be no escape. Pleased with her plan, she headed to the shower, whistling.

Molly tossed and turned all night, the events of the day had taken their toll on her body and on her mind. She awoke in an anxious state, thinking about Tracey, and vowing not to let her become the next Amanda. She sat up on the edge of the bed, her favorite of Cole's t-shirts tangled around her waist, her sleeping shorts uncomfortably bunched around the tops of her thighs. She began to stand, and a searing pain shot through her ankle. She wiped her eyes with the back of her hand, the bandage scratched her eyelid. She sighed and turned to wake Cole just as the radio sang out in alarm.

Cole rolled over and reached his arms around Molly's waist from behind. She pried his hands away, feeling guilty. Cole would never approve of her plan to help find Tracey. She knew that Tracey wasn't Amanda, but she believed that if she could find Tracey, it would help her make amends for what she had, or hadn't done, for Amanda. *Maybe I am losing my mind*, Molly thought. "Come on, Cole. You'll be late," she said, and limped into the bathroom.

"Ankle still bad?" Cole asked.

"Not really," Molly lied. She knew he would tell her not to run, a feat she wasn't even sure she could pull off, but she didn't want to be told what to do. She continued through her morning routine with high hopes of making it to her run.

She caught a look from Cole as they passed each other entering and exiting the bathroom. "It gets a little better with each step," she said, feigning cheerfulness.

"Mm-hmm," he said. "Don't be stupid, Mol. If it hurts, don't run." He stood in the bathroom in his boxer briefs looking very sexy and very sleepy. At forty-three, he still took Molly's breath away. She was reminded of the first time they had stayed together overnight. After hours of newly-finding-each-other sex, they had lain together for the entire next day, reading, talking, and dozing.

Molly turned her back to Cole and lifted her foot onto the bed to begin wrapping her ankle for her run.

"Molly," Cole wrapped his arms around Molly's waist again, turning her to face him. "You'll be sorry if you overdo it. Don't you remember how you hated not being able to run for months on end when you had tendonitis?"

"Yes, I remember," she said, more testily than she had anticipated. "I'm not going to hurt myself this time. If it hurts, I'll just walk." She smiled, "Promise."

He kissed the top of her head, "Good." He walked to the bathroom and turned on the shower, "What's on your schedule today?"

Molly became rigid, fearing the untruth that hung on the tip of her tongue. She'd already calculated the time it would take to scan the papers for updates on Tracey, check out the woods, stop by the police station, and maybe even hand out flyers. Molly was excited to finally have an agenda, even if she knew that this day's particular agenda was one of which her husband might not approve.

After a moment of silence, Cole said, "Mol?" He paused, and the flow of the shower water told Molly that Cole was washing his face. "I know you're worried about that little girl," he said between splashes. "Are you going to try and help?"

That was Molly's in—she wouldn't have to lie after all. She paced, fidgeting with her shirt. "Oh, you know me," she said. "I'll nose around a bit and see what I can find out." She heard the water turn off.

Cole stepped out of the bathroom with a pale green towel wrapped around his waist. "And?" he asked.

Molly looked at his strong body wet with steam, his hair slicked away from his broad forehead, and the seriousness of his eyes. Cole's looks commanded attention, and, whether he was happy, mad, or sleeping, it didn't matter, there was something extraordinary about him—the square of his jaw, the ever-present darkening of the lower half of his face, where, within hours, a five o'clock shadow would settle in, like salt and pepper sprinkled on his upper lip, down his cheeks, and into the little dimple in his chin. He walked into a room and people gawked, women and men alike. He spoke softly and they wanted to align themselves with him, just to be close enough to catch every breath, but when he was upset, his eyes darkened, his stance became manlier, taller, puffed-up. At the moment, Molly was lost in those looks, but her growing desire was quickly quelled by her guilt—guilt for knowing she was omitting the relentless resolve she felt toward finding Tracey. "I'll do what I didn't do, what I wasn't able to do, for Amanda. I'll help."

A look of pity stole over Cole's face. "Mol, what happened to Amanda wasn't your fault. You have to let that go." Cole wasn't used to dealing with the old demons anymore. They'd subsided in the past few years, and he felt a bit rusty trying to deal with them now, but he knew the potential they had to cripple his wife.

Molly grew sullen and looked away.

"Mol," Cole said again, "I get it. I was there, remember? Amanda's gone. You can't save her. Tracey's not Amanda."

"I know she's not Amanda," Molly snapped. "Don't you think I know that?" Molly pleaded with him to understand. "I have to do this, Cole. I just want to help."

Cole threw his hands up. "Fine, Molly, but I'm worried about you. It feels like we just got back to normal, and I'm not sure we can make it through that again." He walked to Molly's side. "Please, Mol, think about this. You weren't at the point of abduction. It doesn't come down to you saving this girl. The whole damn town is looking for her." He gestured with his arm as if to encompass all of Boyds.

Molly knew he was right about their relationship. After Amanda, she'd become useless, and hadn't trusted herself to make decisions. Cole had been supportive and understanding. He'd taken her to therapists, was patient when she would have a near panic attack at the sound of a crying child, and finally, with no other choice, he'd agreed to pack up their family, leave his practice, and move to the country. Molly was thankful, and she knew her recovery would not have been possible without him by her side, but something in Molly needed this. It was something that she had to do.

She was non-committal, "Don't worry. I won't do anything stupid."

"It's not stupidity that worries me," he said. "It's your damn drive and determination. Once you get something in your head, you don't let it go."

The Boyds Country Store had been in business for decades, and Molly could imagine, as she pulled up to the front of the store, that the old wooden bench and the three men who sat upon it each morning had been there just as long. Harley Mott, Mac Peterson, and Joe Dillon, or as Molly liked to call them, the Boyds Boys, were the eyes and ears of Boyds. They'd grown up together, each in their sixties now, and if the stories that Molly had heard were true, they knew intimacies about residents that paralleled teenage gossip.

Molly greeted the men with a smile, "Hey, guys!"

"Hey, girl!" Harley said, a term of endearment that had taken Molly two years to get used to. A burly farmer with slicked-back graying hair, he had an imposing presence and had become protective of Molly for reasons she never understood.

She grabbed copies of the *Washington Post* and the *Frederick News-Post*, scanning them on the porch of the store. Tracey Porter was front-page news, "Boyds Girl Still Missing, Foul Play Suspected." Molly shook her head. She had hoped they might have found Tracey and that the Knowing had been wrong. She glanced up and into the three tired faces of the Boyds Boys. Molly knew their reputation for being bad boys in their younger days, and yet she wasn't able to reconcile that reputation with the three fatherly types that sat before her.

"Have you heard about this?" she turned the newspapers toward them. Immediately their faces hardened—Mac, a small, squirrel of a man, who never had much to say and always appeared a tad bit nervous, pursed his lips and looked away, Harley fiddled with his coffee cup and stared into the dark liquid, and Joe sat between the two, huddling toward the back of the bench.

Molly gave Harley an inquisitive look.

Harley shuffled his feet, his heavy boots scraping against the concrete of the porch, and took a long sip of his coffee. "Well, Molly," he said quietly, "it's just that…well…it's too much like what happened twenty years ago is all." He looked toward Mac, who shook his head and looked away. "It's a little too close to home."

Molly's heart leapt in her chest, *It's not your fault.*

Pastor Lett pulled up in her blue corvette, a car that Molly believed was a little too flashy for a woman of the cloth, though Pastor Lett's argument was that just because she spoke to God did not mean that she had to be as invisible as Him. Children loved Pastor Lett's car. She often took them on rides up and down White Ground Road after the children's services at church. Pastor Lett was very supportive of their activities, showing up at their baseball games, gymnastic meets, and even Girl Scout and Boy Scout outings.

"Good morning, Pastor Lett," Molly said, still distracted by Harley's disclosure. "How's Mrs. Porter doing? Any news yet?"

Pastor Lett walked nervously past Molly, giving her a brief nod, "Molly." She shot the Boyds Boys a contemptuous look and walked into the store.

Molly bristled at the brush-off and looked toward Harley. "What's up with that?"

A knowing look passed between the Boyds Boys. Molly did not like to be ignored. She sat herself down between Harley and Joe, purposely making them uncomfortable. "It's okay, I can wait," she said.

Joe, who had probably been somewhat of a lady's man in his day, with his Gregory Peck good looks and quiet demeanor, cleared his throat, and Harley took another sip of his coffee. Molly didn't budge.

Pastor Lett walked out of the store, orange juice in hand and a newspaper under her arm. She didn't look back at the four of them, packed on the bench like sardines. She got in her car, started her engine, and backed out without ever looking up.

"Okay, guys, spit it out," Molly said. Tension thickened the silence between them. "What the heck, Joe?"

Joe looked away.

"Mac?" Molly said, forcefully.

Mac looked down at his boots.

"Oh, for God's sake," she said, angrily. "Harley?" she caught his gaze and held it, ignoring the twitch that long ago had claimed his left eye.

Harley looked down and fingered the ends of his frayed flannel shirt. He turned his body to face Molly, and said, in barely a whisper, "Kate Plummer. She disappeared about twenty years ago—same way." He looked at Joe, who scowled at him. Mac let his breath out loud and hard in displeasure, and nodded so slightly that had Molly not been scrutinizing every move, she may have missed it.

"What do you mean, 'same way'?" she asked.

"She was playing at the preschool playground. You know the one behind the church on White Ground?" he looked down again, and his voice held a hint of anger. "They never found her."

Molly jumped to her feet, shocked by the news. She looked at the three men, who sat in silence, again avoiding her eyes. Her mind raced with questions. "What happened?"

"She just disappeared," Harley began.

Mac interrupted, "She lived right here in Boyds, by the old Wade farm."

"That's right," Joe said. "The Plummers were mighty upset," he shook his head. "They stayed around for about five or six years, hoping she'd come back, or turn up somehow, but they just couldn't take it, I suppose." He swirled his coffee in the Styrofoam cup, watching it intently. "Moved away, Missouri, I think, back where the wife's family was from." Mac and Harley nodded in confirmation.

Molly paced across the porch—her mind reeled. "How does that happen at such a small playground?" She turned in the direction of the preschool, envisioning the tiny playground, no bigger than a one-car garage.

Harley filled her in. There had been a birthday party with several children playing and a few parents watching over them. "Late September, if my memory serves me correctly."

Mac confirmed, "Remember, they were late harvesting the corn that year because Ned broke his combine machine, and Harley here had to fill in after he finished Hannah's fields."

Harley nodded in affirmation, "Yup, September," he sipped his coffee. "Anyway, I guess the kids were playing hide and seek, and when they got in their cars to leave, they noticed she was missing."

"Where were her parents?" Molly asked.

"Mrs. Plummer, Bonnie, she was ill," Joe said. "Had the cancer, you know? She'd had it for about a year by then. They operated, did some chemo, you know, she was real sick. So Kate was taken care of by neighbors, mostly. Other moms would take her to school, take care of her after school, run her to Girl Scouts, and whatnot. They were a tight-knit group back then, the moms."

Molly asked about her father, and Harley told her that Paulie had worked two jobs just to make ends meet.

"That type of thing never happened," Harley's voice trailed off.

"It never happens anywhere, until it *does* happen," Molly was screaming inside, incredulous on the surface.

"Anyway," Harley began, "they searched, but they ain't never found no sign of her." Harley finished his coffee and crushed the Styrofoam cup with his hand.

Mac got off the bench and threw away his cup. He went to the end of the porch and leaned against one of the wooden columns, his back to the others.

Joe kicked his shoes against the concrete and cleared his throat—when Harley looked over, Joe shot him a stern look. Harley shrugged.

Molly picked up on the cues. "What?" Her eyes darted from Harley to Joe and back again.

51

Harley drew in a deep breath, and let it out slowly. "Well," he said, "they never found Kate, but they knew who did it."

After a long, uncomfortable pause, Molly prompted, "Well…who did it?"

Mac's words fell fast from his lips. "Pastor Lett's damned younger brother, Rodney."

Molly was bewildered, "Pastor Lett has a brother? I've known her for years and never heard her talk about him."

"*Had* a brother. Rodney," Mac said. "He died that year, too."

Molly thought about Pastor Lett, the way she'd hurried past, the look she'd given them. "What happened to him?"

Joe suddenly became enraged, "He knew too much, Molly!" He paced across the porch, muttering under his breath, "Goddamn killer."

Harley explained that shortly after Kate had gone missing, Rodney had been outside on his front porch when a reporter had stopped by, looking for the pastor. As he spoke, Harley rubbed his hands on his jeans, which appeared permanently stained from that specific move. "He looked right at the reporter and just starts sayin', 'She's in a dark place. She doesn't hurt.'" Harley sat back down on the bench, as if preparing himself for a tiring story. "Everything seemed to fast forward from that point. The police arrived, reporters, angry residents." Harley sighed. "They took Rodney to the station, and he told them that Kate was with her mommy, which you know meant that he'd killed her— that he buried her somewhere to go to heaven like her mother eventually would, Bonnie, you know?"

"Well if he was saying all those things, then no wonder the police arrested him, but if he knew where she was, why didn't they find her?" Molly asked.

"They didn't have enough evidence to keep his ass in jail. I have no idea how these dumb-ass police work, but they let the son-of-a-bitch go!" Mac threw his cup into the trash and said, "They have a guy telling them that she's in a dark goddamn place, and they let him *go*?"

"But you said he died. How'd he die?" Molly asked.

When the three men remained silent and avoided Molly's eyes, she pressed for an answer.

Harley lifted his eyes, met her gaze, then turned away. "He was beat to death," he said quietly. "People don't take too kindly around here to a little girl being killed, or stolen, or whatever."

Molly felt light-headed. "If she was alive, then no one could have found her anyway after Rodney was killed. Whoever beat him up should be ashamed. That poor girl never had a chance after that." Molly's words were angry, but the tickle down the back of her neck held the truth. There were many times, since Amanda's death, that she wished she'd had the courage to find her killer—and the strength to do the same thing.

Seven

Tracey kept her arms close to her body to avoid touching the dirt walls. The confined space of the tunnel made her heart race, her breathing hindered. She knew she'd be punished for fighting back the evening before. She couldn't stop her body from shaking or the tears from pouring silently down her cheeks. The ground was cold and wet under her bare feet. She gritted her teeth together, trying not to let her captor see her cry. *Crying girls get punished.* Tracey saw candles burning up ahead. Relief flooded through her as she realized that she was not headed toward the bad spot but rather toward her captor's praying place.

Three candles burned. She knew from the prior evening that one candle was for her captor, one was for her captor's mother, and the last one was for her. When Mummy had told Tracey about them, she had acted nice, but when Tracey had asked where her mother was, her captor had gotten mad and yelled at her, *Don't you speak of my mother!* Her eyes had burned through Tracey's, and her face had contorted. Tracey didn't ask any more questions.

Tracey followed her captor's lead and knelt on the cold earth. She held her hands together tightly to stop them from shaking. It didn't work. She wished she were invisible.

"That's Mummy's girl," her captor said. She handed Tracey a Bible and spoke in an eerie whisper, her voice so confident and the words spoken so smoothly, Tracey felt as if she were sitting in Sunday School. "John 8:42. The Children of the Devil. Jesus said to them, 'If God were your Father, you would love me, for I came from God and now am here. I have not come on my own; but He sent me. Why is my language not clear to you? Because you are unable to hear what I say. You belong to your father, the devil, and you want to carry out your father's desire.'"

Tracey felt eyes boring down on her and kept her own eyes trained on the candles. She didn't dare look up. *Daddy is not the devil!* Tracey wished the woman, who was as big as any man she had ever seen, would just go away. She wanted to go home. She was so tired that it was hard to keep her eyes open, and yet she knew better than to close them. Tracey hated her captor, she hated her words, *I'm your mummy now,* she hated her lies, *If you come see me, alone, I'll give you back your necklace,* and she hated the smell of her breath, like she'd caten too many Slim Jims. Tracey snuck a peek in her captor's direction.

"He who belongs to God hears what God says. The reason you do not hear is that you do not belong to God," Mummy prayed.

Tracey grew angrier as she listened to Mummy pray. In her mind she heard her mother calling her during their last game of hide and seek, *"Tracey Lynn, Emma Elizabeth, where are you girls? You hide better than fish in a pond!"* Tracey swallowed hard.

Eight

Molly felt as if she were being thrown back in time. She could barely wrap her mind around the fact that the small town she'd chosen for its safety and charm had been home to the exact thing she thought she had escaped. Maybe Cole was right. Maybe she should close her eyes and walk away, just not think about Tracey, or Amanda. *It's not my fault.* She drove by the church, vacillating between trying to go for a run and doing a little investigating, finally giving up on the idea of running on a bum ankle. She rationalized that she could keep her promise to Cole by walking instead of running. He didn't have to know that her chosen path was because of Tracey. She headed further down the road toward the Hoyles Mill Conservation Trail.

Molly put her cell phone in her back pocket, threw her pack over her shoulder, and faced the well-hidden trail. It struck her as odd that she'd lived in Boyds for so many years and had never before been on the Hoyles Mill Conservation Trail. She picked up a stick and made her way down the trail, refreshed by the sounds of the birds and the smell of the leaves. It crossed her mind, briefly, that she had been able to drive down White Ground Road without encountering the Knowing, and as much as she disliked the impact it had on her, she also wished for answers about Tracey. She wondered if the episode on White Ground had simply been a coincidence, and if Cole was right, that she was setting herself up for another heartache, or worse.

She quickly came upon a little bridge that crossed a stream. She tossed a stone in just to hear it land and savored the light *plink!* Molly told herself that she wasn't really looking for clues about Tracey, but just taking a walk to replace the run she'd skipped. If she could convince herself of that, than surely she could convince Cole. The foliage increased, and the path became harder to follow as she pushed through vines and made her way deeper into the woods. An hour of walking caused her ankle to ache, and Molly found the absence of the Knowing strangely and painfully disappointing.

Eventually, she came to a clearing, a large meadow that eased up a hill and edged a cornfield. *Great*, she thought, *now I'm lost at someone's farm.* Exasperated, she made her way up the small hill, angry with herself for wasting her morning. At the crest of the hill, the rear of Kerr Hall came into view. The small, concrete building used for the preschool was situated directly behind the Boyds Presbyterian Church. The playground where Kate must have disappeared stood bare, the swings swaying in the gentle breeze. Molly swore under her breath, realizing she'd gone in the wrong direction when she had lost sight of the path. *Or did I*, whispered through her head. She sighed and began the trek down the hill, through the cornfield, toward the church. A noise startled her. She froze, listening. The sound pierced the air again, growing into what sounded like a child crying. Molly yelled out, "Tracey! Is that you?" Her heartbeat quickened, pounding through her with hope. There was no response. She ran toward the sound, "Tracey? Is that you? Tracey!" Still no response. She heard rustling, like a small child running through the cornstalks. Molly was shorter than the stalks and couldn't tell which direction to search. "Hey!" she yelled. "Wait, I can help you!" In her haste, she stepped in a ditch and fell to the ground. She tried to stand, but was incapacitated by the throbbing pain in her ankle. "Shit!" she yelled. "Shit, shit, shit!" She remained on the ground to ease the pain and reached for her cell phone, flipping it open as fast as she was able. She held it up—no bars, no service! "Goddamn it! Piece of shit!" she yelled. "Tracey!" She looked to the sky and screamed out of sheer frustration.

The crying had stopped, the rustling had stopped, and the area around Molly was silent. Her ankle throbbed. She pushed herself up to her feet and yelled, "Tracey? Tracey Porter?" There was no response. Adrenaline pumped through her, enabling Molly to hobble toward the church, flinching with each step. Painfully making her way out of the cornfield, she reached the parking lot just as Nelly, a teacher for the pre-school, came out of Kerr Hall.

"Nelly," Molly yelled, waving her arms. Nelly looked in her direction, squinted, then walked towards Molly.

"Molly," she looked her up and down, "what on Earth happened to you?"

"You wouldn't believe me," she said. "I heard a crying sound in the cornfield. Can you call the police to come check it out?" her words rushed out of her. "Maybe they can bring dogs or something. Maybe it's the little girl, Tracey Porter," she tried to catch her breath.

"Oh my! Let me go call." She turned to go, then turned back toward Molly. "Are you sure you're okay?"

Molly waved her on. "Of course! Go! Hurry!" She turned back toward the silent cornfield, praying that Tracey was in it, safe, unharmed. Molly limped to the red painted picnic table, its wood etched with children's names from years past. She laid her pack on the worn bench and suddenly realized how much her life had changed over the past twenty-four hours. She pulled out her cell phone, hoping to have service, and dialed Cole's number, cursing that her phone had not connected when she had desperately needed it. She filled him in on what had transpired, gracefully accepting his initial chastising, "Geez, Mol. I told you to stay out of the woods!" After a pause of silence, he added, distractedly, "Maybe they'll find her. Are you okay?"

Molly rubbed her ankle. "I guess, yeah. I hope they find her, Cole. You know, the longer it is with no clues, the harder it gets, until…" She found it too difficult to think about what came next.

"They'll find her, Mol, don't worry. It's a small town, someone probably saw something."

The way his voice trailed off, Molly knew that he'd realized what he'd said, and what it meant to her. He was trying to remain hopeful about Tracey, she knew, but this wasn't about hope. She'd seen something. She'd failed Amanda, and they both knew it. Her inability to let go of that guilt lay between them like a great chasm.

Within fifteen minutes of Nelly's emergency call, the fields were swarming with police officers. They weaved in and out of the fields, walking in neat rows so as not to miss the smallest hint of a child. They filtered into the woods in groups of three, some called out Tracey's name. Others just yelled out, "Hello!"

Suddenly, the officers converged on the lower field, less than fifty feet from where Molly had fallen. "Get back!" Molly heard someone yell. "Give us some room!" This was followed by loud gasps and murmurs.

Molly felt supremely frustrated—watching from afar and longing to run into the field. She tried to stand, but her ankle sent a sharp pain shooting up her calf. Nelly ran out of Kerr Hall, where she had been tending to the children, and said, "What happened? I heard yelling."

"Over there," Molly pointed to the area where the search party had gathered. "They found something. Oh God, Nelly, I hope it's Tracey! Go see, please!" Molly watched her run toward the commotion. She hadn't made her way halfway through the field when the crowd began to disperse. Nelly stopped to talk to a middle-aged police officer. Molly watched as Nelly's shoulders dropped. She feared the worst. Nelly ran back to her and sat down on the picnic bench, out of breath.

"They found..." she paused as she caught her breath, and Molly held hers.

"What? What is it? Did they find her?" she asked. Nelly's face was drawn, as if she carried horrific news.

"They found a family of foxes." She put her hand on Molly's knee. "I'm so sorry."

Molly exhaled, confused. She looked toward the field and could feel her entire body deflate. Her renewed hope dwindled. Tears rolled down her cheeks, leaving thin wet streaks. "What…" she whispered, "what about the crying?"

"The mother fox is injured. It looks like she has a broken leg, and when she heard you coming she must have been trying to get her cubs to safety. The crying must have been her screaming in pain as she moved them along."

The enormity of the disappointment devoured Molly. She could barely focus on what Nelly was telling her.

"They said they'll probably have to put her down. I don't know about the pups, though." Nelly stood up, "I'm going to get you some juice. I'll be right back." She started toward Kerr Hall, paused, and turned back to Molly. "The oddest thing, though, one of the baby foxes had one of those Airhead candies in its mouth. When they approached the pup, he dropped it and curled up around it." She looked toward the field. "Weird, huh?"

Molly reached for the picnic table as the world around her began to spin. The taste of apple candy pooled in her mouth.

Molly was sitting at her computer, her leg elevated, and a bag of frozen peas perched atop the swollen protrusion that was her ankle when she heard Cole enter the den. She didn't look at him, for fear of hearing those dreaded words, "I told you so." She feared she'd cry, the devastation of the foxes still rode the surface of her emotions.

He walked behind her and rested his hands on her shoulders, kissing the top of her head. "Hi," he said sweetly.

She craned her neck back and looked up at him.

"I brought you something," he said, handing her a plastic bag.

Molly loved presents, even the smallest of gifts—a card, a token from an airport—she was appreciative of the thought behind them, and Cole always seemed to give her a little something at just the right time.

She grabbed the bag and reached her hand inside, curiously. "What is it?" She grasped the gift, recognized the feel of it, and said, "Oh no! You have to stop doing this." She pulled the sack of Hershey's Gold miniature candy bars from the bag, "I didn't even get to run today. I'll be as big as a cow soon!"

"I figured you could use a pick-me-up," he said, and started toward the family room. "Besides," he called over his shoulder, "you can put them away and eat just one each day."

"Yeah," she called back, laughing, "you know how that works. I'll hide them from myself, then spend every two minutes jumping up to get one, as if there's a spring on my butt, until the entire bag is gone." She stuffed the candies in her desk drawer and locked it. "Thank you!" she called out.

Molly spent hours researching "ground-emitting heat" on the internet, to no avail. She had skipped dinner, asked Cole to fend for himself because of her ankle, a convenient excuse, and had Cole take their dogs for their nightly walk. She had dismissed the call from her mother, and once again put off calling Erik. Frustration brewed within her—there didn't seem to be any plausible reason for the phenomenon. She read about the greenhouse effect, heat flux, man and nature, physical geography as modified by human action, and several other topics that a week before she couldn't have cared less about.

She spun around on her chair and decided to take a different angle. She accessed the library resources, which made the old microfiche archives seem like the dark ages—a skill she learned from her technological-virgin of a husband, who had learned it from his library specialist at work. She searched "Kate Plummer" and immediately found several sites referencing the little girl's disappearance. She scanned through as many as she was able before fatigue set in. The only new information she gained was that the investigation had ended shortly after Rodney Lett had been killed.

Molly leaned back in her chair, listening to the sounds of the television filter in from the family room. She sat up suddenly, disliking herself as she turned back to her laptop and googled "Hannah Slate". Nine pages of data were found. The new search renewed her energy, and she scanned the materials until finally finding something relevant to the Hannah Slate she knew. A local *Gazette* article in the Community News and Events section recognized her for her many contributions to the community regarding equestrian issues and lobbying efforts, and noted her twenty-plus years of employment at the Department of the Navy. It also noted her recovery from a hospital stay for "undisclosed trauma." The article was from the same year as Hannah's divorce. Molly recalled attending a prayer meeting, at the urging of Pastor Lett, when she had moved to Boyds. It was there that she had first met Hannah who'd been attending the prayer group since her divorce. Molly shuddered, remembering how she had wanted to run from that room, the religious overtone too strong for her at a time when she had been so angry at God.

Molly's eyes grew tired, and she scolded herself for thinking that Hannah could have been involved in Tracey's disappearance.

Molly shut down her computer and put the bag of watery peas into the freezer. She hobbled past Cole, asleep in the family room, and gingerly mounted the stairs. She crawled into bed and quickly fell asleep. She was awakened an hour later as Cole wrapped his warm body around hers like a cocoon. Her body settled against his, and she fell asleep, comforted by his embrace.

Nine

Molly woke with a start at dawn, covered in sweat and shaking all over. She sat upright in bed, took a deep cleansing breath, and tried to maintain the flow of air to her lungs, a sickeningly sweet syrupy taste swam in her mouth. As she'd done many times before, she leaned over and grabbed her notepad and pen from the wooden nightstand. She began quickly sketching the images as they flew through her mind: *a dark cavernous hole, trails leading out of the hole and into other shadowy cavernous rooms, a wooden box the size of a crate of wine, sealed with nails.* Just as Molly's throat began to relax, her mind was assailed again, thrusting her body forward. Cole rolled away from Molly, unaware of her difficulty. The image of a shovel flashed before her and was blacked out by a thick mass of trees. As quickly as Molly was overwhelmed by the Knowing, it vanished, leaving her exhausted and energized at the same time. It had taken Molly thirty years to understand the difference between dreams and visions, thirty years to realize that looking out a window after a dream washed it away, leaving a mere shadow in her mind, while nothing could erase the images from her visions which lingered for days, taunting her and leaving her feeling adrift, helpless, and curious.

As her body began to wind down, she curled against Cole once again, causing him to stir. "I love you," she whispered, as she often did when she was scared. He turned to hold her, as he often did when he knew she just needed to be held. Molly lay safe and warm, unable to sleep, and unable to swallow without tasting the sweet flavor of apple candy.

The sun began to rise just as Pastor Lett finished boarding the last window on the Perkinson House. *This should keep the kid inside*, Pastor Lett thought. Her arms ached from hammering during the cover of the cold night. Balancing herself on the ladder had become trickier as the morning had approached and the roof had become slick with dew. She maneuvered down the ladder, her mind drifting back to the previous evening. She had approached the cellar in the same careful manner, and she'd thought for sure that there had been another incident—her warnings perhaps were not sharp enough. Inside, she had found the kid curled up on the mattress, fast asleep. The kid must have been exhausted from all of the fighting the evening before. Pastor Lett had noticed the bruises on both wrists and arms, and her heart wrenched. She had explained the importance of heeding her warnings and avoiding danger. "They wouldn't understand my need to take care of you, to protect you," she had said. She had reached her hand out, but the kid hadn't budged. The kid had just looked at her, unsure, scared. Pastor Lett had seen that look before, and she didn't let it sway her duty then, any more than she did now. She had turned away and left the dark room, locked up, and had gone to work on the long, tedious job of sealing up the windows and adding locks to the outside of the doors.

With her tools neatly organized, she made her way, exhausted, down the overgrown knoll toward her car, thankful that she had decided to park at the enclave just before the bridge, where fishermen and families parked near the edge of the lake. She threw her sweater over her shoulder, her turtleneck just warm enough for the chilly morning air, and retrieved a handful of sunflower seeds, gnawing them into tiny bits. The last ten feet to her car seemed like a mile, the import of what she'd done weighed heavily on her heart. Exhausted, she leaned against the car and looked back toward the Perkinson House—no telltale chimney showed above the trees, no worn pathway snaked its way up the knoll from the lake. It was as if it didn't exist, though she was thankful it did. She whispered, "God, forgive me for what I've done," and headed home to escape the nightmare that had become her life.

A quick visit to the police station revealed that they had no suspects in Tracey's disappearance. Even worse, they appeared to have no real clues, either. Though the officer at the desk gave Molly the usual line of not being able to give out pertinent details, as it might hinder the case, it was clear to her that the search was at a standstill.

Molly had also inquired about the previous disappearance of Kate Plummer, which she knew was pushing her luck, but that didn't stop her. Most of the local law enforcement officials had not been around long enough to know about the Kate Plummer case; however, there was one detective who remembered the case and was willing to speak to Molly.

A short, plump man ambled toward Molly, his hand outstretched, "Officer Brown," he said, as if he were bored.

Molly couldn't help but see a resemblance between Officer Brown and the Pillsbury doughboy, minus the cheery attitude. She swallowed her chuckle and said, professionally, "Molly Tanner, President of the Boyds Civic Association. There's been talk around the community? Residents are trying to draw correlations between Tracey Porter's disappearance and the disappearance of Kate Plummer. I was hoping you could shed some light for me, help me calm their fears."

Officer Brown rolled his eyes and motioned for Molly to follow him. He led her down a stale gray and pale green corridor, turning back to look at Molly every few steps. They entered a small room with a square metal table, no bigger than a desk one might find in a cubicle, and two metal chairs. Molly was mildly surprised to see what she was sure was a stereotypical two-way mirror in the center of the far wall. Officer Brown motioned for Molly to sit down. He must have read Molly's mind, because at that moment he said, "This is our interrogation room." He motioned with his chubby hands around the small enclosure. "It all happens here: confessions, lies, manipulations." His round face was a strange mix of excitement and weariness. His pink cheeks overlapped the sides of his mouth, and he breathed hard from the long walk down the corridor. His brown hair was matted on the top of his head, like a schoolboy with a bad case of hat head.

His arms rested on his protruding belly, and he acted as if he thought he should be abrupt but couldn't quite pull it off.

"Thank you for taking the time to speak with me," Molly rested her arms on the table and smiled. "I'm sure there's probably no link here, but I've only just learned about Kate…and Rodney Lett, and, well, the cases seem similar. You can see why the residents are talking. I was hoping you could fill me in so I can waylay their fears."

Molly expected him to give her the song and dance of not being able to reveal details of the case, but he surprised her, "Well, let's see." He looked at the ceiling, thinking. "That was about twenty years ago, if I remember correctly." He pursed his lips, as if he were trying to figure out the details in his mind. "Odd boy, he was. A man, really, but with a boy's mind."

"That's what I've heard, sort of," she offered.

"He wasn't retarded, not that we could tell anyway. It seemed he was just slow. He would talk slow, move slow, he even thought slow, taking sometimes ten minutes before he would answer questions, but when he answered, he was, or he seemed, one hundred percent certain of his answers."

"Did anyone in the community have trouble with him before Kate Plummer went missing?" Molly asked.

"No, no, not really." As he shook his head, his chin jiggled. "Never heard much about the boy." Detective Brown looked thoughtful. "It wasn't till the Plummer case that we had any trouble with him." He looked away, then back at Molly, "But then again, they never do appear dangerous, now, do they?"

Molly shrugged noncommittally.

Officer Brown continued, "But he knew the details about little Kate Plummer, that's for sure."

"Do you think he heard someone else talking about it, or that there could have been some other explanation?" she asked.

He gave her a stunned look. "He did it. He took that little girl and killed her." He stared at Molly until she became uncomfortable and looked down.

Molly bristled at the coldness of his words, and began to feel sick to her stomach. *The body of six-year-old Amanda—*

"Pastor Lett," he let out a little laugh, "she was really something. She kept insisting that Rodney had some sort of sixth sense."

The hair on the back of Molly's neck stood on end. She gathered her courage and reminded herself that Amanda was not Tracey. "Sixth sense?" she asked.

"I don't know. It sounded like a load of horse manure to me. You know, the older sister trying to save the younger brother type of thing." He looked around the room, fidgeted as if he were getting tired of the conversation. He leaned back in his chair, which Molly was sure would send him flying backwards, but it didn't, and said, "The guy didn't really have an alibi, either, if I remember correctly. I think he said he was at home when Kate was taken. I don't remember anyone being able to corroborate that story for him." He sighed heavily, "People came to fear him very quickly."

Molly readjusted her position, feeling as though she wanted to run out of the room, cover her ears, and forget the whole thing, but Officer Brown's voice reeled her back in.

"Pastor Lett found him that night and took his body to Delaware before we could even file a formal

71

report. Said she was too upset to wait for the medical examiner to come by. Said she couldn't take all of the red tape anymore." He leaned forward in his chair, resting his elbows on the edge of the table. "She was gone within minutes of the phone call to the police, far as we could tell. She called later that evening, saying they were burying her brother the next morning and apologizing for taking off so quickly."

"She must have been upset, but isn't there some protocol for such an event? I mean if he was *killed,* then wasn't there a murder investigation?" Molly asked.

"Yes, indeedy, there was. We searched the house, dusted for prints and all, and came up with nothing more than a broken window in the rear, which is how we think the murderers got in. We found boot prints in the house, several, in fact. Farm boots, the type that all the men in these parts wear. There were no solid leads. It sort of died out. In fact, people were happy to have closure at that point, and the Wilmington Police Chief followed up with the Lett family on their end."

"But, Kate, what happened to her?" she spoke quickly, wanting answers faster than he could give them.

"Well, we continued the search for her. Took his clues, in fact, of a dark cold place. We searched the woods, crevices at Sugarloaf Mountain, trails, and boroughs. We found nothing at all. After a few weeks, we all assumed she was gone—dead, I mean—and that he had disposed of her. The case on Kate Plummer is closed, although the file will remain open until her body is found—if it's ever found."

"But—"

Officer Brown stood abruptly, "Mrs. Tanner, you just tell the residents that there's no connection between the two cases. Rodney Lett is dead and buried."

Molly knew when she'd been dismissed.

The bell above the door chimed as Molly entered the Country Store, and she shouted out her usual, "Hey, Jin!" and limped toward the coolers. Jin didn't answer. Molly looked around the small store, four aisles of household necessities and snacks, but no Jin. She walked toward the rear of the store and called out again, "Jin?" He and his wife, Edie, had owned the store for twenty-five years, and Molly had yet to find the store attended by someone other than Jin or Edie. Molly admired his level of responsibility but in no way wanted to mimic it. She was happy that Cole was home with her at night, and even happier that he had been home with Erik when he was little.

The silence of the store pressed in on her. She grabbed a bottle of water and a Power Bar and was about to call out for Jin again when she heard hushed voices coming from the storeroom. Molly's heart quickened. The store was an easy target for robbery, with the glass of the store covered with banners advertising beer and wine, and the old push-button style cash register. Everyone in town knew that Jin had no security or alarm system—he didn't believe in them.

Molly stood near the storeroom door, "Jin, are you okay?"

"Be right out," Jin said, hurriedly. His Korean accent was as strong as ever. Molly heard Edie say something in Korean, and relief washed through her. Jin's voice became loud and harsh. Molly turned to walk toward the cash register as Jin opened the door, carrying a towel in his right hand. His pants hung off of his slim waist, and his thick black hair was cropped short and combed neatly to the side. "I ring you up," he said impatiently.

"Is Edie...alright?" Molly asked.

"Oh yes. She upset, that's all," he walked behind the counter. "The little girl that is missing, she worried about her," he said.

Molly was relieved by the simple, appropriate concern. "Do you know the family?" she asked.

"No, no. I see the girl before," he was calm and thoughtful, "but I did not know her family."

Molly paid for her purchase, began to leave, then hesitated, "Jin, did you know Pastor Lett's brother, Rodney?"

Jin looked up and away, saddened. "Ah, yes," he said. "I know Rodney." He busied himself straightening up shelves that lined the wall behind the counter. "Poor Rodney. He no kill that girl." He looked at Molly and held her gaze.

The comment took Molly by surprise. "I'm sorry...about him. How well did you know him?" she asked.

"He come here. All the time he come here. While his sister was at work, he walked here," Jin pointed in the direction of the train tracks, and looked toward the back of the store, as if a memory were weaving its way into his mind. "He used to come, talk. He was very, very smart." The "r" in "smart" came across as an additional short "a".

"Really?" Molly said, happy to have been told something positive about Rodney, for whom, for some odd reason, she felt horribly sorry. "Tell me about him," she put her bag on the counter.

"He smart. He knew things," Jin pointed to his temple and tapped it a few times with his index finger. "He had feelings about things—good and bad—present, future." Jin looked down at the floor, "That's what got him in trouble."

"Yeah, so I've heard," Molly said.

"People around here," Jin made a guttural sound of disgust, "they so quick to judge. They no like being scared." He looked into Molly's eyes, "They take things into their own hands," he shook his head, "shame."

Molly grabbed the paper bag containing her water and Power Bar, and turned toward a noise in the back of the store. Edie stood in her long black and gold caftan which dwarfed her small frame. She turned red-rimmed eyes to Jin with a mixed look of anger, hurt, and disbelief—as if she had walked in on Jin in bed with another woman.

"Hi, Edie!" Molly said cheerily, trying to ease the tension that had settled in the small store. "I was just asking Jin about Rodney Lett."

"I know," she said sullenly. She spoke Korean to Jin through clenched teeth. Jin did not respond.

"Do *you* think he took that little girl, Kate Plummer?" Molly asked, turning to Edie.

Edie shook her head and moved behind the counter to Jin's side. She stood with her body half-hidden behind Jin's, as if seeking his protection.

"Both of you think he was innocent, and yet, he was beaten to death," Molly was almost talking to herself. Acknowledging her own doubt of Rodney's guilt, she could not understand her loyalty to this man, a possible killer. "Do you have any idea who killed him?"

Jin looked annoyed, "No, but I bet he know before it happened."

"Before?"

"People don't," he hesitated, "no understand him." Edie vanished further behind him. "He know things before they happen," Jin turned and put his arm around Edie, who had her hands steepled together as if praying.

"People say all sorts of things," Molly rationalized.

Jin shook his head, "Told me things that happen in future." A look of longing passed over Jin's face. "Rodney, he know things no one else understand. He could see..."

Edie mumbled under her breath, "Never find her." She turned angry eyes toward Molly, "Never find girl! They kill Rodney because he know things. No proof! No proof that he took her!" she threw her hands up in the air, and stomped toward the stock room.

"I'm sorry, Jin," Molly said. "I didn't mean to upset her, but she's right. What *did* happen to Kate? Did Rodney take her and kill her?" she wondered.

Jin walked up to Molly, standing within inches of her face. She took a step back, uncomfortable around Jin for the first time since she'd known him. He pointed his index finger at the ceiling, and said, calmly, confidently, "Rodney did not kill that girl. Rodney did not take that girl. I don't know what happened—but not Rodney." Then he turned and walked away.

Pastor Lett wondered how long one woman could carry on her ritual. When she had left the Perkinson House the evening before, the kid was rocking back and forth. She could not get the kid to speak to her—it was getting to be too much for her, and yet she found herself compelled to continue. Even if she had wanted to stop at that point, she wasn't sure she could. She felt it was her calling.

As she approached the altar, she reluctantly released the bag of seeds in her pocket, withdrew her hand, lit a candle, and knelt down as she did every morning, though this day it was afternoon, with the sun already perched high in the sky. She had slept late, her arms and legs ached from her recent labor. Her mind, devoid of energy, had acquiesced to a night of dreamless sleep.

She bowed her head and whispered, "Forgive me, Lord, for I have sinned. You know this, of course," she said. "I've been a sinner for so many years that I know I have no right to ask for your forgiveness, but I am going to anyway. Please forgive me, Lord. I love this kid. I know it's wrong—keeping the kid locked away like this." She choked on her words, took a minute to pull herself together, and then said, "People would never understand. I need a sign, Lord. I need a sign that you understand what I have done and why." She rested her head in her hand, her aged fingers splayed across her tired eyes, rubbing them as if by doing so, the simple motion would bring her clarity.

She startled when the doors of the church slammed closed. She jumped up and turned around, hoping her visitor had not heard what she had said. "Molly," she said, surprised, "what brings you to church this morning?" She smoothed down her jacket and walked toward her, trying to read her expression.

"Hi, Pastor Lett," she said, "I...I just wanted to stop by and see how you were doing." The kindness in Molly's voice eased her mind.

As Molly limped toward her, Pastor Lett wondered if Molly could see her fatigue. Molly's head was cocked slightly to the side, as if she were studying Pastor Lett, analyzing her. Pastor Lett wiped her face anxiously.

"I'm okay, Molly," she said uncomfortably. "Worried about the Porters, of course, but doing well, thank you."

Pastor Lett motioned to Molly's wrapped ankle, "Running accident?" she asked.

"This?" Molly lifted her ankle and twisted it, looking it over. "Yeah, kind of," she shrugged. "I'm worried about Tracey, too. As time goes by, there's less of a chance of finding her. My God, it's so scary." She paused. "Oh! I'm so sorry!" she offered quickly.

"It's okay, Molly. I'm sure He understands," she said, motioning up toward the ceiling. "Is something on your mind? Are you feeling a bit overwhelmed? Want to talk?"

"No. Yes," Molly said, flustered. She was feeling overwhelmed, but didn't want to talk about it for fear that she would then have to deal with those feelings. "Pastor Lett, it's your brother."

Pastor Lett stiffened. She turned away to hide her discomfort and settled herself into the rear-most pew. She breathed slowly, unable to find her voice. She had known this time would eventually come.

"Pastor Lett, are you okay?" Molly asked.

She nodded her head in confirmation and managed, "Yes, fine. Tired."

"No wonder, with all that's going on. It's so reminiscent of what happened with your brother. I'm so sorry."

Pastor Lett kept her eyes trained on the wooden pew before her, wondering how much Molly knew about Rodney.

"I'm sorry, that was rude of me," Molly said, bringing her hands together in her lap. "I just recently learned that you had a brother," Pastor Lett felt her glance at her, "and that you lost him."

Pastor Lett's body visibly relaxed as the statement replaced her fear with relief. "Yes, years ago," she said.

"I know. I wanted to tell you that I'm so sorry," Molly said.

Pastor Lett felt the comfort in her voice. "Thank you," she said. "He was a special person."

Molly looked away, then back into her eyes, and said, "I can't imagine how hard it must have been." She hesitated, contemplating discussing Rodney on a level that would expose parts of her past that she'd never discussed with Pastor Lett. "May I ask you a few things about him?"

Pastor Lett repositioned herself in the pew, cleared her throat, "Sure," she said.

"Well, I was told that he 'knew' things about Kate Plummer's disappearance. Do you know about that? Anything about him *knowing* things?" she asked with innocence, not accusation.

"Yes," she sighed as if she had been asked about that one too many times. "He knew a lot of things. Sadly, his gift became his misfortune. People found out." She looked at the stained glass window on the right wall of the church, noticing for the first time how very bright the reds and yellows were against the more vivid greens and blues. The complexity of the colors, like life, made her half-smile, half-smirk.

She looked at Molly, but knew she couldn't talk about Rodney with truth in her eyes, so she lowered her gaze. "He was apparently walking around town, like he usually did when I was running the church, or holding services, and he was repeating what he saw, or rather, what he knew—and I guess a few people heard it and went straight to the police." Pastor Lett shrugged, rolled her shoulders backward, as if she could rid her body of a pesky ache. "I accepted long ago that those people were just trying to protect their own children. Not many people really knew Rodney."

Molly nodded, sitting forward in the pew.

"He was the kindest boy. Never hurt a fly. He was a bit slow. Drove my parents crazy as they got on in years," she looked away, as if reliving a memory. "They passed a few years back. Mom, of cancer, and my father, well, I think of a broken heart. I brought Rodney here with me twenty-five years ago, he was just twenty-one years old then."

At the mention of his age, Molly's eyes grew wide.

"Rodney was...an accident if you will," she turned her head to the side and looked at Molly. "There were eleven years between us."

Molly nodded again, understandingly, she thought.

"He used to help out the residents with yard work, stuff like that, but even those he helped didn't really get to know him. They considered it charity."

"Pastor Lett," she began, "I sort of...*know* things, too. I wanted to find out if he knew things the way I sometimes do."

She smiled, ruefully. *Everyone thinks they're special.* "Well, what do you mean?" she asked, to humor her.

"I have visions—I guess you call them that— sometimes early in the morning when I'm not really asleep but not really awake, other times when I am near a place where there is danger or something is going to happen," she said, her hazel eyes pleading for understanding.

Pastor Lett politely paid closer attention. "Go on," she said.

"I'm not always sure if what I see is real or not," she looked away, as if embarrassed by her admission.

"I've never met anyone else who truly possessed the same power as Rodney," Pastor Lett said. "Perhaps, Molly, your insecurities, or your past, interfere with your present," Pastor Lett said authoritatively.

Disheartened, Molly replied, "No, I'm sure it's not that."

Pastor Lett continued, "When Rodney was a little boy, he used to tell me that things were going to happen. Bad things were going to happen. I never gave any credence to what he said to me, but then, as I got older and started really paying attention, I realized that they had started coming true, and the connection was undeniable."

Molly released a breath, her disappointment subsided. "So it is true. He did know things."

Pastor Lett nodded, "He knew facts and details about catastrophes that he couldn't have read about or predicted by any means." She turned her body toward Molly and looked her in the eye, welcoming the opportunity to discuss this hidden aspect of her brother's life, craving the acceptance, and, she was ashamed to admit, the purging of the burden. "I don't know how to tell if what you see, or what you know, is real, but I can tell you that with Rodney, it was. It was a little scary." She took a deep breath, about to reveal what nobody understood, or cared to try to understand, years ago. "When Rodney was four, he woke up on June 16, shaking and crying. I remember because for years afterwards, every time he cried in the morning I prayed for a full forty-eight hours, even as a young woman, that nothing bad was going to happen. Anyway, he ran around our house yelling, something about a big bomb going off. The poor kid, he spent the whole day— and even slept that night—in the cellar, petrified. The next day, of course, June 17, 1967, China exploded its first hydrogen bomb. Rodney worried for years that they would bomb us and we'd all die." She looked away, remembering Rodney screaming and frightened, as their parents yelled at him to just be quiet and stop making up stories. The memory saddened her.

"Then there was the time, he was about five years old, when he started talking about this man that would walk on the moon in the month twenty. We had no idea what he was jabbering about. He kept repeating, over and over, 'Month twenty, man walk on moon.' He drove us crazy, until July 20, 1969, when he bound into the room and said to me, 'See! Man walk on moon month twenty!'" Pastor Lett let out a little laugh. "We didn't own a television back them. My parents believed television was the root of all evil," she laughed at the thought, pausing to savor the memory. "That's how it was with Rodney. When he knew something, he really knew it."

Molly could barely contain her enthusiasm, but Pastor Lett's comment had subdued her notion of exposing her clairvoyance. The last thing she needed was for Pastor Lett to think she was crazy. She understood what she thought was Pastor Lett's angst over Rodney's visions. "It must have been difficult to bear that burden all by yourself."

She looked at Molly then. *Finally, a little understanding instead of pity*. "Yes. It was hard," she said, "but I loved him—very much. People didn't understand. No one took the time to see past the allegations." Anger crept into her voice as she sat up taller and looked at Molly, "And now it's like he never existed to them. They pummeled him and forgot him— forgetting that he was a person, a brother, a son. Pummeled him and walked away, thinking they were protecting their community from some...monster." At this, Pastor Lett released her anger, "I'm sorry," she said. "I was never able to protect him—not then, and not in the end." Pastor Lett stood up and tried to pull herself together. "Molly, there were things he said that never made sense, too." She looked away from Molly again, drawing into her own mind, "We had times like that, too, times where ramblings meant nothing more than torture to my poor brother, and a mere inconvenience to me."

Hannah meandered aimlessly through her barns. She had felt a sense of unease since the afternoon when she had taken part in the search for Tracey. The woodsy smell of the fallen damp leaves and the fear-stricken faces of the volunteers—faces that she knew hid the secret panic that they might find Tracey's cold, lifeless body—coalesced and reawakened the memories that she'd forced herself to suppress; memories that she knew, at any moment, could send her into a frenzied state of panic and expose her secret. She had thought she could escape her own thoughts—do the deed and then act as though it had never happened—but they mixed with an overwhelming sadness and confusion that she could not keep at bay. And the anger—she could feel the rage mounting inside her with every breath she took. That anger, she feared, would lead to her discovery. She closed her eyes and ran her hand along the rough wood of the stalls, trying to suppress the memories that played in her mind with shocking clarity, like a rerun of a bad horror movie; the fight, the cold evening air, the desperation—*Oh, the desperation*! Tears streamed down her cheeks. She swiped at them with the sleeve of her rough wool sweater which left almost imperceptible scratches on her face. Others might not notice the thin abrasions, but Hannah took the quick piercing scratches as her due, punishment for what she'd done. Suddenly, guilt hit her with such force that it stopped her in her tracks. She stood, staring at her horses and wallowing in her own emptiness, the unfairness of life. She became uneasy and crouched down to gain control of her own body. She glanced up at Hunter, her Appaloosa, in whose curious eyes she saw accusation. Hannah covered her face as sobs wracked her body, her heart breaking all over again. She knew it was wrong! She'd broken rules—rules of society—and it distressed her. *But she was mine, mine! Not theirs, not his!* She slid to the ground, slamming against the hard wooden stall, her legs splayed in front of her.

"Damn you, Charlie!" she yelled, startling the horse. Hannah pounded the concrete floor with her fists until her hands throbbed. She wiped her nose and waited for her trembling to subside. She looked up toward the ceiling and whispered, "I am so sorry, baby. I am so, so sorry."

Hannah pet Hunter and smiled at Gracie, a colt that she had recently inherited from a friend. "I can't bring you guys with me. I have to be quiet this time."

She often treated the horses as people. Hannah spent more time with her four-legged friends than her two-legged ones. "But look, guys," she said as she held up a handful of flowers, "I've got a present for her." Hannah stuffed them into a knapsack and laughed a shaky little laugh.

She made her way through the meadow that ran along the back of her barn, thankful that the only neighboring houses were acres away, and disappeared into the woods. Hannah had made that trek so often that it seemed second nature to her. She was at home in the fields and certainly in the woods. Today, though, Hannah felt as if she were being watched. She nervously scanned her surroundings, thinking about what would happen if she were ever caught. The thought turned her stomach. *What would people think? How would I survive?* Images of hard women flew to the forefront of her mind—big, stocky women with too many muscles and short, spiky haircuts that screamed of a manly presence, women who would circle her, looking her up and down like a piece of fresh meat. She envisioned herself standing there, old and weak, ripe for the taking, or beating, or whatever it was they did to each other in jail. Whatever it was, she was sure she would not survive it. Her head dropped with the weight of the world resting on her shoulders. *I had to take her there. There was no other option. If people had found out she was with me, surely* he *would have come and taken her and done God-knows-what to me.*

Hannah resolved to be strong. What am I doing, living one life during the day and an entire other life that no one knows about? The poor girl. She couldn't know that I had to keep her from them. Hannah wiped her hands on her jeans and said to the surrounding forest, "There's no way they'll find her." She took one tentative step, then two. Her steps grew strong, determined.

Ten

Tracey was again being dragged through the darkened tunnels. She wondered where she was being taken, but after being trapped in the dark, musty room with the mattress all day, she was glad to stretch her legs. It seemed like Mummy was always gone. Mummy had told her that they were going outside. *Outside!* Tracey was excited when she first heard that word, but her distrust of Mummy subdued the excitement. Tracey hurried, hardly able to keep up with her captor's fast, purposeful gait. The speed of their trek gave Tracey an inkling of hope. Maybe she *was* going outside. Maybe she was being brought back to her own mommy and daddy. If they were going outside, then someone would surely see her, and Tracey was confident that her parents were searching for her. This was it! She was about to go home, she was sure of it!

"Keep up, Tracey, Mummy is in a hurry," the captor said.

Tracey liked how nice Mummy was acting, and she was relieved that Mummy had finally changed her clothes and didn't stink so badly. Tracey rushed as fast as she was able—the last day of resting on the putrid mattress had lessened the ache in her legs.

"We're going outside, Tracey! Outside!" Mummy said, cheerily.

Tracey believed this would be a good day. Mummy hadn't read from the Bible today, and she didn't even worship in the morning. Tracey worried about *why* they hadn't gone to the praying place, but she didn't ask.

The passageway narrowed, and tears stung Tracey's eyes, tears of hope, tears of hope that she would not let tumble down her cheeks for fear of upsetting her captor. She held her arms tight against her body, away from the dirt walls. The narrowing tunnel caused Mummy to walk sideways to fit through. Tracey held her breath—the stench from the walls reminded her of wet, dirty puppies, the way they shake themselves off and splatter you with water and bits of dirt.

Oh, my God! Oh, my God! I see it! Tracey's heart pounded in her chest. A smile stretched across her face as the narrow tunnel opened wider and came to an end, slowly narrowing back to the size of a car tire, and winding its way up toward the outside. Streaming in, like a savior, was the sun—the glorious sun! Tracey wanted to jump, to climb through that hole and rush into her parents' arms. She was sure they would be there, waiting, like this had all been a planned-out game of hide-and-seek. Her hands clenched into fists, her arms became rigid at her side, and she bounced from foot to foot, biting her lower lip to keep from squealing. Mummy stood in front of Tracey, looking up toward the beam of light, a smile on her face. Their bodies were so close that Tracey could smell her, a slight metallic, sulfuric smell. It was not so bad, really. Mummy had washed up that morning and had let Tracey wash up, too. They had used a big bucket of water, towels, which appeared to already have been slightly soiled, and a little soap. Tracey had kept her back to Mummy so she wouldn't see her with her clothes off. She had pretended to be playing clean up with Emma, though she didn't think Mummy was watching her at all. Mummy had been hunched over her journal, writing quickly and in deep concentration. Tracey's own mother kept a journal, too. Her mother, her *real* mother, had always told Tracey and Emma that it helped keep her sane, whatever that meant. Tracey thought it meant that it helped her to yell less when she was mad at them. Sometimes, when her mother was really mad, she'd count to ten, tell the girls to go to their rooms, and then her mother would go write in her journal. Tracey really wanted to read that journal one day. She wondered if her mother wrote about how bad she and Emma were sometimes. Maybe she wrote about when they were good, too. Thinking of her mother made Tracey sad. She made a silent promise to herself—she promised that if she got back to her real mommy, she would never be bad again. *Do you hear me, God?* she wondered—and hoped—as she looked up at the beam of light.

Her captor was silent. She looked back at Tracey, and Tracey's eyes grew open wide, she clamped her mouth shut. Mummy smiled, and Tracey shivered with relief and anticipation. Mummy spun around and crawled along the dirt opening. The passageway seemed to engulf her. Tracey wasn't sure Mummy would even fit through the tight cavity, but the sun was shining at the end of the tunnel, pouring in around Mummy's wriggling, large body. Tracey crouched down and enthusiastically began crawling behind her. The dirt was cold and damp, seeping through her leggings and onto her knees, but she didn't care. She was going home!

As she neared the top of the passageway, Mummy reached down, grabbed her hand tightly, and swiftly pulled her up and onto the ground. Tracey took a deep breath of the fresh air; tears of happiness ran down her cheeks. Relief swept through her. Mummy smacked her enormous hands against her jeans to rid them of dirt, and the sound startled Tracey. She flinched, and stepped backward, almost falling back into the passageway, letting out a frightened shriek.

"Hey!" Mummy yelled. "Watch it!"

Mummy clasped her hand around Tracey's spindly arm, yanking her firmly onto solid ground. Tracey instinctively ducked her head and pulled away. She stole a quick look up through her eyelashes and was surprised to see concern, perhaps even empathy, in Mummy's eyes. "I…I'm sorry," Tracey's words were barely more than a whisper.

Mummy released her arm and dusted off Tracey's knees. Tracey stood stock still, her eyes wide. She took in her surroundings, the brambles, thick with thorns, and tangled branches that grew so high they formed a shelter above them. A mottled tapestry of light formed the ceiling where the sun streamed through.

Mummy straightened up and backed away from Tracey. She stood in the middle of the strange den. She stretched her arms out to her sides and then reached for Tracey, pulling her quickly against her body. Tracey flinched, fought the urge to back away. She hated to be touched by Mummy. Unsure and scared, she clenched her eyes closed.

"Tracey, isn't this wonderful?" Mummy whispered. "We are finally outside! Look how beautiful of a day it is!" she let go of Tracey and spun in a circle with her arms stretched out to her sides, her hair lifting off her shoulders.

Tracey wondered if she should run and scream, like Mrs. Tate had told them to do if they were ever in danger, but what if she didn't get away and Mummy took her back to that dark chamber? What if her captor hurt her because she was such a bad girl? Tracey formulated a plan in her young mind. Her mother had always taught her to find an adult when she was in danger. How she wished she had never followed Mummy into the woods in the first place, but she couldn't change what she had done. She couldn't have known that the woman who had played and laughed with her at the park would ever steal her. She remained still, concentrating on her plan. When Mummy took her out of the bramble—when they saw people—then Tracey would run straight to another adult and ask for help. She'd holler and insist they help her. No matter how much Mummy pretended to be her mother, she was not. *She was NOT!*

Mummy had stopped spinning and smiled at Tracey.

"Where are we?" Tracey asked quietly. She was afraid to ask loudly, afraid that Mummy might turn mean again, and they'd retreat back underground.

Mummy rolled her eyes, a look that Tracey had seen her mother do hundreds of times when Tracey asked a question that had an obvious answer, "We are outside, of course," she said.

Tracey swallowed the "duh" that rang in her seven-year-old mind.

"This is where I come to exercise sometimes or just to read. Once, I even saw a family of deer playing right over there," she pointed to a distant thicket.

Tracey searched for something familiar—a parking lot, the park, people. Her hopes were quickly dashed. She looked up, searching the sky through breaks in the branches. Standing directly under a circle of sunlight, she saw a bunch of birds flying overhead in a circular motion. They weren't flying together or in a pattern—they flew in random circles nearly running into each other. She blinked a few times and realized that the birds were actually little airplanes—the smallest airplanes she had ever seen. A smile stretched across her face as her mind settled on an odd noise, a noise that had been there all along, but that she had been too upset to hear: A hum. Tracey concentrated on the humming noise and separated the hum into two distinct sounds—an mmm and an rrrrr. The sounds varied in pitch, drifting from very high to something softer, more distant.

Tracey began to point to the sky, then quickly brought her hand back to her side. Airplanes meant people, and somehow Tracey knew that if Mummy had known there were people nearby, she would take Tracey back to that awful place. She walked around the small clearing, watching Mummy out of the corner of her eye. It was no bigger than the cave where Tracey and Mummy slept. Tracey remembered her father telling her that she was as tall as her arms were long. Mummy was sitting on the ground, fiddling with sticks and looking the other way. Tracey stretched her arms out as wide as she was able, but was not big enough to reach both sides. *I bet me and Emma and Mommy all hooked together, holding hands, could reach both sides.* Tracey decided to see how many of her it would take to reach each side. She spread her arms, then moved to where she thought her fingertips had been. She was sure she was mistaken in where she stood and went back to the side of the bramble and started over—stretching her fingers, then hurrying to where her extended fingers had been. She was startled when Mummy laughed. In spite of her initial habitual flinch, Tracey laughed, too. It was fun being outside. Mummy got up and stood next to Tracey.

"Reach, Tracey," she said, kindly.

Tracey smiled and reached her arms out, the sound of the airplanes faded away in the distance, but Tracey was concentrating so hard on figuring out how many Traceys it would take to cross the bramble that she had forgotten all about the airplanes. Her fingertips neared Mummy's.

"Put your fingertips on mine, Tracey," she said. "We'll see if we are long enough to reach the sides."

Tracey stretched her fingers further, until they were touching Mummy's. Mummy smiled, and Tracey did, too.

"Nope, not quite!" Mummy said. "This is like a mansion for us, huh? Our place isn't this big, is it?"

As Mummy spoke, Tracey's heart sank. The reality of her situation came tumbling back. Her mind ran through the images of the rank mattress where she had slept for the last few nights, the horrid odor of the bad spot, and the worst realization of all—that she wasn't going home. *She's talking about* our *place,* Tracey thought. Her limbs began to tremble, her lower lip quivered, and she frantically scanned the enclosed area. *I don't want* her *place to be* my *place. I want to go home!* Tracey dropped her arms and looked up, searching the empty sky for the planes. She listened, silently pleading that she would hear them—find some connection to the outside world. Gentle scamperings across the forest floor and her captor's breathing were the only sounds she heard. Her shoulders slumped and her head dropped heavily forward. She stared at her sneakers which used to be white but were now soiled with mud, and grime, and red dirt, upon which she now stood. She stared at the ground as a glimmer of hope crawled through her body. *Red dirt!* The ground looked like the dirt that was in the backyard of her friend Cindy's house. Cindy lived by the church in Boyds, and her mother always got mad when she and Cindy dragged that ugly red dirt into the house on their bare feet. Tracey spun around and again searched beyond the trees. Cindy's house was nowhere to be seen. Tracey backed up until her back brushed against the prickly brambles. "Ouch," slipped from her lips, and her captor turned to face her. Tracey closed her mouth tight and tried to keep from crying. She sank down, wrapped her arms around her knees and began to rock.

Mummy walked toward her, stopping just inches in front of Tracey's feet. Tracey stopped rocking. She did not look up. She kept her eyes trained on the ground, feeling Mummy's presence looming. Mummy sat down beside Tracey, and Tracey began to cry, fearfully.

"There's no need to cry, Tracey," Mummy said in an even, flat voice. "I have saved you."

They sat in silence for what felt to Tracey like hours, until the sun dropped behind the middle of the trees—until her captor told her it was time to go *home*.

I can't go back in that place, I just can't! Tracey remained, huddled and silent, on the cold dirt.

"Tracey," Mummy insisted, "we have to go. Now!"

Tracey remained still, paralyzed with fear. Her captor reached down and yanked her to her feet.

"Move it, Tracey," she ordered. She pushed Tracey from behind toward the opening in the ground. Tracey leaned her body backward, pushing into the ground with her heels as hard as she could. She blindly grabbed behind her, taking purchase of her captor's jeans.

"No!" Tracey shouted. "No! I can't!" She kicked and scratched at her captor, hitting her with all of her might.

Her captor grabbed hold of Tracey's shirt, catching it on a bramble, and tearing it apart as she dragged Tracey into the dark hole.

"Get off!" Tracey screamed. She swung at her, slamming her hand into her ribs. Her captor doubled over, keeping her tight grip on Tracey's arm.

"You little brat!" she screamed at Tracey, her eyes as vicious as a cold-blooded animal's.

Tracey's fear turned to rage—the anger of being taken from her parents fueled her with renewed energy and strength. She fought with all the might of her sixty-three pounds, screaming, "I hate you! I hate you! I hate you!" She broke loose and tried to wriggle back up the hole toward the last of the fading light, but was pulled back down by a quick yank of her ankle. Tracey shrieked, "No! I want to go home!" She clawed at the dirt, kicking fiercely at her captor's face, "I'm not going back in there!" Tracey felt her arm being pulled and twisted behind her back.

Her terrified screams were absorbed by the dirt walls of the tunnel.

Eleven

Molly pulled on a gray cotton sweater and her favorite blue jeans—the ones with several patches of mismatched fabric on the knees. She was excited about the upcoming evening, and as she heard Cole's footsteps on the stairs, she was glad that he had made it home at a reasonable hour.

"Hi, honey," she cheerily called out. "I'm getting ready for tonight."

"Tonight?" he asked, as he entered the room. "What's tonight? I'm so tired." He fell backward on the bed, his arms and legs spread wide. His feet hung off the bottom of the bed, and his arms were just shy of the edges of the king-sized mattress. His rumpled scrubs top inched up and revealed an enticing swathe of his toned stomach, speckled with dark hair.

Molly walked over and sat down on the bed next to him, running her fingers over the rough pattern on his cheeks, up around his forehead, and down the soft skin

97

next to his eyes. She smiled, thinking that his face held the innocence of a child and yet the sexiness of a man.

"Mmm," he moaned. "That feels good. Can't we just stay like this all night?" he asked.

"Mm-hmm," Molly responded. She stood up, sighed, and said, "No, no, we can't." She turned away to glance in the mirror, fluffed her thick hair, and scrunched her face in disapproval.

"Why not?"

"We have to go. Newton Carr is speaking about the history of Boyds at the Boyds Negro School tonight. Remember?" She put her hands on her hips, "Don't you remember? We talked about this." Molly was used to Cole's mind, which, though she knew was like a sponge at work, she believed suddenly turned into a sieve when he left the hospital each afternoon.

He made a face, groaned, and said, "Do we really have to?" He stood and walked toward Molly, reaching his arms around her, and looking at her with his big, dark eyes. "I'll buy you Japanese and rub your feet if you let me stay home," he coaxed.

"Honey!" she smiled. "I want to go. We loved his other discussions, remember? Besides, you always like it once you're there."

He made another do-I-really-have-to face.

"C'mon. I'll buy you Japanese and rub your feet if you come with me," Molly urged.

Cole smiled and relented. As he walked toward the shower, he said, "You owe me."

Molly snickered, "Yeah, yeah, I know."

While Cole showered, she told him about Pastor Lett's brother, his link to Kate Plummer's disappearance, and his untimely death. She paused, waiting for a reaction, listening to the sound of the water being shut off, the remaining drips making their way to the shower floor. "She said Rodney knew things about the girl," she hesitated, "I think he was like me." She closed her eyes, not sure if she should continue, but could not control her impulse to share her thoughts. "I don't think he was guilty."

Steam rose off of Cole's body, a thick towel tied around his waist, his dark mass of hair sticking out in every direction, "What do you mean, like you, Mol? And what do you mean, not guilty?" he asked with a serious tone.

Molly looked down at the floor. "You know," she said sheepishly, kicking her foot out and back, off the side of the bed, "like I do? Like with nine-eleven? Remember?" She lifted her eyes and met his, she saw in them his recollection of her visions before the planes had crashed, the fear she'd conveyed, and his disbelief when the event finally occurred.

"Yeah, I remember," he sighed heavily, and sat down next to Molly. "Baby, why are you doing this? Why are you getting involved?" He put a protective hand on her leg.

"I have to. I don't know why." She looked into his eyes, trying to convey her determination, the seriousness of what she was saying, "I dreamed about it, too." The words rushed out of her before she had time to think about if she should say them or not, "I saw a little girl, curled up on the ground, and these...these...underground caverns or something. I saw a lady on a log." She turned and opened her nightstand drawer, removing her dream journal. "It's all in here," she held the journal out to him. He didn't move to take it. She pushed it toward him, "Take it! You'll see."

Cole finally took the journal, looking at her with disbelief.

"And look at this, Cole," she unwrapped the bandages from her hand, "a perfect T."

He continued to look at her, his furrowed brow and his eyes portrayed a certain empathy, as if he felt sorry for Molly.

"Cole! I know what you're thinking," she pleaded. "Look, it's a T—like Tracey—T!" she said emphatically.

"It could all be coincidental." He watched her hopes deflate and suddenly realized how important this was to her. "Okay, okay, so you are serious, and maybe you know some things. Just be careful, okay." He wrapped his arm around her shoulder, pulling her close against his side, and kissing the top of her head. "You're what matters to me. Everyone else is just peripheral." He released her and stood to get dressed. "Let's go listen to Newton."

Molly's stride down the stairs revealed an exhilarated little bounce, happy that maybe Cole was beginning to believe in her, not realizing that he never even opened her journal.

Newton Carr reminded Molly of a schoolboy making his first public appearance. Seventy-seven-year-old Newton's skin was as dark as chocolate and smooth as butter, in stark contrast to his pale and appropriately-wrinkled wife, Betty. He stood before them, avoiding eye contact with anyone and fumbling with his papers— his hands moving from paper to pocket and back again. His short, thick, gray and white hair, small-framed glasses, and semi-nervous behavior accurately reflected his kind, soft-spoken demeanor. He had kept in relatively good shape for a man of his years by walking his little terrier every day. Although he was the unofficial historian and the keeper of all facts relating to Boyds, one was hard pressed to get an opinion about current events out of the man.

Newton was one of the original founders of the Boyds Civic Association, single-handedly saved the Boyds Marc Train Station from sure closure, and could certainly be credited as the most-informed local historian in the county. Newton had lived on White Ground Road in one of the famous Painted Ladies for his entire life. Acres of sweeping fields provided privacy from the road. The separate garage, which mirrored the color and style of the Victorian home, was stacked with boxes and binders. The binders detailed every event that had ever happened in Boyds, to Boyds residents, or had affected Boyds in some way. He kept those binders current and was probably the only person to also have each of these facts etched in his memory. The man was the equivalent of a walking encyclopedia about Boyds, and yet he was humble, downplaying the significance of the records he kept.

As the sun set, Newton stood in the grass before the one-room schoolhouse, built on an undeveloped stretch of White Ground Road, and historically known as the Boyds Negro School. It felt desolate in the cool evening. Twelve residents, most of whom were over the age of sixty, listened intently as Newton spoke of the topic for the evening's discussion: The Hidden Treasures of Boyds. Newton wore his usual dress clothes: tan chinos and a striped sweater. He paced while he spoke and said "um" a few too many times, which Molly found endearing. Molly was excited to learn more about the area where she'd lived for so many years. Like many railroad towns, Boyds had developed around a small nucleus of buildings: the railroad station, the post office, and the country store. Just beyond these, on either side of the railroad tracks, lay the beautiful Painted Ladies of the Victorian era and the Boyds Presbyterian Church, surrounded by incredible shade trees that must have been just barely saplings a hundred years ago. Rippling out from this historic core, the farms were valiantly trying to fight the suburbia that had spread northward from D.C. over the past twenty years.

Molly thought about Newton, and the fact that she was sure that he held the secrets of the town within his own mind, though she was just as sure that he would never reveal any of them. Newton described Pleasant Springs Farm Bed and Breakfast, "Featuring a private cottage of log and frame construction, circa 1768, and listed on the National Register of Historical Places.

"Surrounded by thirty acres of gardens, woods, meadows, um," he looked from his fidgeting hands to just above the heads of his guests, then back at his hands again, "springs, streams, and a farm pond make this, um, well, the uh, the little house is in a world of its own. It's an eighteenth century paradise of peace and solitude," he continued, enthusiastically.

Molly smiled, squeezing Cole's hand. He turned and winked, his thinking obvious, When can we go?

"Hand-ironed sheets, farm-made soap, fresh flowers, and attention to all details make this B and B unique," Newton continued, sounding a little like a marketing pitch.

Molly's mind wandered as Newton began a tangent about the acreage. Her mind drifted from the bed and breakfast to gardens and, eventually, to the woods, Pastor Lett, and, finally, to Rodney. She was pained by the knowledge that he had been beaten to death. She tried to picture Pastor Lett walking in and finding her brother—her ability to hear Newton had dissolved, replaced by the images that engulfed her thoughts. She wondered if that was why Pastor Lett moved out of the manse. Did being a pastor somehow ready a person for those types of life-altering situations—giving strength and the ability to carry on through faith, maybe? Just as she began questioning her own faith in God, her bandaged hand felt hot, and it was getting hotter. She brought her mind back to the present, hearing Newton say, "...the old Perkinson House. Um, it was originally built as a hotel, and remains on the historic registry. Yes, yes, the Winderber Hotel, I believe, back when Boyds was a vacation area consisting of three hotels, a few homes, and a railroad station."

The gash in her hand felt as though it were burning. She grabbed her wrist with the other hand and cringed.

Cole reached for her, whispered, "What is it? What's the matter?"

Fresh tears sprang to Molly's eyes, "My cut. It burns so badly." She shook her bandaged hand, rocking in pain. "I can't stand it," she hissed, trying to keep from crying out.

Newton noticed Molly's red face, the tears streaming down her cheeks, "Molly, are you okay?"

Molly looked up to see thirteen sets of eyes trained on her. She could not stop rocking, the pain shooting up her wrist felt as if it traveled through her veins. Cole was on his feet, helping Molly up.

"I...I have a cut," she said, trying to sound calm. "I think I have to go."

Cole was calm, guiding Molly to the car and assuring the others that she was going to be fine.

Molly turned suddenly out of his arms and faced Newton, holding her bandaged arm up with her strong one. "Newton," she said through the pain, "where is the Perkinson House?"

Newton stood silently, dumbfounded by the pain in Molly's eyes. It took him a moment to figure out what she was referring to. "Oh!" he said, suddenly remembering his discussion. "It's just up the dirt road next to the lake, but you can't go up there. No, no." He shook his head, watching Cole trying to coax Molly toward the car. "Pastor Lett, who is caring for the home, has strict orders not to let anyone up that road, much less to the house." Newton walked a few steps in either direction, as if he were looking for something.

Molly nodded in confirmation and turned to go.

The relief in Cole's eyes was evident. He turned to Newton and said quickly, "Thank you, Newton. Great discussion. I'm sorry we have to leave." He ushered Molly into the car.

Molly collapsed into her seat, doubling over and holding in her screams.

Cole grabbed Molly's hand and unwrapped the bandage. Molly turned away, afraid to look.

"How is it?" she asked. When Cole didn't answer right away, she asked again, "What? What does it look like?" The words tumbled out of her mouth unstoppable and unsteady.

"Mol, what happened?" he asked, his eyes wide.

Molly looked at her hand. The gash was bright red and swollen, the letter T stared back at her, accusing—or pleading—she wasn't sure which but felt the signal with each pulsating pain.

"It wasn't like that this morning, I swear," she said. "What happened?"

In the space of a breath, the pain receded into numbness, the swelling shrank, the redness faded as if it had never been there. The numbness passed into oblivion—gone.

"What the hell?" Cole demanded.

"I have no idea." Molly panicked. "The pain is gone. Gone! My God, Cole, what's happening?"

Twelve

Hours had passed, and Tracey felt like a limp rag doll. She opened her eyes and found her captor sitting on an upended log, the handle of an old pocket knife in her left hand and a partially-whittled wooden bird in her right.

"Mummy doesn't like bad girls," her captor sneered.

Tracey had become numb to the pains that tore through her limbs and shoulder, numb to the treachery of her situation.

"I have to put you in the bad spot now," Mummy said, irritated at the inconvenience. "I have no choice but to put you there."

Tracey shook her head, whispered, "No." She was too exhausted to fight. Her eyes pleaded with her captor.

"You give me no choice, young lady." Her arms rested on her knees. "It will hurt me more than it will hurt you."

Tracey watched flakes of wood peel from the block and glide toward the dirt floor. She glanced from the knife in her captor's hand to the other wooden birds lined up along the edge of the wall where her captor slept and wondered if each bird represented a child she had stolen. Her eyes drifted back to the knife and settled there.

Mummy sat silently shaking her head, whittling the head of the bird. When the beak was complete and the head distinct, she stood, turned, and set the bird down carefully on the log. The knife remained in her hand as she turned to face Tracey.

Tracey gritted her teeth, swallowing any sounds that might have tried to escape. Her eyes remained trained on the knife.

Mummy walked toward Tracey, gripping the knife in her left hand. She reached for Tracey with both arms. Tracey leaned back, closing her eyes. Mummy lifted Tracey gently to her feet, then laughed. "What is this?" she mumbled. Tracey snatched a quick glance at Mummy and saw her staring at the knife.

Tracey's entire body shook. She leaned back, as far away from her captor's body as she was able while being held by the shoulders in a crushing grip. She turned her face away from the cold, sharp knife. Her captor removed her left hand from Tracey's shoulder and raised the knife to her own eye-level. She looked it over, turning it in her hand. Her eyebrows furrowed, as she closely inspected the weapon. Then she let out a *hmph,* shrugged her shoulders, and tossed the tool toward the upended log. She looked down at Tracey and released her grip.

"Let's go," she said in a bored and tired voice.

Tracey let out her breath in a rush of relief. Breathing hard and fast, she followed her captor as she removed the plywood from the opening and headed down the dingy passageway. They neared the entrance to where the bad spot was; Tracey's legs failed her. She couldn't walk toward that awful place. Paralyzed with fear, she breathed in rapid, noisy breaths. Her captor turned to face her, rolled her eyes, and yanked Tracey's arm toward the wretched room.

"No!" Tracey screamed, blinded by her own tears. "I won't do it again! I promise! I'll be good!" she begged to deaf ears. "I'm sorry. I'm sorry. Please, don't put me in the bad spot. Please!"

Mummy began to pray, which scared Tracey even more than the bad spot did. "Hosea 9:7. The days of punishment are coming, the days of reckoning are at hand. Let Israel know this. Because your sins are so many and your hostility so great, the prophet is considered a fool, the inspired man a maniac."

The rancid smell of urine, dead rodents, and fear pervaded the air of the dark room like rainwater seeping into the cracks of an old foundation. Tracey stood straight as a soldier, petrified. She felt a hand grasp her upper arm. Her captor's fingers wrapped all the way around Tracey's slim arm and squeezed—hard. Her other hand pushed against Tracey's back, forcing her forward.

Tracey's feet reluctantly disobeyed her desire to run away. The light from the lantern cast menacing shadows across the floor. Loose dirt, littered with rocks and pebbles, receded into a dark hole in the earth—the bad spot. Despite her best efforts not to, Tracey began to sob, "Please! Please! I'll be good!"

Her captor pushed her forward, "You don't appreciate anything!" Her words were robotic, as if scripted. "You're a spoiled little brat, and you are going to learn to appreciate the things I give you!" Her entire body shook. "I saved you!" she said nastily, thrusting Tracey forward with such force that Tracey fell to the ground, just inches from the hole. Tracey tried to scramble away, clawing at the unforgiving dirt, struggling to move away from the hole, fruitlessly digging into the ground with knees and toes.

Her captor put her foot on the back of Tracey's calf, successfully trapping her. Her captor yelled, "I saved you from being part of that horrible world! Part of the 'people who don't care'!"

Tracey wriggled and sobbed beneath her.

Her anger chillingly eased. "I'll save you. You will be happy." Just as quickly, her voice became terrifying, "You will learn to appreciate what you are given," her final word was emphasized by her bearing down on Tracey's already throbbing leg. Tracey yelped in pain.

In one quick motion, her captor removed her foot from Tracey's leg, yanked Tracey several inches off of the ground, and dropped her into the hole. Tracey landed hard on her feet—her knees buckled and she sank down, her back up against the cold dirt. The narrowness of the cavity forced her knees against her chest, hindering her breathing. She looked up just in time to see the grate—made out of rough branches and leaves—placed over the top of the hole, evoking more tears of helplessness. As the board was eased over the top of the grate, eliminating all but a single beam of dim light, she pulled her legs in tighter to her chest. Tracey focused on the golf-ball-sized hole that was cut in the center of the rotten board. *An air hole*, Mummy had said. Tracey's body flinched with each shovelful of dirt as it fell onto the board. She held her breath, afraid the dirt was going to clog the air hole, but too scared to reach up, for fear she'd be sealed in forever. Urine seeped in between her thighs, puddling beneath her. The light faded in and out of the hole. Tracey concentrated on the heavy thumps the dirt made on the board, the sound of random pebbles as they plunked against each other. *One...two...three...four...* She put her head down on her arms as bits of dirt fell upon her through the air hole. *Five...six....seven.....eight...nine.* Eventually Tracey was met with darkness, silence. Her pulse throbbed in her ear like an Indian drum. Her fear was so great that she felt as if her heart were actually breaking, piece by piece, torn out of her chest. Her stomach hurt. She was starving, though it felt like a rock was in her belly. Her tears drained the energy right out of her ravaged body, leaving her limp, inert—she gave into the exhaustion. *Maybe not waking up,* she thought, *would be easier than being here.*

Thirteen

Cole worried that his wife might be falling back into the unsettled place of her past. Tense and baffled, he watched her as they sat in their car in front of the schoolhouse. He rewrapped Molly's injured hand, then put the car into motion to begin the short drive home. White Ground Road was dark, quiet. With no streetlights and the umbrella of trees blocking the moonlight, Cole drove carefully, his eyes bouncing between Molly and the narrow road that lay ahead.

Molly's hands were pressed against her thighs, shaking. She looked as if she were intently focused, staring straight ahead. "Hold on, Mol," Cole said, silently calculating the time it would take them to get home—or possibly to the hospital.

"Cole, I don't feel so great," she said, nervously.

"We're almost home," he said, squeezing her thigh.

111

"Cole," Molly said, fiddling with her hands, "Cole!"

The alarm in her voice caught Cole's attention. He pulled over just beyond the Hoyles Mill Trail. Molly was holding her hands in front of her face, turning them, touching one with the other, as if she were making sure they were actually there.

"Oh my God! Cole!" Tears sprang from Molly's eyes as she frantically grasped at her face, the dashboard. "I can't see. I can't see anything!" she screamed.

Cole instantly reverted to doctor mode. He reached for Molly's face, placing his warm hands firmly on her cheeks and tilting her head up so he could look into her eyes. "Molly!" he said, sternly. "Can you see me at all? What do you see?"

"I can hear you, but I think…I'm going…"

Cole watched her eyes begin to roll up into her head. "Molly! Stay with me, Mol!" he demanded.

"Can't...feel—" Molly's head fell back against the headrest.

Cole jumped into action. He ran to the trunk and rummaged frantically through the boxes and medical reference books. "Damn it!" he swore as he dug through the mounds of other insignificant crap in his trunk. "Yes!" he found his first-aid kit and ripped the plastic top open. He rushed to Molly's door and flung it open. Molly's body was shuddering, as if she were having convulsions. "Molly! Can you hear me, Molly?" he yelled. Cole tore open the smelling salt package and broke the ampule in half under Molly's nose.

Molly's head jerked backward. "My hand," Molly's voice was almost a whisper. Then suddenly she grabbed her wrist and screamed, "Cole! Fuck! It's burning!" Just as quickly, her body shuddered, then went limp.

"Molly!" Cole yelled again, slapping her cheeks and instinctively taking her pulse. She was breathing, but her pulse was elevated. Cole raced to the driver's side and threw himself into the seat. He slammed the car into Drive and sped off toward help.

Molly's breathing hitched. "Molly!" Cole yelled, reaching over and holding her head back against the headrest. She lifted her legs off of the seat and curled up into in a fetal position. "Hang on, baby, hang on," Cole urged. He gunned the engine up around the corner, turning fast into Hannah Slate's driveway. He threw the gear into Park and turned to Molly, whose eyes were closed, but her breathing had become normal once again.

"Mol?" Cole's words were laden with concern.

Molly opened her eyes. He grabbed her arm and looked over her bandage—he gasped. "Molly?" He reached up and pushed her bangs off of her head—no fever. He held up his finger in front of Molly's eyes. She stared at it as if in a daze. As he moved his finger from right to left she moved her head to follow. He placed his hand firmly on the top of Molly's head, "Follow, Molly," he directed, in full physician mode. "Follow my finger with only your eyes."

Molly closed her eyes. "Cole?" she said.

He sensed her need acutely. "I'm right here, Mol," he said, glad she could not see the tears forming in his eyes. He wiped his eyes with his free hand, "Molly, open your eyes."

She did.

"Track my finger," he insisted.

She did.

He put his arms around her and held her tight.

"My legs, Cole," she began, "they were like ice, but they're normal now." She wiggled her fingers and looked at the bandage on her right palm. The letter T was singed into the gauze. She thrust her hand in his direction.

Cole looked angry, although his anger was at the unknown, not Molly. He turned away, clenching his jaw and breathing out of his nose. *What the hell is going on?* He turned back to Molly and hastily unwrapped the bandage. Her wound was pink, healing.

"It's the Knowing, Cole," Molly said quietly. "There is *something* here," she explained. "Well, something back there," she turned and gazed toward the darkened road behind them.

Cole stared at her in disbelief. He wasn't sure which he disbelieved—her or what was actually happening.

"I don't know why it happened earlier," Molly said, matter-of-factly.

Cole watched her eyes and knew she was already calculating her next step.

"The Perkinson House!" She made fists with her hands and blurted, "It started when Newton was discussing the Perkinson House!"

"What?" Cole was lost. "Why the Perkinson House of all things?" His mind was still sifting through the medical possibilities of what he'd seen happen to Molly.

Molly ignored his question. "I have to get into that home," she exclaimed deliberately. "There's something there—a clue maybe. There must be some correlation to Tracey."

114

"Molly, please." Cole shook his head. "After what I just saw, how do we know there isn't some other explanation—a medical explanation," he grasped for clarification, rationalization. "There has to be some reason you blacked out, Molly. It looked like you had some sort of a seizure, not some…some…"

Molly broke in, "Some paranormal weird type of thing that you can't explain, Cole? Well, I'm fucking sorry, okay, but that's what's going on with me. I'm not sick! God!" She turned away from him. "You've known me forever, Cole. Have I ever had a seizure?"

Cole grit his teeth.

"Why can't you believe me?" she yelled.

Cole, equally infuriated and concerned, continued staring at Hannah's driveway, "This isn't Philly, Molly! Maybe you're losing it again."

He turned toward her just in time to see her recoil as if she'd been slapped, then quickly turned away.

"Look at me!" She grabbed his chin and moved his angry face in her direction. "Cole, look at my bandage." She held the bandage up in front of him, displaying the undeniable T. "You *saw* what happened back there. There must be something in the woods or something…I don't know, some…thing, or connection, here on White Ground Road." Just as Molly finished speaking and looked up, a revelation spread across her face. "Hannah, of course."

Cole turned and spotted Hannah walking toward the car.

The evening seemed endless to Molly. As soon as Hannah had touched her arm she had been assaulted by images: a woman kneeling on the dirt, surrounded by woods—in a forest-cocoon—leaning over a wooden box; nail heads defining a visible edge across the lid.

She'd pulled back from Hannah and urged Cole to take her home. He'd grown angry at her rudeness toward Hannah, and they'd ridden home in another uncomfortable silence. Their relationship had become a roller coaster of emotions, and Molly was unsure how to change its course.

She was exhausted and felt guilty for having ignored her civic responsibilities. She sat down behind her desk and logged onto her Civic Association email account. As she had expected, there were twenty-seven new emails. Molly sighed, glad to at least be comfortable in her favorite drawstring sleeping shorts and Cole's comfy long-sleeved shirt. She pulled her feet onto the chair, beneath her, and reluctantly scanned the messages, passing over the political materials. *Great, only twenty-two more.* She grabbed a chocolate from the desk drawer and focused on the task at hand, prioritizing based on the subject line rather than trying to tackle all of them by dated order. She would get through what she was able with the little energy she had left. The rest would have to wait. Molly felt a presence and looked up to find Cole standing in the doorway. The disappointed smirk on his face was one Molly was becoming increasingly used to.

"Email?" he said flatly.

Molly shrugged, "BCA stuff."

Cole rolled his eyes and walked away.

Molly's heart sank as the fissure between them grew. She knew she should leave the emails for the next day and patch things up with Cole, but she couldn't find the justification to apologize for wanting to help Tracey. If only she'd have had the courage to have helped

Amanda. *Damn it! Cole is my husband! He should believe me unconditionally.* She pushed her anger aside, took a deep breath, and turned back to her computer, listening to Cole's heavy footsteps climb the stairs and flinching when he slammed the bedroom door.

Her eyes were drawn to three responses to her original announcement about Tracey's disappearance. She read the first two—thank you notes from residents that promised to keep their eyes open. Just as she was about to open the next email, Stealth and Trigger suddenly burst into fits of barking. She could hear them clawing at the back door. Molly picked up her mug of tepid hot chocolate, took a sip, and wondered what she'd have to deal with now. She turned back to her computer but could not block out the frantic barking. Annoyed, she went to the kitchen and opened the door, releasing the alerted dogs into the yard—and finding a folded paper taped to the back of the door. Molly snagged the sheet, more annoyed than concerned, and unfolded the simple white paper. The typed message sent a chill down her spine, "FIND HIM AND YOU WILL FIND HER."

Fourteen

Molly woke with a start. She was becoming increasingly used to the fearful state that greeted her in the mornings. She reached for her journal and began scribbling down the horror she'd seen and felt. Her mind reeled from the Knowing while Cole slept, blissfully unaware, beside her. She never failed to be amazed at his ability to not only fall asleep quickly, but to sleep so deeply that her constant trips to the bathroom never seemed to rouse him. She was too hyped up to go back to sleep. The clock glowed red—four A.M. She climbed from the bed and into her gray sweatpants, slipping Cole's Cape Cod sweatshirt over her head.

Stealth and Trigger followed her as she moved downstairs and entered the mudroom. She forced her feet into her pink converse high-tops, grabbed her backpack and her keys, and slipped silently out the door, dogs in tow. She trembled from the cold—or maybe from her nerves—and climbed into the van.

Stealth claimed the back bench seat, and Trigger settled for the floor.

"Thanks, guys," Molly said to them. "I know it's early, but I could use the company." She knew she had been too focused on Tracey lately and needed to clear her mind. She crawled gently through the slumbering town, passing the Country Store and the darkened houses. *Everyone must be sleeping, the perfect time for a criminal to prowl the streets—with no one the wiser.* She shuddered at the thought.

A glimmer on the lake caught Molly's eye. She pulled over and parked on the side of the bridge, causing the dogs to stir.

"Relax, we're okay," she assured them in a quiet voice. The beauty of the evening was not lost on Molly. She reclined her seat and watched the light sparkle across the water. The inlet from which the light emerged began to ripple. Molly squinted and quickly realized it was caused by a canoe. She watched the lone occupant paddle across the peanut-shaped lake, toward the bridge. *Another insomniac,* Molly thought, wondering where it was headed. She watched the canoe until it disappeared under the bridge and then reappeared on the other side. A gentle mist trailed behind the canoe as it streamlined toward the shore. Molly knew most of the residents of Boyds and was intrigued to see who else could not sleep on such a beautiful night. She raised her seat, started the car, and drove up and around the corner. The dogs whined as she came to a stop.

Molly sighed, "Okay, c'mon," and grabbed their leashes. The dogs jumped out of the van and hurried to the short strip of grass that separated the lake from the road. From her vantage point, Molly watched the canoe careen closer to the shore, the dark water rippled silently as it snuck into port. The person on board hunched over in a heavy coat and hat. The dogs picked up a scent, and they made their way further down the bank through the tall grass. A bunny hopped in front of Molly, Stealth and Trigger immediately gave chase. Molly yanked their leashes, and they gave in to their restraints, sulking, but poised to pounce again.

The street Molly had turned onto ran adjacent to the peanut-shaped lake. The canoe came to rest on the shore below Pastor Lett's home. Molly realized then that Pastor Lett must have moved from the manse to the house on the lake after Rodney's beating. *I'd have done the same thing,* she thought to herself. The person tugged the boat onto shore and dragged it up a hill, behind several large trees, and draped a brown camouflage tarp over it. Molly was about to wave when she noticed the person covering the canoe with sticks and piles of leaves. She hurried back up the hill with the dogs. Pastor Lett would be furious to know that someone was using her boat in the middle of the night. She ushered the dogs into the van and drove to the end of the cul-de-sac into Pastor Lett's driveway. She parked at the top of the black-top driveway and was surprised to see the person approaching Pastor Lett's side door. As she turned toward her car, Molly recognized her.

Molly's mind raced, *Does she know it's me? Can I just back up and drive away?* Reality set in as Pastor Lett neared her door. Molly rolled down the window, a little nervous. The dogs stood, alert, protective. Stealth growled.

"Shhh," Molly said, and Stealth lay back down, his ears perched high.

Molly turned back to see the fatigued face of Pastor Lett, her dirty, tired appearance not fitting into place in her mind. "Hello, Pastor," she said, a bit too cheerily for four in the morning.

"Molly," she said.

"I couldn't sleep," she offered. "Thought a drive would clear my head. Then I saw someone…well…you…in the canoe. I didn't know it was you, and I was going to see who it was so I could tell you about it in the morning." She felt like a teenager caught sneaking out at night. "Anyway, so here we are," she laughed, a little timidly.

"I couldn't sleep either," she said. Her words dragged. "Sometimes I just row to make myself tired."

An uncomfortable silence passed between them.

"Well, I'd better go then," Molly said nervously, relieved to be leaving. She smiled one last time, and said on her way out of the driveway, "I hope you get some sleep. It's been a pretty stressful time for everyone."

Pastor Lett nodded, and as Molly drove away from her house, she glanced in her rearview mirror. Pastor Lett remained at the top of the driveway, watching her leave.

Molly drove slowly back across the bridge, thinking about Pastor Lett. She strained to see the inlet which now appeared vacant and still. As she left the bridge behind, she noticed the gated driveway just beyond the lake—the driveway that she must have driven by hundreds of times and never noticed. It was the type of gate used to block off parks at sunset, two green cylindrical metal bars in the shape of sideways Vs which met in the middle and were chained and locked together. *The Perkinson House!* Molly pulled across the lanes and parked just before the driveway. She reached into her backpack and grabbed the flashlight, wondering if she was brave enough to make the trek up the hill. Stealth sat up and barked, startling Molly. She quickly scanned the area.

"What is it, boy?" she asked.

As if on cue, he barked again and pawed at the door. That, Molly could understand—the universal signal for *I have to go to the bathroom!*

With Stealth's needs taken care of, the dogs bounded toward the driveway. Molly juggled the leashes and tried to keep up with the excited dogs while cursing herself for leaving the van parked facing traffic. *I'll only be a few minutes,* she thought. The dogs' noses were on the ground, and there was a bounce in their steps, as if they were on a mission. They reached the bend at the top of the driveway, and Molly stopped, taking stock of her surroundings, trying to summon the courage to continue through the dark woods where the path of the barely-discernable driveway had disappeared. The train tracks lay to her right, but she couldn't see any signs of a house through the overgrown thorn bushes and thick trees. *It must be here,* she thought, thinking back to what Newton Carr had mentioned about a driveway. She continued along the path that wound further up the hill and through the trees, picking her way carefully through brambles, and finally came upon an incredible sight. The house seemed magnified to Molly, the way it perched atop the hill, clothed in ivy, standing sentry, the peaks of the roof reaching toward the sky. Despite the evident disrepair of the structure, Molly found herself in awe of its timeless beauty. She could imagine the Perkinson family sitting on the covered porch over a century ago, sipping cider and listening to the trains go by.

The air was thick with morning dew, gray and misty in the flashlight beam, making it difficult for Molly to see protruding roots through the fallen leaves. She stumbled, finding her balance before toppling over. The dogs vied to be set free—pulling their leashes and, in turn, yanking Molly—the leashes tore out of her bandaged palm. She winced in pain. The dogs trotted happily toward the rear of the property, leashes trailing behind them.

Molly hurried to follow the panting dogs and found them barking at the weathered and chained cellar doors which emerged from the ground, a treasure chest beckoning to be opened. Molly grabbed the dogs' leashes and pulled them away from the doors, shushing their loud barks. As they walked deeper into the backyard, the trees thinned, and a path was exposed. They followed it to a weathered yet elegant gazebo where the dried remains of wisteria wound around each carved spindle.

Trigger pulled Molly back toward the cellar doors. "That's enough, Trig!" Molly snapped. Molly fanned the light across the back of the house, illuminating the newly-placed boards covering the windows. She tugged hard on Trigger's leash and they made their way over the crest of the yard to where she could see the lake. She readied herself for the descent down the slippery hill, pulling the dogs closer to her sides and rolling her shoulders back. She eased down the hill toward the inlet below, the ground beneath her feet softening as she neared the water. The dogs rushed as far ahead as their leashes would allow, and Molly was pulled behind, barely able to keep her footing. At the bottom of the hill, the dogs sniffed at the water's edge. Molly caught her breath and turned back toward the hill. A path of recent footprints in the mud led up the hill and faded into the grassy knoll.

Fifteen

Tracey woke cold and aching. Even the slightest of movements sent sharp pains through her body. Light filtered through small holes in the top of the bad spot. Tracey tried to remember how to get back outside, which tunnels and turns to follow—but it was as if the path fell apart in her mind. She buried her face in her hands and cried frustrated, angry tears.

Tracey's head snapped upward at the dense sound of footsteps above her. She swiped at her tears, took a deep breath, and held it. A shadow cast over the light, and Tracey's heart jumped.

"Tracey, Mummy's here," her voice was cheerful. "Are you ready to come out of the bad spot? Have you decided to listen to Mummy and be a good girl?" she asked.

Tracey let out a whoosh of breath and pleaded frantically, "Yes! Yes! Please!" Her voice cracked. "Please take me out. I'll be a good girl! I'll listen! I won't fight anymore!" she declared, and she meant every word she said.

"Okay, just a sec," Mummy said.

Tracey could hear Mummy brush at the dirt with her feet. She covered her head with her hands and closed her eyes tightly. She remained still, hoping she was really going to be rescued from the bad spot. Dirt spilled through the hole and onto her arms. The sounds of the shovel scratching and scraping against the wood brought her hope. Her captor lifted the wood and Tracey saw her smiling face. Tears of happiness sprang from her eyes. She knew crying made Mummy mad, so she squeezed her eyes shut and tried her hardest to stop. All she wanted was to get out of the bad spot, make Mummy happy, and be a good girl.

"I'm almost there, sweetie, hold on one more minute," she said, as she lifted the tangled twigs.

Tracey reached her arms eagerly for Mummy to grab them. She held on as tight as she could and stood slowly, flinching from the pains that immobility had wrought. Mummy lifted her out of the hole, and Tracey collapsed into her warmth, pushing as far away from the bad spot as she was able. She took comfort in the safety of the arms of her captor. In her relief upon being freed from the bad spot, Tracey said through her tears, "I'm so sorry, Mummy. I promise to be good!"

Mummy leaned back from Tracey, her firm grip softened, her eyes serious. "Tracey, I put you there for your own good, but you see that Mummy came and got you, right?" she smiled and pulled her close again. "Let's get you out of those wet stinky clothes and clean you up a bit, huh?"

Tracey smiled. She was relieved to be out of the bad spot, comforted to be with another person, and thankful to be alive. She held Mummy's hand on the way back to their bathing place, happy to be taken care of again. Her crying subsided, replaced with acceptance—acceptance of her new life—and her new mummy.

Sixteen

Molly approached the rear of the dark house warily, the dogs pulled in the direction of the cellar doors, whining. Just as Molly felt at her wits' end, about to scream at the dogs and drag them by their fur if need be, she glanced down. A chill ran along her spine as she noticed the faintest ribbon of light beneath the cellar doors. A second later, it was gone. Molly froze, panicked. Her hands released the leashes, though the dogs remained by her side, alert, standing guard. Molly lowered her trembling body and peered beneath the doors. She reached her hands past the shiny lock, and tentatively touched the peeling paint of the old, wooden doors. Molly's vision instantly went black and images filled her mind, flashing erratically: *a man being beaten, huddling, cowering, and chanting; the same man sitting cross-legged on a dirt floor rocking back and forth.* Pressure grew against her hands—pressure of a man's thick, rough palms against her own. Molly shuddered. A second later the sensation was gone. Her eyes darted wildly as she grabbed the dogs' leashes and sprinted toward the driveway, literally dragging them behind her.

It wasn't until she started driving that she noticed the parking ticket. Her eyes stung with tears of fatigue and frustration. She cursed loudly into the dark night.

Molly tried to calm her mind as she stripped off her dirty clothes and pulled a t-shirt from the dryer. If it weren't for the bandage, she would have forgotten the wound on her hand. She peeled the dirty bandage off and replaced it with a clean one. The dogs followed her into the den, where Molly flicked on her computer and was surprised to see the time: six-thirty A.M. She moved foggily to the kitchen and made coffee, thinking about the strange night she had been through and remembering that she still had yet to discover why the ground had been hot where Hannah had knelt in the woods. That location, she decided, would be her destination for the morning—*after* her trip to the police station to talk her way *out* of that damn ticket—and maybe a nap. She rubbed her eyes as Cole walked in, dressed and ready for work.

"Couldn't sleep, huh?" he asked, absently.

"Mm-hmm. I keep seeing Tracey. It's driving me crazy."

Cole looked at her sharply, disbelief spread across his face.

"I'm not crazy, Cole," she said, annoyed. "I took the dogs for a drive, but then I saw Pastor Lett—at *four o'clock in the morning*! She was rowing her canoe out from one of the inlets—the one by the Perkinson House that Newton Carr was talking about." She poured Cole a cup of coffee, added cream and Sweet 'n Low, and filled a glass with water for herself.

Cole went to the front of the house to retrieve the newspaper, returned, and sat silently at the table, reading.

"Cole," Molly continued, "I know what you think of my visions. I don't know what's going on, but something is really wrong with...with...well, with everything right now." She leaned against the counter.

Cole lowered the newspaper. He looked at her, but Molly couldn't tell whether it was a look of pity or concern.

"Babe," he said, "I don't know what to think, but I can only suppose that you believe there's something going on. I'm worried about you. I thought the therapy really helped when we were in Philly. Maybe you should try that again, or talk to Pastor Lett, she helped you before."

Molly felt a strong need to validate what she had seen. "Cole, I got this weird note, and then I went to the Perkinson House, and saw, I don't know, something." She paused, thoughtfully, "There's something in the cellar." She rubbed her eyes, pulled away from him. "I think there might be *someone* in the cellar."

"Molly," Cole's tone was dismissive, "do you even hear what you're saying?"

"Cole, listen!" she pleaded, speaking quickly, as if she had to tell him before he could disparage her again. She told him about the visions she'd had in the early morning and the ones she'd had at the cellar doors.

Surprisingly, he said, in a very serious tone, "Well, Mol, it looks like you have something going on with you, though I don't know what." He looked across the table at her disheveled hair, the dark circles under her eyes. "Are you sure you aren't just exhausted?" he reached across the table and placed his hand upon hers. "Your curiosity working overtime, maybe? You know, Mol," he softened his voice, "you're OCD *could* cause you to dream about all of this, dredging up the past."

Molly smirked, inwardly chiding him for blaming OCD—an easy scapegoat for a person who needed hard, tangible facts in order to believe in things.

He quickly recovered. "I'm not saying it *is* causing the dreams. I'm just saying it could be, in combination with…well, you know, that's all." He sat calmly sipping his coffee—far too calm for Molly's racing mind.

"Don't you think I've thought of that?" she asked sharply. "I know she's not Amanda, and I don't think that I'd have such distinct visions if it were just my OCD. I mean," she fiddled with the castaway section of the newspaper that lay on the table, "if it were just OCD, I don't think I would've felt the man's palms on mine or seen with such clarity the area in the woods where I could *feel* her."

He looked at her as a doctor would look at a patient—a look that Molly was beginning to despise.

"*Feel* her? Come on, Molly. Maybe you did have visions—or do have visions—but we have to make sense of them somehow." He placated her, "You always do, you know. You figure everything out sooner or later."

"But later might be too late! There's a little girl's life at stake!" Molly's voice rose as she got up from the chair. "If she's still alive."

She gulped her water. Her determination grew. "She *is* still alive. I can feel it. I just have to find her." She looked out the window at the woods beyond the backyard and said quietly, "I have to find out about that spot in the woods where the ground was hot."

"What? What spot in the woods? What are you talking about?" Cole asked determinedly. "I'm worried about you, Molly, but if you're not willing to get help, then you need to know, I'm not uprooting again."

His cold stare bore into Molly. Too tired to draft another explanation that she knew would be refuted, she conceded. "I'm not asking you to uproot again. I think I'm just overtired." Molly headed toward the stairs. "I just need to rest." Cole didn't respond. Molly watched him shake his head and walk out the front door. As she ascended the stairs, thoughts of the Perkinsons' cellar raced through her mind. *The light was on. The light was off.* She turned back around and headed toward her den. Molly knew that once her mind got started, it was relentless; she'd never be able to rest. She sat down at her desk and drafted an email to Newton Carr.

Newton, I would like to hear more about the Perkinson House. Do you think you could take me there sometime? I'd love to see the property. She leaned back in her chair, and a moment later typed, Does it still have electricity? Thanks, Molly.

Hannah's morning schedule had been interrupted by an overwhelming sense of anxiety that she could not escape. She felt like a caged tiger, needing to break free. The familiar sound of the horses' hooves sporadically clomping on the packed-earth floor of their stalls only momentarily soothed Hannah's anxiety. She breathed in deeply and closed her eyes, relishing the pungent scent of manure and hay—a scent most people would find sharp or unpleasant. Hannah was normally calmed by the smell of her horses. Today, however, she was unable to put her finger on the pulse of her discomfort; it was unsettling, like a bad dream she could not shake. She unlatched Hunter's stall and drew his lean, muscular body into the center of the barn. She stroked his side, and he nodded his head as if telling her that he was ready. Hannah separated the mouthpiece from the worn leather of the headstall and moved it toward his mouth. He instinctively grasped the bit as he had every morning for the past several years—an expert. Hannah settled the face strap. She didn't halter Hunter when bridling him, there was no need. He seemed to find equal pleasure in their rides and never fought the tacking process. Together they walked out of the barn and to the block that Hannah had had specifically built in order to mount her horses. She climbed atop Hunter, bareback. Her body molded to the warmth of him. She leaned forward and stroked his mane. He shook his head from side to side. *Look, leg, rein,* Hannah thought habitually. She turned her head in the direction of the woods, used her leg to reinforce her intended direction, and Hunter moved with her before she had time to direct him.

"Good boy," Hannah said. They trotted toward the woods behind Hannah's farm.

Thirty minutes later, Hannah and Hunter emerged from the trees onto Schaeffer Road, a one-lane, rural road used as a shortcut from the older section of Boyds to the newer side of town. Hannah had used Schaeffer Road often when the trails were too muddy to ride as it offered a nice loop that led back toward her farm. It was a dangerous path for a horse, she knew, between the kids who raced down the road on their way to the airpark and the old-timers who drove ten miles per hour, but there were times that she just had to ride, no matter what the risk. On this day, however, she had needed to go through the trail—to see her. She felt the pull of the child, urging her near. Her thoughts drifted to Newton, and the first time they'd met, more than twenty years earlier.

She had been hanging up a flyer on the cork board at the post office, looking for farm hands, and Newton had been straightening papers on the table in front of the board. His eyes genially washed over Hannah, and he had quickly looked toward the ground as she tried to make eye contact.

"Well, hello there," she'd said, cheerfully. "You must be the wonderful person who keeps our community boards up to date."

"Yes, yes, I am," he had said, hurriedly. "You must be Ms. State? Bought the old Williams farm?" His eyes continued to dart away from Hannah's.

"Slate, with an L—Hannah." She had reached out to shake his hand.

"Well, nice to meet you, Hannah." He had taken her hand in his which was small for a man's hand. His handshake was gentle, not manly, but warm. Although he was shy, he exuded a friendliness that not many people could claim. "Newton, Newton Carr," he had said, finally looking up at her.

They'd chatted for a while and Hannah found herself intrigued by the little interesting man, who reminded her, somehow, of Piglet, with his modest and embarrassed mannerisms and sweet demeanor.

She'd commented on how he must have known everyone in Boyds, and he said, "I could tell you tales that wrap around this town like a ribbon. Hannah, would you have a minute to come meet Betty, my wife?"

Pleasantly surprised, she'd accepted, and spent the rest of the afternoon, and subsequently, many long days and nights with Newton and Betty, getting to know them, listening to stories about the town, the people, and genuinely becoming close friends. Newton and Betty had quickly become like family to Hannah, sharing holidays and urgencies. It had been Newton who'd dropped everything when Hannah had needed him, multiple times, and Betty who would bring soup when she was ill, tending to her animals over the years.

During the snowstorm in the mid-nineties, it was Newton who had begged Harley to plow her driveway first, *Just in case*. Newton had been there when Charlie left her and she'd needed a shoulder to cry on, a person to sit with, and to help her glue the pieces of her life back together. It was Newton who had held her secret and cherished it as much as she had, for so many years. Newton helped her hide from the rest of the world. Newton was her savior in more ways than one.

A thud behind her startled her out of her daydream, inciting a sense of fear. Something inside Hannah suddenly changed. Memories of the past heightened her anxiety and made her sentimental at the same time. She turned away from the annoying sound of the model airplanes hovering above, away from the trail she had been following, and down the paved road that led in the direction of her farm. The one-lane road weaved through the thick shade of the trees. Streams of sunlight stretched to the ground, offering brief, delicious patches of warmth. As they neared their turn, raindrops began to fall from the sky. Hannah held her face up toward the clouds, remembering a time long ago when she and Charlie had first begun to ride together—the dreams that they had woven, the plans they had made as they had ridden on a day that was so similar with a light sprinkling of rain. Dreams, Hannah remembered, of children, laughing and running through the fields, ponies bounding in the pastures, and dogs keeping a watchful eye over their blessings. Hannah let out a brief, harsh laugh. "Yeah, right. Dreams!" she lifted the reins and gave a quick tap to Hunter with her heels. He picked up his pace.

Hannah's dreams had been crushed when Charlie had realized it was all too much for him to handle. He'd become resentful and quick tempered, and he had finally taken off, leaving Hannah to fend for herself. Her stomach panged at the memory of the days just before he had left, the fear of what he would do had he found out her secret, his wrath of anger, which had come on fast and furious, as it had so often toward the end. Out of sadness or old memories, she wasn't sure which, her hand fell to her barren abdomen.

Molly stared groggily at the ringing telephone. She glanced at the nightstand and had a hard time registering that it was eleven thirty-seven A.M.—not P.M. She had climbed into her warm bed for a quick nap—two hours earlier. She answered the phone groggily, "Hello?"

"Ma? Who is he?"

"Erik? Who is who?" she said, smiling as she was brought awake by the sound of her son's energetic, voice.

"Who is the other son—the one you're probably calling instead of me?" he laughed.

"Oh, that one!" she said, loving the game they had played since he had left for college. "Well, he actually lives nearby. He's about your age, and *he* calls *me* sometimes."

"Yeah, right," Erik said. "Whatever—listen, Mom," Erik's voice turned serious, "it's happening again."

"What is?" Concerned, Molly righted herself.

"The dreams—you know," he hesitated.

Molly could hear the anxiety in Erik's tone. She leaned against the headboard of the bed, closed her eyes, and remembered her spontaneous visit to a psychic when Erik had been just five. Her friends had been going—*for the fun of it*—and she had tagged along. The psychic had told Molly that Erik bore the same ability to "see things" as she, but that his young mind was too cluttered to see them clearly. The worry of that being true had plagued Molly for years. She had secretly analyzed Erik's dreams as he had shared them—but other than a few recurring dreams when he went through puberty, they were always typical boyhood dreams. Now she silently pleaded to God not to burden Erik with the Knowing.

"Tell me, Erik," she said.

"There's this guy, Mom," his voice was quiet, yet rushed. "He's in the dark, well, mostly in the dark. He rocks—forward and back, like that autistic kid did in that show you made me watch? Son Rise? He says stuff, too, but I don't really know what," Erik paused, "but I think it's something important."

Molly gripped the phone so tightly that her knuckles were white. "What else?"

"I'm afraid, Mom. I'm afraid of the other things I saw," he was almost whispering.

"Erik," Molly swallowed, then urged, "there's something big going on here at home." She didn't want to upset him, but every sense in her body told her that she needed to hear what he saw. "Please, Erik. Please tell me. It might help."

He took a deep breath. Molly envisioned his worried face, the way the right side of his mouth would quiver with each word and his brown eyes would open wide as he concentrated. Molly saw the troubled face of the boy he was, not the young man he had become.

"I saw a girl. It totally freaked me out." The words tumbled uneasily from his mouth.

"Oh, Erik," Molly said. "I'm so sorry, honey."

"What, Mom?" his voice became louder as his frustration grew. "What the hell is it? Who is she?"

"I think she's the little girl who's missing, but I don't know that."

"Oh, great!" Erik said, sarcastically. "This is freakin' great, Mom."

Molly could hear his panic rise.

"Well, guess what—there's more. The little girl was in some kind of a...I don't even know what," he yelled, "a freaking hole! She was in a freaking hole in the goddamn ground, Mom!" his voice cracked.

"Erik, listen to me," she paused, listened to his breathing. "Erik, you probably—"

"Don't even say it, Mom," he warned. "I'm not *like* you, Mom. I know you're going to say it's a *vision* or something, but it's not."

"Erik, listen. Please, don't hang up!" she pleaded. "It's horrible. This little girl's been missing for a few days, and Erik," she closed her eyes tight, hoping he would not hang up, "I had the same dream."

Her revelation was met with silence.

"Erik?" she said tentatively.

As the phone remained silent, Molly grew anxious.

"Erik!" she demanded.

"What!" he said harshly. "Jesus Christ, Mom. What do you want me to say?" he yelled. "I just freaking saw a missing girl in a hole, and you want me to talk about it?"

"Erik, you can help her. I know you don't really believe in this stuff, but you *can* help her. You *have* to help her. Please!" Molly's heart felt as though it were going to burst through her chest.

"That's just it, Mom," Erik answered, "I do believe in this stuff," he said sheepishly.

Molly let out a sigh of relief.

"But I don't want to," Erik said. "Don't you think I've seen what you go through—what you've gone through all these years? There's always something that you *just know*. Goddamn it, Mom!" he said angrily. "I don't want to be like you!"

Molly bristled. His words stung. "I'm sorry." She wiped her tears, wishing she could erase his memory of the images. "Honey, I know this is hard, but do you know where she was?" she asked.

"Uh-huh, sort of," he said. Molly could hear the tension in his words, his desire not to reveal what he saw.

"Erik, please," she pleaded.

"Fine, whatever! I saw woods and could hear kids in the background, okay? And, no, I don't know where exactly, but it sounded like she was near a park, or a school, or some shit like that." He took a deep breath.

Molly waited.

"There's more. I'm pretty sure I saw Hannah Slate kneeling over her." He spoke through clenched teeth, "What the hell, Mom?"

Molly eyes grew wide. "I'm not sure, Erik." She tried to waylay his fears—and her own, "I'm sure it's nothing. Hannah helped search for her. That's probably what you saw."

"The guy, Mom—you have to find him. I think he's trapped somewhere. I think he needs to get out. I think he was trying to say something important."

"Okay, honey. I'll do everything I can to find him—and to find Aman—Tracey." She decided to go one step further, "Erik, did you *feel* anything when you saw her?"

Erik didn't hesitate. "I didn't feel anything other than being totally freaked out when I woke up—but Mom, find that guy, please. I don't know why, but it's really important that you find him—soon."

"I will. I promise to hunt him down!" She laughed, heard Erik utter, "Jesus Christ!" and added, "Really, honey. I'll try—and if I can figure this all out, I'll call you right away."

He let out a deep sigh. "Good." His voice softened, like the boy he used to be, "Mom, what if she's...you know...like Amanda?"

Molly braced herself against the back of the bed. "She's not, Erik," she closed her eyes and said, "I'm sorry that you have to go through this. I hoped that you wouldn't have these...abilities." Molly's sadness hung in the air.

"Yeah, whatever. You're probably happy that you have a kid who's just like you."

His sarcasm was not lost on Molly, who smiled at his ability to remain positive about something that just might change his entire life.

Molly unwrapped the bandage from her hand and touched the T which had become a simple scar. She wondered how it could have healed so quickly, but like so many other aspects of her life, accepted it without too much deliberation. She poked at it, curled her fingers into a fist, and stretched them as far as she could—the scar did not tear. It had become as sturdy as the rest of her palm. The T had become a part of her—a constant reminder of the little girl who was yet to be found.

Molly showered, turning away from her own naked reflection in the mirror, *Geez, I look like Mom already*, she thought. Molly had always thought she'd be able to outrun the aging process, and as she took in her own image, she realized that age lays claim to a body without any fanfare; a few extra pounds here, a little less muscle there, until one day, in the mirror appears a wrinkled face that seems foreign. She turned away from the mirror to dress and began making her mental to-do list.

At her computer, she checked her email and found one new message from Newton Carr:

Hello Molly. I hope you're feeling better. You looked rather ill the other night. I cannot take you to the Perkinson House. The Perkinson family has requested that only Pastor Lett walk the property. I do apologize, but I must respect their request. Several family members died in their house and with the rumors of ghosts on the property they've had issues with curious teens. I'd be happy to tell you all about it, but I'm sorry I can't take you there.

Take care, Newton.

P.S. There is no electricity turned on as far as I know.

"Great," Molly sat back in her chair, deflated. "Ghosts. That's all I need."

Molly stepped inside the Country Store, and the familiar bell chimed above the door.

"Hello!" Jin called from the back of the store.

Molly poured herself a cup of coffee, "Hey, Jin, how are you?"

Jin came to the front of the store, "Fine, fine, and you?"

"Great. Tired."

"It's late for you. What happened?" he asked.

"Don't even ask!" Molly laughed. "I was up all night. I'm whipped!" she took a sip of coffee and grimaced at the taste.

Jin pointed to the cup, "Coffee? No water?"

"Not today. Today I need some fake energy!"

"No running?" he asked. Molly had become accustomed to Jin's clipped sentences.

The back door of the store opened and closed, and Molly turned to see Edie slip into the office and close the door.

"Tomorrow," Molly said, distracted. "Today I'm making sure my ankle is okay." She paid for her coffee and turned to leave.

"Rodney. He did not kill that girl." Jin's serious tone stopped Molly in her tracks. "He did not do it."

Molly's shoulders dropped at the mention of his name. "Somehow," she turned and said to Jin, "I think you might be right, but that doesn't help him—or Pastor Lett, who has already lost a brother." Hannah walked in as Molly left the store, breezing by her with a quick hello. Molly sat on the worn wooden bench in front of the store. She set her coffee cup on the ground in front of her and sat back, contemplating the sorrow she felt for Pastor Lett. She thought about the Boyds Boys and how nice it must have been for them to be together for all of those years. The hum of the passing cars and the view of Sugarloaf Mountain in the distance calmed Molly. She relaxed into the bench and began to formulate her plan for the day. Hannah hurried from the store, into her car, and drove off with a quick wave. Molly stood, waved, and climbed into her car. She blew out a frustrated breath and stared at the block-lettered message that was taped to her steering wheel:

> *DOWN ON KNEES, SECRETS NEAR*
> *FIND HIM, IT WILL BE CLEAR*

"What the hell?" Molly said. She tore the note from her steering wheel. Suddenly, she was hit with a stabbing pain that shot through her arms and traveled to her chest. She grabbed hold of the steering wheel, her back as straight as a board, her eyes wide open. The vision hit, sharp and swift—followed by a cold burst that ran through Molly's body, prickling her skin: *Tracey knelt in front of candles, unafraid, peaceful. Next to her, a large woman prayed. The woman turned toward Tracey, her face shrouded in shoulder-length dark hair.*

Just as suddenly, the vision ceased. Molly's body pitched forward, spilling her coffee. She felt the warm liquid dripping down her leg but didn't have the strength to wipe it away. A combination of relief and fear settled in her mind—Tracey was likely still alive, but something about the woman with her had appeared unnervingly familiar.

Molly did not like women who played the part of damsel-in-distress rather than taking their due, but today, she was going to try. The last thing she needed was another parking ticket. She swallowed her confidence and timidly approached the male officer standing behind the front counter of the police station. "Excuse me," she said in a quieter-than-normal voice, "I have a question." She laid the ticket on the counter and tried her best to appear embarrassed, lowering her voice to a whisper. "The other night, I stopped my car on the side of the road because I thought I saw a child down by the lake, and it was really late," she lied. "I ran down to the lake to see if it was in fact a child, and I walked around a little, you know, checking it out. When I came back up, this was on my van." She pushed the ticket towards the officer, adding quickly, "I was worried, with the little girl missing and all. I thought I'd better not waste any time. I didn't want to miss a chance to find the poor girl." She flashed him her sweetest smile and shrugged, all the while, hating herself for having to pull such girly crap.

"Ma'am, how long were you parked there?" the young officer asked, in a tone that was more like Erik's than a man's.

"Oh, not long," she eagerly replied. "I ran down, walked around a bit," she glanced up toward the ceiling, tapped her chin with her fingers, as if thinking, "maybe a few minutes, fifteen or so—not so long." Behind her back, Molly's fingers were crossed.

The officer held the ticket in his fingers and scrutinized it, as if the answer to his dilemma were written there. Molly tried to appeal to his maternal side—everyone had a mother. "It's just that," she looked down at the counter, lowered her voice again, "I have a son, and if someone had seen my son who was missing, I would want them to stop and check it out."

"Of course you would," he said kindly.

Molly surveyed him. He couldn't have been more than twenty-three years old. She pushed a little harder. "It doesn't seem like something I should be penalized for, you know?"

The officer gave her a pitying look, as if contemplating what he might do for his own mother. He leaned forward and said quietly, "Let me see what I can do."

Molly was surprised. "Oh, thank you so much," she said eagerly. "That's so nice of you!" Molly's voice seeped maternal gratitude, which she knew would land in his ears the way a proud mother's might. She watched him walk away and mumbled, "Please God, don't get me for this!"

Molly waited nervously for the officer to return. The thought entered her mind that perhaps his superior would come out and lecture her on the inappropriate behavior of a civically-responsible adult. She was relieved when he came around the corner five minutes later. He settled himself behind the counter and leaned toward Molly.

"Ma'am?"

She hurried over, "Yes?"

"It's okay, I took care of it." He smiled, proud of his accomplishment.

Molly brought her hands together and almost clapped, stopping herself and clasping her hands together instead. "Wonderful! Oh, thank you! You are so kind, really! Thank you so much!"

"No problem," he grinned, "but from now on, please park on the correct side of the street."

"I will," Molly said. "I promise,"

He set the ticket aside, then looked back at Molly. "Thanks for checking out the sighting. Did you find anyone?" he asked with genuine curiosity.

Her smiled faded. "I didn't find anyone. It must have been a deer or something. I looked everywhere and didn't see anyone. I was so bummed." Molly turned to leave, and then turned back to the young man, "Thank you again. Do you have any news about the missing girl?"

The officer shook his head, "No, unfortunately not, but we aren't giving up hope, and ma'am, we would hate for you to be harmed. Please, in the future, notify the authorities if you see anything suspicious."

Molly nodded and left the building. She was digging through her purse for her keys when she ran head-on into Officer Brown.

"Mrs. Tanner, fancy meeting you here," he said.

Molly was caught off guard, "H…How are you?"

"Just fine and dandy, though we've got no word on Tracey yet," he said.

Molly glanced hurriedly over her shoulder, embarrassed about talking her way out of the ticket. "I know, I just checked," she said, hoping her cover would negate his need to follow up on her visit with the officer inside. "I'm so sorry that I ran into you!" she said, touching his arm. She quickly reached back into her purse. "I was looking for," she brought out her key ring and jingled it, "my keys," she said.

"No problem," he smiled in a curious way.

Molly could feel his eyes on her back as she climbed into her van.

Molly stepped out of her van and looked around the parking lot of the Adventure Park. She would never have guessed a child had gone missing from the park had she not known. Children played on the equipment, mothers chatted, and no one noticed as she walked down the grassy hill toward the woods. She realized how easy it would be for someone to walk from the woods to the parking lot and vice versa without so much as a sideways glance. It was too easy.

Molly didn't hesitate. She moved quickly to the edge of the woods, stepping over the untethered yellow police tape and expecting to be greeted by the force that she had encountered during the search. Instead, the air held a peaceful, almost welcoming quality. Leaves crunched under her feet as she moved branches and walked deeper into the forest. Molly carefully stepped over fallen timber and tried to weave her way around the thorny sprigs that clawed at her from every direction. She was prying a thorn from her sweater when she realized that she was near the site where Hannah had been crouched—where the ground had been warm. Molly removed her pad and looked over the drawings she had made of the area, noting the three rocks that were arranged in a triangular fashion near a lone green bush. She was sure she was near the spot, although something struck her as being different, out of place. She tucked the notepad away in her backpack which she tossed onto a nearby bush. Molly scanned the ground. A lone flower lay on the earth—a white marigold, brown around the edges and wilting. Instinctively, she reached for the flower, retrieving her empty hand quickly as heat intensified beneath it.

"Pretty flower, huh, Mrs. Tanner?"

Molly jumped up and spun around, ready to flee or fight, whatever the situation might command. Officer Brown stood just a few feet from her, his heavy hands in his overcoat pockets, a smirk pasted on his face.

"My God! You scared me," Molly accused.

"Well, you scared me, too." He walked toward her. "What are you doing, Mrs. Tanner?" He lifted his chin toward the flower. "What brings you here?"

"I…" she searched frantically for an alibi, "I wanted to see if I could find any hint of Tracey." *Yeah,* she thought, g*o with confidence.* Molly pulled her shoulders back and steadied her hands. "I know it sounds silly, but I think these woods hold the answers. I mean, where else could she have gone?"

Officer Brown walked around Molly, stopping only a foot from the heated ground. He turned and bent over from the waist, his large rear end too close for Molly's comfort. She held her breath and stepped backward.

He straightened back up and turned toward Molly, twisting the flower's stem between his fingers.

"Pretty," he said, handing the flower to Molly.

"Y...yes...it is," Molly managed, suspiciously accepting the flower. "I guess someone must have dropped it."

"Hmm," he nodded his head, turned, and walked across the spot where Molly had encountered the heat. Molly stared, mesmerized. "What do you think you will find here, Mrs. Tanner?"

Molly swallowed, answering quickly, "I don't know. A path? A lead of some sort?" she walked to her right, trying to steer him away from the area. "It seems to me that Tracey must have come this way. I mean, her mother and sister were walking *away* from here, so they would have seen her if she had walked toward the parking lot," she shrugged. "So that leaves the woods."

"But why these woods," he pointed toward the woods on the side of the park, "and not the ones over there?"

"They would have seen her. Someone would have seen her, don't you think?" she asked.

"Maybe, maybe not," he moved closer to Molly, stared into her eyes.

Molly held his stare.

"Mrs. Tanner, do you know that most abductors come back to the site of the abduction shortly afterward?"

"No, I didn't know that," she said, taking a step backward. "Good to know," she looked down. Then she turned her eyes back to his. "Surely, Officer Brown," she said with as much confidence as she could muster, "you don't think I'm a suspect?"

"Never said that," he quipped. "Just thought it was interesting that you came by the station this morning, asked questions about leads, and here I find you at the same spot as the abduction, that's all." He picked up a twig and set it between his yellowing teeth, like a toothpick. "Now, why *are* you here?" he asked.

"Jesus Christ," Molly said, with a frustrated sigh, "I am looking for leads, okay?" She stepped away from him, raised her voice, "I think we'll find them here. Why in God's name would I abduct a small child?

I mean, look at my life, it's pretty full, wouldn't you say?"

"Oh, I don't know about that. You seem to have time to wander around the woods during the day," he said in a patronizing way.

Molly was angry. "No! I *make* the time. There *is* a difference," she said, strongly. "I can't believe this. Do you want to arrest me? Or maybe you can't find leads and you feel badly, so you need someone to hang it on? Well, keep dreaming, sir," she said with sarcasm, "because there is no correlation between me and Tracey Porter besides my own desire to help find her." Molly put her hands on her hips, accentuating her firm stance on her innocence. "By the way," she retorted, "have you considered consulting a psychic? Someone who might be able to *see* where she is?"

He laughed a hearty, condescending laugh and kicked at the leaves on the ground. "Oh yeah, and we've invited the Mickey Mouse Club, too," he chuckled. "We thought maybe they could do a dance, and the abductor would magically appear."

For a split second, Molly had considered telling him about her visions, but decided firmly against it the moment the laugh had left his lips. *Thick-minded ass.* "I'm being serious, Officer Brown," she said. "There are people who might be able to help you find her," she pleaded. "Tracey's time *must* be running out—if she's even still alive."

"Well, statistically speaking, yes, you're right. Her time is running out," he said coldly.

"So? What now? Just walk around hoping to find her and accusing innocent people?" she spat the words angrily. "Oh, am I like Rodney Lett now?" she asked. "Well," she said as she turned away from him. "I won't be your scapegoat, Officer Brown. I have an alibi, and I have been instrumental in trying to find her."

"Calm down, Molly," he said, spitting the twig onto the ground. "Calm down. I'm not saying that you *are* a suspect. I'm simply wondering why you're here and letting you know that the abductor usually visits the crime scene shortly after the crime." Officer Brown watched Molly's back as she stopped walking. "Yup, there have been cases when killers have actually been at the scene while the police were investigating, within hours of the murder."

Molly spun around, "Well, let's hope that you are *not* investigating a murder," she said, emphatically.

"Of course," he said casually, and he turned to walk out of the woods, hesitating a moment later. "Molly," he said with her back to her, "let me know if you find anything here, will ya?" he continued walking away.

"Officer Brown!" Molly called after him.

He turned.

"Were you following me, Office Brown?" she asked with a hint of concern. "How did you know I was here?"

"Actually, I wanted to catch up to you, but you had driven away. So," he paused, motioned around with his right hand, "I suppose, yes, I followed you."

"Why?" she asked.

He stared blankly at her, puzzled.

"I mean, why did you want to catch up to me after I was at the station?" she asked.

"Oh!" he said jovially. "I wanted to let you know that I looked into the Rodney Lett thing, and sure enough, he was buried in Delaware, so there's no chance that he's part of this. There's no correlation between the two." He looked pleased with the news.

Molly nodded, processing the information. She couldn't help herself, she felt compelled to throw it back at him, "Well, I wasn't really concerned that Rodney Lett was the one who took Tracey. I was more concerned that whoever took *Kate* might have also taken Tracey."

"I told you, Molly, Rodney Lett is dead and buried."

This is a positive journey I'm on, Pastor Lett reminded herself as she drove toward the Porters' home. She realized that she'd been reminding herself of her role quite often recently. The events of late were reminiscent of her own journey, years ago—like opening an old wound. *Celia is hurting, scared, and probably feels to blame*, she thought to herself. *It's my job as her pastor to ease that pain and to relieve that guilt.*

Anger grew within her as she thought of the procedures the police used to try and find Tracey Porter. The systems currently in place were the same lame checks and balances, in her opinion, as they had been twenty years earlier when they had investigated the disappearance of Kate Plummer. She grasped the steering wheel until her knuckles turned from white to red. Her mind turned to Rodney. *How could anyone have looked at that big lug and thought he could hurt a child?* She clenched her jaw and pulled the car to the side of the road, tears clouding her vision. She remembered Rodney's face contorting with fear and pain for Kate when she had told him she was missing.

Rodney had sobbed. She remembered his pudgy, fisted hands, rubbing his tears away like a child might have done, but it had been Rodney's reaction to the photo of Kate that had rocked Pastor Lett to her core. He had gone still as a statue. He had taken the photo out of Pastor Lett's hand and had stared into the innocent eyes of Kate Plummer, as if he had, at that moment, through the image on the photo paper, connected with her. Rodney had said, "Girl in dark place." Just like that—without explanation, without thought, or so it had seemed at the time. Those four words had terrified Pastor Lett.

She hadn't wanted to leave Rodney that evening, but she had an obligation to the church. She had to complete her work, and then, she had promised herself, then she would focus on Rodney and try to understand those words—but it had been too late.

The phone call from the police had sent Pastor Lett rushing to the police station, chiding herself for having left Rodney at home alone. She had been taken to the interrogation room and had found Rodney sitting at that awful metal table, looking like a child caught sneaking a piece of candy from his favorite store— remorseful for an act he didn't quite understand. The look he had given Pastor Lett when she had arrived— those big dark eyes pleading with fear—had filled her with remorse. Pastor Lett had gone to him, held him, and Rodney had sobbed on her shoulder. "Girl in dark place," he had repeated. Pastor Lett stiffened at the words, having known full well why the police had brought Rodney in for questioning. Pastor Lett had thought, had hoped, that Officer Katan, a past member of the church who had known Rodney well and had been to their home for dinner, would protect her brother—but she was wrong.

The questioning, which had been futile at best, had left the police with little to go on.

"Rodney," Officer Katan had asked, looking at Pastor Lett with an expression of apology, "do you know Kate Plummer?"

Rodney had rocked in his seat, a motion Pastor Lett had known too well—a motion that brought Rodney deeper into his own mind. Rodney had replied, "Girl in dark place. Girl in dark place."

Again, Katan asked, "Rodney, do you know Kate Plummer?" He had taken Rodney's rocking as affirmation of his knowledge.

"Wait!" Pastor Lett had pleaded. "He doesn't know the girl. He's only seen a picture of her!" she insisted. "Katan, he doesn't know her!" Pastor Lett had turned frantically to Rodney, imploring him, "Rodney, tell them the truth. Tell them you don't know Kate!" she had pleaded, but it had been like pleading with a child who knew he was right and didn't understand the parental confusion.

Rodney had rocked harder, stating adamantly, "Girl in dark place!"

Then Katan had asked, "Rodney, where did you put her? Is she alive?"

Pastor Lett had stood abruptly, fisting her hands and breathing heavily. Rodney stopped rocking. He seemed to crawl inside his head for a moment, swimming around and coming out with a deep breath and an answer, "No pain. She's with mommy," Rodney had said.

Katan had hovered angrily over Rodney, yelling at him, "Mommy? Kate's mother is not dead, Rodney.

She has cancer, but she's not dead! What the hell did you do, you big fool?"

Pastor Lett had stepped in between Rodney and Katan protectively. "Don't you dare accuse him, Katan," she had said sternly.

Rodney, confused by the anger, stood up, towering over Katan. Katan had squared his shoulders, staring at the large man's thick chest. "Sit down, Rodney," he commanded.

Rodney had looked down at him and said emphatically, "With mommy. Not in pain. No pain!"

Katan had taken that to mean that he had killed her.

Pastor Lett swooped into action—wrapping her arms around Rodney and allowing Rodney to cling to her, like a child fearing a stranger. Pastor Lett put her hand to the back of Rodney's head, as if shielding him from Officer Katan. "Rodney, don't say what you don't know. You're confusing Officer Katan." She looked at Officer Katan and said, "He doesn't know what he's saying. Surely you see that."

Rodney watched Officer Katan out of the corner of his eyes. "Carla, Rodney not bad!" he said, tears striping his cheeks.

"No, no, Rodney's not bad." Pastor Lett had assured him. The tears she had been holding back broke free.

"Girl in dark place—with mommy," Rodney whispered.

Pastor Lett had grasped for an explanation, her heart beat hard against Rodney's cheek. "Look, Katan. You know Rodney. He didn't do this. He…" she hesitated, her chest tight with fear, "he knows things sometimes." She had tried to explain, knowing full well that Officer Katan might think she was crazy or perhaps arrest them both, but counting on Officer Katan's compassion and his history of knowing Rodney. "He knows things that happen," she said sheepishly, "sometimes before and sometimes after the event—but…it's real."

"What the hell?" Katan had said, throwing his arms up and pacing around the room. "Carla, this is not good. What the hell do you want me to do here, Carla? We have protocols. You know, I could arrest him here and now—probably for murder."

"Murder?" Pastor Lett was in Katan's face again. "You know Rodney would never hurt anyone, much less a child."

As the ruckus in the room grew, Rodney had moved to the corner, huddling on his heels like a cowering chipmunk being preyed upon by a vicious hawk. He rocked, mumbling, "Girl in dark place. Girl in dark place."

Pastor Lett turned to him. She knelt down, rested her hands on his knees. "Rodney, honey, you have to stop this. They think you hurt Kate. Please, stop saying that. Tell them you don't know her."

Rodney gazed up with wide innocent eyes. He continued to rock, fidgeting with his fingers. He shook his head no.

"Rodney, honey," Pastor Lett put her fingers to the bridge of her nose, breathing deeply and closing her eyes. "Sweetie," she said, "you have to tell them. This is not good. This is bad. They think you hurt Kate."

Rodney shook his head. "Rodney no hurt. Girl in no pain. Girl with mommy. Girl in dark place," he said.

Officer Katan stared down at them, shaking his head in disbelief. "Carla," he started, "I'm going to let you take him home. Do not," he said as he looked around the empty, cold room, "I repeat, do not let him out of your sight. I may have to bring him back in tonight or tomorrow morning." He turned his back to them. "This is...unusual. I know Rodney, but..." He shook his head, began to raise his arms, then let them fall in defeat.

On the ride home from the station, Rodney had been a mess—rocking and shaking uncontrollably. Pastor Lett had begged Rodney to tell her what he knew about Kate, to show her where Kate was, but Rodney repeated the same things he had told Officer Katan. He seemed as sure of those things as Pastor Lett was about there being a God—but Pastor Lett also knew that, to others, Rodney's words were the ramblings of a crazy person—one who just might be crazy enough to kill a child.

Pastor Lett remained in her car, staring out the window at the passing traffic, and ruing the memories of that awful night. She covered her eyes with her hand, leaned back against the cold leather seat, and gave in to the crushing memories of Rodney's last excruciating moments.

The living room, which had once offered comfort and warmth, suddenly felt as if it were a holding room. Pastor Lett had drawn the curtains and sat next to Rodney on the floor where Rodney had pulled into his own world. He was unresponsive to his sister's touch, his eyes trained on a speck on the cold wooden floor, traumatized. Pastor Lett had told him how brave he had been to speak to the police. She told him he had been a good boy and that he had done nothing wrong. Pastor Lett's heart was heavy with inadequacy as she watched her brother pull further into his own silent world. Had she led Rodney astray? Had she not been there enough for him? Guilt clouded her judgment, obscuring her eyes with tears, and rendering her unable to see the path ahead, the right thing to do. She had lifted her head toward the ceiling and prayed, Rodney rocking at her side. She could still recall the feel of Rodney's warm hand as it had unexpectedly grasped her arm. She could still hear Rodney's child-like voice when he had asked, "God? God there?" pointing to the ceiling—and she remembered her own reply, "Yes, God is there. God hears Carla."

Pastor Lett pursed her lips and pounded her fist on the steering wheel, wishing she could have changed what had happened next. Wishing she hadn't taken the phone call.

She had trembled as she had lifted the receiver, fearing it had been Katan telling her to bring Rodney back and not certain that she would be able to will herself to do so—but it hadn't been Katan on the phone that dreadful night. It had been a man with a deep, scratchy voice who had said that he needed to speak to Pastor Lett immediately and confidentially. He had said it had to do with Kate Plummer. A rush of hope had swept through Pastor Lett as she agreed to meet the man at the church across the street from her home. She had fretted about leaving Rodney, but, in his current state, taking him along had not been an option. His rounded, thick shoulders hunched over as he held onto his favorite toy, a matted and stained stuffed brown rabbit. It had been the one possession that he had saved after they had left their parents' home in Delaware to come to Boyds.

Pastor Lett had spoken slowly and deliberately to Rodney before she had left. She made sure that

Rodney understood three things: that he must stay inside, he must not answer the phone, and that he was, no matter what the police thought, a good person. Rodney had looked up at her with his trusting eyes, pulling himself out of his altered state, if only for a moment, and repeated back to Pastor Lett, "Rodney understand. Rodney good boy. No outside."

A feeling of relief swept through Pastor Lett as she had approached the darkened church. Though she could not shake the burden of her own guilt—guilt of lying to the police about staying with Rodney—she had hoped that the man she was meeting might be the abductor wanting to confess, or perhaps someone who had a lead and had found out that Rodney had been wrongly accused. She had waited at the church for over an hour, pacing, sweating despite the cool evening, and watching the perimeter of her own home through the small glass window in the front of the church. Eventually, she had decided that whoever had called had gotten cold feet and was not going to show up. She stepped back into that awful gray, stale night, and went in the front door, in case Rodney had fallen asleep in the parlor at the rear of the home where she had left him.

"Rodney?" she had said, listening intently to the suffocating silence. There was no rush of excitement, no gleeful giggle, no "Carla home!" She had rushed into the parlor, nearly collapsing at the sight of her motionless brother, lying on the blood-splattered floor. Her legs had failed her as she'd gasped for breath and fallen to her knees. The sight of her brother's blood-soaked flannel shirt and couch and the smell of sweat sent her mind spinning. "No!" she had screamed, crawling to her brother's side and cradling his lifeless head. "No! Rodney, no!" Tears had fallen onto

Rodney's unseeing eyes. His bunny's ear, torn off and speckled with blood, lay within his hand. Pastor Lett pulled her brother's heavy body into her chest, emptying her soul via the salty water of her tears. Her next actions were robotic—without thought—her body pumped with adrenaline, her mind a blank slate, in shock. She had quickly called upon Newton, and with his fast and efficient help, they'd laid Rodney in the back seat, covered him with a blanket, and rushed back inside. She took the stairs two at a time, threw open her drawers, and stuffed a few pieces of clothing into a suitcase. She flew back down the stairs and scooped up Rodney's torn bunny. She hurried to the kitchen, saw the broken window, the muddy prints layering the floor like stale accusations, and her panic grew. Without picking up the phone, she had fled, escaping through the back door and leaving it wide open. What she had of value had been beaten to a pulp and was going with her to Delaware. They were going home, where their lives had started, and where her brother's life would end.

Pastor Lett threw the car door open and placed her feet on the shoulder of the road. She leaned forward, resting her elbows on her knees. She wiped her eyes on her sleeve, pushed her hair out of her face, clasped her hands together, and pushed them into her forehead, clenching her eyes closed. She tried to erase the image of Rodney's ravaged body from her mind, to chase the horrid thoughts that came roaring into her head like a bullet train—hatred, pure and evil. She knew she must parlay those thoughts into forgiveness. She wanted to forgive, but the terrifying visceral thoughts would not leave her. She wanted to hate, to take revenge. *Didn't they know he had a family, someone who loved him and would miss him?* she futilely thought for the millionth time. *Forgive me, Father*, rolled through her mind immediately after the wretched thoughts. She took a deep breath and tried to quiet the voice she did not like. *I have to be there for Celia and Mark,* she thought. *The pain I felt must not be felt by others.* She yanked the handkerchief from her purse and wiped her eyes, bringing her long legs back into the car and pulling the door shut. She blew her nose. A guttural laugh slipped from her throat. "I'll show them," she said. "No one will take *this* kid away from me."

Molly hurried back to the site of the confrontation with Officer Brown, cursing her own stupidity for leaving her bag behind, and spotted her pack tangled in a bush where she had tossed it earlier. She fumbled with the thorny, tentacle-like branches, breaking loose a few that dropped to the center of the spiny mess, and freed her bag. A sparkle in the tangles of the broken limbs caught her eye as she hoisted the pack over her shoulder. Molly reached for the shiny gold chain that glimmered before her. She gently untangled the treasure, ignoring the burning sensation in her palm. As she released the necklace from the last twig, the pain became unbearable. She grabbed her wrist with her other hand and cursed, dropping the necklace to the ground. The T on her palm burned, red and angry, bulging from her skin. The pain brought her to her knees. She shrugged her pack from her shoulder and thrust her left hand into the bag, feeling frantically for the bottle of water she carried. She moaned in pain as she wildly withdrew the bottle and brought it to her mouth—twisting off the top with her teeth—and poured the water directly on the burning T. The water warmed in her palm. "Shit!" she screamed and shook the water to the ground. She grabbed her pack and backed away, anxiously eyeing the necklace, not wanting to leave it behind. The further away she got from the necklace, the less severe her pain, until it subsided completely.

Molly sank to the ground, breathing heavily. She was determined to get the necklace, sure that there was a connection to Tracey. She steeled herself for a battle with an unknown entity. *You can do this,* she told herself. She walked back toward the necklace, her neck muscles tight, her body alert to every feeling, every sound around her. The burning did not return. She neared the necklace and reached for a fallen branch with twigs at the end, like frail little fingers. Extending the branch, she hooked the golden thread for one hopeful second, then the necklace dropped to the ground—even further away. Molly blew the breath she had been holding and tried again—to no avail. Frustrated, she crouched down on her heels, "Come on, you bastard, come on!" she said through clenched teeth. Maneuvering the branch with her left hand was far more difficult than she had expected. The branch hovered above the necklace. She lowered it slowly, easing the longest twig under the chain, and pushed it forward, then quickly edged it up. The necklace hung precariously off the tip of the wavering twig. Molly raised the branch toward the sky, resting the edge on her belly for balance. The gold glistened in the sun, the darkness of the trees creating a perfectly serene backdrop for the tiny heart charm that hung from the end of the necklace, stuck, unable to drop past the hook of the chain. Molly smiled. Warmth spread through her body. As sure as the burning had scarred her palm, she *knew* the necklace belonged to Tracey. Excitement rushed through her. She turned slowly to her left and took baby steps on her toes to a clearing about fifteen feet away. She lowered the end of the twig and let the necklace slip into the cushion of the leaves. She was unable to slow the smile that sneaked across her cheeks. She scanned the woods again, unable to believe her luck—or was it something else? She scooped the necklace up in her hand. Instantly, the T on her palm went cold. She closed her hand around the necklace, wallowing in the cool, healing feeling. She closed her eyes and whispered, "I know, Tracey." Molly slid the necklace into the front pocket of her jeans.

Seventeen

Tracey stood in the dimly-lit room, shivering and sick to her stomach from the smell of urine on her clothes. She was relieved when Mummy came back through the rough-and-ready doorway with a bucket of soapy water and two fresh towels. Tracey wondered where clean towels could have been hidden in the small, filthy room but was thankful and quick to please. She reminded herself that a bucket of soapy water was not so bad. It was much better than the bad spot. Just the thought of the bad spot brought tears to Tracey's eyes. She turned her back to Mummy and promised herself that she was *not* going to cry—this was just a different kind of home. She felt Mummy's fingers on her shoulder and reflexively froze.

Mummy turned her around and pointed to a pile on the floor, "I brought you more clothes today. Did you see them?"

Tears of relief formed in Tracey's eyes. She loved new clothes! She walked over to them, careful to keep her legs apart. Her panties were soaked, so cold that they stung when they touched her thighs.

"Go ahead, honey. You can pick them up," she said kindly. "They're yours. Look at them. I think you'll like them."

Tracey bent over at the waist, trying to keep the wet cloth away from her skin. She picked up the dark green, long-sleeved, cotton turtleneck shirt. It smelled clean, flowery, and fresh. Tracey placed it gingerly next to the pile of clothes and picked up a bright yellow sweater with pink heart-shaped buttons. "Oh, Mummy!" she smiled. "I love this!"

Mummy smiled. "I hoped you would," she said, sincerely. "I like to buy you things, when I can."

Tracey noticed a stain on the sweater but didn't say anything. She didn't want to make Mummy feel bad—and it *was* a pretty sweater—and it *was* new to *her*. She laid the sweater on the turtleneck and picked up a pair of white socks with pink ruffles at the top. "I've always wanted ruffly socks!" she squealed. She looked from the socks to the jeans that lay on the ground. Pink and green flowers decorated the jeans. Tracey was beside herself, forgetting about the discomfort of her urine-soaked clothes, forgetting the fear of the night before, and forgetting that Mummy had stolen her from her own mother. She reached eagerly for the brown furry boots that rested next to the pile of clothes. White pom-poms hung from the laces. She didn't care that they had scuffs and a little tear by the heel. Tracey was beside herself. She had seen boots like these in magazines. Her heart beat with excitement as she scooped up all of the clothes and the boots and held them against her. The itchy, cold fabric of her dress was lost in her joy. "Oh, Mummy!" she said. "I love them!" She did love them. Like any little girl, she loved presents. She flew into Mummy's arms, momentarily forgetting what had led her to her crude new home.

Mummy wrapped her arms around Tracey and kissed her cheek. "Tracey," she gently moved Tracey's hair from her eyes, "I want you to be happy."

Tracey looked down, embarrassed. "Thank you, Mummy. Thank you for the clothes and for getting me out of the bad spot." When she said those words, there was a sharp pain in her stomach. "I'll be good from now on. I promise."

Mummy pulled her back into her arms and drew Tracey onto her lap, unconcerned by Tracey's soiled clothes. She bounced her knee up and down. Tracey laughed, becoming more at ease with every fun bounce. After a minute or two, Mummy set Tracey down next to the bucket of water and stood.

"Tracey," she said, "I have to go get us some food. I need you to stay here."

Fear rushed through Tracey. *Alone? Again?* "Please, Mummy. Please let me go with you!" she begged. "I promise I'll be good. I won't run away. I won't scream. I promise!" Tracey's words were frantic, pleading.

"No, Tracey, it's too soon. You need to stay here and get cleaned up. Don't forget about the toxins," she reminded her.

Toxins? Tracey held back her tears and nodded. Tracey worried about the toxins. What were they, and why hadn't her own mother warned her about them? Maybe she *didn't* care about Tracey. Maybe Mummy would not come back because of the toxins. Maybe they'd kill her! Tracey ran to Mummy's side. "Please stay!" she begged. "I don't want the toxins to get you, either."

Mummy knelt down and held Tracey by her shoulders. "Don't you worry, Tracey. I will be back. I know what to do," she said. "You get cleaned up, and Mummy will be back really fast, okay?"

Tracey relented, fearing the toxins more than she feared being left alone. "Okay, Mummy," she said. Her lower lip trembled, but she knew better than to cry. She covered her mouth with her hand and stood up straighter. She could do this! She had to. She had to be a big girl, and big girls didn't cry.

"By the time you're cleaned up, I'll probably be back," Mummy said. "I'll go really quickly."

Tracey nodded. Her legs trembled, and she chewed on the rough edges of her fingernail as she watched Mummy walk toward the tunnel. Mummy turned back to face her. "Tracey, honey," she said, "now don't you try to find our play spot, okay? There could be snakes and other dangerous things. I want my little girl to be safe," she smiled.

Tracey inched closer to the dirt wall of the changing chamber, "Okay," she said. "I'll stay right here."

When Mummy left the chamber, she slid the big wooden board over the entrance. Tracey heard something thud against it. She stood, staring at the board, running her eyes over every inch of it. She was alone—really alone. Just below the board there was a gap between the dirt floor and the board where the ground was uneven. Tracey wondered how Mummy thought that board might keep snakes out and began to worry. She bit her lower lip, then called out, "Mummy!"

She wanted Mummy to fix the gap, but she was answered with silence. Mummy had gone. Tracey panicked. "Mummy!" she yelled again. Tears welled in her eyes. She tried one last time to get Mummy back. "Mummy!" she yelled so loudly that her body shook. She received no answer.

Tracey told herself that since no snakes had come in when Mummy was there, there was no reason to think they'd come in with her gone. She told herself that she had nothing to worry about, that she was being a baby.

She crouched by the tub of water, wet the washcloth, and slowly ran it up and down her shivering arms. The warm, soapy water smelled fresh, clean. It felt good on her arms, but when it began to dry, goose bumps formed. The water turned brown as she continued to wash. *Yuck!* As Tracey reached for her new clothes, she eyed the wood which blocked the entrance and wondered if she *could* find the way back outside. If she were able to find her way, could she run away? *No! Stop thinking about the outside world where the toxins are!* she silently scolded herself. It made her sad when she thought about the outside world, and it was better not to be sad. *It won't be that bad here with Mummy—if I can just be good.*

Tracey finished washing up and dressed in her new outfit and boots, mildly aware of her empty stomach's rumblings. She walked over to the plywood and ran her finger over the rough surface. She thought about the maze of tunnels and knew she could never remember which one led to the bad spot and which one led outside—or even how to get to the worship chamber. The room began to feel spooky, unsafe. The silence was deafening. Tracey went back to the soiled mattress and pulled her knees up under her chin, wrapping her shaking hands around her legs. She rocked back and forth, telling herself to be brave. She rolled onto her side and stared at the barricaded exit, waiting for Mummy to return. Eventually, Tracey's eyes grew heavy, and she drifted off into a dream.

She pumped her arms and ran through the tunnel as fast as she could, her hair lifted from her shoulders with each thump of her feet. Her skin tingled with the feel of the outside air, replacing the stale tunnel atmosphere even before she could see the sunlight. She climbed out of the tunnel and burst into the bramble, spinning around and suddenly realizing she was alone—truly alone. Mummy was not there. She was frightened, shaking, and turned back toward the entrance to the tunnel. "Mummy?" she frantically called out. "Mummy, where are you?" Her questions were met with silence. She peered down the slim tunnel entrance. A force pulled her body away from the tunnel, placing her in front of an almost imperceptible hole in the bramble. She crawled through the hole and into the open forest. She walked at a brisk pace, stepping over vines and branches, around holes, and kicking her way through piles of leaves. Suddenly, she lifted her gaze from the ground, and there were hoards of people, the air filled with voices, conversations, shouting. The crowd was pointing at the sky. Tracey lifted her eyes, shielding them from the glare of the sun. She moved closer to the crowd, squinting to see what held their attention. Then she heard her familiar, comforting voice, "Tracey!" Tracey spun around, her heart pounding with excitement. She ran, fast and hard, into the safety of her open arms, without ever being seen by the people in the outside world. "Mummy!"

Eighteen

Molly drove toward the police station, fully intent on giving the police the necklace she had found, hoping they would search the woods again—more carefully this time—and that this might prove that she wasn't involved in the disappearance of Tracey Porter. She ran through her encounter with Officer Brown and their troubling conversation. *Suspect? Please!* She slowed at the last turn before the station and realized that by turning in the necklace, she might solidify Officer Brown's inclination that she was a suspect; he might turn this evidence on her. Molly was in a quandary, and she didn't like it one bit. Somehow she knew the necklace belonged to Tracey. Her thoughts were interrupted by her cell phone. She pulled the van over to the shoulder and dug through her pack to find it. "Hello?" she said, hurriedly.

"Hey, baby," Cole said flirtatiously.

"Hey!" she smiled, surprised by his playful manner.

"Are you feeling better? More awake now?" he asked.

"Thank goodness, yes. You have no idea!"

"That good, huh? What are you up to?"

She was so excited, she didn't know where to start. "Well, you won't believe this," she said, and told him everything.

"You *what*?" he asked angrily.

She bit her lip, unnerved by his wrath. She continued hurriedly, "Anyway, I, uh…I got the necklace." She reached down and felt the necklace, safely coiled in her pocket.

"This is unbelievable, Molly, really, just…unbelievable." He paused. "You think Erik has these visions, too?" he asked with a mixture of concern and disbelief.

"Yes, maybe, I don't know," she sighed heavily, thinking about the pain Erik might be in for—the agonizing feeling of not knowing when he's innocently dreaming and when he's being given a sign, a message. "Cole, please don't mention it to him. I'm not sure he wants people to know."

"I'm his father, Molly."

Molly heard the hurt in his voice. "Yes, and you're my husband, and how many years did it take for me to admit to you that I had visions?" she paused. "And you still don't really believe me," she said, sadly.

"I won't say anything," he conceded, guiltily, "but damn it, Molly, I don't want him to be as…cra—" he caught himself, then quickly said, "as…wrapped up in things as you get."

The slip up did not go over Molly's head. She swallowed her pride and said, "I know, but there's nothing you can do. Either he will or he won't get wrapped up in things. You can't control what he thinks or how he feels when it happens. I'm telling you, Cole, this…Knowing…it takes over. There's no escaping it."

"So you say," Cole mumbled.

"What?" Molly was getting angry. "What's that supposed to mean?"

"I guess I don't really understand it all. Nothing, *nothing* takes my focus away from whatever I might be doing—"

"Exactly!" she said, not giving him time to finish. "That's what I mean. You focus on what is going on in your life. I focus on what is going on in mine. Unfortunately, I can't change that what's going on in mine is sometimes presented as a vision. It infiltrates my brain. I can't turn it off. No matter what else I'm thinking about, it's always there.'"

"I'm sorry. It's just…" he paused, and Molly waited, knowing it was hard for him, too, "I never know when you're going to focus on this stuff, and it takes you away from everything else, including me."

Molly sighed. She knew exactly what he meant, and he was right.

"It sounds awful, like I'm a selfish bastard, I know, but, Mol, I worry about you going off into the woods at night, getting hurt, falling prey to weird forces, and things I can't see. I never know what's going to happen to you." He paused, and Molly held the phone tightly against her ear, listening to him breathe. "And goddamn it, Molly, how is our marriage ever going to survive this shit? We barely survived Amanda! Am I supposed to just sit back and watch? Wait? So what? One day I'll get a phone call from….from Officer whatever-his-name-is, saying, 'Guess what? She was right. She found the murderer—only this time he got her.'" Molly could imagine him running his hand through his hair, pacing as he spoke. She could hear it in the beat of his words.

Molly answered with the only words she had to offer, "I know, and I'm sorry." She could not promise not to follow her hunches—or the visions—any more than she could promise not to call Erik every week. She'd spent years being helpless against the visions. She'd failed Amanda, and she'd be damned if she was going to make the same mistake twice. Amanda's sweet face appeared in Molly's mind, just as it had in the newspaper when they'd found her body; her blonde hair cropped just below her chin, tilted up toward the camera in a gentle pose. Molly was driven to help and empowered by the drive. She just hadn't realized it might someday become a choice between helping a child and saving her marriage. "I love you, Cole," she said, hoping he could understand.

"Well," she heard the surrender in his voice, "I chose you, so now I'm stuck, I suppose."

Molly was hurt, *Stuck?* She bit back a retort and asked, hesitantly, "So what do I do with the necklace?"

"What do you mean? Give it to the police, of course. Let them deal with it."

"Oh no…I can't. If I give it to the police, then they'll really think I'm a suspect."

"You could be arrested for obstructing justice or something."

"I know, but what if they take me in, make me a scapegoat. I don't know, Cole. Do you really think I need to give it to them?"

"Molly!" he said, frustrated. "You're going to do whatever you're going to do anyway. Why bother asking me?"

Molly didn't have an answer. In the tense silence, Cole pressed his point home. "What if you keep it, and that necklace is the one clue that could have broken the case? You'd feel awful if she wasn't found because you were too selfish to turn it in."

"Selfish? Selfish! Is that what you think?" she screamed into the phone.

"Who are you doing this for, Molly? For Tracey? For Amanda? Or are you doing this for you, so you can fix whatever warped part of your mind thinks you killed Amanda?"

His words stung, and Molly could feel the truth in them, which hurt even more. She was unclear who she was doing this for, but she didn't care. She was moving forward. "One night, Cole, one night, that's all I need. It might bring me more information. Tomorrow, I will bring it directly to the police station. I promise. " Molly didn't need Cole's approval but desperately wanted it to ease the guilt of doing what she knew was wrong. The line went dead in her hands.

Molly had intended to go home, but, on a whim, she found herself driving toward Hannah's. Passing the vast soybean fields brought a sense of calm to her otherwise anxious day. She rolled down the windows and let the breeze wash over her, the stress of the morning fading away. She passed Harley's farm, the hayfields pristine, the grass perfectly mowed, and waved to Harley who stood by his truck in the driveway. Her levity fell away as Harley's unnerving stare, his face awash of any emotion, followed her down the road.

Molly parked at Hannah's and stepped from the van, forcibly pushing aside the uncomfortable feeling of Harley's glare. "Hannah?" she called out, and was answered by two dogs that came bounding toward her: a large, long-haired black dog that Molly thought resembled a cross between a Saint Bernard and a Great Dane, and an older hound dog. "Hey, guys," she said as she scratched their heads. "Where's your mama?" The horses came to attention as she entered the barn, undoubtedly looking for carrots and treats. Molly caressed their cheeks.

"Hannah?" she called out again. The dogs' ears perked up at the sound of their owner's name. Molly looked in the well-organized tack room, calling out in a sing-song voice, "Han-nah?" She walked to the garage, dogs in tow, where she found Hannah's car. Molly scanned the fields, but Hannah was nowhere in sight. The other horses, however, had gathered along the far end of the pasture where the fence edged the woods.

"Molly!"

Molly turned around, relieved to see Pete standing in his dirty jeans and flannel shirt. Pete had boarded his horses at Hannah's farm for fifteen years. Molly had known him for ten of those years but had never gotten used to his diminutive stature. His smile brightened his dark, weathered face.

"Hi, Pete," Molly said. "Do you know where I can find Hannah?"

He ambled over slowly, wiping his hands on a towel that hung from his belt. His skin was slick with sweat. He nodded toward the woods, just past the gathered horses. "She went for a walk."

The walk through the pasture was much further than Molly had anticipated. She leaned against the fence to rest near the four horses. Somewhere from the recesses of her mind, she pulled a memory that horses, like people, have favorite spots where they like to spend their time. As she leaned against the fence, her arms against the prickly wood, she looked down and noticed that the fencing had clear boot markings, as if it had been climbed over in that exact spot for many years. That was not out of place, Molly figured, because Hannah was an avid hiker as well as rider. She had likely climbed over the fence many times. Molly turned to the woods and, sure enough, there was a well-worn path leading into the forest. Molly rubbed the horses and took to the path which was lined with fall flowers, marigolds and blue-stem goldenrod.

The path faded gently, becoming overgrown yet still discernable. The tree branches hovered over the natural trellises. Molly reached up and ran her fingertips through them. She glanced behind her but was unable to see Hannah's farm or hear the gentle noises of the horses and dogs. All was quiet. *No wonder Hannah frequents this path.*

She had been lost in thought when a noise disturbed her reverie, and she suddenly realized that the path she thought she had been following had not been a path at all. In fact, the forest around her looked as if it were a maze of overgrown paths. She pushed aside her rush to find Hannah and decided to enjoy her walk instead. She reassuringly touched the bulge in her pocket where the necklace was safely tucked away. She quickened her pace and crossed the rutted pavement of White Ground Road coming to the entrance to the

Hoyles Mill Trail. Molly considered returning to Hannah's, then she briefly wondered where Hannah had gone and why they hadn't yet crossed paths. She was enjoying the exercise and was not yet ready to relinquish her peaceful escape. She checked the time and decided she'd have enough time to walk to the church and take the main road back to Hannah's farm.

Molly skipped over rocks, bending down to miss a vine here, a branch there, and when she came to an area that she didn't recognize, she ventured to the right, hearing Cole's practical voice echo in her head, *It's a right-handed society.* It didn't worry Molly that she wasn't quite sure where the path would end up, as Boyds was such a small area that she knew eventually she'd come out either by the church, by the farm just beyond it, or onto one of the country roads that encircled the small town.

The sunlight was beginning to fade as Molly came across a clear fork in the woods. Again, she veered right, and what she saw just beyond the bushes startled her: a man-made clearing surrounded by mature oaks and pines. Two picnic tables, the wood gray with age, splintered and rough, names and dates sloppily carved into the benches, were set about ten feet apart in the center of the clearing. A bird sat atop one of the tables, pecking at sunflower seeds. It flew away when Molly took a step in its direction.

Along the edge of the clearing were four large plywood boxes, with angled, green plywood roofs and bowed, unpainted sides. The roughly-built boxes were layered with cobwebs and ivy. Molly tried to lift the lid of the box nearest her which stood beside a small creek. Its weight surprised her. She peered inside, and a field mouse scurried across the bottom. Molly dropped the heavy lid and jumped back, letting out a meek yelp, the slam echoed in the darkened woods. She sheepishly looked around to see if anyone could have heard her little squeak.

"Jesus Christ," Molly said, shaking her hands as if flinging off water. She wiped them on her jeans and approached the box again. "I can do this," she said, and lifted the lid slowly, peeking inside. Cobwebs hung from the corners. A two-by-four shelf ran the length of the box, mouse nests tucked into the corners. In one of the nests, the tiny mouse huddled. Roughly-cut logs were tucked under the shelf. Molly dropped the lid, simultaneously stepping backward and cringing from the loud thud. She took in her surroundings—picnic tables, grates in the ground covering shallow holes—the scene reminded her of childhood camping trips. She smiled at the memory. Molly instantly liked the secluded area.

Darkness began to close in around her, and she started to worry that she may not be able to find her way back to the road after all. She reached for her cell phone, realizing only too late that she had left her backpack in the van—at Hannah's. *Hannah, where in the world are you?* Molly worried about Cole, whom she knew would be upset with her if he knew she was lost in the woods. *Am I lost?* she wondered. She looked around for a path leading out of the clearing. Between two large trees, there was a clear path with…tire marks? She walked toward the clearing and caught sight of a flicker of white and green on the bottom of one of the boxes—out of place in the otherwise clean area. As she neared the box, her senses were assaulted by the sweet taste of candy apples. She rolled her tongue across the roof of her mouth—every drop of saliva carried sweet apple candy.

Molly crouched down near the wooden box, curiously peering at what she recognized as an Airhead candy wrapper. She reached for the shiny piece of trash with her left hand, and instantly her right hand burned.

"Damn it!" she yelped, knowing exactly what she was in for. She backed away from the wrapper, holding her burning palm in her healthy one. "Damn it! I got it, okay? I understand!" she yelled toward the sky. She backed away from the box, shaking her burning palm up and down, trying desperately to cool it off as she retreated up the path and further away from the camp. Her injured palm began to cool. Molly sat down at the crest of a small hill, just outside the cleared area, the ache lingered in her palm. She was not surprised to see the scar reddened and angry. Her hands shook, and guttural, frustrated sounds poured from her mouth. "Tell me already!" she yelled angrily. "Tell me where the hell she is!"

Molly sat for a few minutes, cursing the Knowing and trying to figure out how the signs, the notes, the candy wrappers, and the visions were tied together. She stared down at the clearing, compelled to return to it. It only took one thought to push her past her fear and toward the clearing: *Amanda*. Her senses heightened as she neared the area, she waited for her palm to burn, but was met with nothing—no heat, no pain, no oppressive feeling around the clearing. She breathed a little easier, dropping to her knees an arm's length away from the wooden box and the candy wrapper. She reached her left hand out tentatively, snagged the wrapper, and pulled her arm back quickly, holding the playing-card-sized piece of wrapper between her fingers. She shoved it in her pocket with the necklace and patted the lump on her thigh. "I got you guys," she said. "We'll find her." She froze at the sound of a man's voice.

"Hello!" a deep and concerned voice called out.

At first Molly didn't respond, she had gone on instant alert.

"Hello? Who's there?"

Recognition set in, then confusion. "Newton?" Molly yelled.

Over the crest of the hill, where she had just been sitting, came a figure, shrouded in a long dark overcoat, a hat pulled over his eyes.

"Who is that?" he asked.

"Molly Tanner," she said, unable to make out his face in the dark.

"Molly?" he said. "What in the name of heaven are you doing over here in the dark?"

Molly sighed, relieved. "Newton," she said, rising to her feet. "I was walking in the woods and kinda got lost." She motioned with her arms to the clearing.

"I thought I heard someone yelling," he said, coming down the hill towards her. "Here, I've got a flashlight." He offered his arm to her on her way up the hill, handing her the light. Molly accepted the kind gesture.

"It was me," she laughed. "What is this place, Newton?"

"You, my dear, are, um, in the campsites for the Girl and Boy Scouts. Sometimes the church groups use it or other local nonprofit groups, but it's mainly for the scouts. It, uh, belongs to the church."

They made their way down a tire-worn path that cut through the overgrown field. The field to their right was vast, edged by a cornfield. Beyond the field was an old farmhouse and barn. A silo stood tall in the distance. As if her eyes had a mind of their own, they drifted beyond the silo, above the trees, to where the turret of the Perkinson House peered above the treetops like a voyeur. "Where are we, Newton?" Molly asked, curiously.

"At the church, of course." Newton shone the flashlight beam down the hill, illuminating the grass between the field and the park—the park from which Kate Plummer had disappeared.

They headed down the hill toward Newton's car, the sole car in the church parking lot. Molly asked when the campsite had last been used.

"I don't know. Let's see," he looked to the sky, his hand fidgeted around his lips, "probably August or so. I think the Girl Scouts have a jamboree around that time." He turned to her, "Where's your car, Molly?" he asked.

Molly's hand flew to her mouth. "Oh, my gosh! I left it at Hannah's house," she said, having completely forgotten. "Would you mind giving me a ride?"

"Of course not—come on."

Molly slid into the front seat of the old car. There was not a single scratch on the interior. The back seat, however, was littered with writing papers, binders, and loose articles, the floor stacked high with binders.

"Adding to your historical binders?" Molly motioned to the back seat.

"Oh, yeah," he said, embarrassed. "I like to keep up on things around Boyds." Newton took a loose article that was on the console between them and looked

CHASING AMANDA

at it, longingly, "What a shame this whole thing is—
what a shame." He set the article on one of the binders,
and Molly quickly glimpsed a photo of Tracey Porter
and part of the headline, "Missing Boyds Girl." Newton
started the car, his eyes trained on the road ahead of
them, gripping the steering wheel with both hands. The
bumps on White Ground Road were difficult for any
driver to maneuver around, but Newton appeared to be
having a particularly stressful time.

Molly closed her eyes as she felt the oppressive
pressure of the Knowing engulfing her, as it had the
night before. She gripped the door handle with her right
hand, the edge of the seat with her left. Her body began
to tremble. "Please," she said, breathlessly, "can you
drive faster?" Molly's eyes rolled back in her head as
the visions hit like pictures projected in an old-
fashioned slide show: *Tracey, alone in a dirt chamber,
staring into the darkness; a wooden plank; a thicket in
the woods.* Fear shivered across Molly's skin, and the
memories came crashing in. It was Tracey she saw in
the vision, her face, her body, her hair, but those cold,
dead eyes were Amanda's, staring accusingly, directly,
at Molly.

She could hear Newton calling her name from a
distance, but she couldn't respond. She felt the car
accelerate, her body slumped against the door, jerking
her mind back into the present. Her body swayed with
the turns in the road, first left, then right.

"Molly?" Newton continued to call out to her.

"I feel a little...sick," she managed. As they
neared the intersection at Hannah's road, Molly's
breathing returned to normal, her sight became clear,
and she was able to right her body in the seat.

Newton took the right turn slowly, "Molly, are you okay?" he asked.

"Yeah," she said, trying to minimize the episode. "I'm fine now, thanks. That part of the road gets to me sometimes," she waved her hand, dismissively, "a little carsickness, you know?"

Newton let out a sigh of relief, "Me, too. It scares me sometimes. It's so narrow, and it's in such poor shape. You'd think the county would do something about it." He shook his head.

Molly realized with relief that he hadn't seen her clearly, hadn't realized the import of her experience.

Newton approached Hannah's driveway, and Molly turned toward the rear of the car.

"Newton? May I?" she asked, reaching for one of the articles.

"Oh, be my guest," he said.

She picked up an article. Loosely taped to the back was an old photo. As it fell to the seat, she was able to make out the shape of the grand old house. While the colors had changed and the porches seemed smaller than she had remembered, it looked familiar. "Newton, is this a photo of the Perkinson House?"

Newton spun his head around, nervous, a look of shock and horror on his face. "What? Oh, surely not," he said as he parked the car and gathered the loose papers, along with the photo, and held them on his lap.

"May I see it?" Molly asked, reaching for the photo.

"Oh, Molly. I'm certain it's not the Perkinson House." He clutched the mass of mixed-up papers and the photo to his chest so tightly that Molly could hear the papers crumbling. He laughed, nervously.

"Well, it looked like it might have been the house that you described when you held that discussion the other night. I thought maybe it was one you showed to everyone after I left or something," she rationalized.

"No, no," he said, shaking his head. "I didn't show a photo that night. I, uh, I just talked is all." Straightening the papers, he slipped the photo in between. "It's nothing, really, probably an old photo that fell out of one of the old albums."

"Okay," Molly stepped out of the car. "Thanks for the ride. I'm not sure what I would have done if you hadn't come by. I might have curled up in a little ball and slept on a picnic table!" she laughed, turned to her van, and heard Newton's relieved sigh as she walked away.

Once in her van, she scribbled the visions she'd just had in her notebook. "Where is this child?" she wondered aloud. She put the notebook and her iPod in her backpack and retrieved her phone: seven missed calls. She scanned the numbers: Cole, Hannah, and several from a number marked Private. *What now*? She clicked on the voicemail icon to retrieve the five new messages.

"Hi, babe, just checking on you. Love you," Cole's voice soothed over the recording.

"Molly, it's Hannah. I just noticed your vehicle in my driveway. Are you out running?" She paused. "Well, I guess I'll see you sometime soon. Have a good run."

The next message was garbled with heavy static which continued for almost a full minute. Molly debated hanging up, but curiosity got the best of her, and she remained on the line. Just as she was about to delete the message, a scratchy voice said, "He knows."

More static punctured the air like bullets. Molly pressed the phone harder against her ear, hoping to make out more words, to recognize the voice. When the words finally escaped the static, they made her dizzy. She leaned back in the driver's seat and pushed the number one on her phone to replay the message. The words, "Save...Tracey," were just as painful the second time around. Molly's fingers shook as they hovered over the number nine on her phone, checking it again and again before pushing the number, making sure she was saving the message rather than deleting it. Molly's heart skipped a beat as the next message began with the same sinister static. She listened intently for three minutes, hoping to hear a few words, a hint of who had called. She was met with the spine-chilling noise of cellular airways unwilling to release the voices that they were paid to carry. Just as she was about to give up, there were two voices in the background—one male and one female. The symphony of their conversation rose and fell—an argument, though what about, Molly could not decipher. The voices were muffled, the words unclear. Her heart pounded in anticipation of a clue, some hint to who had been calling her. The message clicked off, and Molly pulled the phone from her ear.

Tracey awoke frightened and cold. "Mummy?" she called out, hoping she had returned while Tracey had napped. There was no answer. The candle had gone out, leaving the room pitch black. Tracey rose hesitantly from her mattress and felt her way along the dirt wall to the makeshift table. She fumbled for the matches and nervously fingered the rectangular match box. She didn't want to get in trouble for lighting the match, but she was terrified of the darkness. She bit her lower lip and withdrew a wooden match. Her fingers felt their way along the thin match, recognizing the bulbous head, and then gripping the opposite end. Tracey trembled as she struck the match along the side of the box, just as her father had showed her the last time they had made a campfire. A tiny spark flittered in the darkness. Tracey released the breath she had unconsciously been holding, and a frustrated, strangled sound followed. She removed another matchstick from the box, again she searched with her fingers for the swollen end. *Please, please,* she prayed. She instinctively stepped back when the flame came to life, then she lowered it quickly against the candle wick.

Tracey squinted into the lightening room, noting the wooden plank, still in place, the ghostly shadows dancing on the wall behind the candle. She felt a presence behind her and turned slowly, frightened, her body covered with goose bumps. She stood rigid while her eyes adjusted to the darkness. Her gaze dropped to a bulging image that lay on the other side of the room— they hadn't been there when Mummy had gone—a tall figure loomed beside them. Tracey was not alone.

Nineteen

Molly threw her backpack on the kitchen table, glad the dogs were in the yard and not at her feet. The *Washington Post* sat folded before her. *Cole,* she sighed. Tracey's smiling face covered the upper right quarter of the page, and around her neck, sparkling like a flash of metal at sea, sat the necklace that Molly held in her possession. Molly withdrew her notepad from her backpack with a sigh. She took it into the family room and sat on the couch, exhausted. Her head flopped back onto the soft cushion. She let her eyes fall closed and took a deep, relaxing breath, wondering why she had ever stopped meditating. She thought about how quickly her life had changed. It seemed to her that one day she was trying to keep up with a three-year-old, her every second wrapped around his needs, the days weaving in and out of each other, some blending so smoothly that it was hard to tell when one ended and the next began, some so terribly hard that she couldn't wait for a reprieve—a little breathing space, a few minutes to think her own thoughts, accomplish her own grown-up tasks. And then her life had been interrupted. There had been Amanda, and the years when functioning became a goal rather than a given—the lost years. Molly sat up and sighed, remembering the therapy, the fights, the fear in Erik's eyes when he realized that he couldn't count on his mother for her strength or safety, and the way that look felt like a knife in her gut, initially sinking her further into depression. Eventually, that pain became the catalyst to her lifeline, her reason for pulling herself toward solid ground. And now that she had it all together—direction, confidence, her son's trust—she was throwing herself right into the heart of an investigation.

"What am I doing?" Molly curled her legs up beneath herself and skimmed through her notepad. *Visions,* she wondered, *or just scenes made up by a delusional mother's subconscious?* She was too tired to deal with Cole's suspicion that her visions were just her mind working overtime, a thought she could not make go away, no matter how hard she tried. She put the notepad down and withdrew the folded messages that she'd tucked in the back of the pad. She stared at the creased pages, pages she knew she had not fabricated. They were tangible evidence that someone, somewhere, knew she was trying to find Tracey. She wondered why the person wouldn't come forward and simply go to the police. She folded the papers, frustrated, knowing she had memorized them the first time she had read them. Molly was too irritated to relax. She wondered if Cole was right, if she should go back into therapy, try to deal with the remaining guilt of losing Amanda. The dogs barked and pawed at the rear door. Molly walked through the house feeling useless. She let the dogs in and walked back out the front door to retrieve the mail.

She leafed through the junk mail and set the rest in a pile on the counter. She let out a sigh, her hopes of finding a catalogue, or something distracting to leaf through, dashed. She'd have been happy with a coupon flyer. She fed the dogs and felt as if she were moving robotically through the motions.

Molly ran a warm bath, pouring in extra bubbles so she wouldn't have to see her aging body distorted through the water. She pulled off her jeans and felt the unfamiliar bulge in her pocket. She gently removed the necklace and candy wrapper, and sat down on the edge of the tub in her underwear. She laced the necklace in and out of her fingers, dragging the chain across her palms. The cold metal felt lonely, hollow. The heart trinket was smeared with dirt. She walked into her bedroom and placed it, along with the candy wrapper, under her pillow. Molly finished undressing and lowered her body into the warm bubbly water, a consolation for a hard afternoon's...*What?* she wondered. *Work? Research? Search?* She quickly decided that she had no idea what to call the way she had been spending her time lately but reassured herself that the bath was still her due. She lay back and closed her eyes.

She had been drifting toward sleep when the phone rang.

"Damn it," she said, opening her eyes and bracing herself to stand up.

"I got it!" Cole yelled up the stairs.

Molly sighed with relief that Cole was home. The clutter of her busy mind had finally been waylaid by the contentment of the soothing bath.

"Baby," Cole whispered, his breath was warm against her cheek. "Have you been doing a little shopping?"

She sighed and opened her eyes. "Hi."

"Tired?" he asked.

"Mm-hmm," she said, closing her eyes again.

"Sweetie, you've got a package." He held up the padded envelope, swinging it teasingly in front of her.

"I didn't order anything," Molly said. "Your baseball cards? Ebay maybe?"

He shrugged and ripped open the package, shaking the contents, an old newspaper clipping, into his hand. Molly raised her eyebrows.

Cole scanned the article, "It's an article about Rodney Lett."

Molly read the concern in his eyes, heard the annoyance in his voice.

"It says that he was beaten to death and that he was responsible for the abduction of Kate Plummer. Mol, this is from October 1989."

"Who sent it?" she asked, nervously rising to her feet and draining the water from the tub.

"Who knows, Molly?" he said agitated. "What exactly are you doing? Trying to get yourself killed?"

Molly tried to calm his anger and temper her own growing concern, "It's probably nothing. It's a gag or something. No one even knows what I'm doing." She leaned her naked body forward and put her arms around his neck, ignoring the irritation on his face. "C'mon," she pleaded. "Don't ruin tonight."

Cole resisted her efforts.

She kissed his cheek, his neck. "Don't be mad at me, Cole," she said between kisses. "I didn't write the note."

"You need to tell the police," his tone had softened.

"Mm-hmm." She felt the tension in his shoulders release as he pulled her toward him and kissed her lips.

"Whoa, wait a minute," she laughed, "we have to get ready. Hand me a towel?"

Cole stood in front of her, leering lustily, and holding the towel just out of her reach, "Not so quickly."

Molly blushed, turned away from him, and feigned anger. He wrapped his arms around her, the water from her wet body soaked his clothes. Standing in the bathtub brought her closer to his height. Embarrassed, Molly pushed him away, "Okay, towel, please."

He playfully tossed her the towel, grinning like a Cheshire cat. As he walked out of the bathroom, he picked up the torn package and looked it over. "Mol, there's no return address." He ripped the package completely open and inside was a yellow Post-It note. Cole's face swiftly changed from lovingly playful to clearly annoyed once again. "Molly," his tone was serious, angry, "what the hell is going on?"

She looked at him in confusion.

He crushed the note in his fist and threw it, and the torn package, into the trash can and stormed from the room. Molly hurried over to the can to retrieve the crumpled paper, unfolding it as quickly as she could. Scrawled in pencil were the words:

LET SLEEPING DOGS LIE.

Pastor Lett stood against the wall, waiting for the right time to let her presence be known. The kid stood like a statue in the dimly-lit room. She watched the kid turn slowly on trembling legs.

Her eyes met the kid's. "Honey," she said in a low, gentle voice, "it's me. It's okay."

The kid stared at her as if she were a stranger. Guilt rose within her, and she pushed it away as her irritation grew. She walked closer to the kid, leaving the garbage bag behind on the dirt floor.

She had thought they'd established an understood vow of compliance, an acknowledgement of how things had to be in order for them to live happily. What had changed? Why, she wondered, had the kid reverted to fear? But she knew why. She knew she had crossed the line, scared the kid—perhaps beyond repair. She moved closer, slowly, crouching down so she wasn't too imposing. "Honey, it's okay. I'm here to take care of you, to keep you safe. We're going to be happy." She reached toward the kid, but the kid pulled back, out of her reach. "God put me on this Earth to care for you," her voice rose, and she tried to gain control of her emotions. She wiggled her fingers, urging the kid toward her. "C'mon, it's okay." Slowly the kid moved, hesitantly, toward her.

"That's right, sweetie. Come to me." Pastor Lett reached out and pulled the kid's reluctant body close, "What were you doing, honey?"

The kid stared up at her—big round beautiful eyes, innocent and scared. Pastor Lett held the kid at arm's length, her heart pounded with love and admiration, mixed with an underlying grief. She hated holding the kid hostage like that. She knew the kid should be outside, enjoying life, not stuck in this damn dungeon.

She whispered, "Were you getting ready to pray? Talking to God?"

The kid nodded nervously.

"It's okay. We all talk to God."

The kid looked up, acknowledging her words with a sense of relief.

"What were you praying for? Do you need something?" Pastor Lett asked.

Her question was met with silence.

"What do you want from God? Are you not happy?" she asked, desperately wanting to make things as comfortable as she was able.

The kid began rocking, barely noticeable at first. Pastor Lett had seen it before, a slight rock back and forth, almost non-existent, yet she understood the message—the kid was uneasy, frightened.

"Sweetie, let it out. I can help," Pastor Lett urged. "Let's see what I've brought you!" she said, reaching for the bags. The kid eyed the bags curiously. Pastor Lett reached deep inside the bag and pulled out a stuffed bunny. The kid's eyes lit up, and Pastor Lett handed the prize over, gratified. The kid held it tight, then tucked it under one arm.

"There's that smile I love," she said. "Let's see what else I've brought you." The kid moved closer, less afraid, renouncing the rocking for the promise of gifts.

Pastor Lett reached into the bag and pulled out a brown shirt and white sweater. "What is this?" she teased. "It looks like clothes." Pastor Lett held the clothing up, pretending to inspect them. "Hm, they look to be just about your size." She glanced at the kid,

"Let's just see if they might fit." She held them up. "Yup. Perfect. They must be yours!"

The kid snagged the clothing from Pastor Lett's hands. Pastor Lett watched the kid smell the clothing, smile. Her spirits lifted. As much as she loathed material items bringing joy, at times it was all she had to offer. She was well aware of what she had done, what she would continue to do, but people had forced it upon her. She was compelled to live a lie. It was unfair, and she knew it. The kid was often left alone, and she hated that, but she knew, or at least she hoped, that God would look over their place, protecting them from harm, protecting them from the cruel, unforgiving world.

The kid stared at the bag, wordlessly asking for more. Pastor Lett pushed aside her melancholy thoughts and laughed a little. "Oh, you want to see what else I might have brought? Don't you have enough yet, kiddo?"

The kid smiled.

"Okay, well, let's see," she said, trying to keep the mood lighter than it had been. She put her arm in the bag and pretended that the item was stuck, cringing and pulling backward. "I can't get it out," her voice was strained as she pretended to use all of her strength to retrieve the contents of the bag.

The kid's face contorted, painfully waiting for the prize to be revealed.

"It's stuck in here," Pastor Lett said. She pretended to be yanked into the bag, flailing her head and arms and falling to the floor.

The kid laughed.

Pastor Lett's voice was muffled by the bag, "Help! Help! Honey, I'm stuck!"

There was a moment's hesitation—then Pastor Lett felt warm hands on her back as the kid tried to pull her from the bag. She used all of her strength to remain in the bag, continuing the game, relishing in the kid's delight. After a minute, they both fell backward, tumbling together, laughter filling the dimly-lit room. Slowly, their laughter faded, and Pastor Lett peeked in the bag, creating a dramatic scene—eyes wide, arms outstretched. She turned to the kid, "No way am I going in there again." She sat back on her heels. "You go," she instructed.

The kid approached the bag tentatively, looking into it, then back at Pastor Lett. A shake of the head and a smile egged her on.

"Uh-uh," she said. "Why do I have to do all of the dirty work? It's just not fair!" she said, pretending to pout. "You can do it. You're strong," she urged.

Again, the shake of the head.

"Okay, okay, fine." She resigned her stance and dove into the bag so fast that the kid jumped up and down excitedly.

Finally, a single word escaped the kid's lips, "Funny!"

Pastor Lett felt her heart melt like chocolate on a warm afternoon. She wanted to grab that one word and tuck it away safely in her pocket. Instead, she scrambled around in the bag, like she was wrestling with an animal. Suddenly, she stopped thrashing and backed out of the bag, cradling a small box in her hands. She sat on the floor next to the kid whose eyes were wide with anticipation. The kid reached for the box, crouched next to Pastor Lett, and looked over the box, slowly lifting the lid, and removing the gold chain. The kid stared, mesmerized. Tears of joy slipped down the kid's cheeks. Pastor Lett had never imagined that a necklace would evoke such a reaction. The token, an icon of Pastor Lett's love, hung from the chain like a star in the sky, sparkling and bright.

The kid clutched the necklace as if it might disappear. *Not to worry*, Pastor Lett thought to herself. *I will be here to make sure it stays right where it belongs.*

When Molly finally made her way downstairs, she found Cole stewing in front of a football game. She came to sit on the coffee table in front of him, blocking his view of the game. She held his gaze until he abruptly clicked off the television and gave her his full, enervated attention.

His eyes said, "Well?" but she didn't know where to begin to fill the breach. The tension was deafening.

She tentatively reached for his hand and said, placatingly, "Cole, how could I know that this would happen? No one even knows I'm looking for her, really."

"No one even knows," he said, mocking her. "Someone does," he said, accusingly. "That little present you just got," he sneered, "is a threat."

Molly peeled her gaze away, "I don't think..." she began timidly. "Maybe it's not really a threat," she tried, lamely.

Cole threw his arms up in the air. "What?" he yelled. "Do you know, do you even have a clue, how dangerous this is?"

She stood with her hands at her side, wanting to say something, anything to make him understand why she had to pursue this, but words failed her. Finally, she took a deep breath and, deciding not to tell him about the other notes, released the air slowly, trying to keep control of her emotions. She turned and looked into his scornful eyes.

"Oh, Cole," she began, "I can't help it. I feel like I *have* to find her."

Cole let out a hiss of anger. "Molly, why do you think you can find this girl? You couldn't help Amanda, and you can't help Tracey!" he yelled.

Molly was too hurt, too angry to speak.

Cole looked away, momentarily ashamed, but the anger came raging forward, "How much more do you know than the police? It sounds like you're all over the place—in the woods, at the Perkinson House. Don't you think if she were in the Perkinson House, someone would have found her? Why don't you just ask Pastor Lett? I'm sure she'll tell you she's not there."

Molly fumed.

"For God's sake, Molly, she didn't take her. I have no idea how you can live like this, wondering, tracking things down. Where do you get the energy, much less the desire? She's not even your daughter."

"I know she's not my daughter, Cole!" she yelled through angry tears. "What if I *can* find her? The police didn't find her necklace, *I* did. What am I supposed to do? Turn my back on this little girl? Walk away like I know nothing when clearly someone, somewhere is trying to send me messages about her? Let her die like I let Amanda die?"

Cole sat on the couch, his eyes focused on nothing.

Molly was caught between walking out and never coming back, and trying to bridge the gap between them. Cole dropped his head into his hands. Molly eyed the foyer, then looked at the photos littered around the room of them in happier times. She walked over to Cole, stood between his legs, put her hands on his shoulders, and leaned her forehead against his. She whispered, "What if it were Erik, and one person was being given details, and that one person ignored them? Would you want that to happen?"

He whispered back, "No, of course not." He pushed Molly aside and walked out of the room.

Molly listened to the rhythm of Cole's heavy footfalls and the hum of the treadmill. She settled in front of her computer and opened an email from Hannah.

Molly, I saw your car here today. Sorry I missed you. Were you out running? Hannah.

Molly replied, responded to a few other emails, and was relieved to reach the last one which was from Newton Carr.

Molly, I'm glad I found you today. I thought everyone knew about the campsites, but I suppose not. You should stop by some time. I can fill you in on much of the history of Boyds. I can even show you Colonel Boyds's grave. He was an amazing man.

Take care, Newton.

P.S. The photo you saw was actually of another home in Boyds that no longer exists. As I mentioned before, Molly, please stay away from the Perkinson House. Grant the Perkinson family their privacy.

Molly clicked back to her Inbox. "That was fast," she said when a new email from Hannah arrived.

Molly, I'm glad you enjoyed your walk through the woods. Next time, though, why don't I go with you? Hannah.

Molly replied, *Sounds great!*

The newspaper clipping nagged at Molly. She retrieved it and scanned the article.

Relief of one sort was provided today to the family of Kate Plummer. The prime suspect, Rodney Lett, was found beaten to death in the home of his sister, Pastor Carla Lett...The body was taken to Delaware for burial in the family plot...The body of Kate Plummer has not been found. Rodney Lett's confession included a statement that the girl was with her "mommy." Police interpreted the information to mean that she was dead. Mrs. Plummer, a cancer patient, is alive, though it is unclear if Rodney Lett understood that at the time of Kate's disappearance.

She tossed the article on her desk, "So that's their proof?" Molly was disgusted with the realization that the police could lead such a shallow investigation, and that the search would be dropped without ever finding Kate's body.

Frustrated by the fight with Cole and her internal conflict, Molly decided to try and put their argument behind them. She went downstairs to their exercise room. "Almost done?" she asked.

"Yeah," he huffed. Cole hated to run, but as he did with most aspects of his life, he did what he was supposed to do because it was best for him, not because it was something he enjoyed.

"How would you feel about dinner out tonight? I sort of need to clear my head." Molly asked, flopping, defeated, onto the couch.

"Sure, whatever you want," he said, as Molly had expected he would.

"Café Miletto okay?"

"Sure, whatever, I'll be done in a minute."

Molly dressed for dinner and then looked beneath her pillow, confirming that her evidence was still in place. She thought of Tracey, out there somewhere, terrified, hungry, cold. Molly ran her fingers over the necklace, then picked up the candy wrapper. Instantly, she tasted apple candy. Her palm became warm, and she could feel Tracey's soft little hand grasping the wrapper. She could feel her fear, her breathing becoming rapid, shallow. She closed her eyes, hoping for more—slowly, gray images came to her: *trees, leaves, the wooden boxes.* The wrapper grew cold and fell from her hand.

Molly jumped when Cole put his hand on her shoulder. She pushed the pillow down over the wrapper and the necklace. "Good God, Cole," she said, "how long have you been standing there?"

"Long enough," he said.

Café Miletto was quiet. There were four other tables with patrons, two young couples, one older couple, and a couple who appeared, from behind, to be middle aged. They sat in the corner with their backs to Molly and Cole. Molly reached for Cole's hand across the table, trying to mend the widening abyss between them. Cole withdrew his hand.

Molly blinked back tears and gazed out the window, inadvertently listening to the couple that sat nearby. Their voices were hushed whispers.

"I don't know what to do. I think someone has been there," the woman said.

"Oh no, I'm sure not," said the man.

"It's just been so long, you know?" she paused. "How long can I do this?"

"As long as you have to," the man replied. "If you come out now, can you imagine the terror it would bring to the community, the distrust?"

Molly recognized the voices and chided herself for listening. At that point, she couldn't help it, she was drawn into their conversation, listening for the sake of curiosity.

"You did what you felt like you had to do. People will be angry, maybe try to railroad you. Send you to jail even," Newton whispered adamantly.

"Look what I've put the kid through." Pastor Lett sounded beaten down.

Molly looked over, her heart speeding up.

"I've put that kid in a prison and for what? Somehow, what started to be about the kid, ended up really just about me. I'm so selfish."

Molly was riveted by their conversation. Cole looked at his menu, unaware of her fixation. He reached across the table and grabbed Molly's hand. The relief she felt was overshadowed by her curiosity.

"And look what I've put you through," Pastor Lett said.

Molly suddenly felt like a voyeur. She pulled her hand away from Cole's, who looked up, surprised.

"What?" Cole asked.

Molly hid behind her menu. She tilted it sideways and looked into Cole's eyes. "Shhh," she whispered, motioning with a finger in front of her lips. She pointed behind him and mouthed, *Don't let them see you.*

Cole angled his body to the side, crossing his legs and stretching. He recognized them instantly, spinning back and leaning over the table toward Molly. "Pastor Lett and Newton—so what?"

"Oh my God! So," she whispered frantically, "they're talking about something awful that Pastor Lett did, about a kid kept in a prison!" She lifted her finger to her lips again.

"Damn it, Molly. Let it go," he seethed.

The waitress brought Pastor Lett her check. She reached for it and handed the check and a credit card back to the waitress.

Cole and Molly sat in silence.

They stood to leave, and Molly quickly pulled her menu in front of her face again. Cole tried, but failed to mimic her speed—Newton's eyes met his. Newton anxiously wrung his fingers, looking from Molly to Cole, then down at the ground, then at them again.

"Well, Molly, Cole," Newton's eyes shifted toward Pastor Lett, then back at Molly. "How are you?" he asked in a shaky voice.

Molly stretched a sleepy arm underneath her pillow, reassured by the feel of the necklace and candy wrapper. She wondered why they hadn't brought her more information, more visions. She turned toward Cole, who was sleeping soundly, and snuggled next to him, but her mind was already too alert, making it impossible for her to sleep. She moved gently off the bed and padded downstairs, dogs in tow.

"Okay, guys," she said quietly to the dogs, "but I warn you, it's cold out there." She opened the door and let them run out. Seconds later, Stealth was scratching to come back in. "What did I tell you?" she smirked and let Stealth back inside. Molly filled a glass with water and took it to the family room, where she curled up under a blanket and clicked on the television, catching the tail end of a local news clip about Tracey Porter. The reporter stated that they were looking to the community for answers. Molly fought the urge to call the police and recommend that they question Pastor Lett and Newton Carr.

Molly jumped when the phone rang. She answered it tentatively, "Hello?"

"Mom, it's me," Erik's voice was wrought with purpose. Before Molly could ask, he said, "Don't worry, everything's fine. I just need to talk to you."

"Okay, okay, slow down. What is it?"

"I saw that little girl on TV tonight—you know, Tracey."

"Yeah, me too," Molly said, relieved that he was okay.

"Mom, she's alive. I know she's alive. I can feel it. Can you feel it?" he asked, hopefully.

"I do think she's alive, Erik. I'm just stuck on where to find her."

"Mom, every time I think of her, I see this guy. He's big, like Dad," he paused, and Molly knew he was pacing the floor, just as his father did when he was on the phone. "I don't know who he is, but I know he's big. Who could it be?"

"I don't know, honey. I'm trying to figure that out, too." She thought about telling him about Pastor Lett and Newton, then quickly reconsidered. She didn't want to taint his feelings against them in case her suspicions were wrong. "I found her necklace, I think. It's a gold chain—"

"With a heart—I know," Erik said.

"How did you know? Did Dad tell you?"

Erik's voice was hesitant, "No, Mom, I just *knew*." He quickly grew angry. "I hate this. I really hate it. I can't put it away or turn it off. Something just happens. It's like seeing Hannah in the woods. Mom, how do you ever know what it all means?"

Molly heard the fear in his voice and wanted nothing more than to wrap her arms around him, engulf him with love and safety, and somehow protect him from the infiltration and pain of the Knowing. "I don't," she admitted, sadly. "I hate it too. I can only believe that we're given this information to save her." Molly paused. "Do you see anything else? Do you feel anything else?"

"Yeah, she's scared sometimes, terrified. I know that. Sometimes I'm sitting in my classes, and this fear comes over me, and when I try to figure out what I'm afraid of, all I see is darkness."

"Oh, Erik."

"Sometimes I see candles, and once…once I saw that big man with his hands stretched up, like he was…I don't know, reaching for something? It looked like he was reaching for the sky, but I know that sounds stupid."

"I saw that too, Erik. Can you see anything else, like where she is?" Molly asked.

"Not really. Sometimes, I see an old creepy house, and sometimes I see just darkness, like she's in a hole or something. I can just sort of *feel* that she's there, but not really see her," he paused. Molly could tell that he wanted to say more.

"What is it, Erik?"

"Once…once I saw Tracey outside." His voice grew quieter, "I just don't know where outside, and that's killing me, but I saw her, and it was like I was seeing out of her eyes or something. It scared the shit out of me. I was in the woods, with one of my lab partners looking for samples, and suddenly it was like I was her. I can't explain it. God! This is so frustrating!" Molly heard him swear under his breath, then return to the phone. "I saw woods, thickets—like the ones where Dad and I used to hunt?"

Erik became silent. Molly grasped the phone tight against her ear. Knowing that Erik would be powerless to walk away from the visions pained her.

"I don't know what it means. I wish I could take it away. When you were little, I could blow on your scrapes and you thought I was magical, the pain would blow away with my breath, but, well, you know. I'm not magical. It kinda sucks. I'm powerless, and I'm so sorry."

"It's okay, Ma. I guess it's kinda cool, too. Maybe one day I'll see some really hot girl as she gets undressed. *That* would be worth it!" he laughed.

"Haha, Erik, I wouldn't hold your breath on that one," Molly said, smiling. "Listen, you get some sleep. Maybe together we can solve this thing."

"Okay, Ma."

"Erik, one more thing," she said to him. "Are you pretty sure it's a guy with her? Are you pretty clear on that? You don't think it's a lady that looks like Hannah?"

"I'm not sure, but I keep seeing this guy. It's like I just know he's reaching out to her, but he's also kind of not there. Shit! I don't know, Mom." Erik drew a deep breath. "I don't know about Hannah, either, because sometimes I have flashes of her sitting on a log, or someone that looks like her. Sometimes she's in the dark. It's just freaky, Mom. I don't know."

"Okay, honey, go get some sleep," Molly said, "and Erik, I'm glad you called. I love you."

206

"Love you more, Mom. G'night."

Molly leaned back against the couch and pet Stealth, and then remembered Trigger was still outside. "Come on, boy," Molly said to the dog, "let's find Trigger."

At Trigger's name, Stealth was instantly alert, on his feet, and bounding to the door.

Molly opened the door. Stealth pushed past her and darted outside. Molly stepped onto the back porch and looked up at the stars, which sparkled across the dark sky, beseeching her to reach up toward them, which she did. Suddenly, the heat of large palms, the same palms she had felt at the cellar door of the Perkinson House, weighed heavily against her own. Her body was frozen, arms outstretched toward the sky. Molly's heart beat faster. The dogs ran toward her barking frantically. She squinted, sure there was a formidable being in front of her, sure of the pressure on her hands growing stronger, and just as sure that she was alone.

Twenty

Molly had been riding the current of emotions for days. Between the daily battles with Cole and the guilt that consumed her, the guilt she thought she'd dealt with years ago, she didn't know what, or whom, she could trust anymore. She began doubting her own determination. Molly put on her jogging clothes, the familiarity of them felt like an old friend returning, giving her renewed energy. She once again buried her doubts and decided to focus on the day before her. She looked forward to a quick trip to the police station, and then a much-needed run. She parked in front of the Country Store and greeted the Boyds Boys as she entered the store for a Power Bar and a bottle of water. She found Edie bent over a group of boxes.

"Hi, Edie. How are you?" she asked, tentatively.

"Fine," Edie said, curtly.

"Did I offend you somehow, Edie?" she asked.

"Not you, Molly. It's not you," Edie stood. "I want to know where Kate Plummer is. Why Rodney have to get hurt? I just don't understand." Years of bottled up anger came tumbling forward. Edie looked as if she were on the verge of tears.

Molly reached out and touched her arm. "I don't know," she said.

"Why no police investigate? No body, no proof!" she demanded. "Where Tracey? Where that little girl?" Tears fell from Edie's eyes.

"I'm just as baffled as you are, Edie," Molly said.

Edie walked away. Molly swore she heard her say, "He knows," when she brushed past her. The hair on the back of her neck prickled with a frisson. She walked hurriedly to the front of the store, paid for her items, and escaped.

Molly hurried down the concrete steps toward her van. Harley yelled behind her, "Running today?"

Molly held up her bottle of water in answer.

"Molly?" Harley's tone stopped her in my tracks.

"Yeah?" she replied, distracted and miffed by the glare of the day before.

"Careful poking a sleeping bear. I wouldn't want you gettin' hurt."

Molly thought she could walk into the police station, hand over the necklace and candy wrapper, and turn around and leave—a five-minute trip. She was surprised at how wrong she felt when she walked through the door and found the same young officer manning the front desk. A spark of recognition passed between them.

"Hello, ma'am, nice to see you again," the officer smiled.

"You, too," she said, mildly embarrassed. "Is Officer Brown in today?" she asked.

A voice boomed from behind her, "Just who would like to know?"

Molly turned around and looked into the round face of Officer Brown, his hands clasped atop his protruding belly. He smiled as if there were no ill feelings between them. Molly tried to smile, to cover the angst she felt at seeing him again.

"Officer Brown," Molly reached into her backpack, protectively touching the treasures she'd tucked away, and thinking about Harley's comment.

"What brings you here *today*?" he asked.

His shoes were dull, his brown pants wrinkled, almost as short as they were wide, and his jacket had a coffee stain on the front. Why, Molly wondered to herself, was she so worried about this unkempt man? She stood up straighter and decided that she would not be intimidated by him.

"I was wondering if we could talk for a minute," she said, trying to summon her business voice from her Philadelphia days.

"Well, we surely can," he said. He waddled in front of Molly and led her down the hallway towards the interrogation room. He winked as he passed her.

You wish, Molly thought, cringing inwardly.

Molly followed him, feeling oddly like a school girl walking to the principal's office, unsure how to turn over the evidence without appearing guilty. Her mind wrestled with the pros and cons, but she could not bring back her resolve to give up those pieces of Tracey.

"After you, Mrs. Tanner," Officer Brown held the door open.

"Thank you," Molly said, clutching her backpack.

Molly sat on the same cold chair, in the same stale room, facing the same two-way mirror, and felt even more like a suspect. She reminded herself that she was there by choice—she could get up and leave if she wanted. She held the backpack in her lap, realizing that by not turning over the evidence, she was, in fact, a criminal. She rationalized in her mind that she could keep them for one more day—in case there were more messages to come, even though she knew that doing so would cause strife in her marriage. Her marriage—that was another thing Molly couldn't worry about at the moment.

Officer Brown sat across from Molly, staring expectantly at her, his hands resting across his stomach.

"Mrs. Tanner?" he smiled. "Do you have something to tell me?"

Does he think I am here to confess? Molly was taken by surprise. "Excuse me?"

"I assume," he adjusted his too large body in the too small seat, "that there is some reason you're here."

"Of course—sorry," Molly said. "I was just wondering," she paused, having difficulty concentrating. She glanced around the room and images came at her fast, stealing her concentration: *An image of a mother crying, while her teenage son sat across the very same table, head in his hands, ashamed; an image of a large man, his veins bursting with anger, arrested after raping a young girl.* They came at Molly with such power that it took her a moment to regroup, so

211

long, in fact, that Officer Brown had asked her if she was alright.

"I'm sorry. I guess I'm a little sidetracked, Officer Brown," Molly sat up straighter, scrambling to come up with a reason for her visit.

Officer Brown looked up at the ceiling, rubbing his chin with his left index finger and thumb. His neck jiggled with each movement. "Mrs. Tanner?"

Molly jumped in her seat.

"Is there something else, Mrs. Tanner?" he asked.

Molly leaned her elbows on the table and leaned forward. "Officer Brown, no one was charged in Rodney's murder, right?"

He frowned, a little annoyed, "Right, yes. We've been over this before." He straightened his back, looking at her more seriously.

"But you never found Kate Plummer, either?"

"Right, right, Mrs. Tanner, where are you going with this? That case is over twenty years old. This case, the Tracey Porter case, has no relation. What is it that you want? I don't have time to talk to every Tom, Dick, or...Molly," he emphasized her name with sarcasm, "about closed cases." He leaned forward until Molly could smell his stale breath, "Unless, of course, you are trying to get me to look the other way, look for others who might be involved."

"Excuse me?" Molly pushed back from the table. "Officer Brown, you cannot possibly believe that I might be a suspect," she said angrily. "That's a load of horse shit and you know it!"

Officer Brown sat back slowly and looked at his stubby fingernails, "Maybe I do." He looked up at Molly, who stood before him, incensed. "But what I can't figure is why you're tracking this case so closely, closer than the girl's parents. What do you have to gain? Or maybe you know the abductor, and you want to keep tabs on the police?"

Molly could feel heat spread up her chest, her face reddening. "That's ridiculous. I'm a mother! I have a son! I would never want harm to come to a child, much less protect someone who caused it!" The nightmares and the face of Amanda's killer flashed in her mind, clear as day. She swallowed the pain of the truth—she had ignored those visions—and turned her back to Officer Brown, hiding the tears of anger that welled in her eyes, "You should be ashamed of yourself," she seethed.

"Then tell me, Mrs. Tanner, what is your stake in this?" he asked sincerely.

"I…" Molly spun around, looked down, and suddenly decided to come clean. She looked him in the eye, "I *know* things." She watched his eyes light up, as if she were going to confess. "No, not because I did them or am involved," she began to pace. "I'm not the culprit, Officer Brown." She stood before him, mustering the strength to tell him the truth, and hoping it would make a difference. "I have visions…visions that I don't always understand. I've always had them."

She recognized the look of disbelief in his eyes, the slack in his jaw. "I know what you're thinking. Either this woman is crazy, or she's in on it." She leaned toward him. "I'm not crazy, and I'm not Rodney. I have flashes of things, which I know is just like what Pastor Lett said Rodney had, but I'm not guilty. My son has the same…gift…if you will." She leaned back, and spoke honestly. "Only it isn't a gift, it's torture. I have seen flashes of this little girl in the dark, of a man

213

reaching for the sky. I just can't make sense of it all."
She looked at him, seeking any amount of belief, but
was met with another blank stare.

"I know how crazy this all sounds. I've lived
with it my whole damn life, but, Officer Brown, maybe
it's not crazy. Maybe we can pull together what I see
with clues you and your team have. Maybe there is an
end in sight. Maybe Tracey is still alive." She was
enthused by the thought.

"And maybe, Mrs. Tanner, you are guilty and
trying to sideline us," he said flatly. "I'm not going to
arrest you. I have no proof, but," he deepened his voice,
"I will be watching you. I'm sorry, Mrs. Tanner, but this
is too crazy. Most housewives," he smirked, "have
better things to do."

Molly knew she should bite her tongue, but the
urge to defend herself was too great, she could not stand
being wrongly accused. Manipulatively, she reached
across the table and grabbed Officer Brown's hand.
"Officer Brown," Molly closed her eyes and focused
her thoughts on the feel of his hand, the heaviness of it,
the clammy texture of his skin. The answers she sought
appeared gently, like a sneaky child putting a slip of
paper into her pocket, then tiptoeing away. Molly
smiled at her own cleverness. "I hope Charlie Cook was
convicted because he did rape that child. Mrs. Jaden's
son did steal the principal's laptop, but he was so
regretful that I hope you let him off easy." She opened
her eyes and looked up at him, surprised that she was
able to find those details with such ease. The room had
become her ally, pulled her through the storm. *Damn!*
Molly thought. *If only I could harness that control for
Tracey—or for Amanda!* She could hear her mother's
sing-song voice, *Be careful what you wish for*, and

could not figure out why she'd gone from a woman who had occasionally experienced a few indiscernible images, to a woman who was receiving multiple, detailed visions. Cole was right, she'd become like a dog with a bone, relentless.

"Excuse me?" he said, stealing his hand from hers.

"I don't know, really. I saw it when I came into this room. I have no idea who those people are, or even if I have the names right, but when I walked into this room," she motioned to the room, stood, and her voice grew louder, "when I walked in, these images came to me. I couldn't make these things up. Why don't you just go check, and we'll see. Who knows, maybe I am crazy—but I have faith in my visions. I have to—for Tracey's sake."

"You're crazy," he made no effort to move.

"Officer Brown," Molly tried to persuade him, "check it out—please. If I'm wrong, you can arrest me or send me away, and I'll never bother you again— whatever you want. Just please," she pleaded, "please! Rodney got killed over this. You can make things right. Just do this for me. It will only cost you a walk down the hall."

He sighed and looked away, then back again. "Mrs. Tanner, you are really pushing me," he said testily.

"I know," she said, almost giddily. "If I don't push you, I'm afraid Tracey might never be found. You need to look outside of the virtual box. Don't you see? If you pigeon-hole me as a crazy nut, or as the culprit, when clearly I'm not, then you're only hurting Tracey—Tracey, Officer Brown, not me."

He reluctantly pushed his chair out from the table and stood. He looked her in the eye and pointed to the table, "Sit," he commanded, "but if you're wrong, I will have to take the next step."

He left the room, and suddenly the air became less stifling. Molly took a deep breath and nervously curled her lips into a smile, hoping and praying that what she had seen was right. What-ifs sailed across her mind. What if there were no such cases? What if they *do* want to consider working with her? What if he finds out that she has the necklace? She leaned back and took a deep breath, staring unseeing at her reflection in the glass panel on the opposite side of the room.

Ten minutes later, which seemed more like an hour to Molly, Officer Brown entered the room looking clearly displeased. He stood next to the table, silently. Molly's heart raced as she waited for him to speak. He looked over her, then shook his head. Molly's heart sank. He walked around the table and sat across from Molly, crossed his arms, and said, "Mrs. Tanner. I don't know what your game is." He sighed heavily. "Those cases did indeed take place in this room. At least the questioning did—last week."

Molly breathed hard, relieved.

"I have no idea how you have done this, but you have. I don't know if I believe in your...visions...but—"

"Okay," Molly's voice shook, "but I didn't take her. Can we work together? Can we try to figure these things out together?" She was excited about the prospect of actually having a plan, working with the police, with their resources.

"I'm sorry," he said. "We have protocols, certain ways of doing things. We can't just open up the investigation to anyone off the street."

"I see," Molly said, disappointed.

"Though I can't advise you to impede our investigation, we do have a lead system set up." He slid a business card across the table. "You can call this number at any time, anonymously or not, and tell the officer who answers what your thoughts are. Every lead is followed up."

The great blow-off, Molly thought.

"Mrs. Tanner, I want you to clearly understand that this does not mean that you are off my radar screen. Like I said, I don't know about all of this *vision* stuff. Also, what happened with Rodney Lett remains as it was. I do not doubt what the officers in charge did, or how they handled that investigation. If you claim to have visions, that reflects on *your* abilities, not his." He waved his hand in dismissal. "I remain constant in my support for the investigation of Kate Plummer. The case is closed."

Molly turned to leave, but when she reached the door, she put her hand on the doorknob and said, "I know she's alive. I can feel it."

Officer Brown rose from the table and looked evenly at Molly. "Mrs. Tanner, if you have a solid lead, something other than a *vision*," he said the word sarcastically, "you can call me directly." He handed her a business card.

Molly walked into the depressing hallway and swiftly came to the realization that she was once again on her own. A stocky, brown-haired man walked out of the neighboring office and leaned against the door, arms crossed, his eyes trained on Molly. Officer Brown appeared in the doorway and nodded at the other man. Molly hurried toward the exit, hearing Officer Brown's hushed voice behind her, "Keep your eye on that one."

Molly was anxious for her morning run and desperately needed to clear her head, but as she neared White Ground Road, she hesitated. After the morning she'd had, she wasn't up to taking a chance on another vision hitting her. Instead, she parked along the road that crossed the lake. She focused on her upcoming run and vowed not to think about Officer Brown. She tied her van key to her shoelace, secured her iPod armband, and began to stretch.

The sun warmed her face as she ran across the bridge, heading toward the gated entrance to the Perkinson driveway. She tried not to look toward the house but couldn't stop herself. Despite her firm resolve to ignore it, her feet carried her past the rusty black mailbox, around the metal gate, and up the overgrown driveway.

She reached the top of the hill quickly and scanned the yard. She veered into the woods, following a metal clanking sound that rang out from the rear of the house. Her heart jumped at the glimpse of someone disappearing around the far side of the house. Molly sprinted to the front of the house, Cole's warnings whispered to her, chilling her bare arms. She ducked behind a bush just in time to see Hannah and Pastor Lett coming around the corner. Molly crouched as low as she was able, hoping the leaves beneath her wouldn't give her away.

The house loomed behind them like a blind sentry, the windows boarded up like two eye patches. Hannah walked up the front steps and tried the door, touching the heavy metal lock, and turned back toward the front yard. Pastor Lett motioned to Hannah. Molly watched from the bushes. Crouching further down, a twig snapped beneath her feet. Hannah's head snapped in Molly's direction, and she moved toward her. Pastor Lett reached out and touched Hannah's arm, saying something Molly could not hear. Molly closed her eyes, hoping she hadn't been spotted. When she opened them, they were nowhere in sight.

After waiting in the bushes for what felt like hours, Molly snuck back down through the woods and decided to visit Pastor Lett and lay it all out on the table. She was going to get to the bottom of the situation one way or the other. Surely Pastor Lett would have a good explanation for the lights in the cellar. Molly trusted Pastor Lett, didn't she? Yes, she decided, she did. She drove the short distance to the church and pulled into the empty parking lot. Newton's minivan pulled in along side Molly's car.

Molly waved.

Newton climbed out of the van, "Molly. How are you?"

"Great, thanks. Just looking for Pastor Lett."

"She's not coming in today." Newton replied.

"Oh," Molly looked perplexed. "I just saw her," she caught her mistake, "earlier. I saw her earlier today. Just thought I might catch her here."

A skinny, old black man walked out of the cemetery and toward Newton and Molly. His army jacket was zipped to his neckline, and he had a woolen hat pulled tight over his head, though the weather didn't call for such warmth. He moved slowly past them, as if each step took great effort, and Molly cringed at the odor that followed.

"Hello, ma'am. Mr. Carr," the man said in a raspy voice.

"Good day, Walter," Newton said.

Molly turned and watched him walking across the parking lot toward the road. His jeans dragged along the asphalt with each step.

Newton whispered to her, "You know Walter?"

Molly shook her head, guiltily feeling like a gossip.

"Walter Meeks. Seventy years he's lived here. Thirty of it right off of Peachtree Road. He, um, he's always kept to himself. Had a wife and child—a girl. Doesn't drive, you know, afraid of cars."

"Why?" Molly asked.

"Not really sure why, just is. Walked to and from work each day when he worked for the mines. Came home one day and his, uh, his house was burned to the ground."

"How awful."

"Some people thought it was arson, but they never figured it out. His wife left him right after that. Took the child with her."

"That poor man. He lost his house and his family?" Molly followed Newton as he walked toward the cemetery.

"She just up and disappeared. When the house burned down, they went to his aunt's house for the night. In the morning, she and the girl were gone." Newton was uncharacteristically forthcoming with Walter's background. Molly paid full attention. "He was married to a white girl. Their daughter was, um, light skinned, too—dark hair, prettiest little thing." He stopped walking, and stared into the cemetery, thinking. "If I recall, his house burned down in the late sixties, somewhere 'round there. A real shame. His wife was a loner, too. She was real sick." Newton shook his head.

"Her father passed away from an asbestos-related cancer, meso-something-or-other, and she was exposed as a little girl." Newton put his hands in his pocket, then pulled them out again, fidgeting. "Said she could cure anything herself. Some said she was into voodoo, witchery, that type of thing. Not sure I believed it, though. Surely never saw any of it." He looked at Molly and said, "Sorry. Too much information, I know."

"And all this time I thought that he was just some old guy that never made anything of himself. Now I feel badly," Molly said, always amazed at the font of information that was Newton Carr.

"Well, he wasn't the brightest tool in the shed, that's for sure, but he was dependable. Yes, ma'am, the mining company was really unhappy when he left. He worked for them for over twenty years. Had a big party for him, in fact, right in the field across from the gravel lot, behind that cornfield." He pointed to a field on a hill behind the church.

They walked silently through the graveyard, and Molly realized that Newton knew far more than just the history of Boyds.

"You know about the quarry, right, Molly?" Newton asked, clearly changing the subject.

Molly was oddly relieved. "Well, I know there was a community battle to keep it out of Boyds, and that it ended when a local resident bought the property."

The simplification of the story brought a smirk to Newton's face. He asked Molly if she'd like to walk with him through the cemetery, where he was headed to check on the upkeep of the graves. She anxiously agreed. "That property there," Newton pointed toward the fields, and then in the direction of the railroad tracks. "The mining company that was trying to put the quarry in? They used to own all this land. The tunnels were over there," he pointed, again, to the fields. "Until, uh, Martin Chambers scooped it up."

"Tunnels?"

"Well, there's debate about if the tunnels ever really existed at all. Rumor has it they dug tunnels clear through Boyds as a means of trucking their gravel without causing problems on the roads. The roads, they were the big issue back then. I suppose they thought that if they alleviated that worry, then the residents wouldn't mind them being here. Anyway, they owned seventeen or eighteen hundred acres. Come to think of it, I believe there's an old abandoned mine shaft in the Black Hill Park area, too. That area used to be called Gold Mine Farm back when the Wicks owned it."

"Chambers bought all eighteen hundred acres?" she asked.

"Yup, sure did. He put about eight hundred acres into conservation land right away—the Hoyles Mill Conservation Park and Trail? We have him to thank for that. He really saved Boyds, if you ask me. Yup, we're mighty fortunate that someone like him would come to our little town and be willing to tie up so much capital to preserve the area."

They walked along in silence, Newton bent down to pick up bits and pieces of debris along the way. They came upon a small grouping of graves. Newton pulled a few weeds and straightened flowers that had been left on the graves. He crouched over a pink headstone, which was unreadable, cracked, and weathered. He looked sad.

"This here is Colonel James A. Boyds's grave. He was born in Ayrshire, Scotland, December 22, 1823. Died here in Boyds, December 21, 1886."

Molly crouched down next to Newton and dragged her fingers across the gravestone's dips and valleys. It was easy for Molly to envision Newton as a younger man, just back from his stint with the army, and wondering how else he might serve his country, his home town

He led Molly up a hill to another group of headstones and stooped by the grave of a child. He ran his hand over the headstone. The sun beat down on them. In the distance, a soft drone of cars from the nearby roads hummed. The headstone bore no name, only dates: 1979-1979.

He tilted his head toward Molly. "There's no baby here, just a headstone, in memory of a dear friend of mine's child. Didn't live more than a few minutes."

"I'm sorry, Newton." Molly touched his shoulder, thinking of Amanda's funeral, which she'd watched from her car across the street—the way Amanda's mother's shoulders had hunched and shaken from her sobs, Amanda's little brother's spindly arm hanging onto his mother's dress, thumb in his mouth, and the tiny coffin, perched and ready to be lowered into the ground forever.

Newton turned, and Molly followed him further up the hill to the rear of the cemetery where the grave of Cathy Mall overflowed with photographs, trinkets, flowers, and stuffed animals. A metal frame cradled an eight-by-ten photo of Cathy, standing in that very spot, with her arms reaching toward the sun, or was she reaching for heaven? Newton told Molly that Cathy had been the founder of the preschool, and that when she was told her breast cancer was malignant, she had chosen that particular grave so she could watch over the children. He explained how Cathy had asked that her insurance money be used to build the playground behind Kerr Hall, a church-owned building that was built just behind the church. Molly wondered if children still played at the simple playground with the massive Adventure Park just five minutes away.

Molly's heart ached for Cathy, wondering if Cathy somehow knew that Kate Plummer had disappeared from the very playground where her dreams for children had come true. The sadness closed in on Molly's heart, creating a pressure in her chest. She closed her eyes, willing it away, and just as she realized it was not sadness, but the Knowing, she was met by a slow montage of images and smells: *A lanky, dark-haired girl, wearing a flowing dress, walking into the cornfield, the stalks split before her, as if she had followed someone. Then she was gone. The powdery fresh smell of her lingered like smoke from a fire.* Molly stared straight ahead, the images still playing before her eyes—*children, oblivious to the girl's disappearance, playing, smiling. Adults gathered in a group, talking, completely unaware.* Molly had an urge to scream, to run toward the image she'd seen, and warn her, *No! Don't go!* But she was rooted to the grassy hill, an onlooker to a past tragedy.

Tracey clutched the new clothes to her chest, her heart beat excitedly. She ran over and gave Mummy a big hug. "I love them!" she exclaimed. "Did you get yourself anything, Mummy?"

"Yup," Mummy said, and she reached deep into her pockets, then splayed her hand out for Tracey to see.

"What are those for?" she asked, wondering why Mummy thought quarters were a fun gift.

"They're for our other worship chamber—our deep chamber. We leave them as gifts, and God grants our wishes." She put them in a pile on the makeshift shelf.

"Deep chamber?" Tracey asked, envisioning the bad spot and growing increasingly anxious.

"The one where my mummy is." Mummy sat down on a log and reached for Tracey's hand. "We'll go there soon," she said.

Tracey touched her necklace, the best gift of all. The charm rested comfortingly between her two collar bones. She ran her fingers over the chain and smiled. Mummy had told her that she had been such a brave girl, staying in their sleeping place all by herself, that she deserved it. She was going to be good, she'd decided. She would make Mummy proud of her.

Mummy told her that it was time to thank God for the things they had.

"Tracey," she said, "remember when I told you that little girls sometimes get sick out in the big world?"

"Yes," Tracey looked up through the fringe of her hair.

"Well, sometimes little girls get sick, and they don't know it. Sometimes they don't know until they are too sick and ready to die." She looked right into Tracey's eyes and squeezed her hand.

"Why, Mummy? Why does that happen?" Tracey asked in a quivering voice, sure Mummy had been referring to her.

"I don't know—no one knows—but that's why we have to keep you away from all of the toxins that are out there. We never know just what will make you sick." She patted Tracey's hand with her free hand. Tracey leaned her body against Mummy, scared.

"Okay," she said, relieved, and silently hoping that she wouldn't get any of the bad toxins in her when they went outside to the bramble place.

"I'll take care of you," Mummy assured her.

"Okay," Tracey whispered.

"C'mon, Tracey, let's put on your church dress," Mummy pulled the dress out of one of the green bags. Tracey was surprised, and happy, to see that it had been freshly washed.

"Do I have to change?" she asked in the least whiney voice that she could muster.

"Today we're worshiping, and we need to show respect to God. Come on now. It will look pretty with your necklace."

Tracey felt for the necklace and smiled at the now-familiar feel of it. She took the dress and went to the corner to change her clothes. She had gotten used to changing as quickly as she could, using her arms to cover up her body. She brought her arms across the front of the dress, walked to Mummy, and turned around. Mummy hummed as she zipped Tracey's dress.

Mummy spoke as they left their room and headed toward the worship chamber, "That my heart may sing to you and not be silent. O Lord, my God, I will give you thanks forever."

Tracey walked nervously with her arms wrapped tightly around her—the dirt walls intimidated her. She could see the worship chamber up ahead and was happy when Mummy sped up her pace.

Tracey stood quietly in the doorway while Mummy lit the candles. "Come now, Tracey," she beckoned. "Let's give thanks to the Lord for keeping us safe." She patted the ground next to her as she knelt down.

The scratchy cold feeling of the dirt on Tracey's knees made her sad. She didn't want to get sick, but she was still a little scared to be underground. Mummy steepled her hands, and Tracey followed. Mummy didn't have to tell Tracey to close her eyes, she knew the routine, closed her eyes, and listened to Mummy whispering.

"Hebrews 12:28. Therefore, since we are receiving a kingdom that cannot be shaken, let us be thankful, and so worship God acceptably with reverence and awe."

Mummy rested her hand on Tracey's thigh. Tracey recoiled, opened her eyes. Upon seeing a smile on Mummy's face, she relaxed again and closed her eyes.

"Dear God, thank you for bringing me Tracey to take care of. She needed me. Thank you for allowing me to keep her safe, keep her healthy. She's a wonderful girl, and I am thankful to have her as my family."

The word "family" made Tracey bristle. She stifled the urge to cry. She had almost forgotten how much she missed her real family. How could she have done that, she wondered. *Have Mommy and Daddy forgotten about me? What about Emma?*

Mummy lifted her hand from Tracey's thigh, "Tracey, honey, what's wrong?"

Tracey didn't realize that she had clenched her eyes shut. She opened them, and tears spilled onto her cheeks. She knew better than to cry in front of Mummy. She wiped her eyes and clenched them shut again.

Mummy took Tracey in her arms and held her quaking body, fresh tears landed on Mummy's shoulder. Tracey tried to fight the tears, but she was powerless—she sobbed in Mummy's arms. Mummy rocked her and hummed the same tune she had hummed earlier, a tune Tracey did not know.

"It's okay, honey. You don't want to get the sickness and die, too. You *belong* with me. You *needed* to be saved. "

No, Tracey thought, *I don't want to die from the toxins!* She didn't know what they were, but she thought of them as little bugs that got under her skin and traveled through her body. She grabbed Mummy's hand and held it tight.

Mummy whispered, one big hand on Tracey's back, the other patting her hair, "God told me, Tracey. He told me, 'Exodus 15:13. In your unfailing love you will lead the people you have redeemed. In your strength you will guide them to your holy dwelling,'" she said. "So you see Tracey, I was put here to find you and love you and keep you safe. This is *our* holy dwelling. Nothing can hurt you here."

Safety, Tracey thought, *safety from the toxins*. She sniffled and pulled back from Mummy so she could see her face. She wanted to be kept safe. She wiped her nose on her arm and was overwhelmed with relief that she hadn't gotten in trouble for crying.

Mummy smiled at Tracey. "I am safe. Look around us, there are no toxins here, nothing to hurt us or get into our bodies. We have each other. We have safety. We have the Lord."

Tracey slipped off of her lap and positioned herself to pray. She whispered, "God, if you can hear me, thank you for saving me. I want to be healthy." She spoke quickly. "Thank you for my necklace, too." She reached for the necklace, and held the cool gold tightly in her fingers. Mummy opened her arms, and Tracey went to her, willingly, thankfully. In the back of Tracey's mind, she wondered why her own mother hadn't wanted to keep her safe from the toxins. She wondered if her own mother had really loved her at all.

Molly arrived home, let the dogs out, and went straight to her office to review the notes, drawings, and other clues that she had compiled. A stream of sunlight illuminated her desk, highlighting the drawings in her notebook. She wrote a list of each item in her notebook, and tried to decipher the clues. Her cell phone rang three times before she reached for it, and was met by a deep, unfamiliar voice.

"Mrs. Tanner?"

"Yes?"

"This is Sergeant Moeler from the Germantown Police Department. Officer Brown asked me to follow up on a few leads that you might have regarding the disappearance of Tracey Porter."

"Okay," Molly replied, curiously.

They agreed to meet that afternoon. Molly confirmed her address and then picked up the phone to call Cole.

"Hey, you!" she said, happy to hear his voice.

"How was your run?" he asked.

"Okay. I ran into Newton, and we talked for a while."

"Did you go to the police station?" he asked.

"Yes," she said.

"Did you give them the necklace and the candy wrapper?"

Molly was silent, fiddling with her pen, trying to figure out how to answer without lying.

"Molly? Did you give them the stuff you found?" he repeated more sternly.

"I went there," she said coyly.

"Mol, I thought we agreed that the best thing to do was turn that stuff in. You can get in so much trouble!" His voice sounded flat-out angry.

"Well, I went there with every intention of turning it in!" she insisted.

"Mm-hm."

"I did! I was going to, and then when I got there, Officer Brown was…I don't know…annoying me, and I got to thinking—what if I gave them the stuff, and they just filed it away? You know how they let cases just die out? And then I thought, well, maybe there's more that I'm supposed to know—to gain—from the necklace and wrapper. Maybe I just haven't looked hard enough yet."

"Give it in, Molly. This is no time for bullshit. This is real trouble. You're withholding evidence!" Molly waited to hear if his voice would soften. It didn't. "Molly, what do you think will happen when they find out? They'll go, 'Oh, it's Molly Tanner, no problem, we'll overlook it!'"

"No!" she protested. "But…I just thought that a few more days wouldn't hurt. Maybe I'll track her down today, maybe tomorrow. Who knows? But something didn't feel right," Molly paced her office. "It felt like a betrayal to give it to them. They aren't even doing anything to find her!" she said too loudly.

"Do what you want, Molly, but just think of Erik and me, okay?" Cole asked, his every word biting. "What will we do while you sit in jail wondering how you could have been so stupid?"

Molly's bravado deflated. She knew he was right, to an extent. "Cole, they don't know I have it.

They could never know how long I've had it!" she pleaded. "When I turn it in, I'll say that I just found it. Besides," she took a deep breath, and mumbled, "the fingerprints would be gone now anyway."

"What?"

"The fingerprints," she raised her voice. "They'd be gone now anyway! I've touched it! It's been in my bag! I screwed that up!" The admission weighed heavily on her. She had screwed up—again.

"Great!" he fell silent.

The silence was worse than when he had been yelling at her. Molly closed her eyes tightly, her tentative voice sliced through the silence, "I think I saw Kate Plummer disappear today."

"Tell me," he said flatly.

Molly told him the details of the vision, which he promptly told her was probably transference—that she had taken the details that she already knew, coupled with the guilt that she still carried for Amanda's death, and that her mind had run with them.

Molly rolled her eyes, *Always the fact man.*

"I saw her dress. If I could find out what she was wearing when she disappeared, that would tell me if it was her or not," she retorted.

"And how does that help find Tracey?" he snapped.

"I don't know!" she said, exasperated. "Look, I've got to go. The police are sending someone over. I'll call you later." She hung up the phone before the tension could grow any thicker. She stared at the phone, wondering how she'd ever be able to repair the damage that she was creating in her marriage and knowing she wouldn't let another child's life end if she could help it.

Molly pushed aside her frustrations with Cole, and mentally raced through her to-do list:

1. Look up Kate's clothes when missing.

2. Who was in the cellar?

3. Call Hannah.

Molly turned on her computer, and, while it booted up, she walked into the kitchen to get a glass of water. She leaned against the sink and looked outside where Stealth and Trigger sat by the back door. She let them inside, and Stealth pushed his body against her leg as he walked by. The comforts of home settled around her, making her feel sad for Tracey, for Kate, and for Amanda. Their safety had been abruptly stolen away from them.

The phone rang, and Molly immediately hoped it wasn't Cole, then hated herself for the thought. Reluctantly, she reached for it, cursing herself for choosing a decorative phone instead of one with caller I.D.

"Hello?"

"Molly Tanner?" The voice sounded like a teenage girl's.

"Yes? Who is this?"

"Someone wants you to know there's a guy who can tell you what happened to Kate Plummer."

Molly's heartbeat quickened. "Who is this?" she asked anxiously. "What guy?"

"I don't know," the girl was irritated, rushed. "I just know that I'm supposed to tell you that, like, you have to find the guy."

"Where? Where do I find this guy? Who are you?" Molly pleaded desperately.

"She paid me to tell you this," she said in an annoyed, exasperated teenage fashion. "I don't know where to find the guy. I don't know anything about this," the girl spat her answers. "She said, like, he would know about Tracey, too."

"Who paid you? I'll pay you twice as much to tell me who paid you!" Molly said eagerly.

"No, I can't. I want no part of this. I…I have to go—"

"Wait!" Molly yelled. "Just tell me who told you to call."

The caller covered the phone. Molly heard muffled voices. When the caller returned to the phone, she asked, "Who is Kate Plummer?"

Molly sighed, deflated. The girl was merely a pigeon—a messenger. "Who paid you? Please tell me!" she pleaded. "A child's life is at stake."

"What?" Molly heard fear in the girl's shaky, unsure voice.

"A child has been abducted—Tracey Porter. If you know anything, please, please tell me. This is life or death!"

"Jesus, I've heard about that girl," she said. "I saw her on the Missing Children flyer that came home from school. Fuck! I don't want no part of this!"

"Wait! Who told you to call me?" Molly begged. "She may be involved. I may be able to save the girl! I'll pay you! I'll do anything you want!"

"Shit! Fuck this shit!" The girl yelled distantly, as if holding the phone at arm's length. She pulled the receiver close again, "I don't know, alright!" she yelled. "Some woman! That's all I know!"

Molly's heart sank with the resounding *click*. She yelled, "Goddamn it! Give me a fucking break!" Molly stared at the phone as if it were evil, "Goddamn you! Help me find her! This is goddamn bull shit!"

For the next hour, Molly played the phone conversation over and over in her mind, like a bad rerun. She had tried to use *69 to trace the call, to no avail. She had called the operator only to be told that they didn't offer a tracing service—she'd have to go to the police. When the doorbell rang, the dogs went crazy, barking and jumping up at the front door. Molly was frustrated. She tried to ignore the door, hoping the person would just go away.

There was another hard rap at the door, "Mrs. Tanner?" a deep voice boomed through the door. "It's me, Sergeant Moeler."

"Just a minute!" she called out, remembering their appointment and trying to decide if she should mention the phone call, knowing they'd tap her phone if she did. Undecided and flustered, she answered the door.

The stocky man she had seen when leaving the interrogation room stood before her looking serious, then quickly smiled, revealing large, square, white teeth. Stealth and Trigger's tails wagged excitedly next to Molly.

"Heel!" she commanded, and they obediently came to her side. She managed a smile, "Hello, Sergeant, thanks for coming."

"Sorry I'm early, ma'am. I had a break so I decided to head over." His face was warm and his blue eyes friendly. His neatly-combed brown hair and ironed uniform gave him a youthful look. He extended his hand to Molly, and Molly shook it, pensively.

She stepped aside. "Come in. They bark but don't bite unless they hear the secret command," she smiled.

They sat in the living room, and he pet Stealth and made playful sounds toward Trigger. Molly was confused by the relaxed man who sat before her. His personality in stark contrast to the stern look he'd given her in the hallway at the police station.

"They think anyone is fair game," Molly attempted small talk.

"I love animals. I have a Great Dane and a Pomeranian."

Molly lifted her eyebrows.

"I know, strange mix," he said. "The Dane was mine, and the Pomeranian belonged to a victim. I just couldn't let it go to the shelter. Anyway, they're best buds now. Rex, my Dane, thinks Tippy is her puppy. She's very protective. Cutest thing when they're curled up together."

Molly was surprised by his open and bright demeanor.

In a more serious tone, he said, "So tell me about these leads."

She was no longer on edge from the phone call, relieved to hand over the worries of the day to someone else for a while.

Molly started to explain about the notes she had received, and Sergeant Moeler cut her off. "I'm interested in the notes, but quite frankly, Mrs. Tanner—"

"Molly."

He nodded, "Molly. Mike," he smiled again. "You were dead-on in the interrogation room."

"But how—" Molly shook her head, then it dawned on her. "Two-way mirror?"

He shrugged.

"So Officer Brown sent you over because he thinks I'm crazy? Or party to the crime?" Molly turned away angrily.

"No," Sergeant Moeler said, then corrected himself, "maybe, but that's not my intent. I came because I'm curious. How did you know about the interrogations?"

Molly stewed in her growing anger. "If you'd like to talk about the anonymous notes I've been getting and how they might lead to Tracey, that's fine, but I'm not going to discuss my visions anymore. I'm not a circus freak. I seriously wanted to help, but I can see that no one at the police station takes me seriously." She stood, as if ready to walk him to the door.

He didn't move.

She put her hand on her hip, "Sergeant Moeler, I don't know what you expect to find out about me."

He stood, his body relaxed next to Molly's tension-ridden self. He spoke easily, "Molly, I'm not trying to cast you as a circus freak, and I'm sorry if you felt that way. I'm not curious out of voyeurism. I'm curious because we never know what lead will take us to find the missing girl."

Molly questioned his motives, staring silently.

He handed her a business card, "Look, here's my number. When you're ready to talk, I'll listen," he paused. "Do you want to show me those notes?"

Warily, Molly acquiesced. When she returned with the notes, she asked, skeptically, but with a sense of hope, "So what do we do now?"

"*We* do nothing. I have to hand this over to the officer in charge." Sergeant Moeler gathered the notes and stood to leave.

"Officer Brown?"

"Do you have a problem with Officer Brown?" he asked, one eyebrow raised.

"Well," she hesitated, ran her fingers along the desk as she looked in the distance, "not a *problem*, really. It's just that...well, let's just say that I'm not sure he is really going to take me seriously, and I don't see him as a go-getter. I get the idea he's more of a sit-and-let's-see-what-happens type of guy."

Sergeant Moeler laughed, a quiet, confirmatory laugh. "Well, at least you read people well, but there's more to him than you see. I've worked with him for three years, and it never fails to amaze me how it appears he's doing nothing all day, and then he solves cases," he snapped his fingers, "just like that. I don't have a choice, Molly. I have to give him the information. He'll delegate it, probably, and I'll try and stay on top of it."

Molly fell onto her living room couch, propped up her feet, and questioned her motive for not revealing the phone call, which seemed to have slipped her mind the minute Sergeant Moeler had walked into the house. The dogs panted in Molly's face. She shooed them away. Reluctantly, they sulked to the other side of the room and lay down.

Just as she began to relax, her cell phone rang. She debated letting it go to voicemail and begrudgingly pushed herself off of the couch to retrieve her phone; *Hannah Slate* flashed on the screen.

"Hello?" she could not hide her irritation.

"Molly!" Hannah's voice was overly enthusiastic.

"Hannah, hi, how are you?" Molly faked levity.

"I'm just fine, thanks," she said. "I was just going out for a walk and thought you might enjoy coming with me. I was so sorry to have missed you yesterday."

Molly's first inclination was to decline, but then she reconsidered.

"Hannah, I hope you know where we're going," Molly said, "because I'm totally lost."

"Of course I do," Hannah laughed. "Did you think I'd bring you out in the woods and leave you here to find your way out?"

When she paused after her strange statement, Molly knew a moment of nervous fear—half wishing she had left a trail of crumbs like Hansel and Gretel.

"Come on, Molly," she tugged on Molly's sleeve. "I've been in and out of these woods for over thirty years. We're nearing Schaeffer Road by now, I would say."

"How the heck did we get *there* without crossing White Ground?" Molly asked, perplexed.

"We did cross it, at the other end of the stream. You were just too busy to notice," Hannah stopped to rest.

Molly set her backpack on the ground and crouched next to a stream that snaked through the woods.

"This is one of my favorite places," Hannah said. "Come here a minute. I want to show you something." She walked up the slight incline, looking carefully at all of the large trees.

Molly watched Hannah from behind, her ponytail swayed with each step, her body tall and strong. Hannah splayed her hands on a large beech tree, gazed upward.

"Look here," Hannah beckoned Molly to come forward.

Molly looked at the tree curiously.

Hannah pulled Molly gently to the spot where she had been standing. "Now do you see it?"

"I see something," Molly squinted.

Hannah's voice grew quiet, and her eyes, introspective. "That, my friend, is a heart that I carved into this tree when I first arrived in Boyds."

Molly looked at the bark, where it had curled back from the grooves. "Your and Charlie's initials?"

"No. What's inside that heart is sacred—but it's not me and Charlie. Some people aren't meant to be remembered."

They crossed another section of road. Molly recognized the one-lane bridge, so small it almost didn't exist, and the creek bed that grew slender as it passed under the bridge, then widened just beyond. The bridge linked White Ground and Schaeffer Roads. They climbed the grassy bank and headed back into the seclusion of the woods. The roar of several small motors broke into the silence.

Hannah crinkled her nose and looked up toward the sky, "The model airpark. The bane of my existence."

"Boyds has an airpark?" Molly was intrigued.

"You're right next to it, Molly." Hannah blocked the sun with her right hand, and pointed with her left beyond the bushes. "They have limited times that they can run the planes, but when they do, they sure are noisy."

Molly had a nagging feeling that she should have known about the airpark.

They turned away and continued on their hike, eventually reaching the Schaeffer Farm Trail, another place Molly had never seen. "This is beautiful," she said. "I love Boyds."

"There's a reason I'm still here, you know," Hannah said.

Molly listened intently, hoping for what? A confession? Hannah was her friend. She didn't want Hannah to be guilty of anything, but she couldn't shake the feeling that Hannah was hiding something.

They talked about Tracey's disappearance and how similar it was to Kate's. They shared their sadness for Pastor Lett's loss of her brother, and Molly asked Hannah if she'd thought Rodney had been involved.

"Don't be silly. I knew Rodney fairly well. He was kind and gentle, like Carla. I still don't know what possessed the police to drag him in for questioning. Just like that, they were the catalyst for his murder." As she spoke, her voice became agitated.

"What do you think happened to Kate?" Molly asked.

"I don't know. Some people say she was taken by someone from out of town. Others say she's holed up somewhere with a child molester. If she is alive, I just hope she's okay." She looked beyond Molly and grew silent. "Shhh, listen," Hannah whispered.

Molly listened. Shouts and children's laughter carried almost inaudibly through the air. The sun, high in the sky, had long ago tipped over the noon time ridge.

"The Adventure Park," Hannah said in an annoyed, sharp voice, and pointed beyond Molly. "It's right over there. I was not pleased when they put the park in. It ruined a perfect setting."

They continued in the direction of the Adventure Park, and eventually Molly came to recognize where they were. Hannah walked right over to where Molly had seen her crouched down on the day of the search— to the hot spot. Hannah knelt and patted the ground. Molly watched, stunned. The look on Hannah's face baffled Molly—she looked as if she might cry. *Guilt?* Molly pretended not to notice, unsure of how, or if, she should approach her.

Hannah closed her eyes. Molly turned away, thinking of her biggest regret, the secret she'd kept.

Hannah stood and walked back the way they'd come, leaving Molly to stare at her back, bewildered.

Pastor Lett took the keys from around her neck and methodically unlocked the back door, first the padlock, then the deadbolt, and finally, the scratched and rusty doorknob itself. The heavy oak door creaked open, releasing a rush of frigid, stale air. Pastor Lett drew her coat tightly across her chest and stepped onto the worn, wooden floors. Her footsteps echoed in the sparsely-furnished house, giving it an aura of hollowness.

She ran her fingers along the cracked plaster walls, her mind hovering anxiously between relief and panic. Her fear of exposure grew worse with every passing day. She felt her time with the kid was coming to an end and feared not for what that would mean for her, but for the kid, for Newton, and for Hannah. She moved slowly, trancelike, through the kitchen and into the musty living room. At the bottom of the wide staircase, she knelt down, as if guided there by an unseen will. She clasped her hands over her knee, bent her head, and just before she closed her eyes, she caught a glimpse of the family portrait that hung on the wall next to the staircase.

"Please, Lord, do not take this kid from me." She prayed with such devotion that she believed God could not ignore her, unless He did so willfully. "Please do not expose our sins to the world around us. Keep this introduction silent and let us continue to find our way together, as we've done for so long." Shamefully, she continued, "I realize, Lord, that this is selfish, but it is for the best. Please forgive me for what I have done, for how I have done it."

She opened her eyes and raised her head, her gaze settling first to the windows next to the stairs, and then higher, to the top of the stairs, where looking down upon her was a woman and a young girl—an apparition. She wiped her eyes, certain she had not seen what she thought she had. She staggered to her feet, her breath caught in her throat. At the top of the stairs, stood Mrs. Perkinson, whom she recognized from the portrait, and a young girl. The figures were transparent, yet discernable. The woman's eyes locked with Pastor Lett's, her floor-length dress and light apron, tied around her waist, moved as she beckoned her with her arms—motioning her to come forward. Pastor Lett's legs felt like lead as she moved toward the stairs. She lifted her foot to the first riser, certain her legs would fail her, and yet they carried her up the long staircase. The little girl clung to her mother's leg, peering out from behind. Pastor Lett stood three steps from the landing, holding onto the railing, her eyes wide, disbelieving. The woman turned and walked down the hall, toward the far bedroom. The little girl held her hand, looking over her shoulder once, then forward again. Pastor Lett forced herself to continue up the risers, and finally, onto the landing. She watched the tail of the woman's dress disappear into the bedroom. The silence pressed in on her. She made her way slowly down the hallway, telling herself that what she had seen was not real—that she was exhausted. She forced the lessons that she had been taught, that the spirit lived beyond the heavenly body, to the back of her mind. She stood at the entrance to the bedroom and pushed the heavy wood door all the way open. It creaked and knocked against the wall, startling her. In the center of the room, the little ghostly girl played with a wooden dollhouse, a dollhouse that Pastor Lett had seen many times—an exact replica of the Perkinson House. The figures in the house were set up in various rooms of the tiny diorama. The girl moved them with her transparent fingers. The tiny mother figurine stood in the kitchen, next to a miniaturized stove. The father figure was placed in the study, surrounded by a desk and shelves that were perfectly scaled. The inhabited rooms were on the middle floor of the dollhouse. The top floor of the dollhouse had four rooms, each one equipped with a miniature-sized bed and nightstand, a small figurine of a girl lay on a bed in the center of one of the bedrooms. The first floor of the dollhouse had indistinguishable rooms, just bare open spaces. The last figurine, a boy, was placed in the open space of the first floor, next to a plastic candle. Pastor Lett took those images in quickly; mere seconds had passed.

The little girl looked up at her and smiled. Pastor Lett blanched, she could barely breathe.

The girl mouthed, "Thank you."

Pastor Lett blinked rapidly and swept her eyes toward a movement at the far end of the room. Mrs. Perkinson stood in front of the boarded-up window. Each board appeared to be an oddly integral part of her body. Her hands were clasped in front of her. She nodded, as if in slow motion. A sudden chill whisked through the room, and the woman and child faded away. Pastor Lett remained still, only the ends of her hair moved with the sudden gust of air. Just as suddenly, the chill was gone, swallowed by the walls.

Twenty One

Molly pulled into her driveway to find Steve Moore, the roofing contractor that Cole had hired a few weeks before, sitting in his truck in front of her house. Molly parked her car and walked to the driver's side door. Steve leaned over his clipboard, cell phone pressed tightly against his ear. He held up one finger to Molly. Molly sifted through her memory trying to recall if Cole had mentioned that he'd forgotten to pay him. A moment later, Steve rolled down his window. Even his large truck seemed too small for his six-foot-five frame. He smiled, a kind, open smile that held no pretense or hidden agenda, simply a welcome greeting.

"Sorry, Molly," he said. "Cell phones: you gotta love 'em, you gotta hate 'em." He waved his phone in his enormous hand.

Molly smiled, "What's up, Steve?"

"I came by the other day to check on a leak. I just wanted to make sure that everything was okay, that there were no issues."

Molly told him that they hadn't had any other leaks and that she appreciated his stopping by. On a whim, she turned back and asked, "Steve, do you know anything about the Perkinson family or their house? The one near the lake?"

"Sure, I've worked around here for so many years that there ain't much I don't know. Which is good and bad if you get my drift," he cracked a wicked little smile. "What do you want to know?"

"I don't really know. I just have a funny feeling about the house, that's all."

"It used to be a hotel, and I've heard that it has ghosts, too." He started the engine of his truck.

"What do you know about the ghosts?" Molly asked excitedly.

He laughed. "Well, I don't know them personally, if that's what you mean. I've heard rumors of old Mr. Perkinson walkin' 'round the house, on the grounds, and of the late Mrs. Perkinson sittin' in a rockin' chair, knittin'."

"Really?"

"Well, there were a few stories that went around for a while, but I doubt they were true. Oh, you know how these things go, everything from Lizzie Borden to the Amityville Horror."

Molly looked intrigued.

"I'm not sayin' that it ain't true, I'm just sayin' that I've heard about a daughter who didn't really exist, and a son that was born when they were really old, but I ain't never seen no proof." He looked away, guffawed, "Stories, they grow like trees around here."

"Well, you never know what happened back then."

"You know Newton Carr? He never lets things go undocumented," he rolled his eyes. "He s'posably asked old Chet Perkinson, you know, to validate the facts? Anyway, according to Newton, old Chet Perkinson ain't as *with it* as he used to be. Said the child was never born. So who knows where these stories come from.

"One thing I do know," his voice grew quiet, "they all died in that house, one by one. They didn't believe in no hospitals. It's a wonder old Chet left." Steve paused, then cheerily said, "Speaking of hospitals, I guess you know about the big indoor yard sale up at the private school to benefit Children's Hospital. It's been going on all week. I went up a couple nights ago."

Damn! Molly had forgotten all about it. "How was it?"

"It was great. I saw Newton there. He was picking up a bunch of kids' stuff, probably for his grandkids, pants, shirts, dresses—even bought toys."

Molly recalled the photo of Newton's grandchildren in his living room: two boys, about ten and twelve years old.

Molly made her way inside, lavishing the dogs with soft strokes and kind words before opening the door and letting them romp outside. She thought about Steve's mention of ghosts at the Perkinson House, and wondered if she were chasing a ghost, chasing Amanda's memory. *Maybe Cole's right*, she thought. *Maybe I am trying to right my wrong.* Frustrated, she buried her face in her hands, *It wasn't my fault!* she thought, then she stood up straight and said, "I can't think about this right now." She leaned against the counter looking for a distraction—anything to take her mind off of Amanda. The blinking light on the answering machine fulfilled her wish.

"Hi, Ma, it's me," Molly smiled at his need to announce himself—as if she wouldn't recognize his voice after listening to it for eighteen years. "Did you find the guy yet? Call me. Oh, and Ma, can you put twenty bucks in my account? I'm a little low. Thanks. Love you. Bye." Molly's finger hovered over the delete button, then she quickly pulled away. She knew she was ridiculous, but she always liked to have his voice nearby. Before checking the next message, she pulled out her cell phone and texted Erik, *Got ur msg. Dating money?* She knew the message would cause an eye roll from him. A moment later her cell vibrated with a reply, *Haha.* She smugly resumed checking messages.

The second message was a hang up, and the third was from Officer Brown. "Mrs. Tanner, this is Officer Brown with the Germantown Police Department," his tone was professional, distant. "Just wanted to make sure Sergeant Moeler came by today. Please let me know if he has not yet contacted you."

The message gave Molly pause. Officer Moeler had left hours ago and said he would have to provide the information to Officer Brown for direction. Molly retrieved his card and quickly punched in his phone number—she was redirected to his voice mail.

"Sergeant Moeler—hi," she paced the kitchen nervously. She was not known for her patience, and that trait had caused her trouble in the past. She knew if Cole were there he'd caution her against bothering Sergeant Moeler—but Cole wasn't there. "This is Molly Tanner. You were here this morning to get some information on leads? I just received a message from Officer Brown wondering if you were here yet. So...I'm just wondering what's happening with the notes I gave you. Thanks. I can be reached on my cell. Bye." She hung up the phone and pressed her lips between her teeth, hoping that he wouldn't think she was the nagging type. Her mind shifted, worrying that maybe he was one of those people who said all of the right things but tended to drag their heels unless someone was sitting on them every second. She let out a long, loud breath, "No, Molly, he isn't like that," she said out loud, mocking herself. She grabbed an iced tea from the refrigerator and headed to her computer.

Molly didn't have long to ponder the comfort of her chair before she received a near-frantic phone call from Erik. He wanted to know if she had found the guy that he had told her about.

"No, not yet," Molly answered, "but I'm working on it."

"Mom, you *have* to find him! Soon!"

"I know. I'm trying." Erik's rising anxiety worried her. "What's going on Erik? Why are you so worried?"

"I just have an awful feeling, like, like...we're going to lose her, the little girl. You *need* to find this guy. I can almost feel her slipping away, like...like...hell, like when I was little and I had that box kite at the Cape, remember? And the string slipped through my hands? Remember? And it was like slow motion as it rose in the sky, until we couldn't see it anymore? That's what it feels like, like I knew it was gone forever, and instead of fighting it, I just accepted it."

Molly closed her eyes, remembering the kite he had loved so much. "I'm sorry, Erik. It's all my fault."

"What's your fault?"

"This! Those feelings! You feel it all because of me, who I am, because I have that sixth sense, or whatever it is they call it. If it weren't for me, you wouldn't have to deal with it at all."

"So what? I don't care about what I have to go through. Who cares about that? I just want to find the girl," he said urgently. "Ma, I gotta go. I have a lab this afternoon."

"Okay. I'll call you when I know something."

"'Kay. Love you," he said.

"Love you more." Molly waited to hear the line go dead before she hung up the phone.

Twenty Two

Tracey couldn't tell if today would be a good or bad day for Mummy who was already dressed in jeans, a blue turtleneck, and a blue sweater. Tracey had gotten used to the cool air of their sleeping chamber—the smell, too; she barely noticed it anymore. Now it just seemed like home—like when she'd walk into her grandma's house, and it had a smell all its own.

All morning, Mummy had been busy collecting things in a basket. She had her Bible and other worship books, bottles of water, and the quarters that she had lined up on the top shelf. Tracey remained still under her blanket—partly for warmth and partly because it was fun to peek at what Mummy was doing. She watched Mummy pull two picture frames off of the top shelf. She smiled when she looked at them, then placed them back up on the shelf. She felt sad as Mummy's hand drifted to cover her heart, as if it hurt. Tracey wondered if Mummy missed her mother. Tracey felt a pang in her heart, but tucked it away with annoyance—she still couldn't believe that her own mother hadn't wanted to keep her safe from the toxins that were outside—and what about Emma? Would she die from them? Maybe they were already sick, and that's why her real mom wanted her to be with Mummy. Maybe her real mother set it up so that Tracey would be saved by Mummy.

Tracey reached for her new doll. Tracey held her doll tight against her chest and touched her necklace. She smiled, relieved that it was still there. *Thank God,* she thought and liked the new way that she had come to think of God. She liked thanking Him, knowing He was watching over them.

"Good morning, Tracey," Mummy said sweetly.

Tracey lowered the blanket and smiled, "Morning."

"Guess where we're going today?" Mummy asked, settling herself on the edge of the mattress.

Tracey looked at her, asking with her eyes.

"We're going to see *my* mummy."

A shiver ran up Tracey's back. "But," she said, tentatively, "I thought she was dead."

"She is, honey, but we still go visit her." Mummy handed Tracey the sweater and pants she'd worn the day before and walked to the other end of the chamber. Tracey dressed under the covers to avoid the cold. She wasn't scared of their dirt room anymore. Something had changed inside of her. She now thought of their chamber as warmly as she thought of the cabin in *Little House on the Prairie*—one of her favorite DVDs.

"Tracey, you have to eat a good breakfast today. We're going to do a lot of walking, and I don't want you to get tired."

"Okay," Tracey said.

Mummy busied herself making breakfast. She removed the butter and milk from the little blue Igloo cooler. She prepared the cereal first, set it on the table, and placed one of the three spoons they owned next to it. Tracey tiptoed across the cold dirt floor and hopped onto the upended log, her feet dangling. She began eating and listened to Mummy mumbling her prayers.

Tracey nibbled on the crust of her bread, wondering how she could ask the question that was on her lips. Should she ask? Was it a stupid question? She gathered her courage and asked timidly, "Mummy? How did you learn *how* to talk to God?" She held her breath, unsure if Mummy would be upset that she didn't innately know how to talk to God.

Mummy looked away. The pit of Tracey's stomach suddenly felt heavy. Her courage slipped away like a rumor. "I'm sorry, Mummy," she said. "I didn't mean to make you sad. I'm sorry. I won't do it again." Tears instantly formed in Tracey's eyes, the memory of the bad spot raced through her. She hoped she wouldn't have to go back there. She had done something bad. She had made Mummy upset.

Mummy turned toward Tracey, her mouth set firmly in a thin line. Tracey closed her eyes and readied herself for what was sure to come. Mummy grabbed her by the shoulders, not hard, but strong. Tears streamed down Tracey's cheeks; she'd misread Mummy. She was mad, not sad. She pleaded, her words shaky, fearful, "Mummy, I really am sorry. I didn't mean to—"

Tracey's chest rattled with each hiccupping breath. She felt herself being pulled into Mummy's chest, her head resting on the pillow of her breasts. Mummy's large hand caressed the top of Tracey's hair.

"Shhh," she whispered. "Oh, Tracey, I learned a long, long time ago how to talk to God. I learned before I even came here." She knelt down, her eyes met Tracey's, and she reached up and gently wiped Tracey's tears away. "Take a deep breath, honey," she said. "It's okay."

Tracey slowed her tears and drew in a jagged, hitching breath, confused. "But how did you learn?" she asked in a whisper. "How do you know what to say?" She wanted to make Mummy proud. She wanted to learn to talk to God just like her. Maybe if she prayed hard enough, Emma, Mommy, and Daddy could be saved, too.

"Well," Mummy offered a hand to help Tracey up from her perch, and then gathered the basket that she had filled, "I listened very carefully to what my mummy was saying, and she gave me lessons, too. Every day we studied the Bible. I repeated the words of God until I knew them all by heart—and when I didn't read it right, or I pouted about learning my teachings, I got punished, too. So, you see, Tracey, the bad spot helps you remember what's important, what you need to learn, and how you need to act."

"You did?" Tracey asked, relieved. She sat on the mattress and pulled her socks over her cold feet, then stepped into her boots.

"Yes, I knew that I had to learn how to talk to God the right way in order to be saved. I would read and read, even when we weren't having a lesson. My mummy was very proud of me. Some nights, I read

254

until my eyes stung and all the words on the page just ran together in one big blurry line."

Tracey couldn't imagine reading that much. Tracey would try, but she wasn't very good of a reader yet, and that worried her, but she'd do just about anything to stay out of the bad spot.

"Don't you worry," Mummy said, turning away from Tracey, who had crouched over the chamber pot in the corner of the room. "I'll make sure that you know exactly what to say to God. We have a lifetime together, and many, many years to learn to do it right."

Tracey wiped herself, pulled her pants up, and straightened her sweater. The basket Mummy held now had a lantern and candles in it as well. She carried a backpack over her shoulder, and Tracey wondered what was in it. They must be traveling far, she thought, to need all of those supplies. They were leaving the chamber and entering the first tunnel when Mummy asked Tracey to wait for a second. She headed back toward the chamber, and returned quickly.

"Here," she said, handing Tracey her new doll. "I don't think you want to leave this behind."

Consciousness arrived with the sound of the shower. Molly rolled over in bed and reached for Cole. Her hand flopped across the empty, wrinkled sheets. She sighed, relieved. The tension between them the evening before had been too thick to bear. Cole had hounded her over the threatening note and her determination. She'd escaped the argument by going to bed earlier than he had, and feigning sleep when his head finally hit the pillow. She stretched, throwing her bare legs over the side of the bed and wishing she were still folded neatly away in the dream that she could no longer remember.

She sauntered sleepily toward the bathroom, nervous for the first time in many years, and pushed open the bathroom door; steam greeted her like warm mist from an ocean, clearing the morning chill.

"Hey," she said hesitantly. Cole's silhouette paused behind the shower curtain, then moved once again. He did not respond. Molly turned away, feeling hurt, torn. She brushed her teeth, then turned back toward the shower, mustering courage. She slipped out of Cole's t-shirt and dropped it into the hamper. She parted the shower curtain looking pensive. Cole stared at her, and she'd worried she'd made a mistake. A heartbeat later he reached for her hand and led her gently under the stream of water, falling softly across her breasts and dripping down her legs. He washed her, lovingly caressing every fold of her skin, every dip and curve that was her body. His touch never failed to arouse her, melting away any upsetting thoughts she might have had. He turned her around, slowly soaped her back, and ran his large, strong hands along her bottom, her thighs. Her breath caught. He bent down to soap her calves, kissing her lower back, her sides. He stood, pulling her against him—the spray of the shower binding them like a love song.

Hannah pulled into the parking lot of the Boyds Post Office just as Newton was walking out of the building. She parked her car and hurried over to him. He scanned the parking lot, walking quickly toward his car even as Hannah approached him. "Newton," she called out to him. "Thank you for bringing me all those clothes and things the other day. Carla said that they were just perfect!"

"Oh, it's no problem, Hannah," he said, looking down at the ground, then back up at Hannah. He fidgeted with his hands. "We all have to do what we have to do, right?"

"Yes, I suppose," she said. Hannah felt the weight of the world resting on her shoulders and was thankful that Newton and Carla were there to help her carry the burden.

Newton opened his car door and lowered his elderly body slowly into the driver's seat. Hannah leaned down, whispered, "Do you ever worry, Newton? About…well…you know?" she asked.

Newton put his hands on the steering wheel, gripped it tight, staring straight ahead. He looked up at Hannah for just a second, as if he were going to speak, took a breath, and then looked away again, rolling his lips tightly between his teeth. Hannah was used to his odd mannerisms, his constant state of unease. She also understood his ability to keep silent, as they had decided they would do so long ago. *The pact*, Hannah thought— a silent, unspoken pact, but a pact all the same. She knew she was now breaching that pact. Out of fear? Out of self preservation? She wasn't certain, but for the first time in twenty-some-odd years, she felt the need to be free of it, to be released from the confines of the secrets that had become her life. They had all held up their ends of the bargain, did what they were duty bound to do. It had taken its toll on each of them, first Carla, then Newton filling in when Carla had her crises and had no one else to turn to, and then, her, of course, because who else had Newton known so intimately? Who else had he known for so long that he trusted with his own children? Who else could he possibly have had watch over his wife during her gall bladder operation and subsequent infection? Newton was like a brother to Hannah. More so, in fact—he was like the husband that she'd never had, the one that would have been kind and caring, the one that would never have taken her for granted, screamed at her, or given her up. He'd tended to her in her time of need, reading medical manuals and calling his colleagues in other cities, the ones that he'd known from his military tour, for medical advice, guidance. He was a gracious man, and Hannah knew she had put him in a horrible position, something he would never do to her. As he turned to her to answer, opening his mouth to speak, she interrupted him.

"Wait. I'm sorry, Newton. I didn't mean to...you know...to speak of it. Please, don't say anything. Somehow if we do, it makes it more real, more difficult. What we're doing seems so right, most of the time. Yet sometimes, it seems so very wrong." She watched his eyes hunt for something, his mind formulating an answer, an apology maybe? Again, she stopped him.

"Newton, it's rhetorical. Keep your peace." Hannah turned to leave and felt his hand gently touch her arm.

"Hannah," he said, his eyes apologizing, empathizing, agreeing with her thoughts. Newton sat nervously, opening his mouth as if to speak, then closing it again. "You are a good woman, Hannah. Charlie was a fool." He looked up and said, "What we've done? It's been necessary."

Though she knew he was right, she wondered, as she had so many times before, how and why she could have let herself become involved in such a life of deception.

Molly ran past the old Victorians on White Ground Road. She slowed as she came to the manse, the house where Rodney Lett had been beaten. She stopped in front of the ordinary-looking red brick house. It was not much different than the others on the street, though notably the only brick Victorian. Molly knew the idea that pressed her forward was probably not a good one, but she let her legs carry her across the street and to the rear of the property. The back of the house was also quite typical, save for the windows—three stories high with ornamental, old wavy-glassed panes. Three steps led to a small screened porch. The screening, stretched and gapped, as if it had been pushed out from the inside and pulled tightly in other places. The stairs were constructed of 2x8 pieces of wood, gray with age, streaked with fine lines, yet sturdy. The door to the porch was made of plywood and screen and had a small, rusty metal handle, which Molly drew open, cringing at the sound of the door creaking. She stepped cautiously onto the porch, eyeing the newer window to her left, wondering if it was the window that the attackers had broken through. She put her hand flat against the cool glass, surprised that she wasn't met with some sort of energy—there was no vision snaking its way from the glass to her body. She leaned forward and cupped her hands against the window, peering into the kitchen. Surely the interior of the home would have changed since the Lett murder, the floors would have been refinished, the walls repainted. Molly thought about the odd couple who lived there now. Who could move into a home that had such a ghastly event take place within its walls? She went back to the steps and looked around at the small green yard. Molly rubbed her arms against the cold air that had broken through the heat of her perspiration. She rounded the house and looked up when she reached the road. Pastor Lett stood across the street in front of the church, glaring at Molly.

Molly jogged up the hill that ran between the two cornfields next to the church, heading toward the campground. Blood pumped hard through her body, driven by adrenaline—a nice side effect from her visit to the manse. She caught her breath at the top of the hill, letting her eyes drift across the fields, down toward the main road, and over the rooftops of the encroaching neighborhoods. Through the gap of trees just beyond the neighborhoods, she realized, must be the Adventure Park. A brief second of sadness swept through her as she thought of Tracey. She glanced in the direction of the Perkinson House. The tips of the turrets were barely visible.

Molly jogged the remaining length of the path and down the slope to the inner circle of the campground. The wind slipped through the trees, making eerie, scratching sounds as branches and leaves commingled. The surrounding trees were imposing, as if they had wrapped their branches around the secluded site and were protecting it from outsiders. Molly walked to the wooden box closest to the path where she had found the candy wrapper. She waited for the taste of apple candy to return, simultaneously relieved and discouraged when it did not. She laid her palm against the rough splintering wood on the outside of the box, the ridges and grooves filled the soft creases of her hand. She waited, hoping for the Knowing to take hold.

CHASING AMANDA

She closed her eyes and opened her mind, willing it to come forward, to bring details of Tracey's whereabouts. The sound of the wind whispering through the trees swirled around her, the crackling of leaves scattering across the ground created an eerie accompaniment, but she experienced no other sensation. There was no tingling, no fading vision, not even so much as a single goose bump on her skin. She felt bare, hollow— disillusioned.

Molly withdrew her hand, the T scar still blending neatly into her palm. "Damn," she said, looking up at the sky. "Come on, damn it!" she said through clenched teeth. "I know there is something here!" she pleaded. "Just show me the way, I'll do the rest." Her arms and legs shook from the cold. Her undergarments stuck to her skin, wet with sweat, her forehead beaded with perspiration. She jogged around the edges of the campsite, around and around she ran, warming her body and trying to piece together the puzzle of the area. She moved to each box, placing her palm flat against the side, anxiously waiting, hoping for a sign, something to give her pause. When there was no sensation, she lifted each lid, as she had before, and scrutinized the interior. The weight of the lids mirrored the heaviness of her heart. Molly's frustration grew. She paced the campsite racking her brain with what-ifs. Not for the first time in her life, she wished she could control the Knowing, demand that it come forth, as she'd been able to in the police station.

Molly sighed heavily, defeated. Anger rose in her chest, pushing tears from her eyes. Molly hated when she cried, feeling like a weak child. She sucked in a deep breath of the cold air and sprinted up the incline and down the path toward the church. She ran right onto

White Ground Road, hoping the Knowing would find her there. She pushed her ear buds into place and ran to the rhythm, fast and hard.

They had been walking so long that Tracey's legs ached. Weaving in and out of the tunnels confused her, but the metal tracks that appeared in the tunnels farthest from where they slept were more bothersome than the pain in her legs. She had to step in the narrow path between the tracks. Every few steps Tracey would forget to watch her feet and the side of her foot would slip into the crevice along the track, causing her ankle to twist a little. She had no idea how Mummy could walk between the tracks so easily with her huge feet—she never slipped into the crack. Each time they passed an entrance, a hole cut through the dirt wall, Tracey peeked to see if it led to a room or another tunnel. They were all pitch black, until Mummy lifted the lantern and light flowed in, revealing what lay beyond. Tracey thought of each area that wasn't a tunnel as a room, even though most were no bigger than the size of a closet. A few of them were larger—not as large as their sleeping place, but large enough to have a few rectangular carts stored side by side. The carts were old and dirty with rusty metal and dented sides resting upon a wide base of aged and scarred wood. Tracey was taken with the eight small wheels under the carts, four on either side. She had wanted to play with the carts, take one back with them to their sleeping area—she thought it might make a good doll carriage, even if it was a little heavy—but Mummy had said no. She said she had asked her mother the same thing when she'd first come to the tunnels, long before her mother had died.

Tracey lifted her doll to her chest and hugged it. She had sort of forgotten that she was carrying the doll. She had dragged it part of the way, and now the doll's toes were brown with dirt. She twisted her body from side to side, as if nervously rocking the doll. "I'm sorry your mom died," she said. Tracey had heard adults say they were sorry when they talked about someone who was sick, and she thought it was the perfect time to use what she had learned.

"It's okay," she said. "We had a lot of fun together." She turned to Tracey and smiled.

"But she was sick."

"She was sick. She told me that she was born sick, and that I wasn't, so I wouldn't have to worry about getting sick." She stretched her long arms out to her sides, almost touching each side of the dirt room. "Healthy as can be! And you are, too, little missy." She tapped the tip of Tracey's nose lightly with her index finger. Tracey giggled.

"Thank you," Tracey said.

"For what?"

"For saving me. I'm glad I won't get sick and die."

"Well, everyone dies, Tracey. You know that, right?" she asked.

"I know, but not until they're really, really old, usually. Like my one grandma? She's really old and she's still alive." Tracey twisted her doll's hair. "Hey, how come the toxins didn't kill her?" she asked.

"Because they don't kill everyone. Sometimes people are just fine, but I had to make sure that you weren't one of the ones that got sick," she smiled. "Remember when we used to play at the park?"

"Yes," Tracey remembered the two of them playing tag around the big castle.

"Well, I knew you were just the type of little girl that I should save, someone just like me."

Tracey cocked her head and looked at Mummy, wondering in what ways they were alike. *She is big, and I am little. She doesn't have a mom anymore, and I did, do*, she thought.

"You and I, we got along so well, Tracey." Mummy rested her arm around Tracey's shoulders. "I knew that you should be saved. I saw how much fun your mom had with Emma and how sometimes you looked really sad. I didn't want you to be sad. I knew you deserved to be happy, to be saved."

Tracey couldn't speak. A giant lump expanded in her throat, tears burned the back of her eyes. She missed Emma and her mother. She missed playing with them. She missed their breakfasts together and the way she and Emma used to stick together when they were bored. She even missed when she used to fight with Emma. Tracey tried not to cry, and Mummy drew her in close.

"It's all right, Tracey." She stroked Tracey's back, her hair, just like Tracey's own mother used to. "It's okay to be sad sometimes. I'm sad sometimes, too. My mummy is gone, too, remember?"

Tracey nodded, sniffling back the tears.

"But now I have you!" she stood up and held Tracey's hand. "You'll see, Tracey. You'll see how much I can teach you about God and how to talk to Him. You'll see how much fun we'll have—and when you're a little bigger, I'll even let you play with the carts!"

Tracey smiled.

They walked for what seemed to Tracey to be forever. She asked Mummy if she thought there was gold in the tunnels, and she stared at the ground, hoping to be lucky enough to see a shiny nugget of gold. The tracks had become deeper set in the ground, almost even with the dirt. Mummy slowed her pace, eventually stopping and settling her backpack on the ground.

"Tracey," she said, "to get to where my mummy is, we have to go down a long, dark, narrow tunnel—much narrower than what we've been in before. It's a little scary, but when we get to the end, it's beautiful, like a garden." She knelt before Tracey and stared into her eyes. She looked like she was mad, but her voice was sweet. "I need you to stay right with me, okay? I need for you to be quiet, too, as we enter her resting place. Do you understand?"

Tracey nodded, fear and excitement swirling in her belly. She wanted to see the garden. She wanted to be outside. A worried look crossed her face. "What about the toxins?" her voice shook.

"There are no toxins where we're going, only a great big, deep well."

Tracey reached for her necklace, calming herself. "Okay," she whispered.

"I mean it, Tracey. You need to stay with me. Don't get too scared, don't try to run away. I'll keep you safe." She pulled her against her chest. Her hair swept the top of Tracey's head, her arms held her so tightly that Tracey was sure Mummy could feel her heart pounding.

She put her arms around Mummy and looked up at her. Mummy's dark hair was like a curtain around her face. "I promise, Mummy. I'll be good," Tracey said, and she meant it. She wanted to make Mummy proud. She wanted to be safe.

"That's my girl. I knew I could trust you! That's why I gave you the necklace—to show you how much you mean to me."

Tracey fingered the cool gold chain.

The tunnels closed in on them, becoming narrower with each step, until they were barely able to fit Mummy's body without her turning sideways.

"Mummy, I'm scared," Tracey clutched her doll in one hand and clung to the back of Mummy's sweater with the other.

"I know, pumpkin. Just stay with me. We're almost there," she answered.

Tracey concentrated on the back of Mummy, a mantra running through her head, *We're almost there. We're almost there.* Her feet moved fast, shuffling across the ground, three steps to every one of Mummy's.

Suddenly Mummy turned around and whispered, "Do not move."

Tracey became rigid. She moved her head to the side, looking around Mummy, and eyed the opening at the end of the tunnel. Mummy peered in, moving just the top of her body forward. She lifted the lantern, illuminating an enormous cavern carved into the earth. The floor, covered with wood chips and rotted chunks of logs, was also, surprisingly, covered with plants and flowers—white flowers with yellow middles, blue and red flowers, big orange flowers. The garden before them seemed unreal, unimaginable in a place where there was no sunlight, no water.

Candles rested on dirt-carved shelves throughout, shrine-like. Mummy moved slowly forward. Tracey tried to follow, but she stood mesmerized, watching her captor move from candle to candle, lighting each one, and with each flame came a harder beat of Tracey's heart. The flames from the candles threw dancing shadows on walls that were littered with white drawing papers and old newspapers, torn and nailed directly into the dirt. Tracey leaned forward, trying to discern the scribble, unable to make out the words drawn before her.

Mummy prayed as her match dimmed, "Place me like a seal over your heart, like a seal on your arm; for love is as strong as death, its jealousy unyielding as the grave. It burns like blazing fire, like a mighty flame." She turned slowly toward Tracey. "Now, my God, may your eyes be open and your ears attentive to the prayers offered in this place."

The smell of must and incense filled the room. The candles flickered, as if there were a draft, though Tracey could not feel one. Tracey turned big, wondrous eyes toward Mummy, who walked toward her, silently taking her hand.

"Follow me," she whispered, "but don't say a word, okay?"

Tracey nodded fast and hard, wanting to figure out the big, magical chamber. Mummy walked her to the center of the room.

"Wow," slipped from Tracey's lips. Mummy squeezed her hand, giving her a stern look.

She turned Tracey around. Tracey gasped, taking a big step backward, afraid she'd fall into the deep dark hole that looked to her like a big evil eye. Mummy dropped Tracey's hand, and in that split second, Tracey wondered if she was in trouble. Mummy bent down, resting her knees on the plush green below them. Tracey followed. Mummy put her hands in a praying position, and Tracey did the same.

"The Lord is my rock, my fortress, and my deliverer; my God is my rock, in whom I take refuge, my shield and the horn of my salvation," she began. "He is my stronghold, my refuge and my savior—from violent men You save me. I call to the Lord, who is worthy of praise, and I am saved from my enemies." She reached out and took Tracey's hand in her own. "We listened, oh Lord, we took heed in your direction; 'Follow my decrees and be careful to obey my laws, and you will live safely in the land. Then the land will yield its fruit, and you will eat your fill and live there in safety.'"

Mummy's hand was warm and strong. Tracey darted her eyes, looking at the flowers—the sound of their breathing, the only rhythm in the room. Mummy let go of Tracey's hand, and Tracey quickly closed her eyes tight, unsure if she would be in trouble, unsure if she should have kept them closed. Mummy touched her arm, gently, beckoning them open again. She reached in her pocket and withdrew the quarters she had brought with them. She kissed each one of them, tossing them gently into the hole, one by one. Tracey listened for the soft *Plink!* as they hit the water, but it never came, almost as if they had disappeared into thin air, like magic.

"Tracey," she whispered, "this is where my mummy is." She lifted her chin toward the hole. "We bring the quarters as an offering to God—to repay Him for all that he does for us."

Tracey barely heard the last sentence, she was too focused on the first. "In there?" she asked.

"Yes. This is our holy well. God has blessed this well with fortune and riches. You see, my mummy was…well…sort of magical."

Tracey's eyes grew wide.

"She could put spells on things and make things happen."

"Why didn't she just make herself well then?" Tracey asked, confused.

"She couldn't change the path of people's lives like that. If God had decided to make a person sick, well, she couldn't really go against his wishes and change that. She tried to make sick people well, but it wasn't to be."

Mummy turned around then, stood up, and motioned around the room. "Look around you. Look what she's created: Life. She's created life where there was none." She moved slowly across the carpet of greenery. "She once brought me a book on plants. These are like the orchids of the genus *Lecanorchis* or *Galeola* type. I remember reading about them. Or what was the other one called?" She looked around, like she was trying to pull the answer out of the air. "Oh yeah!" she exclaimed. "*Pyrolaceae* of the genus *Monotropastrum*! They're called saprophytes."

"Sapro what?" Tracey asked.

"Saprophytes. They're plants that don't need sunlight because they rely on dead plant or animal residue to live, like from decaying wood." She bent down and picked up a chunk of rotting wood. "See? Like these. As they rot, the plants eat them. I think that's how they work anyway."

Tracey bent down and smelled the white flowers, "Mm, they smell like spring!"

Mummy pointed to the walls, "Do you see these symbols and drawings?"

Tracey nodded.

"She made these, too. They represent passages from her own Bible. See her writing, here?" she pointed to one of the papers. "She wrote her spells to keep the plants alive. See? She told me, once, that the flowers would live on forever, marking the Earth where she last stepped." She walked around the room with her arms spread wide, a smile on her face. "She came here in the days before she died and danced. She danced all around the ground, then she blessed the seeds of these plants and told me to plant them all—every last one of them." Tracey listened, spellbound. "So, I did as I was told, and a few days later, when Mummy died, they each came to life. Can you believe it?" she asked.

"It sounds like a fairy tale!" Tracey said, excited.

"The Lord keeps them for us, so we will always remember her, remember her spirit, remember to dance when the end is near. Remember that if God's will is for you to be with Him, then that's where you shall go, and you shall accept it." She smiled, touching each plant as if they were precious gifts.

"But...you put your mom in a well? Isn't that kind of...mean?" Tracey asked cautiously.

"It wasn't mean at all, actually. That's where she wanted to be. She chose this place. She told me exactly what to do with her body so the Lord would accept her, and I followed her wishes, and I hope you will do the same for me."

"Where did she go?"

"She went into the water, into her burial place. She's still in there."

A chill ran up Tracey's spine.

"The well is so deep that even when I put my mummy in, I could barely hear her hit the water. It was as if she became a spirit before she actually landed."

"I don't know if I could do that," Tracey said, stepping further away from the hole.

"It was what she wanted. It wasn't a bad thing." She put her hand on Tracey's shoulder and bent down to look her in the eye. "Tracey, when someone is buried, they are put in the ground, right?"

Tracey nodded.

"Well, my mummy was put in the ground, too, only she has water which is better. She won't have animals and bugs all over her. She's just here, safe, with us. There's no one to walk over her grave, no snow to make her bones cold. This is a good place, not a bad place. It's what she wanted."

"Oh," Tracey said, although she still wasn't sure she could ever put someone in a hole. "Were you with her when she....when she died?" she asked.

"Oh, yes, until the very end. I held her hand and sang to her." She smiled, rubbed Tracey's hand. "We prayed a lot, asking the Lord to accept her, to take care of her, and to watch over me. When she died, she was happy. She closed her eyes like she was sleeping and just didn't wake up." She stopped rubbing Tracey's hand and held it in her own. "After she died, I prayed for her soul to be accepted by the Lord. I prayed that she would always be with me," she covered her heart with her hand, "here, inside me, and I know she is. I can feel her. She's beautiful."

"You're beautiful, too," Tracey said, shyly.

Mummy reached out and took Tracey in her arms again, hugging her tightly against her, sharing her strength with her. The embrace felt good to Tracey, it felt right. She hugged her back.

Twenty Three

Molly ran much further than she'd anticipated, rounding out the three-mile loop down Barnesville Road, and heading toward the Country Store, giving a quick wave to the passing cars that veered to the opposite lane to give her room to run. The lack of a shoulder on the rural roads was hazardous, and Molly appreciated the kindness of the drivers. She picked up her pace as she ran down the final hill, passing in front of the Country Store, where Edie stood in the window wearing a strange look of dismay. The Boyds Boys sat out front.

"Hey, guys!" Molly yelled, waving.

Harley turned away, Mac looked down, and Joe began to lift his arm, then, with a quick nudge from Mac, he lowered it and looked down at his feet. Molly was becoming increasingly annoyed by their behavior and began to wonder if there was more to their reputations than met the eye. Her run came to a halt at the bottom of the road where fire trucks and police vehicles blocked the entrance to the Perkinson driveway and lined the road near the lake. The grassy areas were roped off. Yellow tape, announcing, *Police Area Do Not Cross,* hung from the thick ropes. Molly ran across the road and sidled up to one of the officers wearing not only his uniform but an orange traffic vest as well. He looked to be about Molly's age, dark hair, graying at the temples, and a pinched face.

"Hi," she said, waiting for him to acknowledge her.

He looked over and down, his blue eyes settling on her, annoyed. "Ma'am," he said. His mouth quickly formed a fine line across his face.

"Excuse me, but can you tell me what's going on?"

"We've got divers in the lake, ma'am."

A helicopter hovered overhead. "For what?" she asked. Molly instantly thought of Hannah kneeling over the ground in the woods.

"Looking for a missing party, ma'am," he said, sternly.

"Does this have to do with the little girl who is missing, Tracey Porter?"

"I can't say, ma'am. We're checking the lake."

"So you think she's in there?" Molly crunched her face, as if protecting herself from hearing the news.

"Just doing our jobs, ma'am."

"The helicopter?" she asked. "Is that part of the investigation as well?"

"Yes, ma'am. It has heat-seeking devices. They can track bodies in the water." He planted his hands on his hips, rigid.

Molly realized how annoying it must be for him to answer questions like hers over and over. "Thank you," she said and began jogging toward her car. She turned on her heels and said, "Sir?"

He reluctantly turned toward her.

"How long does something like this take?"

"Not sure, ma'am. Could take a full day or even two depending on what they do or don't find."

"Thank you again," she said and continued jogging.

Molly settled into the van and let her head fall into her hands. Tears burst forward as if they had been trapped behind a dam that had suddenly cracked. Her body shook with sobs. *How could this be happening again?* she wondered. She pounded on the dashboard, "She's not dead," she said to the rearview mirror. "I would know. I would have felt it."

Molly sat in her car for hours, watching the divers come up empty handed, the helicopter hover and dip, spraying water like scattering bugs. A crowd of spectators had gathered at different points around the lake. Finally, at around five P.M., the divers were out of the water, the helicopter had flown off to the south, and Molly made her way back to the officer with the graying temples and the traffic vest.

She tapped him on the back, noting his surprised look when his eyes settled on her once again. "Well?" she asked.

"Ma'am? You're still here?"

"Yes. Did they find her?"

"No, ma'am, they didn't."

Molly's heart skipped a beat of hope, and she was sure she saw a faint smile in the officer's eyes.

"For sure?" she asked cautiously.

"For sure," he nodded, laying his hand on her shoulder, heavy, reassuring. "She's not here, ma'am. That much we know."

Molly turned away without a word. She didn't realize she was crying until she climbed back into the van and looked in the mirror.

Molly arrived to a darkened home, Cole's car in the driveway. She called to him when she opened the front door, the dogs vied for her attention. Soft music sifted through the quiet. She followed the sound to the candlelit dining room. Molly put her backpack down and headed upstairs, "Cole?"

No response.

The shower ran in the bedroom, and Molly hurried in and gathered a black sweater, jeans, and clean undergarments, then raced into Erik's shower to rinse off. A few minutes later she was greeted at the bottom of the stairs by Cole, who held a glass of White Zinfandel in one hand, extending the other toward her.

"I thought you could use a little relaxation," he said, kissing her cheek.

"You have no idea how much," she took the wineglass and came down to the bottom riser, almost eye-to-eye with Cole. He stood so close that she could taste the toothpaste on his breath. "Hi," she whispered.

He kissed her, softly, on the lips. "Hi," he said, leaning his head to hers.

They stood that way for a long moment, forehead to forehead, toes to shins—not an uncomfortable silence, but a testing of the waters.

"Thanks for doing all this," she said, making her way to the dining room.

"I didn't," he said. He disappeared into the kitchen only to return carrying sashimi, California rolls, and sushi arranged artistically on one tray, salad and miso soup on another. "Tsukiji's did," he smiled.

They sat quietly for a few minutes, sipping their wine and letting the stress of the day dissolve, until Molly couldn't stand it anymore, she had to talk about what she'd seen. She asked him if he'd seen the fire trucks, which he had. They discussed how scared Tracey's parents must have been, and Molly told him of her feeling that she would have known if Tracey were dead. Molly saw the stress return to Cole's eyes.

"I know what you're thinking," she said, carefully. "This isn't Philly, and she's not Amanda. We've been over this," she looked away, pained. "I couldn't help her. But maybe I can help Tracey."

"I don't know how you make it through each day as wrapped up as you are in all of this," he said, his voice rising. "I can barely make it through my own stuff, and here you are gallivanting around town trying to do the police officers' jobs."

"I'm not trying to do their jobs," Molly said, playing with her chopsticks. "I just feel…compelled to help find her. I know you think it's weird, or twisted, or whatever you think, but there's something there, Cole," she said defensively. "There's something that won't *let* me let go of this search. It pulls on my mind whether I'm concentrating on it or not. It's like…it's like it's pleading with me to figure it out."

"I know you *feel* that way," he said, dismissively, a little sarcastically. "That's how it starts, and soon you'll be wandering around the house unable to find any direction to your days, and wondering where you went wrong."

277

"Thanks for the vote of confidence." They stared at each other from opposite ends of their beliefs, neither having the ability to change the other. Molly's need to find Tracey and Cole's need to bring her to her senses hovered in the air as if caught in the silk from a spider's thread, fragile, yet unyielding.

The phone rang, and Molly jumped up to answer it, relieved by the distraction. Cole turned away, annoyed. She was met with an unfamiliar foreign voice.

"Who's this?" Molly said cautiously.

"Edie. From store."

"Edie?" It took a moment for Molly to reconcile the voice and name with the Boyds Country Store.

Edie spoke fast, her voice carried a hint of fear. "I want to talk to you. You meet me?"

"Sure, Edie. I'll come by the store tomorrow," Molly said, thinking it odd that Edie would call her.

"No. Not store. You meet me at Blue Fox. One hour." It was not a question.

The line went dead.

The restaurant was an inconspicuous little brick rambler with brown shutters, a brown roof, and a small wooden deck out front, adorned with several small wrought-iron tables and chairs. Molly walked in, still wrestling with Cole's last comment as she'd walked out the door, *You didn't kill Amanda, Molly, but you may be killing us*. It took a minute for Molly's eyes to adjust to the dim light. The flames of small candles in shot glasses rose from the center of each small empty table and flickered with the change in air as she closed the door. An older, thin man wearing a tattered vest that looked like it had seen better days, stood behind a small bar, just feet in front of the entrance. Molly smiled at him. He grimaced, whipped a white cloth napkin off of his shoulder, and began wiping down the bar.

Molly turned at the sound of an uneven gait. A small, hunched-over woman walked through a swinging door with black letters that read, *Kit hen*. She wore an apron around her thick waist, and a red and white polyester dress that was made not a day earlier than the bartender's vest. On her tiny feet she wore black shoes and white socks. Molly felt as though she had stepped back in time into some small rural establishment of years past, before electricity, before fashion. The woman stood before Molly, a scowl on her face, her head the height of Molly's chin. Her back was bent in such a way that she could not look up at Molly without twisting her entire body to the left, which she did. Molly smiled. The woman did not smile back.

"This way," the woman directed, gruffly.

Molly wondered how the business remained open with such a gloomy environment and less-than-stellar service.

"Excuse me," Molly said, politely.

The woman stopped walking, and Molly almost tripped over her. She twisted her body up towards Molly again, scowling.

"I'm sorry," Molly said gently, "but I'm meeting someone here."

The woman made a guttural sound, turned around with difficulty, scuttled back to the table next to the door, snagged another menu, and, mumbling, trudged back toward Molly, then right past her. "Come on," she said gruffly, motioning for Molly to follow.

Molly suddenly saw the comedy in the scene and stifled a laugh. The table she was led to was one of six. The square wooden table rocked with the weight of

Molly's elbow. Headlights flashed through the front window of the restaurant. A moment later, the front door swung open, and Edie stepped in, a black hat covering her dark hair. Sunglasses and a brown knit coat completed her disguise.

"Edie, don't you think the sunglasses are overkill?" Molly joked. Edie approached the table.

Edie glanced suddenly and suspiciously behind her. She took off her coat and sunglasses but left her hat pulled tightly down over her head. "I didn't want to take a chance. Didn't want no one to recognize me," she said.

"Well, there isn't anyone here," Molly pointed out. "I think you've picked the one restaurant that throws you back in time."

Edie looked at the bartender, who continued washing the glasses, but lifted his chin in a slight greeting.

The old woman returned to the table. "Drinks," she said in a monotone.

Molly ordered water with lemon and Edie ordered tea. The woman turned around without acknowledgement and hobbled away. A moment later she hobbled back out with the drinks.

Edie ran her finger around the rim of her mug, avoiding Molly's eyes.

"Edie, what's going on?" Molly asked.

She didn't answer. She looked down, and then, slowly, up at Molly. "I should not tell you," Edie said, sipping her tea and looking away.

"Should not tell me what?" Molly asked, becoming annoyed at the cat and mouse game.

Edie stared blankly at the table and said with no emotion, "I wrote notes. I pay girl to call you."

Molly's jaw dropped. "Why?"

Edie continued looking down, avoiding Molly's accusatory gaze.

"Edie, I just don't understand." She was becoming angry. "If you know something that might help Tracey, you have to tell me! There's a little girl's life on the line," Molly pleaded.

Edie's gaze held both fear and hope. She took Molly's hand in her own trembling one. "You no understand, Molly," she began. "There are many people's lives at stake here, not just Tracey." She bowed her head and mumbled something in Korean, then released Molly's hand.

"Edie," Molly said, frustrated. "Why are we here? Who are we hiding from?"

Edie made a low growling sound. "Jin must not know I'm here," she said, firmly. "Ever!"

"Okay, okay," Molly held her hands up in surrender.

"Many years ago," she began, her hands clenched around her mug, "a very bad thing happened, a very, very bad thing."

"Rodney's murder?"

She nodded. "Rodney, Kate, it was all very bad. Rodney did not kill that girl." She paused, "He did not hurt that girl. He did not take that girl. He did not."

"I hear you," Molly said.

"Rodney was a good boy. No trouble to anyone. He just…different." She gave Molly a knowing look. "You know this, Molly. You know why he different."

"Yes," Molly said. "He was slow."

"No, no, no!" Edie hit the table with her fist. "Not because he slow!" Her dark eyes pierced Molly's like daggers, a vehemence Molly had never before seen in Edie, alarming her. "He *different* like *you*," she said with conviction.

"Wait, Edie, what do you mean?" Molly's heart raced, her eyes darted from Edie to the bartender and back.

"*Different*. You know, Molly. *Different*," she accused.

Molly tried to laugh it off. "We're all different, Edie. What does that have to do with Rodney?"

"I *know*," she tapped her temple with her index finger. "I know about you. You like Rodney. You *know* things."

Molly stood, nervously pacing, crossing and uncrossing her arms. Her movement caused the old woman to walk toward them. Molly held her palm up, staving her off. She took a deep breath and rejoined Edie.

"Okay, so you know. How?" she asked.

Edie stared at Molly, silently tapping her temple.

Molly felt as though her life had become a comic strip—this was some type of sick joke.

"Something about you…just like Rodney," Edie said.

"Great. He's dead." Molly threw her body against the back of her chair, her arms crossed tightly across her chest. "That gets us nowhere."

"Rodney knew about Kate Plummer," she said. "He knew things about where she was."

"I know that, Edie. That's not new."

"He only knew some details, not all of it. But the two of you," she looked at Molly, "together, you might know about the girl."

"What does that mean, Edie? He and I can't do anything together. He's dead."

Edie folded her trembling hands in her lap, and spoke in a hushed voice. "Rodney is only one that can help."

"Edie," Molly said, exasperated.

Edie leaned forward, "What I tell you, you no hear from me."

"Okay," Molly said, believing she'd found someone crazier than herself.

"You no tell anyone. You no tell Jin," she said Jin's name with a faltering, quivering voice.

"I promise, Edie," Molly said.

Edie looked around, as if expecting someone to suddenly show up, catching her in the act of telling her secret. "Rodney didn't take her. He just saw her, here," she pointed to her head. "People think he took her, think he hurt her, because police take him in."

"That's why they killed him," Molly nodded.

"Yes, beat him."

"Awful," Molly said, sadly.

"His sister take him away, back home. She take him that night. Pack him in the car and go, before he got more hurt."

Molly perched on the edge of her seat, *More hurt?*

"His sister take him to Delaware, but his parents no want him. Too much trouble. They—"

"Wait!" Molly interrupted. "He was dead. What do you mean *too much trouble*?"

"He no dead. He almost dead, still breathing."

"What?" Molly said incredulously.

"He no die," Edie said.

"He lived? Rodney is alive?" Molly was in disbelief.

Edie nodded.

283

"He might be able to lead us to Kate's body," Molly said anxiously.

"No!" she said, thumping the table again with her fist. "He no involved!"

Molly grabbed Edie's hand. "Edie, you have to help me. If Rodney knew things, maybe you're right, maybe together we can find Tracey and figure out what happened to Kate."

Edie suddenly looked five years older than she did when she had walked into the restaurant. "I don't know where he is," she said.

"Damn it, Edie, come on," Molly said loudly. "What are you worried about? You must know where he is."

Edie shook her head. "If police find him, they arrest him again. Or worse, Rodney beat again," she hissed.

"I won't tell the police, Edie. I promise," Molly pleaded, her mind raced through the possible outcome: finding Kate's body.

Edie looked around the restaurant nervously. Molly urged her again, using Edie's own thoughts, that together, Molly and Rodney could find Tracey. Finally, Edie conceded. "Very dangerous, you involved, Molly. Very dangerous." She looked down at her tea once again, "Pastor Lett, she know where to find Rodney. I not see Rodney. I just know he alive."

The Perkinson House, Molly thought, remembering the locks on the windows and the sensation of the strong hands upon her own at the cellar doors. Molly knew that she would not keep her promise to Edie. She had to call Sergeant Moeler.

"Why, why, why?" Pastor Lett sobbed, repeatedly hitting the back of the couch with her fisted hand. She raised her arms toward the ceiling, "Why? Why do I have to go through this again?" She paced, frustrated, saddened once again by the ghost of a brother she once had, once cherished, and still loved. She knew what she had to do. She'd seen Molly in the woods, spying on her. She gathered her store of empty boxes, pulled on her overcoat and gloves, and picked up the phone.

Hannah's voice was soft, tired, as if she were on the edge of sleep and had been brought back to wakefulness, "Hannah, it's Carla. I'm sorry to bother you so late."

"What's wrong, Carla?"

"We need to talk. Can we meet at your house, right away?" she asked, urgently.

"Yes, yes, of course. Are you going to call, or shall I?"

"I will. Just be ready. We need to move fast." She was thankful for Hannah's lack of questions. She hung up the phone and dialed again.

"Newton, it's Carla. We have an issue. Trouble."

"Carla? Okay, yes. Um, where?"

"Hannah's house. I'll meet you there." She hung up before hearing Newton's reply.

As Pastor Lett drove through the empty streets of Boyds, she felt as though she were being watched through the darkened windows of the homes she passed. She went by Molly's house, and she envisioned her stewing over the whole situation. She couldn't blame her for wanting to find Tracey. She didn't like to have harsh feelings towards others, but she was hurt, maddened even—seeing her at her house in the middle of the night, then at the manse. The pastor side of her wondered how she would get past the ill feelings that brewed within her to find her way to forgiveness.

Newton's car was already in Hannah's driveway when she arrived. She rushed up the back steps. The dogs barked as she rapped three times on the door with her gloved hand. Hannah's tense face greeted her, her dark brown hair piled in a loose bun on her head. She guided her silently to the parlor where Newton sat fidgeting with his keys, his Members Only jacket zipped right up to his chin.

"Thank you for meeting me," Pastor Lett said quickly. "We have an issue, or at least, I think we might have an issue. I'm not certain, but just in case, I think we need to move swiftly." They eyed one another seriously.

"What is it, Carla? What's happened?" Hannah folded her hands in her lap.

"Molly Tanner's been snooping around," she paced nervously, "asking about Rodney." She poured a cup of tea from the silver pot that Hannah had set out for them, and took a slow sip. The warmth of the liquid calmed her nerves.

"Molly?" asked Hannah. "Why would Molly ask about Rodney? I just don't understand." She adjusted her sweatshirt, flustered.

"Why, she'd have no reason not to trust you," Newton said, quickly.

"I don't think she's causing trouble, really, but I want to take precautions."

"Carla, what exactly are you worried about?" Hannah asked.

Pastor Lett stood and walked behind Hannah's Victorian sofa, looking out the window, running her hand through her hair, then down her face, trying to figure out exactly what she *was* worried about. She returned to the sofa and sat down, bracing her hands on her knees. "I don't know," her words were rushed, frustrated. "I'm worried that they'll search the Perkinson House." She ejected a sigh of relief. She'd finally said it, after all of those years of hiding behind each other's glances, behind the safety of their carefully-executed stories. It had been released, laid naked on the table before them.

"The Perkinson House?" Hannah asked.

"She saw me, one night, when I had rowed over there."

"Oh, Carla," Newton said, fidgeting with his hands. "This is bad, real bad. What are we going to do? After all these years. The Perkinsons trusted you. We have to do something." He spoke quickly, as if the taste of the words would cause him pain.

"I know that, Newton!" Carla said sharply. "We need to go there, to make sure the cellar is secure, and, if they get a search warrant, to make sure there are no....holes for them to find."

"Yes, yes, right. We need to go right now." Newton stood to leave.

"What should I bring?" Hannah asked.

"No, Hannah, you stay here. It's late and cold. I don't want you out there in this weather. Besides, Carla and I can handle this," Newton said, protectively.

"Nonsense, Newton. I'm coming, and that's that. Now, what do we need?" Her hands on her hips told him that she had made up her mind.

"I'm really sorry that I got you two involved in this," Carla said thoughtfully. "It was wrong of me."

"Nonsense," Hannah snapped. "We have to watch out for one another." She and Newton exchanged a knowing glance.

Newton lowered his eyes. "Yes, yes we do. Carla, you couldn't have done this on your own. Why, you had to rely on us." He picked up the one large box he had been carrying and nervously changed the subject, "Well, um, let's move on, shall we?"

Pastor Lett asked Hannah for supplies, "Extra food and water. Anything that you think the kid will need over the next week or so, just in case they watch the house, and we're unable to get there." Carla thought of the kid, listening to people rumbling around in the house, fearful of making a sound. "Hannah, do you have a small CD player with earphones? Something to eliminate the noise when, and if, the police come rummaging around?"

"Just a minute. I might have just the thing." she hurried from the room.

They loaded Hannah's car with supplies, and drove toward the Perkinson house, deciding along the way to park in the Huntington Brothers' truck yard, which was on the same side of the road as the railroad tracks. They parked Hannah's car behind the maintenance building and gathered their supplies. The three of them stood at the edge of the dark woods that separated the maintenance yard from the Perkinson property, nervous, but determined. Without a light to guide them, they felt their way through the woods. Hannah headed their trek, advising them, *Careful of this branch. To the right, here. Newton, watch your step!*

At the crest of the hill, the house loomed before them. Pastor Lett's heart ached at the lies that lay within the walls of the magnificent structure.

Pastor Lett watched Newton with appreciation and guilt, remembering the long and painful deliberation she'd endured when she'd first brought Newton into the fold of her situation. She'd worried that Newton might not want any part of it, and she wouldn't have blamed him, either. After a month of consideration and worry, and the date of Carla's visit back to Delaware at her heels, she finally decided to chance it. She'd asked Newton to visit her at the church one evening and disclosed what she'd been doing, her clandestine meetings, the reasons, and finally, about the kid. Newton had acted pleased. He'd secretly worried, he'd said, about what had happened to the child.

It was Newton, with his knowledge of tinkering, electricity, and plumbing, things Carla knew nothing about, who installed the commode in the cellar. It had been a long, daunting process. Thank goodness for the dirt floor. Carla had been in awe of Newton's knowledge, his ability to follow the Do-It-Yourself handbooks. They had worked for a full month of nights, digging trenches for the PVC piping, connecting it to the septic system, and rigging up electricity from the lines at the Huntington Brothers truck site, unbeknownst to them, though Pastor Lett wouldn't have put it past Newton to have asked permission and made up some story that would sit well, yet cause no concern for inquiries.

It was one year later, when timing had, once again, become an issue, that they let Hannah in on their secret. They were the two most trustworthy people that Carla had ever known, and she cared for them both a great deal. As she watched them now, she felt guilty for burdening them with her responsibilities, and yet, she couldn't imagine how she would have made it through this many years without them by her side.

They crossed the grass and stacked their supplies next to the cellar doors. A cold gust of wind against the sweat on Pastor Lett's face made her feel alive, alert. She took the key from around her neck and unlocked the substantial metal lock from the heavy chain, and glanced up at her conspirators, who hovered above her, watching her every move. A chill rushed through her body as a fleeting image of the child in the dollhouse danced through her mind. She hefted one door upward, then the other. The chamber below was dark. She lowered herself down the crooked steps, and from behind the shelves, behind the plywood, she heard the kid.

After the long and tedious job of securing the area was taken care of, they replaced the plywood and shelves, each moving slower than when they'd first arrived, each feeling the weight of the situation, the sadness of it. Newton climbed the cellar stairs last, and before Pastor Lett could close the cellar doors, he threw old pieces of wood, sticks, and leaves onto the cellar floor and steps.

"This will make it look like the Perkinsons stored wood here." He gathered more leaves and threw them into the cellar, asking Hannah to hand him the small box that he had left at the top of the cellar stairs. Hannah looked around, found the box, and handed it to him, feeling something scurry inside of it.

"When you called, I had an idea that we might have to do this. So I took some precautions of my own." He opened the box, and lifted one live rat by the tail and tossed it gently onto the steps. Then he reached back into the box and withdrew two dead rats, throwing one to the floor and the other on the steps. The stench was so bad that Hannah moved away.

"Goodness, Newton. Where did you get those?" she asked.

Carla covered her nose. "Newton, that's awful!"

"That's the point."

They locked the heavy metal chain in place and began their long trek back.

By the time they reached Hannah's car, it was after two A.M.

"Carla, you don't look very good," Hannah said.

"I'm just exhausted. This…this whole thing. Sometimes it feels so wrong," she said.

"We all wish we had done things differently in our lives," Hannah said, supportively. "Some things we do because we have to, and other things, we do them because they're the right thing to do. And sometimes, what starts out feeling right, changes as time passes and lives change," Hannah leaned against the car, her side touching Pastor Lett's, "but by then it's too late. Then it is what it is and we carry on." She smiled at Carla, and then they climbed back into the car—each lost in her own thoughts, each pretending it was just another normal night.

Twenty Four

Weekend mornings always felt like mini-vacations to Molly. No matter how great of a running morning it might appear to be, her body wanted to lie around a little longer, move a little more slowly, and welcome the morning more gracefully. The sun peeked through the curtains in a streak across Cole's body which was stretched across the bed. She curled around him, feeling as safe and warm as any secret she'd ever held. She suddenly realized how soundly she'd slept. The turmoil of the night before crept into her mind, trying to settle there, but was met with resistance—resistance of wanting a few moments' peace without the invasion of real life.

Cole reached around her, drawing her closer, and moving his upper body over hers, his handsome face looking down at her, his eyes smiling, hair tousled.

"Hi, stranger," he said, brushing her wavy bangs off of her forehead.

"Morning," she said, wrapping her arms around his neck and lifting herself up to kiss his cheek.

"What time did you get in last night?" he asked, running his index finger down her right shoulder, sending goose bumps down the length of her arm.

"I don't know," she said, trying to keep focused on their conversation and not the warm sensation growing beneath her skin. "Late."

"Mmm." He gently kissed her forehead, her eyes, and then her cheeks.

Molly lay with her eyes closed, thinking of the feel of Cole's whiskers tickling her skin, when the sound of the ringing phone slashed through the moment. Cole stretched across her chest, reaching for the phone.

"Hello?" Cole said with a strained voice. He moved off of Molly, handing her the phone as if it were a dirty diaper. "For you. Mike Moeler." Cole reached for his book.

"Hello?"

"Molly? Mike. Thanks for the call last night."

Molly rested her head on Cole's shoulder. Cole tensed. "You won't say anything to Edie, will you?" The pit of her stomach hurt when she thought of her betrayal.

"We'll talk about that later. They put another officer in charge, Officer Rozutto. He wants to meet you."

"Why did they do that?"

"We get moved around based on other cases that come up. Rozutto's a fine detective. Can you meet us? Now?"

Molly heard the urgency in his voice, "Of course." She sat up and turned to Cole with a look of apology. He rolled his eyes.

"Panera Bread? Half hour okay?" Mike asked.

Molly agreed, and hung up the phone.

Cole shifted his gaze above his book. "Well?" he asked in a disappointed tone.

Molly snuggled closer to him. "I know this really stinks," she laid her head on his shoulder, "but I have to meet them. The detective wants to talk to me."

"Do you want me to come with you—wherever it is that you're going…with Mike." Mike's name held a quip of annoyance.

Molly turned to face him. "First of all, *Mike* is Sergeant Moeler, a cop, and second of all, no, I'll be fine, but thank you." She put her arm across his chest.

"Uh-huh," Cole said flatly.

"Cole," she said, trying to rein in her anxiety over the pending meeting and her ailing marriage, "how can I make it up to you?"

"That's a good question," he said and looked back down at his book.

Molly shook the outstretched hand of Sal Rozutto, his olive skin and thick dark hair as stereotypically Italian as his name.

"My pleasure," he said with a voice smooth as butter and thick with culture. His demeanor was friendly, yet keenly in charge. "I appreciate your meeting with us. It's people like you that are *in tune*, shall we say, with things that help to solve these cases." The smile remained on his lips even as he spoke.

Molly lifted her eyebrows, "Well, I don't know how in tune I am with it, but I'm glad to help."

"It's my understanding," he said a little quieter, moving closer to her, "that you are very in tune with the issues surrounding this case, that you have seen things."

The way he said it, quiet, like an inside secret between the two of them, touched Molly. She liked this man. "That is very beneficial to us, Mrs. Tanner."

He must have noticed the surprise in Molly's eyes, because he added quickly, "We don't often use...seers, but, in a case like this, where time is of the essence and a life hangs in the wings," he paused, thoughtfully, "in a case where we need every available lead to pan out before we lose a child, well, such a case may deem it appropriate, if the...seer...appears to be a safe and sane individual."

"But Officer Brown said—"

"Let me worry about Officer Brown," Sal said.

"I don't know what you've been told."

"I've been told enough to know that you know what you're talking about." He glanced at Mike.

Molly took a deep breath and felt a blush warm her cheeks. *Validation.* "Well," Molly began, "I'm not sure what I can tell you. I mean, the things I've seen," she leaned forward, spoke a little softer, and hoped the other patrons would not overhear their conversation, "they haven't really been that clear, you know?"

"I don't know, but I do understand that this is how these things work. Have you kept a record of any of it?"

"A record?" Molly gave a little laugh and told them about her journal, "But I can tell you what I've seen. I've got most of it right here." She pointed to her head.

Sal nodded.

Molly was torn between trust and deceit, "Sal, I have no trouble talking about it, but I want to make sure of something first."

Mike looked at her questioningly.

"Officer Brown basically said I was a suspect. If that's why you're talking with me, I want to know up front. I don't play games, and I won't be party to any, either. If I'm a suspect, come out and tell me, and I'll get a lawyer, and then we can talk," she spoke confidently, almost defiantly.

"I didn't realize that Officer Brown thought you were a suspect." He looked at Mike.

Mike chimed in, "Don't look at me. He never directly conveyed that to me."

"Regardless," Sal interrupted, "right now, you are not considered a suspect. You have my word on that, but obviously someone wants to convey things to you, whether it's someone who is involved or knows who might be."

"The notes," Mike said.

"I'm interested in what you know that might help us find Tracey—and hopefully find her alive and quickly."

"Okay, good." Molly surveyed the surrounding booths, making sure that there was no one she knew within earshot. She stared out the window, trying to figure out how, or what, to tell them.

"Molly," Sal touched her arm, "are you okay?"

She sighed, "I'm fine. It's just that…well....sometimes, it's not easy describing visions. There are many parts to them, some that will make no sense at all, others that, in the end, will have nothing do to with the vision itself." She squeezed lemon into her water and added a little Sweet 'n Low, making lemonade. Mike and Sal watched with questioning eyes. "*This* is my caffeine," she smiled.

Molly steeled herself for disbelief, then she began to describe the images she'd seen of a man being beaten, the three men hovering above him, the pain and the overpowering sadness that she'd felt. She stopped several times to collect her thoughts and figure out how to describe the depth of what she'd felt, the horrible sinking feeling in the pit of her stomach returning. Mike and Sal's slack jaws and incredulous looks made Molly feel as if she were speaking obscenities. Her voice faded to a near whisper.

At Mike's urging, she went on to describe the apple candy taste, which brought saliva to her mouth as she spoke. She detailed the cold, dark, cavernous holes and passageways that she'd seen, the image of Tracey and the dark-haired woman on their knees, praying in front of many candles, and the peaceful feeling that Tracey emitted, the sheer lack of fear that Molly had recently felt coming from her, the strange calm which had seemed out of place and, somehow, wrong.

Molly's energy was draining. She felt queasy, as though she'd been telling tales that should not be revealed—as if, by voicing them, she were making them real. She knew she had to push herself to continue, replaying for them the evil that overtook her as she'd run down White Ground Road. She swallowed the bile that rose in her throat and continued to describe the image of the girl she'd seen in the flowered dress, the girl who walked happily into the cornfield next to the church, only to be swallowed whole and never seen again. Mike and Sal took notes but did not say a word. Molly thought they were afraid to speak, afraid she might stop divulging her secrets.

Molly's breathing had become shallow. She had one vision left to describe. She took a deep breath, finally, and told them of the sensation of the large palms against her own at the cellar doors of the Perkinson House.

Molly leaned onto the table for support, her visions splayed out before them like a bad dream. Molly's head felt heavy and ill fit. She lowered her face into her hands as unexpected tears streamed down her cheeks, leaving her empty, and feeling as though she'd somehow betrayed her own mind—rendering her depleted, sad. She barely registered Sal's strong, even voice as he spoke to Mike.

"Get a warrant."

Pastor Lett sat on the rear deck of her home, gripping her warm mug of coffee, looking upon the lake but thinking of the past. She thought of the days before Rodney's beating, before she had taken the course of deception. She remembered fishing at the lake with Rodney, when Rodney was just a boy, the way his feet dangled over the dock, his toes wriggling in the water, and the way he had pulled them out quickly, worried that fish would bite them. No matter how many times she'd tell Rodney that he was scaring the fish away, he'd continue with his toe-wriggling game. They never caught a single fish. Yet every Saturday morning, before the mist would rise off of the lake, before the birds would leave their nests in search of food, she and Rodney would make their way to the docks, dressed in full fishing garb: tan vests with multiple pockets and lures attached, rubber boots that they'd discard as soon as they hit the docks, and tan and brown floppy fisherman hats, which Rodney called "fish heads." The memory brought a smile to her lips.

She watched the flurry of activity across the lake—the officers' cars arriving, police dogs on leashes.

She shouldn't have been surprised, she knew what lay ahead; nevertheless, her hand began to shake. A splash of coffee spilled onto the deck, and she watched it spread like a horrible lie. She thought of Molly and the long talks they'd had, the intimate details of Molly's depression they'd discussed, and felt the weight of sadness in Molly's sudden mistrust.

She stood and walked inside, looking around, for what, she wasn't sure. Hints of who lay in wait at the Perkinson House? There were no visible hints in her home—except for the sole legal paper, hidden in the locked metal box on the top shelf in her den. The key, tucked behind her shirt, suddenly felt cold against her chest. *Nerves.* She moved methodically, retrieving her heavy coat from the closet and setting it on the small maple table near the front door.

As a car pulled into the driveway, she rushed upstairs, taking the photo of Rodney down from the mantel in her bedroom—the photo of Rodney sitting on the living room floor of their childhood home, playing with a wooden train and smiling at the camera. She would carry the innocence of that photo with her as things became more difficult to handle. She said a small prayer and promised to keep Rodney safe, no matter what happened to her. There was a loud knock at the door. Pastor Lett held the photo to her chest for one last second, placed it carefully back on the mantel, aligning it with the other knickknacks, and walked calmly down the stairs.

"I'm coming, just a minute," the tranquility of her own voice startled her.

On her front stoop stood an officer of the law.

Sergeant Moeler briefly introduced himself. "Pastor Lett," he began, "we have a search warrant for the Perkinson property." He handed several papers to Pastor Lett, who took them with a trembling hand— suddenly too nervous and angry to read them, much less decipher them.

"We would like to gain access to the premises now, please."

Pastor Lett drew in a long breath, thinking of Hannah and Newton. "No problem at all," she said. She walked to the French doors, using each measured step to compose herself. She locked the doors and, on her way back toward the front door, paused to straighten a magazine. Thoughts of the kid ran painfully through her mind as she put on her coat and went out.

"What exactly will you be looking for?" she asked as they walked toward Sergeant Moeler's car.

"Rodney Lett, ma'am," Sergeant Moeler answered.

Molly found Pastor Lett standing on the Perkinson driveway, watching the war-like scene before them unfold.

"Good Lord," said Pastor Lett. Heavily-armed police officers moved in and out of the woods, search dogs in tow. She watched the house that she had so carefully boarded up be ripped open and invaded by strangers and lowered her face into her hands, "What have I done?"

"Is someone in there?" Molly asked, urgently.

Pastor Lett shook her head without looking at Molly. "I take care of that house! That is my responsibility! And now...just look! It's being taken over, people are walking all over it, shouting, mussing up the floors, disturbing the balance!" She paced, the grief in her face undeniable; wrinkles settled in around her eyes, her mouth, drawing her face downward.

Molly watched the ensuing commotion, listening to the sounds of disruption and envisioning the dogs running from room to room, scratching the floors with their nails, closets being thrown open. A few scattered voices rang through the thick, stressed air, "Clear! Here!" Her senses were overwhelmed. The unmistakable smell of Pastor Lett, Ivory soap and sweet perfume, mixed with the fresh scent of the cool outdoors.

Twenty minutes later, Sergeant Moeler came down the hill.

"Good, you got my call," he said to Molly. He turned to Pastor Lett, "You've got a rodent issue in the cellar."

Molly watched the two of them. Their efforts to avoid looking at one another were painful for her to witness. Their distrust was blatant, her guilt, distressing.

"The house was clear," Mike said, turning to Molly with an annoyed look.

"Clear?" Molly asked. Mike nodded. She turned to Pastor Lett. "If Rodney *is* alive, he might be able to help find Tracey Porter," she pleaded, knowing full well that if she'd hidden her brother for that many years, she was not going to give him up easily.

"Molly," she said confidently. She covered her eyes with her index finger and thumb, drew in a deep breath, and said, "Rodney can't help you."

"Molly, the house was clear. Leave the poor woman alone," Mike said firmly. He shook Pastor Lett's hand and went to join the search team as they descended the hill.

Molly pursued Pastor Lett, "This girl has one chance, like Kate Plummer did." she watched the muscles in her jaw tense. "The police made a mistake the first time. Kate may have been found if Rodney hadn't been fingered as a suspect, and then…well…"

"They cost him his life, Molly," she said, heatedly. "His life!" She turned away.

Molly called out to her again, "Think of the little girl. Think of Tracey."

"Think of Rodney," she spat back. "Think of *his* family."

Pastor Lett stared at Molly. The silence drew them together, linking them in an uncomfortable moment.

Sergeant Moeler's voice broke the silence. "Molly! I told you to back off. If Rodney is alive, we'll find him."

"But—" she said.

Pastor Lett interrupted, "Sergeant Moeler, my brother was *killed*, murdered, because he was a suspect, because he *knew* things. Not because he hurt Kate Plummer! Not because he killed Kate Plummer! He was murdered because of insecure people in our little town, the town that I have served for over twenty-five damned years—the town that I have given my heart and soul to—the town that I thought I could trust with my own flesh and blood."

Molly stood between the two of them—the chasm between them impassable. She felt torn, "I'm sorry!" She raised her eyes to Pastor Lett's and was struck by her venomous look. "Pastor Lett, I am truly sorry. It's just…" her voice broke off, shaking. "It's just that if we can save Tracey, we need to. You need to."

"That's where you're wrong, Molly," she said. "He needs to." She pointed to Sergeant Moeler, who stood ready to take the heat. "He needs to find Tracey. It's certainly not *your* job, or my job, or, for heaven's sake, Rodney's job. It's *his* job. The police need to find Tracey!"

Mike walked toward her and said, "You are absolutely right, Pastor Lett. It is our job to find Tracey Porter. It was our job to find Kate Plummer, though I was not part of that investigation, but if Rodney is alive, it is imperative that we find him and speak to him. It does not mean that he would be placed under investigation for Tracey's disappearance. We just want to talk to him."

"Do you *know* what happened when my brother was *questioned* by the police, Sergeant Moeler? Do you have any idea what it is like to come home and find that your brother has been beaten?" her face reddened, her arms flailed wildly with her angry words. "To walk into a room and find your own family member lying on the floor, not moving, barely breathing, covered in his own blood? Do you have any idea the pain one endures experiencing such a spectacle?"

Sergeant Moeler fumed, "Yes, Pastor Lett, I do know exactly how that feels. My own wife was killed two years ago, and I was the one to find her. I know the pain that doesn't go away, that follows you when you are awake and permeates your dreams." He walked to within inches of Pastor Lett, unable to stop the hurt from spewing out. "I know, Pastor Lett. I know just how badly it hurts. I know the rancid taste of it that doesn't leave your tongue, the taste of death. I know the smell of it, Pastor Lett, the smell of blood and dying flesh."

Molly watched, horrified, as Sergeant Moeler, wrought with anger, spat his angry words.

"I know, Pastor Lett, the loneliness that you live with day after day—the what-ifs. What if I'd been home? What if I hadn't run out for milk and eggs? What if I had come home earlier?" Tears welled in his eyes, his voice faltered. "I also know, Pastor Lett, that if someone had a chance to stop me from feeling that pain, if someone had an inkling of how to save her, I wish they would have—and believe me, if I'd found out afterward that someone could have helped her, and didn't, I can't tell you that I wouldn't have harmed them for not stepping in."

Pastor Lett's body sagged, as if all the energy had been sucked out of her. A silent moment passed between them—a stand off. When Pastor Lett spoke, she sounded defeated. "Sergeant Moeler, I am the pastor of the church. This is my community. Do you think that I would lie about something so critically important to finding that young girl?" Pastor Lett's voice was low and surprisingly calm, reassuring. "The Lord once said, 'The soul who sins is the one who will die. The son will not share the guilt of the father.'"

Molly tried to decipher what Pastor Lett was saying. Sergeant Moeler turned to join the other officers as they retreated down the hill. Molly felt a pang of guilt as she watched Pastor Lett's discomfort. "Pastor Lett? I know it seems like I don't trust you, or that I'm accusing you, but—"

She cut her off mid sentence, "Molly, you have done nothing wrong. You have been led to believe a lie, and you are simply trying to save Tracey. I understand." She smiled gently and held out her hands to Molly in supplication, "We're all in this together—you, me, and the Lord."

Molly contritely placed her hands in Pastor Lett's, beginning to feel as though she might be telling the truth about Rodney. At once her chest grew heavy, her lungs constricted. Through Pastor Lett's hands, she received an electrifying jolt, hitting her with such force that she almost fell backwards. Her vision wavered, and she heard her name from somewhere far away. She floated above the voice, as if carried by a cloud. An image appeared in her mind—a very large man, huddled in a shadowy room, rocking back and forth. Chanting came from his direction, "Dark tunnel, dark tunnel." Molly grappled in vain for Pastor Lett's wrists just as the vision disappeared and her legs failed her. Her body sagged to the ground, her cell phone ringing furiously in her pocket.

Twenty Five

Tracey awoke to find Mummy sitting on the edge of her mattress. "I made you some warm milk this morning." Tracey smiled as the steam rose and warmed her face. "You were quite a trooper last night. Were you scared?" she asked.

Tracey shrugged. "A little," she said.

"Before we start our day today," she said, "we have to talk to God, Tracey, thank Him for taking care of us last night." Mummy's hair brushed across her shoulders as she spoke.

Tracey thought Mummy looked pretty with her hair swinging like that. She wriggled out from underneath the covers, excited to learn how to talk to God the right way so that she wouldn't get sick. She took a sip of her milk and set it on the floor next to her mattress. Her happiness faded as she thought of the church dress she'd have to wear. "Mummy," she put her hand on Mummy's arm, smiling at the softness of the brown sweater she wore. "I'm cold today. Can I pray in my regular clothes?" She bit her lower lip, expecting Mummy to get upset.

Instead, Mummy placed her palm flat against Tracey's forehead. "No fever." She pressed her lips against her forehead, "Nope, cool as a cucumber." She smiled. Then she put her hand under Tracey's blanket and took hold of her small foot, yanking her hand out quickly. "You *are* cold! You have ice feet!" she laughed. Tracey giggled. "It's a good thing I brought warm socks for you today!" She held up the fluffiest socks Tracey had ever seen and placed them in the center of her blanket.

Tracey scooped them up and brought them to her cheek, "I love them!"

"Since you were such a good girl yesterday, and you're like an iceberg today, you can wear your regular clothes to pray."

Tracey scooted under the covers and slipped her feet into the new socks. She dressed in the clothes Mummy had given her. The shirt was a little too snug, and the sweatshirt was a little too big and had a stain on it, which looked like ketchup, but Tracey didn't care—it was red, one of her favorite colors, and she was warm. She pulled on clean panties and corduroy pants that were as brown as Mummy's sweater. They matched, and Tracey felt a pang of happiness. She reached down and grabbed the mug from the floor, drinking the last of the tepid milk.

"Maybe we'll go outside a little today," Mummy said.

Tracey's eyes lit up. "Really?"

"Really!" she said. "I have to run some errands today, so maybe we'll go outside for a little while before I do that. I have to get a few things on the outside."

"Can I come with you?" Tracey asked.

"I'm sorry, pumpkin, but I can't take you with me today. It will be very boring and very tiresome. Besides, I don't want you exposed to those toxins any more than you have to be. Going outside to play is a worry in and of itself, but I think it's worth it. I don't want to risk it for boring old errands." Mummy moved to the table and set out Tracey's drawings, papers, and crayons for Tracey to use while she was gone.

Running errands did sound boring to Tracey, but the idea of doing something different appealed to her. She weighed the excitement of doing something new against the chance of getting exposed to the toxins, and opted not to press the issue. "I hope you don't get sick," she said.

"I'm big and healthy. I think I'm pretty safe, but I don't want to be out there all the time, that's for sure!" She moved to the cooler, sliced an apple, and handed it to Tracey. "I have to get us some food, and I wanted to find some more warm clothes for you."

"Where do you get our clothes?" she asked.

"Oh, different places. There are people who give clothes to those of us who…who are a little less fortunate, and I have some friends that I've met at the park and other places, and they give us hand-me-downs."

"What about our food? You don't work, and there is no daddy. How do we buy our food?" Tracey asked.

Mummy reached over and put her hand on Tracey's leg, whispering furtively, "Don't you worry about things, okay? Mummy has friends, and they let me do some little jobs here and there. We will always have enough food. There are places that give us food, too."

Tracey looked at her sideways, "You don't steal it, do you?" Her eyes grew wide with the thought.

"Of course not! My mummy taught me never to steal—and don't you ever steal, either. That's no way to live!"

They ate the rest of their breakfast in silence, and Tracey wondered if she'd make a good mom one day, if she'd be able to keep her kids safe—if she'd even be able to have kids. Didn't you need a daddy to have kids? As Tracey's mind wandered, she gazed at Mummy's coat thrown carelessly on the mattress. Her happiness went away as she realized that soon Mummy would leave for her errands, and she'd be left alone once again.

Shortly after Mummy had left to run her errands, the candle had burned out, and Tracey was unable to relight the wick, becoming more frightened with each passing second. She'd frantically grabbed at the table, desperately feeling for the flashlight she hoped Mummy had left behind, and knocking her drawings onto the floor. Mummy returned from her errands to find Tracey huddled in the center of the room in a fit of panic, sobbing so hard she could not understand the words Mummy yelled. Tracey gripped the sides of her head with her hands, pulling her hair, like needles from her scalp, she rocked back and forth, shutting out the darkness that surrounded her. Then Mummy had fled, leaving Tracey alone in the dark once again.

Hannah sat across from Newton in the café, recalling the memory of the cold and dreary night twenty years earlier, as if it were yesterday. Fear still resonated throughout her body. It had been just months after Charlie had left her, and she had been petrified every minute since, terrified that he would come back, that he would find out her secret. She had kept watch as she ran errands, to make sure she wasn't followed, and Newton, God bless him, would drive by the farm at night, a few times each night, as a matter of fact, and make sure that Charlie wasn't parked outside. Though it was Charlie's choice to leave, he had a hair trigger of a temper, and Hannah was never quite confident that he wouldn't return. On that particular night, she'd just come in from feeding the horses and her body ached all over, her back, her legs, even her arms hurt. It was too early for the baby to come, so she hadn't been worried about early labor. She'd thought that she was coming down with a bug. She'd gone inside, bundled up with a cup of tea, and decided that she'd desperately needed rest. As usual, she'd called Newton to tell him that she was in for the night, reported how she was feeling, and said that she was going to try and sleep. One could set their clock by their nightly calls, but Newton and Betty insisted. They had wanted to know she was safe, and she'd appreciated their concern.

It was near midnight when she'd placed the call. Newton and Betty were at her bedside in minutes with medical manuals, fresh towels, and ice chips. None of them was quite sure what to expect—Newton had not been in the room when Betty had given birth to their son, Sam, and Betty had been highly sedated. Newton paced the room, shaking as if his shoes were vibrating. He tried so hard to convince Hannah to go to the hospital, begged her, in fact, but she'd stood firm. She couldn't risk Charlie tracking down this baby and taking it away from her.

The pain had lasted for hours, Hannah's screeches mirrored by Newton clenching his face and shoulders so tight that Betty had worried about him, as much as she had about Hannah, but she also knew Newton was a strong man, and that his strength would carry him through this ordeal. Hannah writhed from the stabbing pains that seared across her lower back and engulfed her protruding belly with the force of two giant hands, squeezing, pushing with so much pressure she'd thought she would surely burst open, but the baby would not come, and Hannah was not sure she was able to continue—part of her wanted to die, right then and there, leaving behind the fear of Charlie, the pain of childbirth.

Betty constantly wiped her brow with a cool cloth, soothing her with supportive words and rubbing her shoulders. Newton, on the other hand, pleaded with her to go to the hospital, get some real help. When Hannah refused with such determination that Newton finally understood the futility of his efforts, he became her ally, breathing in tune with Hannah, right through each powerful contraction, sweating bead for bead, spinning tales and telling jokes to take Hannah's focus off of the gut-wrenching pain that gripped her. Suddenly, the contractions had stopped. Hannah's breathing slowed, Newton's followed. The three of them watched Hannah's belly, waiting for the next contraction, waiting, it seemed, for hours, though in truth it was only mere minutes. Newton placed his hand on her belly, and Hannah watched his mouth move in prayer. Then, as if someone had kicked her in the lower back, Hannah let out a wail so loud she was sure to wake the sleeping cows across the road. She arched her back and pushed as hard as she was able, and out she slipped, tiny feet first. Newton was there, with his gloved hands outstretched, and a blanket laid across them, pillows below, *Just in case*. He'd caught Hannah's dear baby daughter, bundled her up, and set her gently in Hannah's arms. It was Newton who heard her first gasp of breath, and it was Newton who saw her last—the same as her first. The first was a shallow, labored breath in, and the last, a long, breeze-like breath out. She was beautiful, with a mop of brown hair, little cherub face, and scrawny little body. Her arms and legs had hung like a rag doll's, pink and soft. Ten little fingers and ten little toes—Hannah had counted them, each with the tiniest little nails she'd ever seen—but she had come too early. *It had not been her time*, Hannah had said—or maybe it had.

Hannah was brought back to the café by the warmth of Newton's hand on her own, "Hannah?" he said.

Hannah blinked, shook the memory from her mind. "I'm sorry." She wiped the fresh tears from her cheeks.

The short drive was familiar, comforting. Pastor Lett thought about Rodney's life, what he'd been like when they were growing up, and how she had stood by her little brother and protected him since the day he was born. Her mother had told her that she had Rodney for her, so she would not be alone. Pastor Lett had taken that responsibility very seriously, protecting Rodney when neighborhood kids made fun of him, trying to teach Rodney how to read and write when it had been a daunting, almost impossible task. She had cared for him as if he were her son, rather than her brother. When she had moved to Boyds, she couldn't fathom leaving Rodney with their parents, who told her often how much of a burden Rodney was to them. She had no qualms about being a sole provider for Rodney. As a young woman in her twenties, she'd felt ready to shoulder the responsibility. Rodney had never questioned Pastor Lett's role of caregiver. He only became uncomfortable when she had other duties that took her away from him. It had taken years for Rodney to come to understand that Pastor Lett *had* to run the church, often leaving Rodney alone in the manse. Rodney had a fear of crowds, even the small community gatherings at the church made him fret. In time, Rodney came to prefer staying at home. Pastor Lett had often made the effort to walk Rodney through the historic road on which they lived, introducing him to the neighbors, making him feel more comfortable in his surroundings. It hadn't come easily—many times Rodney had turned on his heels and run back to the manse, leaving Pastor Lett alone in the effort. Pastor Lett had seen the value in Rodney becoming adjusted to people, and she forged forward, eventually breaking Rodney's fear almost completely.

Rodney's favorite walk was the one that led to the Boyds Country Store. He had taken instantly to Jin and Edie, who had reciprocated the fondness. Pastor Lett had shown Rodney the safe way to get there, using the pedestrian underpass. She taught Rodney how to listen for oncoming trains, and never to cross the tracks. Rodney had been hesitant, at first, to believe that he would indeed come out of the underpass on the other side of the tracks. Pastor Lett had made a game of the lesson. She'd run through the tunnel, appearing across the tracks with an overly enthusiastic smile and waving her arms, then doubling back to show Rodney that he could, and would, appear right before her once again.

Pastor Lett had spoken to Jin and Edie about Rodney, asking if it was okay that he visit them daily, and assuring them that she would step in at any time. She'd made it clear to Rodney that if he became a burden, the daily visits would end. That day never came. Edie took care of Rodney, loving him like a son. She made sure he was eating well, and generally happy. Jin had looked forward to his visits as well, keeping an eye out for him at the same time every day, standing on the back stoop of the store, watching for his large head to pop out of the underpass, and calling to him when he appeared. They were a comfort to both Rodney and Pastor Lett. Their love for Rodney enabled Pastor Lett the freedom to run the church, without worrying too much about whether Rodney was okay. She knew that Jin and Edie would be there for him. It was an unspoken, appreciated, trust. On the rare days that Rodney did not visit them, Jin would call Pastor Lett and inquire about Rodney's wellbeing.

The thought of her betrayal to Edie and Jin made her sad—and angry. It seemed that in her effort to save Rodney, she'd inadvertently hurt many people.

Throwing caution to the wind, she pulled up the long driveway without a care about being seen.

Pastor Lett entered the small dark room, already on edge from the weight of her past—twenty years were closing in on her. A disturbing sound emanated from the contorted face of her charge, who rocked furiously, forward and back, sobbing, in a frenetic state. Crayon pictures littered the floor—twenty, maybe thirty drawings, scribbled with a heavy hand and, clearly, dark thoughts.

Pastor Lett had seen this disturbing state only once before. She grabbed at the drawings, leafing through them quickly; black crayon streaks, thick and uneven.

"What is this?" panic raced through her. She tried again, hysterically raising her voice, "What is this?"

Pastor Lett raced from the room, *What have I done?*

Molly lay on the couch, having collapsed after her emotional morning. She grabbed her phone and exhaustedly dialed Cole's number.

"Hi, honey, what time do you think you'll be home?" she asked when she heard his voice on the line.

"I'll leave now, since I know you're home," he said cheerfully. Molly smiled, relieved. "What do you want to do? Go to a movie?"

"Whatever you want. I would just love some down time with you," she said, pleased by his effort at reconciliation.

His reply was interrupted by a loud knock at the door. The dogs raced through the foyer, barking excitedly. "Honey, hold on a sec," she said to Cole.

Another knock, urgently sounded. "Who's there?" she called to the visitor.

The answer stopped her in her tracks. "Pastor Lett?" Molly reached out to answer the door, the phone still up to her ear.

"Don't answer it, Molly. After what Edie said, I don't trust her," Cole said sternly.

"I can't just not answer it, Cole. Relax," she said into the receiver, surprised at his sudden mistrust, his possible support. She settled the dogs and opened the door.

Pastor Lett stood on the porch, the afternoon sun failing to warm the cool day, a blue knit scarf hung around her neck, a dark hat atop her head. Her overcoat was buttoned from top to bottom, and her hands fidgeted nervously at her sides. "Molly, may I come in?" she said urgently.

"Don't do it, Molly!" Cole said.

Molly stepped aside, letting Pastor Lett into the foyer. Stealth and Trigger sniffed at her legs. From her cell phone she heard, "Molly? What does she want?"

Cole was calling her name as she lowered the phone, "Pastor Lett?"

"I know...about what happened at the search today. I've seen that look a thousand times—with Rodney." She slipped a few sunflower seeds into her mouth.

Molly bristled. *Of course you have*, she thought. Her palms grew sweaty. She gripped the cell phone tighter, beginning to panic.

Pastor Lett looked at her hand, then turned her head upward, toward the ceiling, and whispered, "Give me strength to do this, to do the right thing. Please, Lord," She dropped her gaze to Molly, and she opened her mouth, revealing pieces of her habitual seeds, but no words came out. Instead, she reached into her pocket.

Molly's heartbeat sped up. She took a step backwards. Stealth growled, Trigger followed, alert by her side.

Pastor Lett withdrew several child-like drawings from her pocket, flattened them against her leg, and handed them to Molly.

Pastor Lett was clearly disturbed as she raced through the streets of Boyds. Molly sat warily beside her, Cole's angry words ringing in her head, "Molly, don't be stupid! Do *not* go with her!" and silently cursing herself for her terse reply before hanging up on him, "Stupid? Consider me gone!" She flipped nervously through the dark drawings, her heart in her throat. "I knew she was alive," she said under her breath, recognizing images of Tracey; drawings of a little girl surrounded by a cornfield, kneeling in front of candles, and walking through dark tunnels—drawn as narrow alleys colored black except around the girl, creating a halo of white around her. Molly's breathing quickened—flashes of her visions mirrored the drawings before her.

They pulled into the familiar driveway, and Molly turned warily toward Pastor Lett, guarded, mistrusting once again.

They drove up the steep hill and parked in front of the old Victorian home.

Molly looked down again at the drawings that covered her lap. Her hand shook as she lifted one drawing and exposed another. "Look at th—" Molly's voice dropped off. "Oh my God—look at this." She held the disturbing picture up for Pastor Lett to see. The anguish in her eyes was undeniable. Molly's mistrust was beginning to fade.

"It looks like she's in a hole," Molly's voice cracked. "Where is she?" she demanded. She pressed the drawing to her chest. Her chest grew tight, and the smell of cold dirt and urine swirled around her. Tracey's fear melded with her as if it were her own. Her heart beat so fast she thought her chest might explode, and just as suddenly, she felt a release, as if Tracey had given up hope and accepted her situation, succumbing to her captor.

Shortly after Mummy had left to run her errands, the candle had burned out, and Tracey had been unable to relight the wick. Mummy had returned from her errands to find Tracey huddled in the center of the room, scared and crying. Mummy had yelled something, but Tracey was too frantic to recognize the words. Then Mummy had fled, leaving Tracey alone in the dark once again. She'd been gone only moments before reappearing with fresh matches.

Mummy lit one candle, mumbling a prayer as she brought the flame to the wick, then went to Tracey's side, comforting her, making sure she knew she was safe.

Tracey eyed the candle that lit so easily for Mummy. She knew she had to be able to learn to light the candles—she never wanted to be in that awful position again. "Mummy, can I light the candles today?" Tracey asked timidly. She'd watched Mummy for several days and was sure she could learn to light the candles.

"Maybe we can do it together," Mummy said.

Tracey perched on her knees next to her while Mummy struck a match. She was mesmerized by the sudden spark, the instant bright red and orange flame, and her favorite part, the low hiss that lasted only a millisecond. The smell of sulfur rose to her nose. Tracey put her hand on Mummy's, and, together, they lit the candles. She knew what to say this time. She was proud of herself and began to speak at the same time Mummy did, their words blending seamlessly together.

They spoke quietly at first, "Heavenly Father," Mummy's eyes widened, surprised to hear Tracey saying the prayer, "we thank You that these things are written in Psalms 91, that we can dwell in the secret place of the most High, and we thank You that we can."

Tracey forgot the next words and looked nervously down at her peaked hands. Mummy continued praying, her lips parted in a wide grin.

"Abide under the shadow of our Almighty God. We thank You that we can say You are our Lord, our refuge, our fortress, and our God, whom we can trust. We thank You for delivering us from the snare of the fowler and from the deadly pestilence. We thank You for covering each of us with your feathers. We thank You that we can walk under your wings and take refuge. We thank You that your faithfulness and truth is our shield and armor. We thank You that we are not afraid for the terror by night; nor for the arrow that flieth by day; nor for the pestilence that walketh in darkness; nor for the destruction that wasteth at noonday. We thank You that a thousand shall fall at our side, and ten thousand at our right hand; and none will come near us."

Tracey remembered what came next. It was her favorite part. Her voice grew louder as her confidence grew. The words flowed as easily as a nursery rhyme. "We thank You for giving your angels charge over us to keep us in all ways and that your angels' hands will lift us up so we do not dash our foot against a stone. We thank You that we can tread upon the lion and serpent and trample the young lion and the dragon under our feet. We thank You that when we call upon You, You will answer us, be with us in trouble, deliver us, honor us, satisfy us with a long life, and show us your salvation."

Mummy took her hand, and together they said, "Amen!" She pulled Tracey in her arms and hugged her tight. Tracey was proud of herself and gleamed with excitement.

They climbed the stairs, Molly following Pastor Lett down the dimly-lit hallway. Tormented sounds came from the room at the end of the hall. From her visions, Molly recognized the burly mass of a man who sat huddled on the floor of the dark room, rocking furiously, forward and back, forward and back, his head bent over his lap, his hands clasped firmly together. The weight of his upper body propelled him, picking up momentum with each forward motion.

"Rodney," she whispered.

Pastor Lett looked at her with almost imperceptible relief, "Yes, this is my brother, Rodney."

"How long has he been like this?" she asked.

"I don't know. I found him this way," she spoke with concern.

"Does he always do this? Rock?"

"Only when he has visions—but never this hard, and he never...he never cries," Pastor Lett's voice rose with her elevating panic.

Molly looked down and noticed wet stains on Rodney's thighs and tears that streaked his face. Pastor Lett moved closer to Rodney, reaching her arm around her younger brother's back. Rodney was completely unaware of the familiar touch.

"Honey," Pastor Lett said, "what is it? What's wrong?"

Rodney didn't acknowledge her presence.

"Rodney, let me help you," she urged.

There was still no response.

Rodney made no move to look at his sister or at Molly. He rocked harder, faster. Molly moved to his side, compelled by the connection of the drawings to her visions. She placed her hand on top of his. Rodney opened his eyes and lifted his gaze. His body shifted slightly, out from the safety of Pastor Lett's embrace. He spoke in a quiet monotone, "M...Molly." Molly gasped, alarmed, and stepped backward. Rodney dropped his gaze again, his rocking pace quickened.

Suddenly he stopped rocking. "Rodney know Molly!" he said in a hushed, serious tone. "Molly see bluebirds," he cocked his head, as if waiting for an answer. Molly stood stock still. "Rodney see bluebirds," he said, slowly rising to his feet, and towering over Molly. She stepped backwards once again, aligning herself with Pastor Lett. Rodney reached his enormous hands out and grabbed Molly's hands. Molly stiffened. He lifted his hands and placed his palms flat against hers. A look of wonder crept across his face. "Rodney know Molly!" he crooned.

"It was you," she whispered, feeling the perfect fit of his giant paws against her own small, shaking hands.

"Molly find girl." He stared at Molly expectantly, lowering his hands to his sides.

Images raced through Molly's mind. Her brain somehow confused Amanda with Tracey, and suddenly she couldn't separate the two. *I'm okay. It's not my fault*, she told herself, grappling to remain in the present and not slip into the past. She lifted the drawings of a woman with a child—eating, playing, walking one in front of the other, on their knees praying—the harshly-drawn pictures of trees and bushes, the forest floor, and in an uneasy voice, Molly asked, "Who is this, Rodney? Who is this little girl?"

Rodney stared.

"Do I know this girl?" she persisted.

His chin dropped—half a nod.

"Amanda? Is this her, Rodney?" she said, accusingly.

Rodney touched her arm, and in that second she understood. It was not Amanda. It was Tracey. Her eyes darted quickly to Pastor Lett. "Is this the girl that's missing?"

Pastor Lett simply lifted her eyebrows.

"Not missing," Rodney answered flatly. "Girl not missing. Girl in dark place," he said. "You see them, too."

Molly saw Pastor Lett lean forward, listening intently. She bit her lower lip and took a deep breath. "See who?" she asked, fearing that even she'd forgotten her path.

"The girl. Mommy."

"Who is the girl, Rodney?" Pastor Lett asked.

"Molly *know* who girl is!" Rodney looked at Pastor Lett sternly and said in an angry, guarded tone, "Carla not know. Molly know!" Rodney turned away from them.

Molly's eyes darted between the giant man before her and Pastor Lett, who paced, clenching and unclenching her eyes, fisting her hands. A moment later there was a loud *thud*. Rodney had dropped to his knees. Molly ran to his side. Rodney rocked, emitting a short, low moan. Instantly, the movie Son Rise flashed in Molly's mind. She dropped to her knees next to Rodney, and began to rock at the same fast pace. "Is it Tracey?" Molly asked.

At the sound of her voice, Rodney stopped rocking. He made no move to look at her, but sat still, tears dripping from his chin. He began rocking again, slowly. Pastor Lett stood by, anxiously frustrated. Molly was on the verge of tears, her nerve endings afire. She reached for her bag and withdrew the necklace and candy wrapper, silently placing them on the floor in front of Rodney. He closed his eyes, and he stopped rocking again. Pastor Lett stopped pacing, her eyes trained on her younger brother, concern written all over her face. Rodney reached his bulky hand out and covered the necklace and wrapper slowly, not touching them, but cupping his hand over them, as if he'd caught a mouse. He began to moan, a long, low, sorrowful sound, which broke only as he took a shallow, almost invisible breath. He rocked slowly again, leaving his hand protectively over the treasures.

Molly knew she was crossing dangerous territory. She had no idea how Rodney would react, only that he would. She spoke in a calm, measured voice, "Rodney, tell me."

The moan continued. He scooped the items into his cupped hands and lifted them to his face. He breathed in deeply through his nose, his eyes firmly shut. Molly's thoughts were scattered, consumed by both excitement and fear, she knew all too well the gripping, gut-wrenching feeling that he was sure to be experiencing.

His hands began to shake, and the moaning grew louder. Pastor Lett rushed to his side, but Molly put up her hand and shook her head. His moan turned to sobs, wracking his body, his large chest heaved up and down as his hands remained cupped below his nose. He sobbed so hard that Molly wanted to beg him to stop. Just when she felt she could no longer fight the urge to comfort him, he turned to her and opened his eyes. He lowered his hands. Constant tears streamed down his cheeks.

"Rodney?" Molly whispered.

He shook his head. Tears welled in Molly's eyes, fearing the worst. Rodney moved his hands under hers, her hands rested on the thick base of his thumbs. Molly closed her eyes and was met with an insistent force, one that she could not escape, a force that was more powerful than anything she had ever experienced. The taste of candy apple filled her mouth, saliva pooled below her tongue and seeped around her teeth. Images came at her at an alarming rate, almost too fast to recognize: *the image of a young girl passing through a familiar wooden opening. Pitch dark tunnels, and a deep, hollow hole—a lantern illuminated a tall woman with dark hair and a small girl.* A rush of ease and acceptance passed through Molly, which she knew came from Tracey—a contentedness, which scared Molly even more than if she'd been terrified. Molly's breath caught and somehow she realized that the moaning she was hearing was now coming from her own throat.

Rodney pulled his hands away, and Molly opened her eyes, instantly finding his and holding his stare. The Knowing passed between them like a secret. Rodney turned Molly's hands over, placing the necklace and candy wrapper in her palms. He withdrew his hands and nodded. Molly stood on shaky legs, clinging to

Pastor Lett as if she were about to slip underwater. "I know where she is," she whispered.

Twenty Six

The afternoon seemed to Tracey to go on forever, and she was anxious to get out of their small room and play. She was proud to have remembered the words to their prayer this morning. Seeing the joy in Mummy's face, feeling her happy embrace at her success had given Tracey confidence. She watched Mummy write in her journal, mumbling under her breath.

"Mummy, can we go outside?" Tracey asked.

Mummy turned to her, a faraway look in her eyes, opened her mouth to speak, then turned silently back to her journal.

"Mummy?" Tracey asked again.

Mummy's pencil stopped moving. She kept her eyes trained on the full page. "They didn't want me," Mummy said quietly, then scribbled furiously in the journal.

Tracey bit her lower lip, confused. "What Mummy?"

Mummy did not answer. Tracey knew better than to push. She sat quietly on the mattress watching Mummy, and wondering why Mummy was acting so weird. She stretched out on the mattress, her head resting on her forearms.

Mummy stood up and paced. Tracey rolled over and watched her. As if she'd just realized Tracey was in the room, Mummy abruptly stopped pacing and glared at her.

Tracey sat up and pulled her knees into her chest, new fear forming.

Mummy shook her head. "That won't do," she said.

Tracey panicked, "I'm sorry!" she said breathlessly.

A funny smile crept across Mummy's face. "Yes, let's play."

"I haven't told anyone where he is. Not even our parents knew." Pastor Lett's eyes remained on the road before her. "They believed he was dead and buried." There was a coldness to her voice, the shock of where they were headed still fresh.

Molly didn't know what to do other than comfort her. "You've held onto this burden for so long."

"It's no burden," she said. "Rodney is not a burden."

"No, not Rodney, I'm talking about the secret. I mean, you must feel the weight of it, like a tether holding you down. You must have wanted to cut it free hundreds of times."

She nodded.

"Your parents—why?" she asked.

"Because if anyone came looking for Rodney, as you did," she looked up at her accusingly, "they would have found him if I didn't have him buried—and he might have met the same fate once again."

Molly asked her how she had been able to fake the burial, and her explanation seemed convenient.

"I told the coroner that I wanted to bring his body in and be with it until it was in the coffin and sealed for his final interment. I was long-time friends with the embalmer. He owed me one. I knew I could trust him." She ran her hand over her face again, as if wiping away the thought of it. "That night we took him to his house, and together we nursed him back to health. He pretended to do the embalming, and we packed the casket with sand bags—a lot of sand bags, Rodney's a big guy. My parents, they didn't want to care for Rodney, not when he started having visions. It was too much for them. In the years he was with me here, they never even visited him, so I didn't figure it was any worse for them if they thought he had passed on."

"Jesus," Molly said, instinctively covering her mouth with her hand, and whispering from behind her fingers, "sorry!"

"It's okay," she said.

Molly watched her reach into her pocket for her sunflower seeds and slip a few into her mouth. Her jaw quickly went to work on the tiny shells.

"Do you see him often?" Molly asked.

She nodded. "I see him often. You see, that's the wonderful thing about being a pastor. No one holds your schedule. There is no time clock. I have freedom to simply tell my secretary that I'll be gone a few hours, and she doesn't question me, ever." She sighed, a long, relieved, sigh.

Silent minutes passed like hours.

Molly's nerves were on fire. Pastor Lett parked the car and Molly asked, carefully, "Does he remember...the beating?"

Pastor Lett shook her head. "He remembers living with me here, in Boyds, and he seems haunted by the little girl who was in a dark place with her mommy. Sometimes it gets really bad, and he goes into his own little world, rocking and saying things over and over, like he used to, but," she smiled, "he's alive, Molly, and for me, that's been all that matters." She stared at the road before them. "But the drawings," she paused, then looked at Molly, "and the state he's in today..."

As they pulled into the parking lot, Molly turned to Pastor Lett, "We have to make a decision. Do we go on our own or call the police?" Molly spoke before Pastor Lett could voice her concern. "I won't mention Rodney. This can be all me—my vision, as far as they know."

Pastor Lett's body visibly relaxed. She pulled Molly's cell phone from her bag and handed it to her. The light of the afternoon had gone, replaced with a cool, gray evening. Molly dialed Sergeant Moeler's number, his voice instantly calmed her. "Mike," she said, relieved.

"Molly," he said flatly.

Molly paused at the tone of his voice, "I need to talk to you and Sal. I know where she is." She listened to Mike sigh on the other end of the phone. "Mike?" she said tentatively.

"Molly, we're not—"

"Mike! This is important. I *know* where to find Tracey!" she said emphatically, annoyed at his hesitation. Something was very wrong.

"Molly, we aren't going to follow your leads right now," he said in a professional, cold tone. "Officer Brown felt that today was a big waste of station time and money."

Molly's jaw dropped. "But—"

"Molly," Mike said dismissively, then spoke in a kinder tone, "Sal and I appreciate all that you're doing. We even think it's possible that you might have these…visions…or whatever they are, but we can't waste resources on hunches."

She was pissed, "Hunches? That's what you think these are? I can't even believe this! I know where she is! Please!

"I'm sorry, Molly."

Pastor Lett gave her a sympathetic look as she cursed at the dead phone line.

"Sorry," Molly said as she dialed Cole's number. She told him what had transpired. "Cole, can you come with me? Please? I need you." Nerves made her chest ache.

"Tunnels, Molly? You really want to go traipsing through some freaking tunnels in the dark? No way. Now you're going too far. This is a job for the police, not you." Cole's voice sounded firm, angry.

"I told you, they won't come!" she said defensively.

"Doesn't that tell you something, Molly?"

"I don't give a flying fuck what the police say, Cole. I know where Tracey is! I saw it all! Will you come or not, because I'm going!" her hands shook. She ignored the incredulous look on Pastor Lett's face. She

330

was consumed with anger, which only fueled her determination to go into the tunnels and find Tracey.

"If you go, Molly, that's it. I'm done."

"What?" she could not believe the threat.

"You heard me. This time, Molly, you're going too far. You're putting yourself in what could be severe danger—and if the police don't believe you, then back off. You have no business in those tunnels, and I'm not going to be waiting around when you come out empty-handed."

Molly had never heard Cole that angry, not once in all the years she had known him. She contemplated his words but could not turn her back on Tracey as she had on Amanda. Molly was haunted by images of five-year-old Amanda's terrified eyes, her screams, as she was shoved into the black minivan almost ten years earlier. The look of the man's eyes as she turned to Molly in the parking lot and said, "She didn't get the dolly she wanted." If only she'd gotten involved. If only she'd followed her gut. If only she hadn't turned her back on the dreams she'd had over the ensuing three days. Maybe then Amanda would still be here, alive, her abductor in jail. She'd be damned if she'd have the blood of another child on her hands.

With no small amount of fear—fear at what looked like the end of her marriage—she said, "You do what you have to do, and I'll do what I have to do." With trembling fingers, she disconnected the call.

The church parking lot was empty, illuminated by two lights perched at either end of the lot. As she drove over the curb and up the grassy hill toward the campsite, Pastor Lett tried to convince Molly not to go forward with her plans, citing the dangers, the unknown, but Molly was adamant. She asked Pastor Lett to wait outside the tunnels, just in case she did not return. On the outside, Molly was confident, determined. On the inside, she was petrified. The thought of losing Cole devastated her, but the thought of Tracey being in those tunnels for one minute more than she had to be, the thought of not finding Tracey alive, drove her to override her own dilemma and push forward. Pastor Lett stepped out of her car and opened the trunk, returning with two industrial-sized flash lights.

Molly nodded, afraid her voice would fail her.

They crested the hill to the end of the tree line that led to the clearing. Molly took long deep breaths to calm herself. She turned to Pastor Lett and said, "I'm sorry, for everything."

She nodded solemnly. They got out of the car and walked down the path toward the campsite, her energy renewed with each step, hope forming in the illuminated path before her. Pastor Lett put a hand on Molly's shoulder. "Are you sure you want to do this? You could be endangering yourself and maybe even Tracey," she tried again to dissuade her. "We could go to the station and convince them, come back later."

Molly took a deep breath. "I'm fine. I'm doing this."

Molly changed her cell phone setting to vibrate, trying desperately not to let the thought of no cellular service in the tunnels scare her out of continuing. She ignored her trembling hands, shoving them deep into her pockets as they walked. Against her will, her mind drifted to Erik, and she swallowed hard against the lump in her throat, knowing she could not turn back.

"What's the plan?" Pastor Lett asked.

Molly approached the first wooden box where she'd found the candy wrapper. The taste of apple candy once again tickled her senses. "If Rodney and I are right, then I think the entrance is in here."

Pastor Lett looked at her as if she were crazy.

"Come on. Help me open it, will you?" she asked, irritated by her look.

They propped the box lid open and peered inside. Molly's heart sank. There was a wooden floor in the box. There was no passageway.

"This is where I found the candy wrapper. This is where she had to go in," she said, frantically looking around.

Pastor Lett cocked her head, "Candy wrapper?"

Molly rolled her eyes, too frustrated to explain, "Nothing," she said. She kicked the corner of the box with her foot, making the lid slam shut. "Shit," she said, and they lifted it up again.

"What in the world?" Pastor Lett peered into the box.

Molly pushed past her to see.

The slamming of the lid had jarred the bottom loose. The left front corner of the bottom plywood had dropped, revealing a gaping dark hole. Molly and Pastor Lett looked at each other, a nervous smile forming across Molly's face, a frown across Pastor Lett's. They lowered the lid, slowly, silently.

"Molly, are you sure you want to go in there?" she asked.

"Hell yes, I'm going in there." She took a step away from the box, thinking not of her fear or her crumbling marriage but of her plan. "Give me your sunflower seeds," she thrust her hand toward her.

Pastor Lett reached into her coat pocket and withdrew a bag of seeds.

"More," she said, pushing her hand toward her other pocket.

She sighed and withdrew another bag from the other pocket. "Why?"

"Bread trail," she walked back toward the box. "I don't know how far I have to walk to get to them, if they're even in there, but if I'm not back out in a few hours, call the police—please."

"Molly—"

She put her hand up, silencing her. "I'm going. I don't know if my phone will work or not, but if it does, I'll text you if something happens." She took one last deep breath and hoisted herself onto the edge of the box, seeing the ominous hole below her as her ally—the only thing keeping her from Tracey now would be her own fear, and she was not going to let that happen. She hopped off her precarious perch and into the hole, landing with a loud thud. Pastor Lett quickly dropped a flashlight down to her.

"Two hours. If you're not back, I'm getting the police," Pastor Lett said.

"Not worried," she lied. She directed the beam of the flashlight in front of her, then back up the eight-foot hole to see Pastor Lett's worried face staring down at her. She shrugged, "Here goes Alice."

Molly's heart thumped in her chest. The entrance behind her quickly disappeared. The tunnel smelled of wet earth. The dirt walls were not much wider than her body, the ceiling a few feet above Molly's head. The flashlight illuminated ten feet in front of her, beyond that it was pitch black. She prayed the batteries would not fail. She dropped her hand to her pocket, feeling the safety of her cell phone. The urge to try it was overwhelming, but she was afraid of making any unnecessary noise, already worried about Tracey's abductor seeing the flashlight. She tried to keep her fear at bay, but could not deny the urge to turn back and run. *Move it!* she told herself. *You're fine. This time it will not be your fault.* She looked into the abyss of the tunnel, and silently prayed, as she knew Pastor Lett was doing above her, that she'd find Tracey and bring her home safely. Quickly, she reached into her pocket and withdrew a handful of sunflower seeds, dropping a few every couple feet.

Molly thought about Tracey and the fear she must have felt that first fateful evening, walking in the dark tunnel, wondering if she'd ever come out alive. She wondered what went through Amanda's mind during the first hysterical moments of her abduction. *It's not your fault.* She wriggled her ankle as she moved forward, determined not to be the weak link in Tracey's rescue. *Rescue.* Molly knew all too well that her search could end up at a dead end, and if so, she'd let her marriage go for nothing.

Damn him! Cole should support my visions! She knew how crazy that thought was, but she also knew that the one time she'd let her guard down, to the police, to Cole, she'd been essentially laughed at, and it infuriated her. Her pace was quick, her senses acute. The only noise was that of her fast footsteps on the dirt and her heart thumping in her chest.

She recalled her vision of Tracey being lowered into the box and felt certain she was in the right place. She worried about the Knowing—what if she passed out and the abductor...or killer...found her? Molly pulled her thoughts away from the negative what ifs and back to the task at hand. She dropped more seeds and noticed something on the ground a few feet ahead of her. She bent down and picked up a tiny white piece of a candy wrapper. Her eyes grew wide, hopeful. She withdrew the other torn wrapper from her pocket, and saw that they fit perfectly together. Molly moved forward with renewed vigor.

Molly slowed as she came to a cross section where tunnels ran in each direction, one to the left and one to the right. She contemplated the path, listened, but heard nothing in either direction. She bent down, inspecting the dirt at the entrance to each of the tunnels. She followed the one to the right, which, by the scuffs in the dirt, seemed to have been traveled more recently. She dropped a number of seeds in the entrance and continued dropping them as she walked. A darkened opening appeared in the wall to her left. She stopped, her fear rising. She listened to the silence, then peered cautiously into the room, ready to run, or fight.

The room was empty, except for a few scattered pieces of wood. She let out a relieved sigh, and pushed on. She followed the same heart-pounding process for each opening, her pace slowed considerably as she cautiously inspected each one, floor to ceiling, looking for any sign of Tracey, of life in the underground maze.

When she was met by another bisecting tunnel, Molly once again sent her light down each tunnel and inspected the dirt. She hoped she was choosing the right paths and knew that if she didn't leave the trail, she would never find her way out of the convolutions. She determined that the tunnel to the left had been recently used and moved in that direction. In her mind, Molly saw a quick flash of Tracey walking away from her, in her belly she felt the pull of the girl. She stopped, flashed her light behind her, ahead of her, then back behind. She turned back toward the tunnel that had been on her right. She gathered the dropped seeds and moved them onto her new path. "Okay," she whispered to herself, "I'm coming, Tracey. I'm coming."

Molly's pace had slowed significantly from when she'd first set out. Her ankle pained her, and her adrenaline had subsided, replaced with a growing fatigue. The air was difficult to breathe, although she'd already become used to the rancid smell. At the next intersection of tunnels, Molly sighed, tired of the decisions, and for the first time, questioned what she was doing. Who *did* she think she was? Maybe Cole was right. As she headed down the tunnel to the right, which was wider and low-ceilinged, she contemplated turning around, finding Cole, and trying to repair her marriage, admitting she was wrong. A muffled noise—a voice perhaps—broke her thoughts. She stopped, turned off her flashlight, and listened—Cole quickly forgotten.

Molly's heart pumped in her ears like a drum. It took every ounce of her concentration to hear past the rush of blood. Her fear magnified when she heard a noise come from the darkness behind her.

"It's for you!" Tracey said, excitedly. She was proud of the picture she'd drawn of a beautiful garden.

Mummy smiled from across the room where she was putting cans of vegetables onto the shelf. "I never knew you were such an artist."

"I'm a good drawer," Tracey gleamed, putting her crayons into the cardboard box that sat in the center of the table. "Mrs. Tate picked my picture out of the whole class's to put up on our classroom door." Tracey yawned.

"Are you tired, honey?" Mummy asked sweetly.

"A little," Tracey said. She stood up from the log she'd been sitting on and turned toward her mattress when an unfamiliar woman entered their chamber. Tracey's eyes grew wide, "Hi!" she said enthusiastically. "Are you a friend of Mummy's?"

Molly could barely breathe. Fear drove her forward, into the chamber, and quickly toward Tracey, taking in the two dirty mattresses, upended logs, and the Bible on the makeshift table. She put her arm protectively around Tracey, her eyes glued to the woman who stood by silently watching, as if in shock. "Are you Tracey?" Molly asked in a rush of breath.

Tracey nodded.

The woman's eyes darted erratically between Tracey and Molly. She began to shake, backing up against the wall. Suddenly she lurched forward. In one swift action Molly pulled Tracey tightly against her chest, threw herself back-first against the wall, avoiding the woman's grasp. Tracey screamed, tears spilled down her cheeks.

"Mummy!"

"Give her back!" The woman clawed at Molly's back. "I saved her! Give her to me!" She pulled fistfuls of Molly's hair. Molly bent over, shielding Tracey, unwilling to loosen her grasp, her scalp searing with pain.

"No!" Molly growled, using her elbows to fight off the large, powerful woman.

The woman grabbed Molly by the back of her shoulders, throwing her down to the ground, and ripping Tracey free from her hands. Molly jumped quickly to her feet and upon the woman, punching her arms, grabbing them. The woman held tight to a screaming, petrified Tracey.

"Go, Tracey!" Molly screamed. "Run! Get away from her!"

The woman back-fisted Molly in the face. Molly tumbled to the floor, scrambling to get to her feet and retrieve Tracey, who was being dragged toward the entrance of the tunnel. Blood poured down Molly's face. She grabbed Tracey's arm. "Let her go!" she commanded.

The woman ignored Molly. "Tracey, run!" the woman said. Tracey ripped herself from Molly's arm and clung to the woman's legs.

"Mummy! Mummy!"

Momentarily dumbfounded, Molly took in the scene—had she made a mistake? With her next breath she lost the doubt and jumped at the woman, who took a step backward with Tracey in her grasp, leaving Molly reeling before her, flailing her hands toward the girl.

"Give her to me!" Molly screamed. She was no match for the large woman. She lunged at her legs. The woman kicked her away—Molly reeled from the blow to her gut.

"Get away from us! Go away!" the woman yelled. She picked up a rock and threw it at Molly. Molly ducked, the rock caught the side of her face. The woman kicked Molly's arms, her chin, and Molly fell to the ground. Tracey's screams pierced the air. Molly looked up just in time to see the woman lift a large log over her head.

"Get away from her!" the woman screamed. Suddenly, the woman was thrust forward and fell to the ground, writhing in pain, the log landed with a thud beside her.

Cole was instantly on the woman's back, pinning her to the earth.

"Get that girl out of here!" Cole commanded Molly.

"Cole?" she looked at him, stunned.

"Get outta here! Now!" he yelled.

Molly picked up Tracey, who flailed and kicked to be released, and ran toward the opening, grabbing her discarded flashlight, and fleeing along the path of scattered seeds.

Tracey's shrieks trailed behind her, "Mummy! No! Mummy, the toxins! Mummy, help me!"

Tracey had lost her will to fight by the time they neared the end of the tunnel. She trembled, clinging tighter to the strange woman's arms with each step as they approached the entrance. The stranger had told Tracey that her name was Molly, and that she was a friend, that she wouldn't let anything bad happen to her, and that she was taking her back to her mommy and daddy. Tracey had not been relieved. She had a sinking feeling in the pit of her stomach, like she was on a roller coaster and had just gone down an enormous hill—*the toxins*. At first Tracey had sobbed at the news of being brought to her parents, *I am home! I don't want to leave! I want to be with Mummy!* But eventually she had calmed, her tears subsided into short, fast hiccups, and later, even, tired breaths. She'd told Molly that she was scared of the toxins, and asked Molly to bring her parents into the tunnels, instead. When Molly asked about the toxins, Tracey became silent, as if their meaning were a secret. After much prodding, Tracey eventually relented, and told Molly that she didn't want to die. She'd said that she didn't really know what they were, but that they lived outside and they could kill you if they got in your body. Molly had simply pulled her closer, shielding the back of her head like an infant's, and told her that nothing was going to kill her. She was safe.

Molly held tightly to Tracey's body with one arm, withdrawing something from her pocket with her other. She held her hand open for Tracey to see. Tracey stared at the heart-shaped charm. She touched her delicate finger to the chain.

"My necklace," she breathed, wonderingly. Her other hand was drawn to the necklace that hung around her dirty, swan-like neck. "I have a new one," she said politely, her little body trembling like a newborn bird's.

"I see that—but you should have this one, too," Molly said, and placed it in Tracey's palm.

A large, curly-haired man lowered himself into the hole just as Molly reached the entrance to the tunnel. She recognized the blue police sweatshirt.

"Molly?" he said.

Molly nodded.

Tracey clung to her, "Who's that?"

"He's a police officer. He's here to help us." Molly set Tracey on the ground in front of her and Tracey spun around, clasping her arms around Molly's legs. "Tracey," Molly said, crouching down so she was face to face with the scared little girl, "It's okay. This nice police officer is going to help you out of this tunnel."

"Are you coming?" she asked in a quivering, unsure voice.

"You bet I am. Right after you, okay?" Molly reassured her.

Tracey nodded and took hold of the officer's warm hand, gripping it as if it were a lifeline. He lifted her up with ease, and they heard welcoming cheers.

As the officer lifted Molly, Mike reached down into the hole to help her.

"Good job, Molly," he said.

As soon as she was pulled from the hole, seven armed men went down into the tunnels.

Molly was not feeling very gracious, stewing over her earlier treatment, and frantic with worry about Cole. He grasped at words to apologize, but she didn't give him a chance. She quickly told him what had transpired. She looked frantically around the campsite, which flurried with activity.

"Where's Tracey?" she asked urgently.

Mike pointed to the nearby ambulance where Tracey sat huddled in a blanket, safe, waiting for her parents to arrive. Molly was instantly moving in Tracey's direction. One paramedic was taking Tracey's blood pressure, the other speaking into a walkie-talkie. Tracey looked up, saw Molly, and tried to get out of the ambulance, but the officers gently held her back. For an instant, Molly saw Amanda's face in the first grade photograph, as it had appeared in the newspaper the day they'd found her; her smiling face, her dancing eyes, and the headlines above, *Body of Amanda Curtis Found*. Molly closed her eyes against the memory, feeling both the guilt and the relief of the moment, and went to Tracey.

"You're going home, little one," she whispered in Tracey's ear.

Between the heightened fear in Tracey's eyes and her tight grasp on Molly's arms, Molly found herself wanting to cry. She hated that Tracey was going to be forever damaged by the past week. She fought back tears, trying to remain strong for Tracey's sake. Molly pulled Tracey into her lap and rested her head on Tracey's dirty, matted hair.

A police vehicle drove along the path toward the scene, slowing to a crawl, and finally stopping a few feet from the ambulance. The back door flew open, and Celia Porter quickly climbed out. She was thinner than Molly remembered, her face had aged ten years since she'd told the story of Tracey's disappearance.

Celia looked in their direction and screamed, "Tracey!" running toward them. Tracey wriggled free of Molly's protection, fresh tears poured down her cheeks. Tracey's father was two steps behind Celia, but he sprinted forward and hoisted Tracey up to his chest. Tracey's spindly legs wrapped around his thick body. Celia threw her body against the back of Tracey, sobbing, gripping her so tightly that Tracey tried to wriggle free, just a little, to take a breath. Mark Porter wrapped his long arms around Tracey and his wife, securely, protectively. Tears sprang from his eyes unabashedly.

Sal had been in the police vehicle with them and stepped out to guide them away from the site of the tunnel. He glanced at Molly sorrowfully, or perhaps he was embarrassed. At that moment, Molly didn't care what he felt. She looked away, her thoughts turning back to Cole.

A strong hand grasped Molly's shoulder, pulling her out of her worried stupor. She spun around. Pastor Lett stood before her. Molly walked into her open arms.

"Molly," her voice carried relief, "are you okay?"

"Yes, I mean, no. I don't know," she admitted.

"You're a brave woman, Molly," she said.

Molly heard her whisper a prayer, and Molly pulled gently back from her, recognizing, for the first time since Tracey's ordeal began, the remarkable person behind Pastor Lett's eyes: a woman of strength and dedication, a woman who cared more for others than for herself. She saw her as she must have been for so many years before the tragedy that had befallen her and Rodney. She saw her as Rodney's older sister.

Molly took Pastor Lett's large hand in hers, "Thank you so much, for…everything. Tracey wouldn't be with her parents if it weren't for you, and I know you risked a lot by helping." Molly reached into her pockets and withdrew the empty bags of seeds. She looked up at Pastor Lett sheepishly, "I'll buy you more."

"No need," she smiled, warmly.

"Cole? How'd he know?" she asked Pastor Lett.

"He came on his own," Pastor Lett said. "He came flying down here in your car," she nodded in the direction of her car, "and said he had to get to you. He was down the tunnel before I could say anything."

Commotion at the tunnel entrance commanded Molly's attention. Two officers lifted Tracey's abductor out with their hands under her armpits. The abductor grimaced, and made a sound in her throat, as if she were in pain. Molly stared into her eyes, and it was there that she saw not pain, not fear, but the hollow feeling of loneliness and despair. Instinctively, Molly took a step backward. Officers immediately converged on the abductor, leading her toward a waiting police car. Tracey was nowhere in sight, and for that, Molly was thankful. As soon as the abductor was safely in the car, Molly rushed to the tunnel entrance.

"Cole?" she yelled as she ran.

Mike, crouched by the tunnel entrance, turned toward her. Molly pushed past him and demanded, "Where is he? What happened?"

Mike stood, "He's coming, Molly. He's okay."

"No thanks to you," she said angrily. She bit her lower lip and paced.

"Molly—"

"Don't talk to me now!" Molly's biting tone cut off his words. "Just…just…" She waved him away and turned her back to him. At that moment, Cole's soundly-set jaw and the worried, welcoming eyes appeared before his strong, filthy body. Relief swept through her. She started to run to him, hesitated, her hands clasping together in fresh panic, remembering his angry words, *I'm done.*

"Baby," he whispered, as his feet hit the ground.

Molly ran to him, almost knocking him back into the hole.

Cole held her as if he'd never let her go, and Molly sobbed, clinging to him as Tracey had clung to her. "I'm sorry," she said, over and over.

"Shhh," Cole replied. "I'm sorry. I should have believed you. I'm so sorry." He reached up and stroked Molly's hair, kissed the top of her head.

"How did you—"

"Erik," Cole replied. "He called after you did. He said you were in trouble. He told me where to find you. He told me, Molly. He knew."

Molly exhaled for what seemed to her like the first time in hours.

Molly's tears drenched his soft gray shirt. She looked up at him, but could not find the words to express her feelings. The happiness in her heart physically hurt. She held onto him for support, drawing

345

out his strength and using it as her own. A tiny hand on the back of Molly's shirt called her attention, and she turned around, her eyes dropping to see Tracey, dirty remnants of tears streaked her cheeks. Her parents stood behind her, each with a hand on one of her shoulders. Molly crouched down and hugged Tracey.

Tracey whispered in her ear, "Thank you."

Her parents cried openly, unashamed, and Molly moved to Celia, taking her in her arms. They embraced with a warmth and need that could only come from a mother's love, only understood by another mother. Celia looked into Molly's eyes, unable to find her voice, and mouthed, "God bless you."

The lump in Molly's throat had stolen her voice. They embraced again, and when they parted, Mark Porter said, "How can we ever repay you?"

Molly shook her head. She hugged Mark and leaned down to Tracey again, whispering in her ear, "You're safe now, Tracey." Molly kissed her forehead, gave her another hug, and watched them walk toward the waiting police car.

"Thank God she's home," Mike's voice broke the solemn scene.

Molly was too exhausted to say what she'd felt when she'd first set out that evening, angry, frustrated, and disappointed. She stared at him, then dropped her eyes as Sal joined them.

"You did it," Sal's words were kind, appreciative.

Cole put his hand on Molly's shoulder. "She sure did," he said in a tough, protective tone.

Sal reached a hand out in greeting. Cole lifted his chin, without accepting his hand.

"We have limited resources," Sal said in explanation. "Mike and I tried to convince Officer Brown, but we couldn't chase a..." he paused, searching for the right words.

"Whim?" Molly asked, annoyed. "Well, my *whim* saved her."

Mike grabbed her arm as she turned away. Cole moved closer, stood taller. Mike dropped her arm, explained, "Molly, we wanted to believe you. We did, honestly, but come on, you have to admit—"

"I know, okay?" she interrupted. "I get why you didn't come running," she looked up at Cole and stepped back from the three of them. "But what the hell? I mean, I had to do this alone?"

"Molly," Cole said.

"No, Cole. I'm thankful that you were there. I *could* have been killed. You were right, all along you were right. I put myself in danger, but I didn't care. Don't you get that?" Her anger returned. She spoke fervently to Mike and Sal, "You're police! If you don't take a chance to save someone, what good are you?"

"And what if she hadn't been there, Molly?" Mike retorted.

"Then I'd have wasted your time, right?" Molly spat.

"Yes! Exactly!" Mike said sternly.

Molly paced, "I don't know, okay? I don't know what you should have done, but I'm goddamn thankful that I went, and even more thankful that Cole showed up!" She moved to Cole, realizing, at that second, that it had taken Erik's visions, his plea, to get Cole's acceptance. Why should it have taken any less to get theirs? Her shoulders slumped, the ability to fight left her, and she sighed, pinching the bridge of her nose with her fingers, struggling to hold back the tears that threatened like a storm on the horizon.

Cole went to her, understanding her body language and held her.

Cole stared at Mike and Sal, indicating his displeasure. They nodded and walked away. Cole silently moved Molly's wayward curls from her eyes, pulling the tresses off of her shoulder and laying them, carefully, behind her back. He tipped her chin up with his index finger, gazing into her red and swollen eyes, and said, each word conveying his love, "Molly, you scared the hell out of me. When Erik called, I had thoughts of all sorts of awful things happening to you." Molly opened her mouth to respond, and he placed his index finger gently across it, shushing her. "I can't lose you, Molly. I adore you. You scared me, but I'm so proud of you. I wouldn't want you to be any different." He took her in his arms again and held her.

Finally, in that moment, the dam burst. She cried. She cried for Tracey. She cried for Amanda. She cried out of thankfulness that Cole had rescued her. She cried the tears that she'd held in for so many nights that week. It was finally over.

Twenty Seven

Tracey's abductor's nerves were afire. Her body trembled. She could not stop thinking about Tracey. *Where was she? Was she okay? Safe?* She worried about her being sad, becoming sick from the toxins. She missed her.

She sat on the cold metal chair in the gray room, her arms wrapped tightly around her torso. She felt small and more alone than she ever had in the tunnels. Gazing at the long mirror that adorned one of the walls, she didn't recognize the woman she saw in the reflection. She'd seen her own image so rarely that the image of a little girl, not a grown woman, materialized in her head. She looked away. The officer had told her to wait, but for what, she wasn't sure. She prayed silently, hoping God would hear her, *"Lord, you have been our dwelling place throughout all generations—"*

The door swung open, and two men moved noisily into the room. She recognized them from the day they had taken Tracey, the day her home was invaded by that woman.

The older man, the dark-haired one, spoke first, "Ma'am, do you understand why you're here?"

She nodded.

"You are under arrest." He paused, looked to the other, younger man who stood just inside the closed door, wearing jeans and a sweatshirt. After a moment he said, "You are under arrest for the abduction of Tracey Porter."

She sat silently, unresponsive.

The younger man read her the Miranda Rights and asked if she understood them.

"Yes," she whispered

"Do you understand why you are being arrested?" he asked.

She raised her eyes to meet his. He had kind eyes, but she still did not understand what was happening. "Yes?" she asked tentatively.

"Ma'am, do you understand that you may have a lawyer present if you wish?" he asked.

She nodded, knitting her fingers together nervously.

"Would you like a lawyer present, ma'am?"

She shook her head and whispered, "No, thank you."

"Okay."

The other man placed a tape recorder on the table, turned it on.

"Ma'am, I'm Sergeant Moeler," the younger gentleman nodded and smiled. "I'm going to tape our conversation. Is that okay?"

"Yes," she said.

The older gentleman said, "My name is Officer Rozutto, and I'm in charge of this investigation. State your name, please," he asked.

She looked down shyly.

The men rolled their eyes. "Ma'am, your name, please?"

"I...I don't really know." An unexpected tear rolled down her cheek.

"Ma'am, you have no idea what your name is?" he asked, trying to determine if she was being a smartass or truly did not know her identity. Sal leaned toward her from across the table where he had positioned himself.

"I...I know my first name, but I was never really told my last name," she admitted.

Sal glanced at Mike, who had settled himself into the chair just to her right.

"Okay," he said, "that's a start. What is your first name?"

"It's..." Her hands shook, her heart slammed against her chest, and tears tumbled down her cheeks. She tried to speak, but could not remember the last time she'd cried so hard—when her mummy had died? Was that it? She had been taught not to cry. The lump in her throat felt foreign to her. "My first name is..." she took a deep breath, which was interrupted by first one sob, then another. She tried again, "My first name is...Kate. My mummy called me Kate."

The two men sat back in their chairs. Sal wiped his hand down his face.

"Well, I'll be goddamned," Sergeant Moeler said.

The sweet smell of hazelnut and cream wafted into Molly's room, gently rousing her from a sound slumber. The evening before had taken a toll on her body which ached in places she didn't know were possible, bruises and cuts served as painful reminders of her struggle. Although she awoke with an overwhelming sense of relief, it was not a peaceful feeling. Something uncomfortable lingered, as if she'd forgotten something on a shopping list. She wrote it off to stress, and, listening to the faint sounds of ESPN from Cole's atrociously-loud television, Molly swung her legs off of the bed and opened the curtains. The morning sun was high in the sky.

Molly joined Cole at the kitchen table, where he immediately commended her on assisting with the search, and asked if she wanted to talk about it. Molly looked at him crosswise. Talking about it was the last thing she wanted to do. The thought of the search taking over any more of their time together worried her. She knew she had lingering duties and wanted to avoid the conflict they might cause.

"What's on today's agenda?" he asked.

"Let's see…nothing…nothing…and more nothing," she laughed.

"Uh-huh, right," Cole rolled his eyes. "Now, what's really on the agenda?"

Molly braced herself and decided to get the admission over with. "Okay, so I know I have to deal with it all today, go to the station, stop by and see Edie, visit Rodney—my God, Rodney," she sighed loudly, frazzled, "and I need to call Erik, but I don't want to talk about it. I need a break." She reached across the table and grabbed his hand. "We need a break."

"We don't have to talk about it. I just thought you might have wanted to. I've already spoken to Erik, so that's one less thing on your list." He leaned closer to her and placed his hands on her cheeks. He gazed into her eyes, and in a warm, protective voice, said, "You'll never have to face anything alone again. I'm going with you."

Pastor Lett knelt before the altar, feeling like a hypocrite. She preached to the community about faithfulness, sins, and righteousness—and yet, she kept such dark secrets, secrets of necessity, but secrets just the same. She closed her eyes and prayed, "Lord, please hear me out. I probably don't deserve any favors, certainly not from You, anyway, but I need one here. You sent me a sign, a sign that I was doing the right thing by carrying on the wishes of those who trust me, but I cannot reconcile it in my mind any longer. I can no longer see the correctness of it, the use for it. Times have changed, people have changed. I need another sign. I can't believe I am being so greedy," she shook her head, as if disgusted with herself. "I can no longer live with myself. I just don't know how to go on, knowing how the kid is living, up there on the knoll, alone. What on this good Earth could be so awful to have to keep him hidden away like that any longer?"

She froze when a gentle hand touched her shoulder. She shielded her face, hiding her tears, and turned around cautiously. She was met with the solemn faces of Newton and Hannah. She stood and reached out to them. *A sign.*

Kate was thoroughly exhausted, physically, mentally, but most of all, emotionally. She felt as if her heart—and her soul—were being violently ripped apart. She thought back to that morning's revelation.

She had been sitting in the remote room with the large mirror, facing the friendly police officer.

"Ma'am, do you think your last name might be Plummer?" he had asked.

The name had sent a chill down Kate's spine, as memories of an older woman and man leapt into her mind from some deeply-hidden recess where they had been stored long ago. She let her face fall into her hands and tried desperately to will away the tears that welled in her eyes. She'd fought the memories for so many years! She did not want to live through them again.

"Kate?" Officer Rozutto had attempted to soothe her. He had reached over and touched her arm. "Kate, do you think your last name might be Plummer?"

The sound of the name again had sent a shudder down her spine. She could feel the blood pulsing through her veins, her heart beating in her neck. From behind her hands and through her sobs, she said, "I don't know. I don't know." The sobs choked her. She took several deep breaths, still hiding her face in her hands, unable to face the officers, the two men who had taken Tracey from her, the two men who had exposed the memories that she'd pushed away for so long in an effort to survive, memories that she'd locked away and refused to revisit, the pain was too great, the longing too harsh. She feared what they'd do about her crying. She knew she should not be weak. She'd been taught not to be weak. She took a deep breath, and slowly lowered her hands until her fingertips rested just below her eyes, her mouth barely visible. She tried to stop the flow of tears, but no matter how much she tried to stop them, they streamed relentlessly, just like the memories. No matter how much she fought them now, pushed them away, she also wanted to spit them out. They were eating away at her, like the toxins.

Kate stared at him for a long time, until it became uncomfortable, and he looked down. Her voice, barely a whisper, said, "It…might be."

"Kate?" Sergeant Moeler said softly, bringing her back from her thoughts.

She could feel his eyes on her, but she was drowning in sorrow, in memories that she'd buried long ago.

Officer Rozutto asked again how she had come to live in the tunnels and where the person who brought her there was.

"My mum…my mother, she died of the toxins. I don't want to die from them." She began to move her hands in an agitated fashion, remembering the promise she had made to her mother, and knowing that now she could no longer keep it. "You have to save Tracey," she pleaded with them. "My mother told me to save her, and I did, but now she might die anyway!" Her voice escalated, fear of the toxins loomed in her mind. She grabbed Officer Rozutto's arm urgently, "Please, you have to find Tracey. We need to save her." She breathed heavily, looking around the room—but for what? Tracey? An exit? She didn't know.

"Kate, it's okay. I think you've learned some things that maybe aren't so true. Tracey is going to be fine. She is not going to get sick, I promise you that."

Kate was confused, worried about Tracey. She closed her eyes and silently prayed, asking God to watch over Tracey.

"Kate, if you are Kate Plummer, you have a mother and father who will be thrilled to see you,"

Sergeant Moeler looked at Kate as though he doubted her word.

Kate folded her hands in and out of her lap nervously.

"We need to verify that you are Kate Plummer. We can do that with a DNA sample."

"Oh, I see," she replied even though didn't really see. Kate was confused. She looked from one officer to the other, then down at the table, hesitated, then asked, "What if I'm not... Kate Plummer?"

"Well, then we'll try and find out who you really are," Sergeant Moeler said confidently.

Officer Rozutto sat in the chair across from the woman, his hands steepled just under his nose, thinking. Eventually he broke the silence that had become uncomfortable for Kate, and said, "Kate, this is going to be very hard for you, and I'm sorry for that, but do you remember how you came to live underground? Can you remember who took you there?"

Kate closed her eyes, flashes of memories played in her mind like a poorly-cut movie. Tears pushed on her closed eyelids. She felt as though she were betraying her mother by talking to them, but something in her mind told her that she had to tell. It was the right thing to do. She'd been taught not to lie, and even though her gut told her not to tell them the truth, she worried what God would think of her if she didn't. She opened her eyes, took a deep breath, ignoring her own tears, and began telling them about how beautiful and kind her mother was, and of her childhood in the tunnels—playing hide-and-seek and listening to their echoes. Her memories of waking up scared at night, as a small girl, and how her mother would wrap her arms and legs around her from behind, and let her fall asleep like that, safely tucked within her confines, their hearts beating in rhythm.

Officer Rozutto asked her again what her mother's name was, and she answered honestly, "I never knew her real name. She never told me, and I don't think I ever asked. She was the little girl in the photograph that you took from our home. I called her mummy, like Tracey calls me." The sound of Tracey's name coming from her own lips sent a pain through her chest. She'd failed her mother. She'd failed Tracey.

Officer Rozutto gently persisted, "Do you remember how you came to live with her?"

Again she closed her eyes, shaking her head. "I know I was wearing the dress that Tracey wears to pray. I remember that flowered dress." Kate's face contorted, as if a painful memory were weaving its way through her mind. Sergeant Moeler and Officer Rozutto looked at each other.

"It's okay, Kate. We can take a break if you need to," Officer Rozutto said.

She shook her head, tears streaming down her cheeks. Her cheeks flushed red. She stood. Sergeant Moeler and Officer Rozutto came quickly to their feet. She paced nervously. "I—" she said, then went silent. Officer Rozutto motioned for Sergeant Moeler to stay back, let her pace.

"I remember," her words came out like broken glass, each one hard to piece together. She grabbed the sides of her head. Officer Rozutto came up behind her and guided her gently to the chair. She sat down, clasped her hands together in her lap and began rocking nervously. She didn't look at Sergeant Moeler or Officer Rozutto. "I remember...I remember playing in the playground by the church. I was there with friends, and I remember trying so hard not to get my dress dirty," she looked up with sad, red eyes. "I had gotten that dress specifically for that party," a crooked, pained smile passed across her lips, then disappeared. She reached up and covered her face. "She came to the edge of the cornfield. She was hidden, and I could only see her face. I was so happy. She had played with me before, and I remember being so happy to see her that day." Tears ran down her cheeks, but she didn't feel saddened by the memory, just confused. "I walked over to her, in the cornfield, and she took me to the campsite. I remember her telling me that her mummy had died, and she really needed a friend, so I went with her." She lowered her hands and raised her voice, "I went with her. I went."

"And she took you underground that day?" Officer Rozutto asked.

Kate nodded, remembering. "She turned it into a game. She said it was her secret hideout, and that no one could find us there, that we could play forever, and I wouldn't have to go to school or do anything I didn't want to do. I remember it being...fun. Until I wanted to go home, then-" she turned away. She wiped her tears and looked down at her hands, ashamed that she had been a bother to Mummy, that she had cried and had to be put in the bad spot. She wondered what Sergeant Moeler and Officer Rozutto must think of her—that she had been a bad little girl, or selfish, or something even worse.

"Did you try to get away? Do you remember?" Sergeant Moeler asked forcefully.

She nodded, giving him an odd look, "I...I don't remember wanting to get away from her," she said protectively. "I just remember asking if I could go home." She looked down again, her voice became faint, "But there was no going home. Mummy explained to me about the toxins, and how they get into your body when you live on the outside, how sometimes you don't even know you're sick until it is too late. She told me that was how her mummy died. She lived for about thirty years on the outside, and she was sick when they went underground, and became even sicker as time went on, but she did it to save Mummy...my mother. She didn't want her to die, and she knew that she was sick a lot, and I guess it was from the toxins, because when Mummy died, she died just like her mother did, in the same way." She was uncomfortable with their eyes trained on her, hanging onto her every word, disbelieving her, she could tell. "And she told me that I had to save a little girl, that it was my job, that God would be waiting for me to save someone, and if I didn't, that He might do something awful to me." She became angry again, "And now I've failed her."

"Kate, I'm sorry you went through all that you did," Officer Rozutto leaned across the table, "but do you understand that taking Tracey away from her parents was just as wrong as your mummy taking you away from your parents?"

Tears burned her eyes again, and she clenched them shut, speaking through clenched teeth, "But she *saved* me. What she did *wasn't* wrong—and I saved Tracey. Maybe her parents don't even know about the toxins, I don't know." She pulled back from the table, swiping at the hair that had fallen across her face. "I *saved* her!" she said fiercely.

Molly hung up the phone and flopped on the couch next to Cole. "It was Mike. He called to apologize, *again*, and then put Sal on. They think Tracey's abductor is Kate Plummer."

"Unbelievable," Cole said, astonished.

"Sal said Tracey's family is pressing charges," Molly added, "but they'll decide what they're seeking for her—help or jail—after her identity is confirmed—or not." Molly turned away, but Cole pulled her close.

"I know you're thinking about Amanda and her family."

Molly blinked away her tears. "She never had a chance, Cole. I wish I had done something, tried to stop that man. I wish I had screamed, called 9-1-1. Something! Anything!" she wiped her eyes. "But I didn't, and I know I can't change that. Amanda's gone."

Cole looked into her eyes, "But Tracey isn't."

Cole had been at the grocery store for over an hour and Molly had lain on the couch, resting, in his absence. She heard the front door open and lifted her body to an upright position, gathering her energy in order to appear a little less exhausted for Cole when he walked into the room. To her surprise, she saw Erik's face instead. She jumped up, energized, and ran to him, throwing her arms around his body, "Erik!"

"Ma! I can't breathe!" he said, laughing.

"How did you get here?" She was overcome with joy. She turned her smile to Cole who popped a grape into his mouth and shrugged.

"I know you, Mol. You needed to see him, to touch him." Cole winked.

Erik grinned, digging into the grapes.

"You guys are so great!" she exclaimed. "How did you get here so fast?"

"I called last night and made flight arrangements. I was sure you figured it out the other night, when you came back from looking for the dogs? When you walked in and I was on the cell phone speaking cryptically?"

Molly gave him a puzzled look.

"I had an airport taxi pick him up this morning and drive him to the Carters'. He's been there for hours."

"But I just spoke to him a few hours ago."

Erik held up his cell phone. "That's the great thing," his dark eyes sparkled. "With a cell phone, you never really know where I am." He put his arm around his mother and kissed the top of her head, very parentally.

Molly reached her arm around his back, which felt broader than it had when he'd left for school just weeks earlier. She *had* needed to see him, to touch him. She had missed his presence.

"Are you hungry? What do you want me to make you?" Molly slipped into mommy mode again so easily, like riding a bike.

"Naw, Dad and I ate a little while ago," his voice was deep and thoughtful.

"Oh, gosh!" Molly said. "I almost forgot. I have to return a call to Pastor Lett. I'm so sorry! Give me just a quick minute, okay?" She saw a look of disbelief pass from father to son.

"Come on, buddy, let's watch a movie. She'll be at least that long," Cole said.

Home is different now, Tracey wrote in her new journal. Everything felt different to her. The warm bubble bath had felt good; the clean clothes, her soft sheets, and her favorite toys comforted her, but she still felt funny. Her mother and father treated her too carefully, as if she could break. Tracey missed Mummy. She wanted to know where she was, if she was okay, and if she was worried about the toxins. She knew she wasn't supposed to worry about Mummy—her parents told her that she was a bad person and that taking her had been wrong, but Tracey didn't think she was all bad. After all, she really hadn't hurt her—and the toxins! Tracey was so confused. She tried to explain to her mother and father about the toxins—how they killed Mummy's mother and her grandmother—but they didn't believe her. Tracey felt sure that they just didn't know about the toxins. Her mother told her that what Mummy had said about the toxins was just a story that she'd made up to keep Tracey with her, but Tracey didn't believe her mother. She really wanted to see Mummy, and she needed to learn the right way to talk to God, just in case.

Tracey's mother told her that they'd have to see the police officers again sometime soon to answer their questions about where she had been kept and how she had gotten there. She said that they'd had loads of people looking for her and everything! Tracey wondered why all those people couldn't find them; they always did in the police shows. She told her mother that Mummy had never hurt her, but she didn't tell her about the bad spot. She didn't want Mummy to get in trouble. When her parents asked her why she went with Mummy into the tunnels, Tracey couldn't tell them. All she could remember was that she'd wanted her necklace. Her mother cried, then, and told Tracey that she needed to understand why she went and that she was sorry that she wasn't a good mother. Tracey felt horrible! She told her mother that she was a good mother, and that even if she didn't know about the toxins, that wasn't really her fault, but her mother just threw her hands up in the air and walked over to Tracey's father and cried. Tracey was trying so hard to be good that she couldn't understand why her mother was so sad. Maybe she was worried about the toxins.

Emma had crawled into Tracey's bed the night before. She came right in when she thought Tracey was asleep and curled up in front of her. Tracey didn't mind. She had missed Emma a lot and grew sad when she'd heard her sniffling, like she was crying. Tracey had reached her arms around Emma and had held her like she was a giant doll. Then Tracey had cried, too.

She and Emma were playing now, but whenever Emma took one of Tracey's toys, their mother yelled at Emma. Tracey didn't need her mother to yell at her. She didn't mind that Emma took her toys except for the dolly that Mummy had given her. That one was not for sharing. It was special.

Tracey wanted to see Molly again, too. Her mother told her that she could, as soon as the people with the big cameras left their front yard. Tracey peeked out of the curtains when her mother wasn't looking— she didn't understand why their house was suddenly so special, but she liked knowing it was on television, even if she wasn't allowed to watch it. She wanted to go outside and let them take her picture, but her mother wouldn't allow it. She called them sharks, but they didn't look like sharks to Tracey.

Who knew this house could feel so warm? Pastor Lett thought to herself as she scrubbed the shelves in the library of the Perkinson House. It was just after four o'clock in the afternoon, and she, Hannah, and Newton had been cleaning the home for most of the day. They cleaned and dusted each room, polishing the floors and scrubbing away years of idle dirt. She was pleased to be making the home livable once again. Pastor Lett refrained from going into the upstairs bedroom, the images of Mrs. Perkinson and her daughter, coupled with her current anxiety, were just too much for her to fathom. Thank goodness for Hannah, who was more than happy to take over the cleaning of the bedrooms, and she had yet to mention seeing anything out of the ordinary. Newton had been busy repairing the outside of the house, rebuilding the steps, replacing rotten wood, and unsheathing the windows. Hannah had brought a few old throw rugs, and Newton and Betty had purchased several pieces of used furniture.

Pastor Lett was once again thankful for the loyalty of her friends. She knew she would not have been able to go through this *coming out* on her own. She stepped outside and the brisk afternoon air refreshed her. The gloom she had felt for so many years around the house began to lift, and it seemed that even the air itself had become lighter and less burdened. She walked off the wide porch and into the yard, astonished at how welcoming the house looked without the windows boarded up—or perhaps it was the relief of knowing the ominous lies that had been tied to the house were soon to be lifted.

Twenty Eight

Molly held Cole's hand as he drove past the Boyds Presbyterian Church, following Pastor Lett's car, on the way to visit Rodney. Molly looked beyond the church to the spider's web of yellow police tape. A chill ran through her. Molly was thankful to Pastor Lett for allowing her to meet Rodney, at the same time, she felt apprehensive about visiting him. She was glad Cole was going with her. She glanced behind her at Erik who was busy texting in the back seat. After so many days of bedlam and confusion, she almost felt a sense of calm.

They drove up to the familiar Victorian home. The front porch had three colorful rocking chairs and a sign that read: *Everyone Is A Friend, And All Friends Are Welcome*. There were green pastures with outcroppings of rocks peppering the ground. An enormous willow reached its long slim branches over a running creek just to the right of the house, with an iron bench under the umbrella of its limbs. Molly was astonished that Newton and Betty had been able to successfully hide Rodney for all those years.

Rodney shuffled out of the front door and into the outstretched arms of Pastor Lett, her eyes aglow with love and delight, her quick pace one that Molly could not have envisioned had she not seen it with her own eyes. She was dwarfed by Rodney, who effortlessly wrapped his arms around his older sister's body and spun in a circle, gleefully yelling, "Carla, come back! Carla, come back!"

Eventually, Rodney released her, and Pastor Lett landed with a thud. Rodney moved like an excited child, his hands wriggling at his sides, his feet marching quickly up and down. The jeans he wore were baggy at the knees and bunched around his ankles, as if he were wearing someone else's clothes, though his shirt was tightly stretched across his enormous chest and fleshy stomach.

Pastor Lett put her arm around Rodney's waist. Rodney's eyes grew wide, spying Molly, and he pushed out of his sister's grip and approached Molly with an enormous grin. In the flash of a second, he swooped her into his arms and lifted her off the ground, laughing, "Molly find girl!" His jubilant voice boomed, ricocheting off of the clouds.

Pastor Lett came to her rescue, pulling on Rodney's arm, urging her release.

"Ma?" Erik yelled. Cole looked at Pastor Lett expectantly.

Rodney continued to spin, and Molly thought she might be sick. "Rodney! Put Molly down!" Pastor Lett demanded.

Betty hurried to Molly's aid, "Rodney Lett, you put that girl down right now," her voice left no room for negotiation.

Rodney stopped, mid-spin, and lowered Molly toward the ground. She stumbled, dizzy, and lowered herself to the safety of the still ground beneath her. Rodney stooped next to her, his brown eyes open wide, concerned. Betty and Pastor Lett had their hands on Molly in seconds, insuring that she remain on the ground.

"Molly hurt?" Rodney asked nervously.

"I'm okay," Molly said in a whisper. She eased herself up to her feet. Rodney rose to his feet and locked eyes with Molly's.

"Rodney hurt you?" he asked sheepishly.

Molly reached out to Rodney and put her hand on his massive arm. "It's okay, Rodney," she said, forcing a smile. "It was fun. I'm okay." She watched the smile spread across his face.

"Molly like it?" Rodney asked in his husky voice.

"Yes, Molly like it," she nodded. She gave Pastor Lett and Betty a look that said she was alright.

"Erik?" Rodney asked simply.

Molly nodded toward her son. "Erik," she confirmed, "and my husband, Cole."

Betty was flawlessly efficient, serving turkey sandwiches and fruit and ensuring that everyone had a substantial amount of food, drinks, and properly-set silverware. She and Molly had a comfortable conversation about how long she'd been caring for Rodney, which, it turned out, she'd been secretly doing since two months after he'd been beaten. Their secluded property had provided the perfect cover. She was cheerful yet proper, sitting with knees bent and her legs crossed at the ankles and jumping up when Pastor Lett could not reach the salt, passing it to her promptly. It was evident that she was a natural caregiver and seemed to enjoy every aspect of it. Betty excused herself to get something from the kitchen, and Molly watched her hustle into the house.

Rodney ate voraciously, as if he hadn't eaten all day. Pastor Lett chided him, "Slow down, honey. Your food isn't going anywhere."

Rodney immediately slowed his chewing to a waltz as opposed to a samba, watching Molly out of the corner of his eye. Molly whispered, "I eat fast, too," which made him laugh out loud.

After lunch, Rodney insisted on showing Molly his bedroom which had windows on two sides and dark-colored sheers parted to let the sun shine through. Molly hardly recognized the room from the last visit when it had been shrouded in darkness. She walked in, expecting the Knowing to find her. She felt nothing unusual. "What a beautiful room, Rodney," she said. Pride filled his eyes.

Suddenly, Rodney darted out of the room as quickly as his large body would allow. He thumped up a flight of stairs, hunching over to avoid hitting his head. Molly, Cole, and Pastor Lett followed him into the quaint, finished attic. There were toys scattered about, and one corner had drawings tacked up on the wall. Molly turned questioning eyes to Pastor Lett.

"This is Rodney's playroom," she whispered.

Molly lifted her chin toward the drawings. Cole came to her side, "Please, Molly, tell me they mean nothing."

She laughed and snuggled into his side, "Don't worry. I don't feel a thing."

Rodney rushed to the stairs, startling Molly. "Rodney go. Find Erik."

They found Erik and Rodney in the backyard. Rodney stood with his back to the house, his eyes locked in a gaze with Erik's.

"Rodney?" Molly asked. "Are you okay?" Rodney did not answer. She moved to Erik's side. "Erik? What's wrong?"

Pastor Lett moved protectively to Rodney's side.

"Mom," Erik's voice was strained, "I kind of still feel the guy."

She turned and looked at Rodney. "Rodney?"

"No, another guy," he shifted his gaze to Pastor Lett.

"What's going on?" Molly asked in Pastor Lett's direction.

Pastor Lett looked down. Erik did not.

"It's her, Mom," he said.

"Pastor Lett," Molly said, in confusion, "what the hell is going on?"

Pastor Lett stepped forward, holding Molly's gaze. "I need to show you something."

Pastor Lett walked with Betty, speaking in whispers, just ahead of Molly, Cole, and Erik. Newton and Hannah were already inside the Perkinson House, and she was thankful for their presence.

"You've done a lot to this house in a day, Pastor Lett," Molly said with feigned interest. Erik hurried around her, toward the rear of the house. Pastor Lett nervously followed him, ignoring Molly's comment.

"Molly," Pastor Lett said nervously as she neared the rear of the house, "how long has Erik had visions?"

"Why do you—" she turned to follow his gaze and saw Erik kneeling at the cellar doors, his palms flat against the cold metal. "Oh my God!" She ran to his side, leaving Cole a few steps behind.

Pastor Lett registered Newton's fleeting footsteps rushing toward them.

Erik's hands appeared frozen to the cellar doors. He looked over his shoulder at his mother, his eyes pleading with her.

Molly kneeled next to him, her hand on his back.

"It's him," Erik said, his eyes falling back down to the cellar doors, the lock.

"Who?" Molly laid her hands on top of his. "My God," she said under her breath. She looked over her shoulder at Pastor Lett, anger in her eyes. "How could you?"

"Molly, it's not what you think!" Pastor Lett said quickly. She had hoped that she would have been able to explain before Molly found out on her own.

Newton moved swiftly between Molly and Pastor Lett. "Molly," he said, "Pastor Lett's done nothing wrong. Please, let her explain."

"Let her explain why there's a man locked in a cellar? Newton, what are you thinking?" she said angrily. Her eyes fell back to her son, who appeared to be unable to move from his kneeling position.

"What the hell is going on?" Cole demanded, seeing the fear in Erik's eyes, the anger in Molly's. No one moved or answered. "Erik?" Cole rushed to his side, then looked directly into Molly's eyes. "Molly?"

"There's a man in there, locked in."

Cole's eyes met Pastor Lett's, cold and angry, filled with rancor. He lifted Molly to her feet, then took Erik by the shoulders, and with all of his strength, and all of his tenderness, he lifted him back, away from the cellar door. Molly rushed to Erik and wrapped her arms around him. Erik stared straight ahead, as if his mind had somehow been damaged by the scene.

Cole confronted Pastor Lett angrily. "Open it!" he demanded.

Pastor Lett could not speak, she was in a state of panic.

"Open the goddamn door, Pastor!" Cole yelled.

Newton came forward, trying to calm the situation, "Cole, please, before this gets worse, please let us explain."

Hannah, hearing the noise, came running onto the back porch. "What is going on out here?" She took in the scene: Erik, shivering and enveloped in his mother's arms, Cole, angrily confronting Pastor Lett, and Newton, soft and small, standing between them, trying to make peace.

"Oh, for heaven's sake, Cole," Hannah said as she descended the steps. She reached out and placed her hand gently on his arm. He shrugged her off. "Cole!" She said in a motherly tone. "You listen to me, Cole Tanner. Carla did nothing wrong. She merely carried out the family's wishes. Now calm your britches and come over here and talk to me, would you?" She spun on her heel and walked toward the gazebo.

Cole pointed angrily toward Pastor Lett, then followed Hannah, venom in his eyes. "You've got my full attention," Cole said to her, hands on hips, body tense with fury.

Hannah wiped her hands on her jeans, her voice calm, direct, "Cole, Carla was asked years ago to care for one of the Perkinsons' kids. You see, he was born retarded, and the family was scared. It all happened right after Rodney was," she turned thoughtful eyes toward Pastor Lett, "beaten. They felt they had to hide William from the community. They were terrified for his life!" She looked from Cole to Pastor Lett, a look of sorrow in her eyes. "They had no family in the area, and they were a reclusive family to begin with. They didn't trust anyone. They kept the child hidden in the house for years and years, until it was all he knew—and after what happened to Rodney, well, it seemed only right to continue to keep him hidden." She looked down at the ground, then back at Cole. "It doesn't seem right now, now that the world has changed, and everyone is accepted for who they are, but back then, in the time when he was born, well...it was what it was. They locked kids up that were different, put them in institutions, and the family didn't want that."

Pastor Lett had moved closer to the gazebo, her shoulders dropped, her head hung low. She interrupted Hannah, hoping not to agitate Cole any further, but needing to speak her mind. "He had run of the house until just recently. I didn't like keeping him there. I came to visit him every day, sometimes many times each day. He is family to me. As I said, while I cared for him, he lived in the house, not the cellar, and then those damned teenagers became curious about the haunted house on the hill." She paused, looking up at the house, wearily. "We had to keep the kid," she said endearingly, "William, secluded to the cellar where he had grown up." Pastor Lett looked down and shook her head. She knew she would have to face the community and that this was just the beginning. Cole's anger wasn't near what she'd expected, but the ache in her gut still surprised her, the sadness for what she'd done engulfed her mind and her body. "It's awful, Cole, and I know that," she spoke from her heart, true words laced with disgrace. "I have wrestled with this for years. You have no idea how painful it is," her voice escalated, "but I am a pastor, and I gave the family my word!"

She looked at Molly, hoping for understanding, forgiveness. Erik sat beside her, worn out, motionless. "It was Molly who made me change my mind. When I saw her with Rodney, I realized then that the kid, that William, needed to have more of a life, no matter what the Perkinson family wanted." The anguish in Pastor Lett's words was clear. "I have wanted to release him from that place for years, but Chet Perkinson was adamant about him remaining there, hidden from the community. I felt locked in a prison—knowing it was wrong to keep him hidden, and yet, I had given my word." She turned away, ashamed.

Cole looked at her, then at Hannah, and Newton. "How could you do this for so long? There's a man in there! For Christ's sake, Pastor Lett, you of all people."

"I know," Pastor Lett said, solemnly. "I cannot reconcile it myself, so I don't expect you to. We're trying to right the wrong we've done, make his life better, provide a real life, no matter how closely we're scrutinized."

"Newton, Hannah? You, too?" Cole turned pained eyes toward them.

Hannah nodded, "Yes, Cole, we all helped take care of William. He's a lovely man, just lovely." She shrugged. "When a family asks something of you, how do you know when it is right to go against their wishes? How do you know when to back out of it?"

"I thought for sure this would have ended years ago," Pastor Lett added. "Another location found, a home with a family possibly, anything, but the years just kept passing by, and then it was such a habit, such a normal typical thing, taking care of him, well...." she let her words trail off with the setting sun and looked away. "I don't expect to be forgiven. He's a man now, physically, but he's still a five-year-old mentally. I cannot tell you how many nights I wanted to bring him home with me, but I was worried that even that would get me into trouble. Once Rodney was beaten, I was unsure of anything in this town. Hannah," she looked at her brown hair waving in the slight breeze, her hands covered with dirt and dust, the understanding that was evident on her face, and the compassion in her eyes, "and Newton," Newton gazed nervously at the ground, hands in his khaki pants pockets, the toe of his sneaker kicked at the ground, "well, they are the only people I felt that I could truly trust with someone else's life." She looked toward Molly, "until the other night, when Molly opened my eyes and made me remember that there are good people in the world, that sometimes giving of yourself, making yourself vulnerable, is the right thing to do at any cost." Her eyes pleaded with Molly, who allowed the end of her mouth to turn up.

Cole paced, running his hand through his dark hair. "What the hell? Molly?" he looked at her, as if she held all of the answers.

"Cole," Molly said, "she didn't have to invite us here." Her voice was quiet, almost a whisper. "She didn't have to expose William at all. It sounds like— and not that I condone her behavior—but it sounds like she was overwhelmed, accepted a responsibility that she came to realize wasn't the right thing to do, and now she is trying to right her wrong." She reached up, tenderly brushing his hair off of his forehead. He leaned down and rested his cheek against hers, as if he would know what was right by touching her, as if the answer would seep through her skin to his own mind.

He turned toward Pastor Lett then, and spoke softly, his hand in Molly's, "Well, what the hell are we waiting for?" he looked around. "Let's get William out of there and get this place in shape for him. The quicker the better." He looked toward the gazebo where Erik sat, the color returned to his face. "Erik, I need you: Stat!"

Erik walked swiftly to his side, "Dad?"

Cole put his hands on his shoulder. "Are you all right, son?"

Erik nodded.

"Good. Can we use your strength to help make this place livable?"

Erik looked to his mother for guidance. She nodded, encouraging him. "Hell yes!" he said.

Hannah sidled up to Molly and tapped her on the shoulder. Molly turned and understood from the pained look in Hannah's eyes that there was more. Hannah took Molly's hand and led her away from the group, to the edge of the woods.

"As long as we're all confessing," Hannah whispered, "I have something to tell you." Tears formed in her eyes and she turned to face the lake. "Walk with me?" They walked over the crest of the hill, descending toward the lake. "Remember when I took you into the woods?"

Molly feared what she'd hear next. "You don't have to tell me anything, Hannah," she said.

Hannah stopped walking and faced Molly. "I want to. I've been carrying this around for too long." She took a deep breath, let it out slowly. A bird landed on the water and Hannah watched the ripples snaking their way to the shore. "That place, where I knelt?"

Molly nodded.

"I...I had a daughter. She only lived for moments, and Charlie was so crazy," her words spewed swiftly, nervously from her lips.

"Hannah, no."

Hannah nodded. "I was terrified. If Charlie had found out he would have done god knows what. I know it was wrong, not to bury her properly, but I did the best I could."

I did the best I could. Molly felt the truth in her words. "I'm sorry," was all she could say.

Epilogue

"Hurry up, you guys, we'll be late for the party!" Molly hustled downstairs. The interwoven sparkles in her clingy black dress gleamed from the lights on the Christmas tree with her every move. She walked up behind Erik and hugged him, remembering the days when he had gone through a stage where he had pretended that Molly wasn't his mother—embarrassed by any public displays of attention. She couldn't believe that the young man who stood beside her, his arm around her shoulders, was the same person—she'd thought the stage would never end. Her heart swelled with pride. "Thanks for coming home for the holidays," she said.

"Ma, where else would I go?"

"Jenna's?" she said, cautiously.

"Yeah, right, like she'd be more fun than you and Dad? I don't think so." He popped an almond in his mouth. "Besides," he grinned from ear to ear, "she had to be with her family today anyway."

Molly gave him a look that asked for more details, and she wasn't surprised when he responded, "Don't even ask." She followed him into the family room where Cole sat in his underwear and dress shirt watching television. "Cole!" Molly chided him. "What are you doing? We're supposed to be there in ten minutes!" Exasperated, she threw her hands up in the air and waited for him to move upstairs. Instead, he turned his head to face her. The light caught his dark, sensual eyes, making it hard for Molly to stay upset with him. The look on his face was sweet, reminding her of all the reasons she'd fallen in love with him in the first place— and fallen in love with him again over the past few weeks as their harrowing ordeal had wound down.

"Why don't you just sit down here next to me a minute?" he said, patting the couch next to him. "You look so beautiful." He reached for her hand.

"Flattery, my friend, will get you nowhere. Come on," she urged him, "the clock is ticking, and I promised. Eight o'clock, remember?"

"Yeah, I remember." He patted the cushion again.

"Urgh," Molly relented, walking around the couch. He ran his hand seductively along the back of her legs as she stepped past him. She settled into the couch, a little agitated, and forced a smile.

He wrapped his arm around her back, placing his other hand on her knee. He gazed into her eyes, reeling her in. "We've been so crazed lately. I just want a minute with you." As he spoke, Erik walked into the room. "I wanted a quiet moment to give you your gift."

She gingerly took a flat box from his hand and excitedly tore it open. Inside was a leather-bound journal with the inscription, *'My love, No more doubting. I believe in you. Go get 'em, Baby! I love you now and always, Cole.'*

"Oh, Cole," she climbed into his lap and kissed his lips.

"Oh, come on! Get a room! I don't want to see this," Erik laughed as he left the room.

Pastor Lett stood in the living room of the Perkinson House in anticipation of the holiday party. She watched Hannah, Betty, Rodney, and William sitting by the Christmas tree, drinking eggnog and eating Christmas treats. She had no doubt that they had done the right thing and wished that they had felt they could have done it years earlier. Part of her worried about forgiveness, but she knew that might be too much to ask. She'd have to wait and see what the Lord had in store for her. There had been a bit of an uproar from the community, and she had undergone an investigation of abuse, but she came out with a slap on the hand and a few harsh words about how she should have known better, done something sooner, made other arrangements, which she knew she deserved, but after a few short weeks, the grumbling stopped. The investigative committee had been surprised, though not nearly as surprised as Pastor Lett had been, to learn that William was the illegitimate son of Chet Perkinson's mentally retarded sister, who had died during childbirth. That had made no difference to Pastor Lett, in fact, she believed it endeared him even more to her. In the end, it was the support of the community and the backing of the Boyds Presbyterian Church congregation that had enabled her to turn the Perkinson House into the Perkinson House for the Handicapped. Lauren, the caregiver she hired, was wonderful. She'd taken to William as if he were her own brother, showering him with attention, patiently listening to his repetitive stories and jokes, and generally making him feel loved and needed.

The police made amends for their mistake, and Pastor Lett, being the good woman that she was, accepted their apologies and forgave them, thankful that Rodney had not perished. The community rallied around her when she'd made the announcement at the church that Rodney had lived. Edie and Jin were beside themselves with joy. Edie told Pastor Lett that she had known he was alive, and that Pastor Lett had told her about him many years earlier, although she didn't remember ever doing so. It brought great pleasure to Pastor Lett to have both Rodney and William welcomed into the community, though she was taken aback by her own feelings, feelings of anger toward the community that had once accused her brother of such a heinous crime and toward Harley Mott, Mac Peterson, and Joe Dillon, the men who had beaten him, but God took care of those feelings, reminding her of forgiveness, of what she had asked for with regard to William. He certainly worked in mysterious ways.

It had been a hard decision for Pastor Lett not to bring Rodney home to live with her, but Betty had felt very strongly that moving him from her home, where he'd lived for the past twenty years, would cause great conflict within him. In the end, she'd given in, leaving Rodney to reside with Newton and Betty, where she was certain that Rodney was not only cared for but was happy. Molly and Rodney had established an even stronger connection in the past few weeks. She visited Rodney with Pastor Lett every Tuesday, and he continued to lift her up off of the ground and spin her as if it were the first time he had ever seen her.

Hannah's confession about her baby, Clara Ann—her birth, and her death—had come as a surprise to Pastor Lett, and sadness weighed heavily in her heart as she watched her friend across the room. She still couldn't imagine the guilt that must have eaten at Hannah every day, living with her child being buried in the woods—like an animal. Newton had, once again, done something remarkable. The headstone he'd had made to mark Clara Ann's passing had gone unnoticed for all those years, waiting for her little body to join it. Pastor Lett hoped that all those years of guilt and hiding had been put to rest with the moving of Clara Ann's body to the church cemetery. She thought of the memorial service that had taken place just days earlier, and she thought she saw a softening of Hannah's face, around her eyes, as she looked in her direction.

Pastor Lett turned toward the sound of laughter. Newton and Betty were busy stringing popcorn, which they had been threading for the last week. They giggled like schoolchildren, laughing at a secret that only the two of them knew. Betty reached down and kissed his cheek, her hand as pale as a dove against his dark skin. He blushed and touched her hand. Pastor Lett didn't think she could have made it through each of the difficult years, all of the trying times, without Newton by her side. He'd made things bearable for her, often reminding her why it was that she was taking care of William, and just how much the family relied on her, and how one day, it would all work out for the best. He had been right. *God bless him.* Pastor Lett leaned against the wall and watched Newton with Betty, his Member's Only jacket still zipped up tight to his chin, even though he was inside the house. Thinking of the old joke, *He's got to be the last member!* brought a smile to her lips. She felt a little like a voyeur and turned away to allow them privacy. A soft knock at the door pulled her in that direction. Molly, Cole, and Erik stood before her carrying Poinsettias and brownies.

Molly handed her a large wrapped box which had been hidden behind her back, and which she would later discover held four large bags of sunflower seeds. She embraced her. "So good to see you," she said.

Rodney heard her voice and lumbered across the floor, his speed in great contrast to his size. He pulled Molly away from his sister and picked her up, swinging her around, laughing, "Molly come! Molly see Rodney!"

She stood on her tiptoes and kissed his cheek. Rodney blushed.

At that moment, Pastor Lett felt as though she were complete: the secrets were out, and she could live each day in happiness, with no more midnight canoe rides, no more locks and chains. At that thought, she glanced toward the front door, next to which hung her old neck chain and keys. She kept them as a reminder of her own weaknesses as a human, but was glad to be relieved of their weight.

When Sal and Mike arrived at the party, Molly was dancing with Cole, her cheek pressed against his chest, their bodies moving in perfect sync. Molly felt a hand on her shoulder before she heard his voice.

"May I cut in?" Mike's voice swept into her ears, and she envisioned his boyish smile.

Cole handed her over to him.

"So," Mike said, as they eased into their dance, "how have you been?"

"Great, and you?"

"Okay. This is a hard time for me," he admitted.

Molly looked into his sad eyes, eyes that she was sure his wife must have longed to stay with as she took her last and final breath. "I know. I'm glad you're here," Molly said. They had become close, and Molly felt that he needed a family to spend the holidays with.

"Did Sal tell you the news?"

Molly shook her head.

"We got the DNA results back. Kate is in fact Kate Plummer, and the two bodies, they were definitely Walter Meeks's wife and daughter, Maribelle and Leah. We just got the call this morning. And the Boyds Boys, as you so kindly call them, have been taken into custody."

Molly was saddened by the news of the Boyds Boys. She had held out hope that they weren't the ones who had beaten Rodney.

Molly watched Cole from across the room. His mouth barely moved as he spoke to Erik. He rested his arm around Erik's shoulder, and once again Molly knew that she and Cole were meant to be together. The song ended, and she and Mike walked toward them. Both Cole and Erik reached out to Molly. Instantly, she understood why she had fought so hard to find Tracey, why she felt so deeply for Kate, and why she hurt so badly for Amanda and for Walter. A glimmer of true love was an astonishing thing, and if an ounce of it was stolen, the emptiness it left behind, that time of loneliness, that time of despair, could never be relived, never be refilled. It remained forever empty, a hole in the soul. Molly knew that she was safe, she was loved. With Cole's support she'd never lose her way again.

"So what happens now?" Cole asked.

A coy smile crept across Mike's face, and he looked at Molly. "Well, you know I've been reassigned to the Cold Case Unit."

Molly's eyes perked up.

Cole groaned.

Tracey loved Christmas! Her mom made ham and scalloped potatoes, Tracey's favorite meal. Tracey's favorite part of Christmas, though, was that she and Emma were allowed to stay up late and watch Christmas movies on television. Tonight, though, they made her sad. She thought of Mummy. She missed her. Tracey had asked her mother if she could give Mummy a present, which her mother had quickly corrected, *Kate, Tracey. Her name is Kate*. She had been allowed to choose the present herself. Tracey had picked out a doll for Kate, so she would never feel alone again, and so she wouldn't have to steal some other mother's little girl. Before wrapping it, she slipped her own necklace, the one with the heart-shaped charm, around the doll's neck.

Tracey's mother had said that Kate would not be sent to jail. They'd made a deal with the police, and she would go somewhere to get help. Tracey didn't understand why Kate needed help, but her mother said that she had been taken from her parents, too, a long, long time ago, and that the woman who raised her underground made her believe in those toxins. Kate needed help to learn the toxins weren't real. Tracey knew her mother didn't think the toxins really existed, but she wasn't so sure. She tried to believe her, but sometimes, like when she'd gotten sick with a bad cold, she worried that she was going to die. Her mother had rushed her to the doctor, who also told Tracey that there were no toxins. She secretly wondered if they just hadn't known the truth.

When Tracey had first come home, she'd tried to see Kate. She had worried about her every day and didn't like the idea of her being alone, or with strangers, but every time she asked her mother if she could see her, her mother would cry. Tracey stopped asking her mother, and asked her father, who told her that her mother would like her to just forget the whole thing, forget her time underground, but Tracey couldn't forget Kate. Finally, Tracey's father spoke to the counselor that Tracey had to see every week since coming home, and she said it was okay for Tracey to visit Kate, and that it might even help Tracey gain closure and also assist in Kate's recovery. Tracey didn't like the therapist very much because she asked too many questions, but she was happy that she would be allowed to see Kate. She and her mother usually picked up Molly, and together they would drive to see Kate. Kate stayed in a place that felt, to Tracey, like a hospital; every wall was white, and it smelled funny, too, like the stuff her mother used to clean out her cuts. Tracey thought Kate looked prettier now than she used to. She was definitely cleaner, and her eyes lit up whenever Tracey went to visit, like she'd been waiting to see her for a very long time. Tracey liked visiting Kate, and every time they visited, Kate would again apologize for taking Tracey away from her mother and father. Kate's therapy was helping her to understand why taking

Tracey had been a bad thing to do. Tracey was happy that Kate was okay, but she secretly wanted to ask Kate about the toxins. She knew, though, that if she did, it might upset her mother, so she refrained. Tracey didn't refrain though, one cold December afternoon, from whispering to Kate that she didn't like the bad spot. Kate had apologized, and cried, so Tracey secretly vowed to never mention that again either.

Sometimes at night, Tracey would close her eyes and try to remember all of the things about her life underground with Mummy, but it was like someone had taken an eraser and erased almost everything. She could remember the dirt floors and walls, and the outside place, but she had trouble remembering what she had done all day and what was in each of the rooms—although she did remember the cart that she'd wanted to use as a baby carriage. Tracey reminded herself to pray for Kate every time she went to church with her family. She couldn't remember the whole prayer she'd said with Kate, and that bothered her sometimes, but she remembered the last part of it, and at night, when she was alone in her bedroom, she'd close her eyes and pray, "We thank You that when we call upon You, You will answer us, be with us."

Acknowledgments

It takes special people to provide unending support and unyielding belief. I'd like to thank all of the people who have touched my life over the past few years. I could not have written such a strong story without the help of my good friend and editor, Dominique Agnew, or without the help of my trusted beta readers, whom I'm sure I drove crazy with varying renditions of the manuscript: Hilde Alter, Doreen Guarino, Cathy Hunter, Ave Parnell, Maria Meyers, Beth Grimmett, Alison Rotich, and, of course, my husband, Les Foster.

A special thanks goes out to all of my site sisters on The Women's Nest who have been there for me during the toughest of times, giving me encouragement to continue writing, and providing their opinions along the way: Clare Karstaedt, Sharon Spearo, Jacklyn Reed, Kian Vencill, Linda Markley, Jessie Ford, and so many other warm, encouraging women.

Many of the historical facts about Boyds were relayed to me by Arthur Virts, a man who knows more than one can imagine about his hometown.

Retired Lieutenant Michael Mancuso of the Germantown Police Department was kind enough to answer my questions, and any and all mistakes about police procedures are mine and mine alone.

A hearty thank you to Clare (Rachelle) Ayala for her exceptional formatting skills and her friendship, and to my "sister," Natasha Brown, for her creativity in helping to create my paperback book cover

I'd also like to thank my good friends Greg and Dale Cassidy and Brooke Rendzio (and her parents) for all of their help in providing cover options.

Lastly, my family has stood behind me, sometimes laughing at me and other times laughing with me. They've helped me to develop scenes, and allowed me to spend endless hours in front of my keyboard. Thank you for loving me enough to see this novel through to publication. I truly believe I'm the luckiest woman on this planet to be blessed with each of you: my mother, Hilde Alter, my husband, Les, and our children, Noah, Zach, Brady, Devyn, Jess, and Jake.

Book Club Reader's Guide

1. Given what was at risk—her marriage, friends, sanity—if you were in Molly's position, would you have continued searching for Tracey? Would you have gone down the tunnels after Cole's ultimatum?

2. Pastor Lett carried with her the burden of living in a small town where her brother had been beaten. Do you think that would have had an impact on her relationship with congregation members, or do you see her as the type of person who would have been able to separate the two? Would you have been able to?

3. Cole was supportive to Molly in many ways, yet he was skeptical of her clairvoyant abilities--maybe rightfully so. How do you feel about the way he treated Molly throughout the book?

4. Tracey experienced Stockholm Syndrome, which became increasingly evident toward the end of the book. As a parent, would you have allowed your daughter to visit the woman who had abducted her given the non-malicious nature of the crime?

5. What are your thoughts on the Boyds Boys, and what should happen to them now?

6. Erik was afraid of his ability to have visions, afraid of becoming like Molly had been after Amanda was killed, and yet he was compelled to follow them and try to find Tracey. What support would you offer your own child in that same situation?

7. Did this book make you think differently about parents/children that you see in public places? Question reasons behind crying children (I hope so!)?

Thank you for choosing CHASING AMANDA. I hope you enjoyed the story. Amazon reviews are always appreciated.

Please enjoy a summary of my next book

COME BACK TO ME

Tess Johnson has it all: her handsome photographer husband Beau, a thriving business, and a newly discovered pregnancy. When Beau accepts an overseas photography assignment, Tess decides to wait to reveal her secret—only she's never given the chance. Beau's helicopter crashes in the desert.

Tess struggles with the news of Beau's death and tries to put her life back together. Alone and dealing with a pregnancy that only reminds her of what she has lost, Tess is adrift in a world of failed plans and fallen expectations. When a new client appears offering more than just a new project, Tess must confront the circumstances of her life head on.

Meanwhile, two Iraqi women who are fleeing honor killings find Beau barely alive in the middle of the desert, his body ravaged by the crash. Suha, a doctor, and Samira, a widow and mother of three young children, nurse him back to health in a makeshift tent. Beau bonds with the women and children, and together, with the help of an underground organization, they continue their dangerous escape.

What happens next is a test of loyalties, strength, and love.

Melissa Foster is the award-winning author of five International bestselling novels. She is a community builder for the Alliance of Independent Authors and a touchstone in the indie publishing arena. When she's not writing, Melissa teaches authors how to navigate the book-marketing world, build their platforms, and leverage the power of social media, through her author-training programs on Fostering Success. Melissa is also the founder of the World Literary Café, and the Women's Nest, a social and support community for women. She has been published in Calgary's Child Magazine, the Huffington Post, and Women Business Owners magazine.

Melissa welcomes an invitation to your book club meeting or event.

www.MelissaFoster.com

CPSIA information can be obtained at www.ICGtesting.com
Printed in the USA
LVOW05s0901180813

348440LV00001B/79/P